Also by Cathryn Grant

NOVELS
The Demise of the Soccer Moms
Buried by Debt
The Suburban Abyss
The Hallelujah Horror Show
Getting Ahead
Faceless
An Affair With God

NOVELLAS
Madison Keith Ghost Story Series
Chances Are

SHORT STORIES
Reduction in Force
Maternal Instinct

Flash Fiction For the Cocktail Hour
(Volumes 1-5)

Cathryn Grant

ALONE ON THE BEACH

Haunted Ship Trilogy Book One

D2C

Published by D2C Perspectives

Mary

Mary Carmichael knew there was a ghost haunting the concrete ship. The S.S. Palo Alto had been built too late to be of use in World War I. It was used briefly for dancing and dining in the early 1930s before a violent storm damaged it and The Great Depression eroded its appeal. It was permanently moored at the end of the pier on Seacliff Beach, decaying under the onslaught of sun, salt water, and thrashing waves.

Very few people believed Mary when she mentioned the ghost, but very few people believed anything an elderly person had to say, if they listened at all. They laughed off her beliefs as dementia, a sad, slightly pathetic longing for the people she'd lost to death. By the age of ninety-one, a person had lost almost everyone to death. Mary's references to a ghost were simply a hope for proof there was some kind of consciousness beyond the grave.

But she'd known there was a ghost long before she grew

old. She'd known since she was a little girl, watching the "cement boat" as it was towed up to the beach. She'd seen it, she'd felt it, and she'd heard it speak.

Haunted

I've been here for a long time — alone on the California coast, near the northern curve of Monterey Bay. I'm the ghostly breath of fog that blows across the water, first hugging the horizon, quickly shrouding the blue sky, blanketing the sand. I'm closer than the pebbles and sand and broken logs of drowned trees. Only a handful of the millions of beachcombers and surfers, swimmers and sunbathers have felt my presence. Only those with eyes. Not the eyes in their heads, but internal eyes.

I'm here, *watching*. I'm here, *listening*. I'm here, *speaking*...if anyone wants to pay attention.

It's commonly believed that ghosts haunt a particular place because they're looking for closure. They want to find rest, they need release from something unresolved so they can pass on to the afterlife. But that's not how it is at all.

One

Most of Corrine Dunning's friends, including Andy, had the opinion that dogs were better than cats. Dogs offered adoration and protection. They went running with you and they looked at you with soft, understanding eyes when you'd had a stressful day.

Dogs were smart and loyal. There was a reason they were decreed man's best friend. A dog treated his master as if he was the most beloved person on the planet.

Corrine thought most dogs were affection whores, offering unconditional love to anyone who passed by. They opened their mouths and their heavy breath swept across their dangling tongues. The moist, loose skin around their teeth pulled back until it was impossible not to believe they were grinning at any opportunity for a head pat. But even well-trained dogs rushed up close, sniffing kneecaps, as if to remind her they were wary animals, only a few DNA molecules removed from wolves, capable of killing without warning. Their caution lasted only for a moment. Once they approved of a scent, they became best friends with a woman or man they'd just met. They were demanding best friends, tireless in their desire for belly rubs and ear massages and neck scratches. A dog would retrieve and return a ball and chase it again until he dropped into a coma.

Corrine saw their appeal. Andy's Rottweiler was loyal and friendly. His eyes glowed with intelligence. She enjoyed stroking the velvet fur on his ears. It wasn't hard to imagine that her morning runs along the edge of the surf on Seacliff beach would be more playful, less about working out and more about loving life, if a dog were running beside her.

Dogs were happy creatures and they taught their owners to love life. Or maybe their owners already loved life, and that's why they loved dogs.

Corrine didn't doubt that she loved life, but she preferred cats. She wasn't anti-dog, as her UC Santa Cruz roommate had accused her of, but she didn't want to own one. She wanted a pet that didn't need her so badly. A cat didn't need anyone. Her cat, which she called simply, Cat, left her alone. Cat slept at the foot of Corrine's bed when it was cold, except when Andy slept over and his Rottweiler, Parker, was in the bedroom. Cat curled up on her lap in the evenings, but otherwise, she demanded nothing. Cat minded her own business, expertly bathed herself, took herself to the litter box without any assistance from Corrine, and was content with a thorough combing every few days. Cats were silent. Corrine's accusatory roommate had called them sneaky, but they weren't. They walked softly and they kept their thoughts to themselves.

Corrine twisted her hair into a coil, folded it on top of her head, and wrapped an elastic tie around it. The pile of hair fell toward her neck, but it was good enough for now. She tore the plastic off a package of fresh linguine. She cut the pasta into manageable lengths, dropped it into the boiling water, and reduced the flame. Andy would walk in the door with a bottle of Zin any minute. She was ready for her first glass now. She liked sipping it while she cooked, and she didn't like it that he was late. But living a block from the beach and working less than two miles from home, while he had to make the congested drive through the Santa Cruz Mountains and down Highway One, removed any justification for complaining. She should have insisted on providing the wine herself.

Cat walked into the room. Her claws, overdue for a trim, clicked on the tile floor. Cat made her way to the stove and rubbed her ribs against Corrine's leg, leaving a sprinkling of charcoal and white fur, then proceeded to her food dish. The crunch of her teeth on chicken-flavored pebbles battled with the sound of the gulls outside the open kitchen window. It was dusk, the breeze getting stronger, the gulls expanding their concentric circles further inland. Occasionally, one of the regal snow-white males would land on the iron birdbath in the garden outside of her kitchen. The French doors from the eating area opened out onto a brick patio. It was filled with potted plants that grew taller than the fence, and featured a teak love seat next to the birdbath. Cat wasn't allowed outdoors — too many coyotes, raccoons, and the occasional mountain lion. That left the songbirds free to enjoy the few inches of water. Except when a gull settled its enormous, sea-worthy body into the bath. The gulls didn't stay long, they were quickly hungry and eager to keep moving. They looked ridiculous sitting there and she wondered whether they knew that.

Gulls were scavengers, unwelcome and overpopulated according to some, but she loved them. They squawked and bellowed like hysterical middle-aged women, but when they soared against a blue sky, or slipped into view from behind a fog bank, they were majestic. When they stood on the beach, a small, soldierly community staring at the ocean, silent and watchful, their eyes seemed filled with wisdom.

She turned down the flame beneath the second pot, filled halfway with clams simmering in butter, garlic, and a generous splash of white wine. Linguini and clams, steamed broccoli, an unpretentious three-bean salad chilling in the fridge, and sourdough bread were all ready. After dinner, they'd go for a walk. It was so domestic and so uneventful she wasn't sure whether she should cry or fall on her knees in gratitude for such a satisfying, pleasurable existence. Usually Andy and Parker stayed overnight on Friday nights, but Andy had a seven o'clock tee time the following morning.

Andy made her feel safe when she was curled up beside him, her head on his chest or his shoulder, or angled in the other direction, her legs extended across his lap. Contentment bubbled inside of her while they ate dinner and shared a bottle of wine. But you didn't work with the elderly, a witness to their withered skin and rapidly fading eyesight, their ability to manage even basic self-maintenance growing weaker every month, and not realize there was no security in life. Still, she loved it, felt honored to be part of their lives, especially the final months and days, or years, no one ever really knew how much time was left. Even she didn't really know. Like everyone, she blindly closed her eyes and thought the future extended forever. She loved touching frail hands, observing skulls that no longer hid beneath layers of thick hair. Old people were real, stripped down to the essentials.

"One hour and forty-seven minutes!" Andy's voice echoed in the tiny entryway. He always sounded proud of the inordinate amount of time it had taken him to travel twenty-five miles from his office to his condo where he'd picked up his dog before driving to Corrine's. It was as if he wanted to one-up himself each time. He appeared in the kitchen doorway and crossed the room in three steps. He put his hand around the back of her head, weaving his fingers through her hair, holding it tight as if he was afraid she'd drift away from him. He kissed her lips quickly but with an intensity that left her feeling a need to sit down.

His energy swallowed the room in one satisfying gulp. He

set the wine bottle on the counter, yanked open the drawer, took out the bottle opener, and removed the cork. He went to the cabinet to the left of the sink and selected two wine glasses. He squatted and rubbed Cat's head. Cat lifted her chin and a rumbling purr came out of her throat. Maybe cats could be indiscriminate affection whores as much as dogs. Corrine smiled.

He washed and dried his hands and poured a splash of wine in each glass. "A quick toast, and then I need to go back to the car and get Parker."

Corrine tapped her glass against his.

"To us," he said.

She took a sip of wine and pictured ninety-pound Parker, pressing his nose against the window in the back of Andy's Mercedes, leaving a gooey smear on the glass. In her mind, she saw his liquid chocolate eyes and his short, glossy fur. If she closed her eyes right this minute, which would be the stronger image implanted on the backs of her eyes — Parker, or Andy's pale skin and blonde, nearly white hair? She wasn't sure. Andy had as much unrestrained energy as the dog. She'd seen pictures of Andy when he'd taken his customers out to dinner, everyone's faces turned toward his, their wine glasses tipped in his direction as if they wanted to capture his words and drink them. But Parker's presence in a room was more... just more. Bigger. Solid muscle, loud breath. A pure animal presence that warned — despite the grinning expression and the eyes that spilled over with the devotion worthy of a god

— he would have his way. He was your friend, as long as you behaved to his liking. But he was an animal. A moderately-trained, friendly animal, but still a powerful carnivore, driven by instinct.

Andy put his glass on the table and left the room. She drained the linguine. A moment later, the car alarm chirped, then the car door slammed. The front door opened and they were both inside. The bulk of Andy's six feet and Parker's excited presence, made her twelve-hundred square foot cottage no longer entirely hers. Cat retreated to the bedroom. At night, when Parker came into the room and curled up on Corrine's side of the bed, Cat disappeared to one of her favored hiding places — the deep, narrow shelf beneath the TV or the laundry basket that always contained a towel or two, sitting on top of the washing machine. Sometimes she wedged herself between the wall and the wide chair that looked big enough for two, but lied.

Corrine put the food in bowls and set them on the table. She turned off the light and lit the two white candles beside the basket of bread. While they ate, Andy told her about a customer he'd met with that afternoon. He looked like he was a twelve-year-old kid, but ran a global technology company. "I'm not bullshitting. Twelve. I'm selling to a child."

Corrine clucked sympathetically, although she wasn't certain sympathy was what he was looking for. She told him about the woman who had passed away that afternoon — Helen. A woman whose family hadn't visited in nearly four months. Every few weeks when Corrine had called the eldest son, he'd apologized with absolute sincerity. His voice had grown weak with tears as he explained that *work was hell*, and their kids' schedules were *nightmares*. Despite months of being upset, almost angry, at the family's badly ordered priorities, she'd dreaded making the call to tell him Helen was gone.

"I'm worried you're too invested in these people," Andy said.

"That's what I do."

"Take on everyone's feelings? As if you're the one who's dying, and at the same time you're the family, feeling guilty for not visiting enough?"

"I have empathy."

"Yeah, but you can't feel every sliver of loneliness and regret on their behalf. It'll eat you alive."

"I can't help what I feel."

He put his hand over hers. He let his fingers creep past the knob of her wrist bone. His grip was warm and solid. "You need to distance yourself."

"I called the sister first, and then…"

"Why couldn't she call the rest of the family?"

"I don't tell you how to do your job."

"Fair enough."

She smiled. Parker's tail beat against the floor.

"Does he need water?" she said.

"He's fine for now. He was only in the car for ten minutes."

"Anyway, after all the emotion every other time I've talked

to him, he was amazingly calm. He thanked me. Thanked Fairhaven for taking such good care of her."

"I'm sure he's relieved."

"Not relieved. I think he was…"

"Relieved."

"I think he really wanted to visit her, it was just hard."

"Wanting and doing aren't the same."

"I know. I suppose he was calm because he'd expected the call for so long, and when it came, it felt like it had already happened ages ago."

Andy picked up the wine bottle and refilled their glasses. "Great dinner. Perfect clams."

"Thanks. Are you changing the subject?"

"No. What you said is true. He felt it already happened and he was relieved that reality finally matched the inevitable."

"He wasn't relieved, he was disoriented. It's so sad they left her alone at the end. That they couldn't find time."

"Getting old sucks," he said.

"It doesn't have to."

"You can't take care of yourself, you have no power."

"It's scary, sure. But it gives you wisdom."

"I'm not scared." He laughed. "It just sucks." He stood up and carried the bowl of clams to the counter.

Corrine got up, wrapped a sheet of plastic over the bowl, and put it in the fridge. She scooped the bean salad into a plastic container and set the serving bowl in the sink. "Let's go to the beach. Parker will like it."

"It's dark."

"I'll bring a flashlight."

"It's not really a good idea to walk when the tide is this high — almost six feet — especially in the dark."

"You always say that."

"Because it's true."

"We'll be fine."

"It has to be quick. I need to get some stuff done and get to bed early."

"I know." She stood on her tiptoes and kissed his jaw.

Andy poured the last of the wine into their glasses. "First, I have something for you."

"What?"

"Go sit on the couch. I'll bring it in."

She sat and sipped her wine while she waited for him.

He returned with a large, cream colored bag. Clouds of turquoise tissue paper billowed out of the top.

"What is it?" she put her wine on the coffee table.

"What's the fun if I tell you?"

She pulled out the paper and let it fall on the floor. Cat appeared beside her feet, drawn by the crinkling sound, not caring whether she ran into ninety pounds of dog flesh. Tissue paper was too alluring.

While Cat dove and batted at the bright paper, Corrine reached into the bag and pulled out a peach colored dress. It was so soft it slid across her fingers like water. She studied the high collar made of gold and pearl beads, holding the front and back together without sleeves, the teardrop cut in the front to show off more than she usually liked. "A dress?"

"You'll look great in it."

"I don't wear dresses very often. Maybe to a holiday party, and this…"

"You should wear them more. You have a fantastic body. You look good in your jeans, but you'll be a goddess in that."

"Okay."

"Try it on."

"After our walk."

"Promise?"

"I guess."

"You don't like it?"

"When have you seen me in a dress?"

"I didn't mean to make you mad."

"I'm not. Thank you. I just…"

"I happen to think you're pretty hot and you'll look amazing in that."

"Okay." She put the dress in the bag and carried it into the bedroom. She put it on the closet floor and closed the door so Cat couldn't get it.

She returned to the living room. Andy put his arms around her. He unwrapped the elastic band and stroked her hair, pushing it off her shoulders so it fell down the center of her back, thick and slightly tangled. He kissed her. She relaxed into him and closed her eyes. In the dim living room light, the insides of her eyelids seemed to be soaked in the same peach color as the dress.

They pulled away from each other. Corrine went to the entryway and shoved her arms into her hoodie. She stood with her hand on the doorknob while Andy went into the bedroom and changed into jeans and a sweatshirt. Parker scrambled across the kitchen floor, suddenly clued in to the fact they were going out.

She called out to the bedroom. "Where's his leash?"

"In the car."

When they opened the front door, Parker dashed to the side of the car and sat expectantly. Andy clipped the leash to Parker's collar. They headed up the street, Parker walking sedately beside Andy, glancing up every few seconds as if he wanted to be sure he wasn't dreaming, grinning, his tail flopping in every direction.

Two

From the top of the stairs leading down the side of the cliff to the beach, the concrete ship was visible. She was positioned with her bow facing to the south, at the end of the pier where she'd been unceremoniously dropped on a winter day in 1930. An access pier was built, and a tugboat had towed the concrete ship into Monterey Bay. She'd been purchased by an amusement company with the intention of creating a unique dancing and dining establishment. For less than two years, she'd provided a brief period of entertainment with a restaurant and ballroom. In the winter of 1931 the ship's hull cracked. When the amusement company folded, she'd been stripped of her upper deck infrastructure. For close to seventy years she was beloved by fishermen and children. As the ocean did her work, the hull cracked further. The concrete was battered by logs and waves, eroded until the rebar was exposed. When she was deemed too dangerous for humans, she was abandoned to provide a sanctuary for pelicans and seagulls.

When Andy, Corrine, and Parker reached the bottom of the wooden staircase, they turned right and walked along the path, past the pier and the ship. Waves crashed against the concrete and roared onto the shore.

"The waves are getting close to the wall," Andy said. He took her hand. "We should stay on the path."

"It's more fun on the beach. Look. Parker agrees with me." The dog yanked on the leather strap, his neck extended as he tried to force Andy to walk faster to the steps leading down to the sand.

"Didn't you see the weather warning about rogue waves?"

"We'll stay right by the wall. Come on." She jogged ahead and hurried down the steps. On the last one, she pulled off her flip-flops and tucked them into the pocket of her hoodie.

Andy followed, stopping on the bottom step. "The water's only a few yards out."

"We'll be fine."

Parker surged forward. "Steady," Andy said.

The dog ignored him, straining at the leash, the collar tight around his thick neck. "No swimming tonight," Andy said. Parker turned and looked at Andy as if he understood. He shook his head and veered back toward the wall, sniffing at a pile of dried seaweed.

They walked for a while in silence, their feet sinking into cool sand. The water roared at their left, the waves rising up like mountains that had come to life, swelling and curling over, crashing on the shore. Andy took her hand and moved away from the lapping foam that crested the ledge that had formed in the sand. Parker followed. The next wave was smaller than the others had been, but it was moving much faster. It raced across the wet sand, easily crested the rise, and ran toward them.

They scrambled closer to the wall. The water was a few feet from where they stood.

"We should go back."

"Not yet. It's exciting," she said.

Andy pulled on Parker's leash. The dog continued straining forward as if he wanted to make his objection known and wasn't going to let any discomfort stop him.

"Why did you buy me that dress?" she said.

"You'll look great in it."

"Don't I look great the way I am?"

"Absolutely, but I wanted to get you something nice. I know you can't afford frivolous things on your salary. It's a gift."

"Maybe I don't want clothes like that."

"I like buying clothes for you. I saw three other things in that store that would look great on you."

"It seems like you don't think much of how I look."

He took her hand again and squeezed it. "Of course I do. But you're undervaluing yourself."

"I'm not a used car," she said.

He laughed.

Another wave ran up the beach, silent, moving so fast they couldn't get out of the way. It swirled around their ankles, soaking their jeans.

"We really shouldn't be out here," he said.

"It's fine. I want to keep walking. I haven't had a lot of time to think about Helen Malvers."

"Who's that?"

"The woman who died."

"Why do you need to think about her?"

"Just remembering her. I don't want her to disappear."

"My jeans are wet, and the tide's coming in." He stopped. Parker stopped and sat on the wet sand. He settled his belly down and looked up, waiting to find out what was going to happen.

"Go on back. I know you need to get to bed early. I'll be fine."

"I'm not leaving you here by yourself. And you were going to try on the dress."

"I'm not rushing back just to try on some slut dress for you." She couldn't see his face clearly in the darkness, but she felt something. Shock? Hurt? "Sorry. I don't know what it is. It's just not me."

"I was trying to be nice. It's a compliment."

She took her hand out of his and shoved her hands in her pockets. She glanced toward the pier. It seemed as if something moved but she couldn't make it out. She turned back toward him.

The dress is hideous. Slut is the perfect way to describe it.

She shook her head and glanced around. She felt as if she'd heard a voice speak the words, but no one was nearby. They'd come from inside her head, but seemed to have sprung up out of some other place she didn't recognize. "It's not me," she said. "The dress isn't me."

"How can you know that? You haven't tried it on. I liked it. I'd like seeing you in it. Isn't that important?"

"I…"

He tugged gently on her wrist. "Let's go back."

"No. You go. I want to walk some more."

"I don't like leaving you here alone."

"I don't need you to protect me." She laughed, trying to ease the hardness of her words.

"Are you sure?"

"Yes."

"I'll call you in the morning?"

"Okay."

"I'll text you before I go to sleep." He put his arm around her and kissed her. As he turned to go, Parker barked, but she didn't pet him this time.

She walked for another quarter mile or so before she turned around. The beach between her and the pier was deserted, nothing but water, swirling in angry curves, carving out wedges in the sand. There were no gulls or pelicans in sight, all of them taking refuge on the abandoned boat or sheltered wherever the shore birds went at night.

The beach was strangely light beneath a nearly full moon. The water glowed as light hit the whitecaps and the foamy edges of the breakers. She'd walked a long way past the area where the wall formed the back side of the beach and was now in front of a row of homes with strategically placed boulders aiming to protect patios and gardens from rough surf. In the most violent storms, the water crashed up and over the rocks and drenched tile and shrubs and outdoor furniture. If she didn't hurry, it might pin her against the rocks. She could probably scramble up them, but it would be slippery and difficult to hold on. Andy had been right to be cautious, but she hadn't wanted to give him the satisfaction. She loved the wildness of the ocean. He preferred it when the water was flat and pale blue, lapping at the shore like the tiny waves of a mountain lake.

The roar and crash had changed into something different. The waves seemed to be shouting at her. She laughed softly. What a ridiculous thought. She'd been on the beach alone in the dark with a high tide racing toward her several times before. This shouldn't be any different. She quickened her pace. Her feet sank into sand that was saturated with water. It was cold and felt like she imagined quicksand would feel — sucking at her heels, her feet buried deep as if she'd punctured the surface of the earth.

She turned slightly and headed away from the encroaching water. As she came closer to the pier, its thick pillars like a grove of trees in perfect formation, she looked up. A woman was on the pier, standing near the end, looking out at the storm-torn ship. That made no sense. The access gate was locked at night. Corrine slowed. Without warning, a silent wave rushed at her, surrounding her with water up to her knees. She stumbled, trying to remain upright while it tugged at her wet jeans. She whimpered softly. She sounded like Parker. She fought as the wave swirled back out, using all its strength to drag her with it.

Because of the icy water, it was difficult to breathe for a moment. She swallowed. Once the water had receded, she looked up again. There was definitely a woman standing there, somehow having found her way past the locked gate. The woman wore a cape. Thick white and gray-streaked hair floated out around the edges of her hood. Of course — the old lady. Since Corrine had bought her cottage in Seacliff, she'd seen the woman on the beach or the pier every day. They'd never spoken. The woman worked hard to avoid even a casual greeting, staring at a point beyond Corrine when they passed within speaking distance.

Corrine called out but her voice was drowned by the crash of the surf. Water rushed at the legs of the pier, tearing past them like it wanted to rip them out of the sand. It wasn't even a storm. She couldn't understand why it seemed so fierce. She jogged toward the steps that led up from the sand to the pathway. She turned and looked. The woman was gone.

She took a few steps back onto the beach. Had she imagined it? Had the woman crossed to the other side, moving out of Corrine's range of vision? She felt the woman must be there, out of sight, because Corrine was overcome with a feeling that someone was watching her. Someone was laughing at her wet legs and her battle with the pull of the water. She called out but the only response was another wave, so loud it sounded like a crack of thunder.

When she reached the top of the steps, she was panting as if she'd been running for hours. She bent over, pressing her hands into her thighs, trying to stop her heart pounding against her ribs, throbbing up into her throat. From where she stood, she could see the entire pier. The woman was nowhere in sight. She was so old, surely she hadn't jumped into the water. Some of the people in Corrine's care murmured occasionally that they wished to control their fate, to decide when enough was enough.

Corrine walked along the path and turned onto the pier. She walked up to the gate and looked through the iron bars, spaced four or five inches apart, impossible for someone, even a small, thin woman to pass through. She stood there for several minutes, listening to the waves crash and recede. After a while, she realized she was shivering. She pulled her hood up over her hair, damp with mist, and started up the hill toward her cottage.

At home she filled the shaker with ice. She unscrewed the cap on the gin, poured a shot over the ice, and splashed in a bit of vermouth. She shook it until her shoulder ached and she thought she might drop it. She strained the liquid into a martini glass, dropped in two large olives and took a sip. She went to the front door and turned off the exterior light. Cat was curled up in the center of the living room floor, announcing the house was once again her domain. Corrine went into the bedroom, took another sip of her drink, and set it on the dresser. She steeled herself to try on the dress. Maybe Andy knew something she didn't. She'd overreacted. The dress was beautiful. She opened the closet door. The cream colored bag, blue tissue paper, and the buried contents were gone.

Three

Mary sat on the bench on the east side of the pier. The fog had burned off within an hour of sunrise and she was happy to be out in the sun and the warmish temperature for a January morning. She sipped the coffee in her metal container, letting the hot liquid sear her throat and warm her from the inside out. Despite the sun, the wind was chilly as it gusted across the pier. It had a way of tearing through her clothes no matter how may layers she wore. It was probably a sign of old age. There were so many.

Water crashed against the wooden legs of the pier. She took a deep breath, glad that today, the rank odor that sometimes permeated the beach on either side of the concrete ship wasn't evident — the odor of too many birds living too close together on the dissolving concrete, chunks falling away from rusted rebar like flesh falling off one of the dead seals that sometimes washed up on the beach. Thankfully, all she smelled was coffee and sea water.

Overhead a gull called and a moment later she heard a splash, but it was heavy, larger than a gull would make. Pelicans were also surfing the waves today.

She leaned back and sipped her coffee. She moved her hands down to the lower part of the container and laced her fingers together. Her skin was dry and so thin she sometimes feared her bones would poke through without any provocation. It was startling, every single day, to see how ancient and depleted her body was. Ninety-one years old. She was only one year younger than the rotting ship. She was confident she was the oldest person who still came to the beach by herself, and proud of the fact. Without her twice daily walks to the water's edge, she would die.

Walking to the beach wasn't difficult. She knew the shape of the path that ran parallel to the water, the various breaks in the rail where concrete steps led to the sand, and the steps up to the pier itself, as well as she knew the skin clinging to the bones on the backs of her hands. Unlike others living in Aptos, she wasn't required to climb the hill or the long flight of stairs to return home. Her house was a narrow, simple cottage next to the sands of Rio Del Mar Beach. Over a lifetime of walking on that sand, and living a few steps from the water, the beach had threaded its way into it all her bones and muscles. The loss of her eyesight hardly mattered. Still, she regretted how she'd walked along the beach and onto the pier so many times, for so many decades, without really looking. She hadn't known what she had.

A fisherman's thick plastic bucket thudded on the boards, followed by the rattle of the latch on his tackle box. She liked the fishermen. She liked the shouting children, chattering questions about the boat, asking why they couldn't go past the locked gate and play on it. She liked the soft voices of couples who saw only the lovely side of the ocean, and imagined it existed solely as a backdrop for their passion. She wasn't so fond of the people who felt called upon to inquire about her health and stability. Total strangers took her elbow and tried to help her down the steps, worrying aloud that she'd been left there alone, disgusted that no one was looking after her.

She didn't need looking after. She didn't need their hard, pinching fingers on her elbow. Their grips hurt. She could navigate each step and bulge of sand better than they could, even as they watched where they placed their feet.

"One of those days you live for, isn't it, Mary?"

The voice was Daniel Sloane's, one of a handful of fishermen she knew by name, if not by sight. Never by sight.

"It is."

"How're you doing?"

"Very well."

"You say that every time."

"It's true every time."

"I have some bear claws with me," he said. "Want one?"

"I'll take half, thank you." She set her coffee container on the bench.

A moment later, the sticky, fluffy dough was in her hand. She inhaled the almond and sugar and took a small bite. The sweetness overwhelmed her, but it was nice, and it made Daniel happy. She'd have to lie down when she got home, sluggish from too much food, drugged with a sugar high.

He's trying to poison you.

She shook her head to dislodge the thought and laughed softly, but not softly enough.

"What's so funny?" he said.

"I was thinking about the sugar high."

"Don't know what you mean. Everyone says that, but I've never felt it myself."

"I wasn't laughing at the sugar. Just the high. Remembering how kids came out here in the sixties to get high. Not that they don't now, but it was something else back then. Newer, maybe."

"Like I've said before, I bet you got stories."

"And like *I've* said before, I'll never tell them."

"I don't know why. Don't you want the world to know about your life, how the world was, before you're gone?"

"No, I don't." She smiled for his benefit.

"Your call," he said. "Sure I can't interest you in the other half?"

"Never."

She felt the movement as he hurled his line over the side. The wheel spun, releasing more line.

"What do you think you'll catch today?"

"Whatever the gulls and pelicans miss."

"I hope it's something good." She ate the last bite of the bear claw. She licked her fingers and picked up her coffee container.

She felt Daniel's mind closing in on itself like a sea anemone, shrinking and tightening around his own thoughts, shutting out the world around him until his body was fused with his fishing pole and the only thing that could penetrate would be the tug of his line.

She took a sip of coffee and let her own mind settle back into itself. The feet of other fishermen thumped past. Buckets tapped the wood, gulls called out to one another, and the pelicans dove for fish, landing with flat, dull splashes. Watching the pelicans was one of the things she missed most. That, and the steady, rhythmic, never-ending, curl of water, over years and decades and centuries, rising up and crashing onto the sand.

She didn't miss that ugly old boat.

The last time she'd seen it, her eyesight dimming so that everything looked gray, or blurred so that she couldn't make out objects at all, the boat had looked terrible. It was cracked and broken, the bow pulling away from the main ship, sinking faster. Water gushed through the torn space, sending up a beautiful spray, but it made the boat look weak. It had looked as if the poor thing had been punched in the stomach. The superstructure had been torn down decades ago, leaving nothing but salt-washed concrete. And yellowing bird shit.

Her mother would have been appalled, in 1930, to hear Mary use a word like that. Shit. Shit. Shit. She spoke out loud, "Shit." No one responded. Most likely, no one even looked in her direction. Maybe they hadn't heard, or it had no impact. How the world had changed.

The boat looked desolate the last time she'd seen it, but it had looked that way for years. Rebar, corroded and deadly, protruded like bones, making her think of the dead birds that washed up on the beach, their bodies broken, the necks bent at painfully awkward angles. Access to the boat was blocked by an eight-foot iron fence. Birds sat on the ship, pausing for a rest in a safe place, staring out at the sea. Some of the birds looked wounded and as close to death as she was. Although she didn't know that for sure — she might not be close at all. She could live another ten years. People did, sometimes more, nowadays.

She longed to outlive the boat. She thought about that a lot. She wasn't sure why it seemed important. She was healthy. She didn't take any pills except occasional pain relievers for arthritis. Her blood was good, her heart was steady. According to her doctor, all her organs were functioning as they should. A lifetime of eating mostly vegetables and fish had kept her body in much better shape than the poor, dying S.S. Palo Alto.

She preferred remembering the ship as it had been when it was young and beautiful and hopeful. It glowed, lights blazing from the dance hall, shimmering on the night sea like a magical floating palace. At least that's what her ten-year-old eyes saw. She'd wanted to go inside but her father said it was a place for grownups. Adult games and dancing. Bootleg liquor carried in metal flasks with screw caps that made hollow sounds when they were twisted in place. The flasks slipped quietly into the party rooms where the contents were consumed even more quietly. She didn't know about the alcohol then, but she figured it out later, when she was old enough to understand her father's vague words that it wasn't a place for children.

The day the ship was towed into position, she and her mother and Aunt Claire had gone out to watch. They'd walked down the hill in the early morning January cold, hoping the sun would push its way through fog and clouds and at least brighten the beach, even if it withheld warmth.

Mary held Claire's hand. Claire seemed more like a sister than an aunt. She was only sixteen, and so beautiful Mary couldn't stop looking at her dark hair, her perfect skin, not like other adult women who had blemishes and moles. Claire was her mother's only sister. She lived with them after Mary's grandparents had died within three weeks of each other. Claire slept on a twin bed in Mary's room. Her combs and her fancy hairbrush, colored glass bottles of perfume and jars of cream, pushed Mary's collection of seashells and pebbles to the side of the dresser. Claire spent a lot of time standing in front of the dresser, using all of her creams and combs, looking into the mirror and smiling at herself.

They stood on the promenade, they called it a footpath now. She smiled at the dull words. Promenade was much nicer. They'd watched all morning as a tugboat moved slowly toward the pier, the massive, gleaming ship following behind like a dog on a leash. The Palo Alto hadn't been allowed to enter under her own power. She'd been stripped of her engine before she even made her way to Seacliff beach. Instead of a proud vessel, she was made into a helpless, dependent, powerless hunk of concrete and metal and wood, dragged from her home and sunk into the sand. Her eventual end should have been obvious then, but no one imagined what the sea would do to her over the decades. She was pristine and full of promises. Like life itself. Like Mary and Claire and her mother had been. She would be a unique tourist feature, a ship that didn't float, offering dancing and dinner, swimming and games. A restaurant was planned for the top deck along with several elegantly furnished salons.

Mary wanted to run down to the sand and out to the edge of the surf, beside the partially constructed pier, to stand as close as possible to the slowly moving ship. Her mother forbade her. Claire squeezed her hand, and Mary knew that if her mother got tired and went home, that's exactly where she and Claire would go. She shut her eyes and prayed for her mother to get one of her headaches, or her queasy stomach, or any one of the other ailments that cropped up often, the afflictions alternating like cards dealt across a table.

Instead, Mary got bored. The ship just sat there as men

prepared for its final resting place. Over the next two days, the Palo Alto's three, three-and-a-half ton anchors were lowered and a steel cable pulled the ship in line with the pier. When she was finally in place, the seacock's in the ship's boiler room were opened and she swallowed vast amounts of salt water until she sank into the sand.

Mary had only seen the ship once at night, but that was the image that remained throughout her entire life, and lingered inside her memory, where she didn't need her sight to view it on a regular basis. Her parents were going to eat dinner and dance to a live orchestra on the boat. Mary was furious that she wasn't allowed to join them. When they were gone, Claire walked with her down to the beach and allowed her to stand there for a long time, drinking in the lights, hearing the faint music coming from open portholes, floating across the sand like mist. It seemed to her like a ghost ship. No human life was visible, only their eerie sounds distorted by the crashing waves and the occasional cry of a gull. The glow of lights added to the impression of a specter, a sunken ship that carried on with music and lights as if it were still floating on the sea.

Now, eighty-one years later, reality had set in. The boat was decaying, and Mary's aging stomach had developed a fierce ache. She never should have eaten the bear claw. Her body couldn't handle that kind of lapse. With all her heart, she wanted to maintain her admirable health, to be able to walk out to the beach every day, sit on the pier, not sink into a rotting pile of bones and skin in a nursing home. If that were to happen, she'd gladly die. But those who suffered that fate didn't get to choose a quick death.

It was imperative she stay strong and well-nourished and self-sufficient. Her sons were scattered across the country — four sons to the four winds, she liked to tell people. Her husband, at least the one who mattered, had been gone for more than ten years. She didn't mind out-living him. She was content. The only thing she feared was being stripped of her dignity and left to decay like the majestic and humble S.S. Palo Alto.

It might have been twenty minutes, might have been an hour. The sky was overcast now, so she couldn't tell by the feel of the sun how long she'd been sitting on the bench. She stood up slowly and tucked the empty coffee mug into her bag.

Daniel didn't speak. Possibly he had his back turned in her direction and wasn't aware she was leaving.

"Good-bye, Daniel."

There was no answer. It must be that he'd moved along the pier, his voice one of many debating the status of the water alongside the boat, the potential for mackerel and bass and salmon to swim close to shore, comparing the number of fish caught so far that morning. It didn't matter. He was used to her leaving without speaking again. And once he had his line in the water, all that mattered were the fish and the others on the same mission as him.

She turned and walked quickly across the rough boards, sure of where she was going, unafraid of bumping into anyone. If you walked with purpose, people moved out of the way. If you walked with purpose, they never noticed you couldn't see them. When she passed the gate, she found the railing and walked down the ramp leading to the footpath. She turned right and moved steadily toward the covered picnic areas. She stopped at the first set of stairs leading down to the sand. She slipped off her shoes, tucked them in her bag, and went down the stairs.

The sand was cool, which she appreciated. It didn't take much sun to make it intolerably hot, but she hated walking across it in shoes, feeling them fill with sand, kicking it onto her legs. When she was near the crest of sand that sloped down to the water, she stopped, took a blanket out of her bag and spread it on the ground. She sat down with her legs tucked to one side. Soon, the beach would be overrun with visitors, but for now, it was empty.

The waves crashed, the sound filled her head as if she were holding a large shell up to her ear. The tide was out and she knew the gulls stood at the water line, webbed feet gripping the damp grains packed like wet cement. Their orange beaks were pointed at the surf and their eyes watched, unblinking. All her life she'd wondered what they were waiting for. They stood motionless, the males with brilliant white feathers and gray and black tails, the mottled gray and brown females, the smaller gulls the color of charcoal. When the tide reached its lowest point, they ran close to the edge of the waves, digging for sand crabs. When they were tired of watching, they made a running start and took off, soaring over the water, watching beneath the surface for the silvery flash of fish.

Their self-contained beauty made her heart ache, even now, able to see them only in her mind. They had a hard life, every hour of the day spent looking for food, but they seemed content as they stood watching, and ecstatic when they floated on the air currents, dipping and turning. When they'd looked her right in the eye, they'd seemed human. She'd always wondered what they saw in her eyes, and now she wondered even more. Did they know she wasn't looking back?

A child shrieked and another one laughed, followed by the faint tap of webbed feet running across the sand, then the flap of wings. When the gulls were above her head, they cried out, scolding and complaining.

She hated it when children chased and taunted the birds. She'd seen it done all her life. From her earliest memory, she'd been sympathetic to the birds, giving them space, staying out of their way. It was cruel to chase them, laughing at their panic. She sat up straighter, turning her head slightly to see if she could pinpoint where the children were. They continued to shout, but they ran in erratic patterns. She felt her head was jerking as rapidly as a bird's, trying to get a sense of how close the children were, what they were up to. There were no adult voices that she could make out.

It was horrible, feeling the birds' small hearts beating even more rapidly than they did under normal circumstances, knowing the terror in their eyes as they scattered. The worst were the children who threw rocks. She had no idea what made them do it. Some streak of cruelty. It was said the entire human race had that potential, it was normal for children to chase birds. Maybe she saw that streak of cruelty inside herself, if she thought back over her life, the horrible things she'd sometimes felt, even if she'd never acted on them. But those feelings were toward human beings who had hurt her first. What had the gulls done? What joy was there in seeing their terror, seeing them run on feet that were well-designed for sitting in the water, but terrible for making an escape on land? They flew and dove and dug from dawn until dusk. They shouldn't be disturbed when they were trying to rest, taking a few minutes to meditate on the source of their food. She hated hearing them flap in distress, tiring themselves further, and possibly exhausting themselves so that diving for fish became more difficult.

Her boys had never been allowed to chase birds. You had to teach children compassion. The first time each of them, in his turn, made a move to chase a gull from its place, she'd gripped his upper arm and told him to be considerate toward the creatures who inhabited the beach. They never did it again. And they grew up to be men who treated other human beings with respect. Even their ancient mother. Especially their ancient mother. She laughed softly, but her eyes were still filled with tears, angry and frustrated that she couldn't reprimand the children who seemed to be shouting on all sides of her. There were only two of them, she was sure, but running and chasing each other and never pausing, never coming close enough for her to speak to them. If she shouted at them, possibly facing the wrong direction, she'd look like she was deranged — a small, withered woman, her only remaining beauty her long, wavy white hair, shouting madly at something she couldn't see.

Four

At least two hours had passed. The heartless children had moved farther down the beach, or maybe they were settled under an umbrella eating snacks. Maybe the family had given up waiting for the sun to return and had gone home. She hoped so. The tide was coming in, but she was certain she was far enough back that she didn't have to move out of its way. She pulled a container of water out of her bag and took a few sips. She pushed the hood of her cape off her head and turned her face up to the sky.

"Hi."

Mary yanked her hand off her lap at the shock of the voice from someone whose approach she hadn't noticed. She clutched the sides of her cape in front of her throat, as if it would protect her.

"I'm sorry. I didn't mean to startle you. I've seen you around quite a lot but we've never met. Do you mind if I sit down?"

"Who are you?"

"Corrine Dunning. I moved here a few months ago. To a cottage in Seacliff."

Mary guessed the woman must have extended her hand, but with the voice coming from several feet above her head, she had no idea how to locate it. "I'm not being rude. I'm blind," she said.

"I didn't realize." The woman's hand touched Mary's shoulder. "And no one's here to help you? They just dropped you at the beach?"

"Don't sound so shocked. I don't need any help. I live right over there." She gestured toward the row of houses lined up beyond where the footpath ended, on the opposite side of Aptos creek.

"What's your name?"

"Mary."

"Mary…?"

"Is that important?"

"I guess not. Do you mind if I sit down?"

"There's not much room."

"I have a towel."

Mary felt the slight shift in the air as the towel flapped open and Corrine placed it on the sand.

"What do you want?"

"I've seen you on the beach almost every day."

"I'm here every day. Usually twice a day."

"How long have you lived here?"

Mary smiled. She wondered if Corrine noticed, or if she was looking out at the ocean. "Forever."

"And no one helps you across the sand? Watches out for you? In case you fall, or someone bothers you, or…so many things could happen."

"I don't need a babysitter. And if you sat here to worry about how I'm getting along, we don't need to talk any more."

"No. I didn't. I'm just…concerned."

"Don't be. I can take care of myself. I've lived on this beach for nearly fifty years, and I've lived in Aptos my entire life." Her hip was stiff. She shifted her legs and leaned on her arm for support.

"I didn't mean to insult you."

"Thank you for saying so."

"I pass you a lot. I wondered why you never looked at me."

"Now you know."

"Yes," Corrine said.

"And what else?"

"I saw you on the pier last night."

"It wasn't me."

"I'm sure it was. You were wearing the cape. Your hair."

"You can't get onto the pier at night. They lock the gate at sunset."

"I know. That's why it was so strange."

"Well you saw someone else." Mary shivered. Her hand had slipped away from the edges of the cape at her throat. She pulled the two sides together again.

"I saw you and then you disappeared. I was worried you'd jumped, or fallen, or…"

"I wasn't on the pier, Mrs. Dunning. Please stop arguing with me."

"It's Ms. I don't mean to argue. But the cape, your hair."

"Possibly you saw a ghost."

Corrine laughed.

"You don't believe me?"

"I'm not sure I believe in ghosts."

"Why not?"

"I don't know. I haven't thought about it much. I've never seen one. I guess when I've heard of people who believe in them, they seem a little off."

"Everyone thinks so, but this place is haunted."

"Have you seen a ghost here?"

"Don't you feel it?"

"No."

"I've seen things on the ship. For years. Most of my life."

"Really?"

"I wouldn't have said so if it weren't true."

"Oh," Corrine said.

"You don't believe me?"

"It's not that."

"Then what is it?"

"I've never known anyone who's seen a ghost."

"You said you had. That they were *off*."

"I misspoke. I've never met someone who's seen a ghost, but I think I've seen stories on the internet, watched movies that claimed to show paranormal activity. Those people seem a little off."

"Everything has to have an important sounding title now. It can't just be a ghost. A spirit. It has to be categorized — *paranormal activity*. It's a way to keep your distance."

"But you've seen something, or felt something? You're sure it wasn't fog?"

Mary laughed. "I know the difference between fog and a being that hasn't fully departed from this world. Are you ever on the beach by yourself?"

"I was last night. Lots of nights. I like it when there's no one else around."

"You feel safe?"

"I do. For some reason, I do. All the houses, the motor homes."

"If you screamed, someone would hear."

"Are you trying to scare me?" Corrine said.

"Not at all. But the ship, doesn't it feel haunted? Decaying like it is? So broken apart. No human life on it for more than ten years now, but it's sitting there, waiting for something."

"That's what I think about the seagulls," Corrine said.

"That they're haunted?"

"No. No. Not really, although maybe, now that you say it. But I always think they're waiting. When they stand along the edge of the water and stare out. It's like they're waiting for a signal that it's time to go, or waiting for a certain time of day when it's best to dig for crabs. I don't know. It sounds silly."

Mary pulled her hood up.

"Are you cold?"

"It doesn't sound silly. I always felt the same way. When I could see them. And now, I know they're there, even if I can't see them. I feel their presence."

"Like a ghost?"

"I suppose."

"Anyway, the woman I saw last night, she wasn't...she didn't look like a ghost. She looked like a flesh and blood woman. In a cape."

"It was not me. And how do you explain her getting past that iron gate? Unless she was young...tied a rope to the pier and climbed it," Mary said.

"No, she was old. She had white hair."

"It was dark. Could have been blonde."

"You think it was a ghost?" Corrine's voice was quiet, as if she was afraid someone might overhear her entertaining the idea.

"I do."

"Who would it be?"

"It was a party place at one time. When I was a little girl. People dancing. Bringing in illegal liquor."

"Do you know someone who died on the ship, when it was open for dancing?"

Mary wasn't sure how the conversation had turned in this

direction. She wasn't about to tell this stranger, a person she would never lay eyes on, her whole life story. The woman was too easy to talk to. The conversation had twisted and flowed, taking its own form and now she felt cornered.

"Do you? Is that why you think it's haunted?" Corrine said.

"I think it's haunted because it's been left to rot. It's ugly and filthy. A death trap. They should remove it."

"I like it," Corrine said.

"I hate it. Once, it was beautiful. Magical. But it died, and now it's haunted. So many birds have died there." She moved her legs in front of her and pointed her toes. She shifted onto her knees, waiting for the blood to flow back to her lower legs.

"Are you leaving?"

"I'm tired. I'm ready for some tea and soon it will be time to fix lunch."

"Can I help you up?"

"No, thank you." She stood up slowly. She folded her blanket and put it in her bag, moving her shoes so they sat on top, ready to slip on when she reached the steps.

"I liked talking to you," Corrine said. "Can I look for you again sometime?"

"And I liked talking to you." Mary held out her hand. Corrine took it. Her grip was firm without pinching, and her fingers were warm and soft. "I'm here every day. For the rest of my life."

Corrine squeezed her hand gently. They walked to the steps

and said good-bye. Mary was sure she could feel Corrine watching her walk away.

Five

During her college years, Corrine visited the Santa Cruz Beach Boardwalk several times every summer. After graduation there had been a few more reunion visits with her roommate and some of the girls in her dorm, then, nothing. They'd outgrown the carnival atmosphere. It had been at least six or seven years. Maybe more. At the age of thirty, what did she need with roller coasters and a not very frightening haunted house? But once her Seacliff cottage had gone into escrow the previous summer, she'd decided she needed to reacquaint herself with the area — the beaches, the restaurants, and even The Boardwalk. Becoming a local in the string of beach towns circling Monterey Bay was thrilling enough to make her overlook the feeling she was acting like a kid who couldn't quite grow up.

Long before Andy was part of her life, she'd met Josh near the end of college. They hadn't become a couple until she was in graduate school. They'd been together for three years, and while Corrine felt she'd become an adult somewhere between graduate school and advancing her career from hourly aide in a care facility to assistant manager in the social support office, Josh was still a bit of a kid. Mostly a kid. Her friends assured her that lots of guys were kids long into their forties, and quite a few viewed themselves as kids their entire lives. Josh's enthusiasm over her suggestion they spend an evening on roller coasters and other adrenaline-generating rides was endearing, but also slightly unnerving.

Josh didn't view a Friday night at The Boardwalk as an ironic experience. He was serious about his roller coasters, Ferris wheels, junk food, and the bone shattering log ride through icy water that Corrine worried was splashing bacteria in her face. Of course, they put chlorine in the water, maybe other chemicals. Still, she didn't like suspect water in her face. Josh told her not to open her mouth and it wouldn't be a problem, but she couldn't stop herself from screaming when the plastic log-shaped cart plunged down the chute.

They'd eaten burgers and fries, saltwater taffy, soft vanilla ice cream with a chocolate shell, and now they stood in line for the Big Dipper roller coaster. It was their second trip careening around the rickety wooden structure seventy feet above the pavement. The line was long. A September Friday night at ten o'clock, a day when there'd been absolutely no fog. If people hadn't crawled over the twisting mountain highway to the coast for a day at the beach, they'd made the last minute decision to drive over at night for a summer evening that didn't require sweatshirts.

She hugged Josh's arm, suddenly feeling less mature and judgmental. "After this ride, let's get some cotton candy," she said.

He squeezed her waist and pulled her in front of him so she was leaning against him. He rested his chin on the top of her head. "Sure."

They inched forward, Josh using his hips to nudge her in front of him as if she were a life-sized rag doll. People flowed past — couples holding toddlers and pushing strollers, younger couples with their arms wrapped around each other, groups of girls shrieking at each other and taking selfies every four steps, and teenage guys who seemed oblivious to the girls.

After a few minutes, they inched forward again.

"How long have we been standing here?" Josh said. "It didn't take this long the last time."

"There are a lot more people now."

A large man carrying four giant drinks bumped Josh's elbow. Soda dribbled onto the back of Josh's hand. "Hey!"

"Sorry, man. Too many people."

Josh's arms tightened around her, but he didn't say anything more. They took four steps forward.

Pop songs blared through loudspeakers. She couldn't smell anything but popcorn. It seemed to be everywhere. Even her French fries had tasted a little like popcorn.

"Hey!" Josh said.

"What's wrong?"

"That guy just cut in line."

"Don't make a thing," she said.

"We've been standing here forever."

"I know, but it's nice to take a break."

"He doesn't get to take cuts."

"Don't get in his face," she said.

Josh let go of her. She stumbled back slightly. He stepped to the side and walked around the three teenage girls standing in front of them, all of their heads diligently bent over their phones, unaware that their rights had been violated.

Josh grabbed the kid's upper arm. He was tan and fit, managing to look clean-cut despite his dreadlocks. His left wrist was circled with leather bracelets and he was barefoot, wearing nothing but cargo shorts.

"No cuts," Josh said, his voice louder than Corrine would have liked.

The surfer held up his hands, forming the hang ten sign. "Easy. It's cool."

"It is not cool at all," Josh said.

"Chill, Dude."

"You cut in line. We've been waiting forever. The end is back there." Josh waved his arm in Corrine's direction, still gripping the guy's bicep with his left hand.

Corrine was surprised the surfer hadn't tried to break free. The girls had put their phones in their hip pockets and were watching, their lips parted, eager to see a fight.

"Come on, Josh. It's…" she said.

Josh held up his hand as if he were a traffic cop. "Get out of line and wait your turn."

So much for acting like an eternal kid. Now he sounded like her father. What was his problem? He was going to make a scene at best, and was in danger of starting a fight. The surfer's words were mellow and his face was slack, but she could see a thread of tension riding across the ripples in his shoulders and chest.

"Let go of me," the surfer said.

Josh glared at him. One of the girls giggled. She slapped her hand across her mouth.

A few people had stopped and were watching, but no one stood up for Josh's effort to keep order, to maintain fairness. They all wanted a fight. She could see it in their eyes. No one could resist a fight, they wanted a winner and a loser, they wanted justice served or aggression punished.

She wanted to approach Josh, touch his arm. Maybe he'd pause and let it go, but she didn't want to lose their place. Then he'd really be pissed. She moved closer to the girls.

To her left, a man appeared. He was good looking, with white-blonde hair, slim and taller than Josh and the surfer by several inches. He wore a black t-shirt, jeans, and expensive-looking leather sandals. "Let's not have this get out of hand," he said. His voice had a conversational tone, nothing that Josh could over-react to.

"I'm handling it," Josh said. His voice also sounded chatty, already looser than it had a moment ago, as if he needed to make himself look equally calm and in control.

"It's a big crowd," the stranger said. "It wouldn't take much to get out of hand."

The surfer twisted, wrenching his arm away from Josh. "What's wrong with you?"

Josh took a step toward the surfer. "No cuts allowed. Move."

The surfer smiled and shoved his hands in his pockets.

"Am I going to have to make you move?" Josh said.

"Chill out. There's always an extra seat." The surfer jerked his head toward the girls behind him. "There's three of them. Easy. A seat left over for me."

She could see Josh's jaw tighten. He wasn't going to back down. "You don't get to take cuts."

The stranger moved around to Josh's left, becoming a slight barrier between Josh and the surfer. "It's not a good idea to provoke someone."

Corrine wasn't sure who the comment was directed at.

No one spoke, but she could feel Josh, and maybe the surfer, sensing the size and strength of the man reminding them they had the potential to start something ugly and ultimately dangerous. Even deadly, if you glanced toward the far side of The Boardwalk where large, fleshy men wearing leather vests, their pockets adorned with chains, had been laughing earlier. They now looked wary, picking up the animal scent beneath the smell of popcorn.

Watching the stranger's face, lacking any definable expression, including fear, Corrine felt he was the only civilized person in sight. Even the parents with children were transformed into protective creatures, their hands clenched around their helpless offspring.

"It's not cool to jump into the line," the stranger said.

The surfer shrugged. "Most people don't care."

"It looks like this guy does care. Very much."

The surfer grinned. He lifted both hands, palms facing the stranger instead of Josh. "Just trying to expedite the seating. No worries." He stepped out of the line and threaded his way through a cluster of strollers, headed toward the beach side of The Boardwalk. In a moment, he was gone.

Rather than looking satisfied, Josh looked angry. Corrine closed her eyes. Most men were not children at all. Only Josh was a child, and she was exhausted from looking after him.

Speaking past the girls who still stared with open mouths, Josh said, "This is bullshit. I'm gonna get a beer."

"You don't want to ride?" Corrine said.

"Not worth it. Too many people. Stand in line for forty-five minutes for a five-minute thrill?"

"I thought…"

He stepped over to the side. The stranger remained where he was, oblivious to the girls who stared at him with widened eyes, flared nostrils, and damp, open mouths.

"Let's go," Josh said.

"We've already waited all this time. I'll save our spot."

Josh shrugged. He turned and walked away. After a moment, he too was swallowed by the crowd.

There was a wide gap ahead of the stranger. He stepped away from the line and the girls walked forward. The crowd pressed behind Corrine, wanting her to fill the space before another line-jumper appeared. Did Josh really want her to give up their place? She wasn't sure whether to follow him or wait for him to return. She moved up close to the girls. The stranger moved with her.

"Thank you," she said.

"It looks like you're without a partner for the Big Dipper."

Corrine studied the crowd. She was no longer sure which direction Josh had gone. She pulled her phone out of her purse — no text message. The stranger waited, smiling.

"I don't know what happened to him," she said.

"He let his emotions get the best of him."

"Don't we all."

"Do we?"

"He's not a jerk," she said.

"Did I say he was?"

"He was acting like one." She smiled, ashamed that she was betraying Josh, and smiling about her betrayal. But the situation could have escalated quickly. Crowds were unpredictable. You couldn't assume everyone saw your point of view. She checked her phone again. The screen was dark.

"Do you want a seat mate?" the stranger said.

"I'm not sure. Josh…"

"He wouldn't like it."

"If the roles were reversed, I wouldn't like him doing that to me."

"Would the roles ever be reversed?" he said.

"It's an expression. I meant, in any situation. I wouldn't like him going off with someone else when I was upset."

"He abandoned you."

It was an extreme comment, yet truthful. Josh was more concerned with his fractured ego, or whatever it was, than staying with her. For all he knew, the surfer had returned and was giving her trouble. Or someone else had taken cuts while everyone was off balance. Josh had walked away as if she didn't matter. And he hadn't sent a text. She looked at her phone again. She could text him. But she wasn't the one who stalked off. She had no idea where he was. Did he even care that he'd left her alone with this very good looking, very charismatic man? Was he thinking about her at all, or only about the attack on his sense of fairness and justice?

The line moved forward. The stranger stood outside of it, waiting for her to speak. She felt as if the next step forward, her next words, would change the direction of her life. It was a wild thought, filled with imagined drama. She wasn't sure if it was the shocking white blonde of the stranger's hair, his utter control over what had happened, and now his control over her, or something else, that was making her feel the next step was so momentous. The line moved again but she didn't step forward.

He slipped into the empty space. She glanced a fourth time at her phone and put it in her pocket. "I thought I'd outgrown The Boardwalk, but it feels good to be a kid for one night. I really wanted to ride again. It terrifies me, but then I want to go again."

"Fear is addictive. I'm Andy." He held out his hand.

"Corrine." The warmth and strong, comfortable pressure of his fingers startled her. She pulled her hand away slowly.

"Do you live around here?" he said.

The question should have triggered a warning alarm. From anyone else, it would have. She knew nothing but the man's first name and his calm in the face of contentious boys. You didn't blurt out personal details to a stranger. Especially one you'd met at a place like The Boardwalk. "I just bought a house in Seacliff. Near the cement boat?"

"Yes. I know it. I live a few blocks from there."

"Really?"

"Really. But it's concrete."

"What?"

"The boat is concrete. Cement is the powder that turns to concrete when it's mixed with water and hardens. It's a concrete ship."

"Everyone calls it the cement boat."

"Everyone is wrong."

"Everyone?" she laughed.

He didn't smile.

A slight chill ran across her scalp. As she studied his eyes, lighter than any blue eyes she'd ever seen, there seemed to be a need trying to hide itself. As if he desperately required her to agree with him. She dismissed the shiver in favor of the warm feeling his desire created in her belly.

They'd ridden the Big Dipper. When she climbed out of her seat, her legs shaking, and checked her phone, there was still no message from Josh. She knew she should be concerned, but instead, she was pissed.

Andy Johnson was in sales with a high tech company. He'd lived in the Seacliff area of Aptos for three years. He didn't surf, and he was at The Boardwalk to help a friend chaperone his nephew's birthday party. The kids were playing miniature golf, so they'd urged Andy to take a break from the shouting boys. He had a dog named Parker and he played golf and admired her career choice although he didn't think he could spend all his time around people so close to death. He liked to run on the beach and looked mildly pleased that she liked to do the same. He was impressed she'd found a house and been able to make a good offer in a market that was getting very competitive. He wondered how much remodeling she'd have to do. When she explained she didn't mind old things, imperfect things, he smiled and said she was a very centered person. He thought it was funny she hadn't named her cat. When she insisted Cat was a name, he said she was cute, but it was not a name. They laughed and tossed their naming points of view back and forth, and toward the end of the evening, she wondered if it was too late to change Cat's name.

Andy was easy to talk to and easy to listen to. She was mildly annoyed at her tendency to swoon every time she looked at him. It wasn't just his appearance, it was his solid self-assurance that managed to avoid arrogance. Even so, beneath all the seeming perfection, there was something in him that showed in his eyes — a need she couldn't fully identify, but it was there. It seemed as if he needed her.

By the time she heard from Josh, she and Andy had gone through the haunted house, eaten cotton candy, and she'd taken her third ride on the Big Dipper.

Josh's text read — *Where the hell did you go?*

She texted back — *I should ask you the same.*

Josh: *Meet me at the car.*

Corrine: *You don't want to ride the Big Dipper?*

Josh: *That guy pissed all over it. Next time.*

She wasn't sure which guy he was referring to, but it didn't matter. She gave her phone number to Andy. He took her hand, lifted it slowly to his mouth, and kissed her knuckles.

The next morning, she'd told Josh things weren't working out. He'd cried, which was unnerving. His tears had haunted her for a few weeks, but not any more.

Andy had filled every corner of her life. He was the guy she'd been looking for. He listened to her as if she were the most charming woman he'd ever encountered. The feel of his skin on hers chased every stray thought out of her mind. She couldn't believe her good fortune or the random nature of how they'd met. It was destiny, a thought she kept to herself.

Six

A ferocious storm lasted two nights and one day. On the second morning, the sun rose in a cloudless sky. Corrine tried to roll over and wrap her arms around Andy, but Parker was between them. The rain pounding the roof had driven him up onto the bed when she and Andy were deep asleep after two bottles of Zinfandel. It had been a cozy evening, but now, she regretted all the wine. Her head ached, and the dog's body was too heavy and too hot, pressing hard enough against her leg that her foot was numb.

She poked the dog's ribs with her knee. He didn't grunt, snuffle, or move. She didn't like him in the bed. He took up too much space by half, and he snored louder than Andy. Even though he had frequent baths, he smelled doggy. She had to take a deep, lung-exploding breath to notice it, but the smell was always there. It seeped into her comforter. She didn't want to be dragging it to the dry cleaner every month. She tentatively nudged him again. She didn't like to give him too big of a poke. A dog woken out of a dream could be unpredictable. She turned on her opposite side, facing the window.

She pushed off the blankets. She went into the kitchen and started the coffee. When she returned to the bedroom, Andy and Parker were both snoring. She wasn't sure she'd ever seen Andy sleeping, at least not during daylight. Most of the time, he'd already eaten something and was on his third cup of coffee when she woke. He looked sweet, a little boy pucker creasing his lips, his hair partially covering his eyes. The dog was another matter. She wasn't sure how she'd ended up in this situation, nearly part owner of a dog who was nice enough, but not what she wanted consuming every room of her cottage every time Andy stayed over. The place had an air of tranquility when she and Cat were the only occupants. She imagined it might have that same air with Andy and no dog, but that rarely happened.

The dog was contrary to everything else about Andy. He was devoted to cleanliness and order. His condo had been completely remodeled in gray and white with touches of turquoise. It was exquisite, and there wasn't a dust bunny or a crumb or a dog hair anywhere on his barren tabletops or tiled floors or plush carpet. He moved with fluid deliberation, while the dog bounded and wagged and slobbered. The dog was Andy's alter ego — a Hyde to Andy's Jekyll. Not that the dog was a monster. He was just too big and too active and too…doggy.

It had been a week since Andy had given her the unwanted dress. He hadn't mentioned taking it back, had never acted as if he was still hurt. It was as if the ocean had closed over any rough spot between them. She'd thought about mentioning it, but that might cause the dress to reappear and she really did not want that. She'd made her point and they'd moved on. Now he understood more about her. That's what happened as a relationship evolved and grew and parts of yourself were gradually revealed. She'd made too much of it, and fortunately, Andy hadn't. More proof of his kind heart.

She went to Andy's side of the bed and kissed his forehead. "Wake up, Prince Charming."

He smiled but didn't open his eyes.

She put her lips against his ear. "The weather is amazing. We should go for a run before all the weekenders get here. They're probably already lining up at the gate."

Andy swung his legs over the side of the bed. He pulled her onto his lap and kissed her. Parker jumped off the bed and came around. He licked her foot. She shuddered and stood up. "Do you want coffee first?"

Andy nodded.

The dog realized they were making plans. He trotted out of the bedroom, headed for his food bowl. "Can you take him out?" Corrine said.

"He'll be fine until we go. I'll be dressed in half a minute."

"I don't want to gulp down my coffee."

"He'll be fine for a while."

Once the leash was hooked in place and their running shoes laced, they headed out the door. Cat watched them go. She seemed to be smiling, knowing she had the house to herself. As Corrine closed the door, Cat turned and walked toward the kitchen, her tail erect behind her. Corrine wondered if she planned to sneak some of Parker's food.

They walked to the stairs and jogged down the 151 steps to the path that extended from the concrete ship to Rio Del Mar beach in one direction, and up a slight hill and past the thirty or forty spots for RVs that lined Seacliff Beach.

They started beneath the pier and ran on the hard-packed sand toward New Brighton Beach. The entire stretch was about two miles, but she doubted they'd go that far today. With groups of children already digging holes, throwing sand and stones into the waves, every other family holding the leash for a dog or two, running became an obstacle course.

They ran fast. Parker stayed to Andy's left, splashing in the foamy edge of the surf. Their feet sank into the sand, slowing their pace. It was only sixty degrees, but the uncovered sun and the lack of a breeze made it hot. Within several minutes, Corrine stripped off her sweatshirt, tying it around her waist as she ran. When the knot was secured, Andy handed the leash to her and pulled off his t-shirt, tucking it into the elastic edge of his running shorts. She handed the leash back to Andy.

They dodged a large pile of kelp, and then jogged up away from the water's edge to avoid three kids on boogie boards.

Before they could veer back closer to the water, Corrine saw something dark, too dark and solid to be kelp, too misshapen to be a large rock. She slowed as the object came into focus. It was one of the cormorants that usually bobbed just beyond the breakers. The beak was plowed into the sand as if someone had tried to make a yard ornament out of it. The slender neck was bent at a hideous angle and its webbed feet were flattened as if the legs were broken. Its feathers were dull and stiff, the eyes nothing but dark holes. She wasn't sure about the last because she turned her head quickly, unable to look. "Oh." She made a sharp left, walking down the sloped wet sand.

Andy slowed and turned. "Why'd you stop?"

She pointed at the bird.

"Ugh."

She put her hands over her face and started crying.

Andy walked back to her. "What's wrong?"

"The poor bird. It's so degrading with his beak like that. I hate it. I hate when I see dead birds! I don't understand." Her tears mixed with her sunscreen, turning her face into an oily mess. There was a pinching feeling in her heart, as if someone had grabbed it and was twisting, refusing to let go.

Andy put his hand on her back. "Don't get so upset. You do this every time."

"Because it's awful! It's so sad."

"There are millions of them. And they die."

"It breaks my heart."

"I wouldn't call a dead bird heart-breaking."

She wrenched away from him. "Why doesn't it upset you?"

"I don't let it get to me."

She looked up at him. His mouth and jaw were hard. Sunglasses blocked his eyes. How could he be so unmoved? The corpse lying in the sand, picked over by other birds, nibbled at by flies, made her nauseous, and unbearably sad and a little afraid. She focused her gaze on his mouth. Perhaps he was as upset as she was, scared of the lifeless decay but he couldn't show that, couldn't even admit it to himself.

"Let's keep going," he said.

"Why are you so cold?" she said softly.

"I'm not cold. Wild animals die all the time."

"I know. But they're so beautiful. They live such uncomplicated lives. The poor thing didn't deserve such a humiliating death. Everyone walking by looking at it, so helpless."

"Stop looking at it." He took her arm. "Let's go."

"You act like it's no big deal."

"I wonder if working with all these people who are constantly dying is getting to you."

"That's not it."

"You were insulated in the suburbs. Life is harsh — we live, we die."

"But it doesn't have to be so horrible."

"Are we going to keep running?"

She wiped her hands across her face. She turned and started running again. Andy followed, then moved to her left so Parker could once again run in the surf. At the one and a half mile mark, according to Andy's running app, they turned and started back. They never talked while they ran, but now it felt different. There seemed to be a vast space between them.

When they were finished, Andy suggested lunch in Capitola and Corrine agreed. Based on what she saw around her, no one was much bothered by death on the beach — murres, cormorants, the occasional pelican or seal. The cycle of life.

Andy took Parker home for a bath, followed by his own shower.

Corrine stripped off her running clothes and got into the shower. She stood under the hot water. The shower floor sloped to the back left corner and there was a cracked tile in that spot, but the water pressure was good, so she didn't mind the flaws. It was easy to close her eyes to things that didn't matter. Why couldn't she close her eyes to the dead birds, and to Andy's lack of grief over their broken bodies? Why did it even matter, why did she need him to feel what she felt? She wanted him to be horrified and upset. She wanted to crawl inside of him and pluck at his heart until it ached like hers.

He doesn't care about any creature but himself.

No. That wasn't right. Not at all. He loved Parker. She turned and let the water run over her face, too hot. Her lips grew soft and pulpy. She sobbed for the broken bird. Hundreds of people walked by dead shore birds, half of them didn't even see the bodies stiffening among tangled seaweed and wet sand. Others barely stepped aside to avoid them. No one cried. No one recoiled. Maybe they didn't show it, locking the feelings inside.

She shampooed her hair twice, as if she needed to dig rotting bird flesh and flies out of her scalp. She scrubbed the rest of her body equally hard and used a new razor blade to shave her legs. She put on a white sleeveless top and silky khaki shorts. She wore flip-flops with black soles and white straps, a rhinestone glued at the joint where they went between her toes. It was strange to be putting on summer clothes during the last week of January, but obviously the weather wanted to pretend it was summer for a day or two.

While she dried her hair, Cat walked around the bathroom counter, lifting her head toward the dryer as if she wanted the motorized air turned on her. Corrine knew better. If the warm blast got within even a few inches of Cat's face, she ran and hid.

The more time Corrine spent with Andy, and of course, Parker, the less she saw of Cat. Watching her tiptoe up and down the counter, walking around the sink, dragging her tail across the mirror, Corrine saw how Parker was taking over her house. Her life. Was Andy also taking over her life? She cared for him very much, maybe even loved him, but she had a slight sensation that she was disappearing, swallowed by

Andy's habits, Andy's preferences for restaurants and wine, even Andy's sleep patterns.

The night she'd met him, he'd seemed like a god. Tall and so good looking it was hard not to stare at him. But it wasn't just his looks that drew her into his vortex. It was the composed look on his face through the brief encounter with Josh and the surfer, the unmoving way he managed to inject a sense of equilibrium that diffused the situation. And since then... He made her laugh, she absorbed his energy and felt it take over her thoughts. He listened to her, he offered thoughtful suggestions for dealing with problems at work, along with the sense he cared about what she did, and that he liked that she cared about it. Except he always wanted things to be slightly different. Maybe she could find a more interesting job. Maybe she could wear a dress — this dress. Her hair would look great if it was cut in layers instead of heavy and thick, straight down the center of her back. Maybe she could rearrange the kitchen and the living room and the bedroom and her life for that ninety-pound dog. But Parker was a good dog. He didn't bark unnecessarily. He didn't harass Cat or jump on Corrine and maul her with his huge paws. He sat quietly whenever Andy attached his leash.

She went into the kitchen and poured half a glass of iced tea. She dropped in two ice cubes and carried the glass to the living room. Twenty minutes until she needed to leave to pick up Andy. She sat on the couch, then got up and went to the garden outside the kitchen. She took a few sips of tea and went back into the living room. Maybe Cat would sit on her lap and they could reconnect, if connecting with a cat was even possible. But Cat had disappeared. She was probably under the bed. Corrine didn't want to get dust bunnies on her clothes trying to lure her out. She finished the iced tea, washed the glass, and wiped down the kitchen counter where a few pieces of grilled corn from last night's dinner were scattered across the counter, unseen until the sun hit them directly.

The restaurant featured a patio looking over Capitola creek where seagulls splashed and cleaned themselves in the shallow water as if they were children in a wading pool. Watching their pleasure lightened Corrine's mood. She wouldn't be upset with Andy. Whatever mysterious quality transformed attraction to infatuation to love, it was happening, despite his imperfections. Love was all about accepting imperfections. He couldn't help how he was any more than she could. She wished he had a more profound respect for the natural world, but he also wished for differences in her. Two people could never be exactly the same. Even if they could be, where was the fun in that?

All the concern over her extreme reaction to the dead bird had been rinsed off Andy's face. He held out her chair while the hostess stood clutching the menus to her chest, grinning like an idiot at his chivalry. Corrine sat down and Andy maneuvered her chair closer to the table and took his own seat on the bench in front of the railing. The hostess handed them each a menu, placed a wine list in front of Andy, and said their server, Janet, would be with them shortly. She disappeared into the restaurant, leaving them alone on the patio. In the covered section across from them, six tables had been pulled together. Vases of flowers lined the tables and two balloons were tied to the back of each chair. She hoped their lunch would be nearly over by the time the party arrived.

"That shirt looks great on you," Andy said. He opened the wine list but continued staring at her.

"Thanks."

He reached across the table and stroked her hair, tucking the left side behind her ear. "Such amazing hair," he said. All her bones seemed to dissolve as his fingertips followed the curve of her ear. He rubbed the two holes in her lobe. "You forgot earrings."

"I didn't feel like wearing them."

He took his hand away. "You look sexy in earrings."

She tipped her head slightly, letting the hair fall over her ear again.

He looked down at the wine list. "Chardonnay?"

"Yes."

When Janet appeared they ordered the wine and two cups of clam chowder. Andy asked for the skirt steak cooked medium rare and Corrine ordered coconut prawns.

They sipped wine until the chowder was served.

Corrine put her spoon in the chowder. It emerged full of

tiny bits of potato and two plump clams. She took a bite. It was warm and creamy and the clams were perfect. She ate another spoonful. "Did I tell you I saw that old woman on the pier? The night we were walking at high tide and you went home early?"

"No."

"She was standing at the end near the boat. I couldn't figure out how she got past the gate. And then she disappeared."

"You thought she jumped?"

"That's what I was worried about. But I saw her the next day. I introduced myself."

"Why?"

"I was worried about her. Walking around on the pier at night, sitting alone on the beach. She's very old and frail. You've seen her."

"She never struck me as frail."

"Have you seen her face up close? She's at least ninety. In fact, she told me she was a little girl when the ship was towed in. So I guess that might make her over ninety, if she was old enough to remember."

"So why did you introduce yourself?"

"I've always wanted to meet her. She's out there every single day. I was curious. And I do worry about her."

"You worry about all the old folks."

She smiled and picked up her wine glass. It was cool, despite sitting in the sun. She took a sip and leaned forward.

"Anyway, I always wanted to meet her, but she was rude every time I passed her. She would never even look at me so I didn't have a chance to say *hi*. It turns out, she's blind."

"And she walks around by herself? I guess that is something to worry about."

"She said she's lived here all her life, it's easy to find her way around."

"I suppose that's possible." He pushed his empty soup cup to the side.

The server appeared and took it away. She pulled the wine bottle out of the ice bucket and poured a splash in both their glasses. Glass crunched against ice as she wriggled it around to nestle it back in the bucket.

"But that's not why I'm telling you the story."

"Okay."

"She insisted it wasn't her that I saw on the pier."

"You said it was."

"I know. She had on the cape. And her hair."

"She's old, she probably forgot she was out there."

"She said it was a ghost."

Andy laughed.

"She thinks the ship is haunted."

"But she was on the pier, not the ship." He laughed again and took a long swallow of wine. "Not that I'm arguing about where a ghost might be seen. Since they don't exist."

"Have you ever heard stories about it being haunted?"

"No. And if I had, that's all it would be — a story. She's

old. She needs something to entertain her. Why not ghosts?"

"Do you think so?"

"Well they certainly aren't real, so what else? Unless she's completely unhinged."

"She seems normal in everything else she says. It was just the ghosts."

The server delivered their main courses, refilled the wine, and asked Corrine if she needed the heat lamp. "I noticed you have goose bumps," she said.

"I'm fine," Corrine said.

"The sun will be gone in a few minutes, so let me know if you change your mind."

"I will." Corrine picked up her water glass and took a few sips. She stabbed the smallest prawn, sliced it in half, and put a piece in her mouth. It was firm and sweet. She chewed slowly.

"I guess it'll be a mystery," he said. "Whoever was on the pier. Maybe it was a bird and you thought it was a person in the dark."

"No. It was a person. In a cape. With white hair. I'm sure of it. But now I don't know what to do."

"Why do you have to do anything?"

"I want to know who it was. Don't you?"

He shrugged. "No." He pulled the wine bottle out of the mostly melted ice. Water dripped on her plate as he poured wine into her glass. He topped off his own and set the bottle on the table.

"Why do you think some people believe in ghosts?" she said.

"They're stupid."

"That's not very nice."

"But it's true."

"Maybe they exist, but if you've never seen one, you think it's fantasy."

"It's wishful thinking. People who are bored, or who want proof life continues after death. That's all. Fear of death turned into a fairy tale. I can see why you're attracted to the idea. Because you're so resistant to death."

"No, I'm not."

"I think you are. It…" He put a piece of steak in his mouth and chewed slowly.

"It…what?"

"I don't remember what I was going to say."

"Well I want to find out more about it — the woman. Or the ghost."

"Knock yourself out." He swallowed the last of his wine. "Should we get another bottle?"

"I have to drive."

"I thought we'd walk around for a while. Go shopping."

"Maybe. Okay." The thought of stumbling through shops, tipsy and thirsty, Andy pressing unwanted dresses on her, was not how she wanted to spend a beautiful afternoon. For a moment, she imagined a ghost sweeping through the restaurant, shrouding them all with her dark cape.

Seven

Sometimes Mary was shocked by her own bravado. She'd spoken calmly to that woman who'd walked up to her on the beach, frightened her, then sat down beside her, uninvited. A total stranger. When Mary was young, you didn't approach strangers. It was expected that a common acquaintance made an introduction. And so nosey. Wanting to know why Mary was by herself, trying to insinuate herself into Mary's life, as if she wanted to become a personal aide. It could be she was a con artist. Wasn't that what they did? Befriended the elderly, made themselves useful, then indispensable, then moved in and took over your life? They put themselves in a position to wrap their tentacles around your finances and suck the marrow out of your bones.

Be careful.

She felt a sharp chill. Careful indeed. Her bravado was unnerving. She didn't need help, but that didn't mean she wasn't so vulnerable that simply thinking about it made her heart jitter like a hundred crickets were hopping about. Relying on her hearing, which was good, but not what it used to be, and her sense of smell, and her nervous awareness of changes in the atmosphere, weren't enough to compensate for the loss of sight. It was downright terrifying to know that anything could be happening right in front of you, and if the participants were silent, you'd never know. A woman could walk up and nearly sit on your lap and you wouldn't know until you felt the weight of her body and her voice jolted you like the stab of a knife.

If she'd been honest with that woman, she would have said ghosts were nothing compared with the terror of living in constant darkness. It was always night.

She reached out. Her hand found the faucet and made its way to the spigot. She pushed the lever gently until a thin stream of water flowed into the sink. She held her coffee cup under it, let the water splash around, then pulled it out. She put the cup upside down on the drainboard.

It was early — six-forty a.m. according to the robotic woman inside the smart phone, a gift from her sons on her eighty-ninth birthday. The device also announced the weather — cloudy, partial clearing by eleven, currently fifty-two degrees. At that temperature on a January Monday, she could count on a deserted beach. An empty beach was much more to her liking. When no one was there, she didn't feel the lack of sight with such intensity. Eyesight wasn't necessary to know the location of the birds, the slope of the sand, and the size of the waves. She put on a wool sweater and leather boots that reached mid calf, guaranteed to prevent hard grains of sand from creeping inside her shoes. She wrapped a scarf around her neck, and put her cape over her shoulders, tucked her single braid beneath the neckline, and pulled the hood across the top of her head.

She stepped out the front door, locked it behind her, and turned left. It was 183 steps along the narrow sidewalk that sloped down toward the beach path. After that, 56 steps to the bridge over the creek, 149 steps to the ramp leading to the sand. She passed it and continued on toward the last set of steps before the pier.

The wind whipped at her cape, but it was well-secured across her chest, every button on her sweater done up in an effort to keep warm. Her nose ran and she patted it with a tissue. When she reached the beach, her feet sank into the wet crust of sand. The tide had been all the way up to the sea wall overnight. Everything smelled clean. It usually did in the morning. One benefit to her loss of sight was she didn't have to see the trash left by weekend visitors. How could they come to the beach, longing for an intimate connection with the earth and the beautiful expanse of sparkling water, but care nothing about the damage they created with Styrofoam and plastic and aluminum and mylar balloons with their deadly ribbons? It was baffling. When she was younger, she'd gone out every Monday morning, even in stormy weather, carrying a large black garbage bag and a pole with pinchers on the end. She'd picked up trash for an hour or more, walking up and down the shore, apologizing to the birds and seals whose lives were threatened by the detritus of human beings.

Now, she left that task to others. It was possible to find trash, either stumbling across it, or walking slowly, patting one bare foot in a half circle around her as she walked, but it was too easy to fall, too easy to land her foot in something dangerous, or something disgusting. The weekend visitors were as careless with their dogs' excrement as they were with their food containers. It wasn't completely fair to place all the blame on visitors. Locals could be equally careless, although in smaller numbers. Some of the mess came from raccoons digging through trash cans, tossing garbage around the picnic areas, and gulls carrying discarded food out over the sand where they dropped the wrappers.

She walked toward the water. It was low tide and she knew the birds were sitting in flocks, like worshippers in a church, looking out at the sea. She moved slowly, careful of where her feet landed on the uneven sand, ensuring she didn't trip over a sand castle or step into a deep hole. When her feet registered the change in consistency from dry to slick wet sand, she stopped and took a few steps back.

The water lapped against the sand like the waves of a lake more than the crashing surf of the ocean. Her thoughts returned to the woman who'd landed beside her and tried to pry into her life. What did she want? Mary couldn't stop thinking about her. At the time, she'd hoped to frighten her away with talk of ghosts, but now, she had a surprising desire to talk to the woman again. Her life could get quite lonely at times. She had her neighbors and her weekly calls from each of her sons. But she'd never filled the enormous hole left when James died. She'd known she never would, and hadn't tried. A man like James only came along once in a lifetime. Memories were enough to keep her company. She still heard his voice in her head — another blessing of losing her sight. She wasn't looking for him all the time. His voice had never faded, as if he were right beside her, whispering in her ear when she woke in the middle of the night, when she ate her meals, and especially when she walked on the beach.

Now, she realized she'd been terribly lonely. His voice wasn't quite enough. She could hear his thoughts, speak hers to him, but he couldn't respond.

The woman had made her feel safe. Was that because she was a very *good* con artist? The woman — Corrine — hadn't laughed at the idea of a ghost. Even if she was a con artist, there was no harm in talking to her. It was important to be cautious. She could never reveal any information that was too personal, shouldn't give the exact location of her home, or the number for her smart phone. But talking on the beach was fine. The woman was one of those types who was driven to help, who needed to help in order to satisfy something inside of her, but that was okay too. Mary didn't need to accept the offer. Corrine could worry over every little step and every possible danger facing a sightless, elderly woman walking on the pier and crossing the sand without assistance, but how would that hurt Mary? As long as Corrine didn't grab at her arm, become too insistent. She hoped Corrine would approach her again, hopefully with a bit of warning this time.

A dog barked with a rapid-fire sound. It was running full speed. She heard the birds' feet slapping the sand, pictured their bodies waddling as legs moved so quickly but covered such a short distance, frantic to outrun the dog. They began crying out and she felt the rush of air as a large group of them launched themselves into the sky. The dog barked louder, filled with the lust for blood.

Mary turned toward the sound. Footsteps pounded the sand, accompanying the lighter touch of the dog's racing feet. Metal tags rattled.

"Please don't let your dog chase the birds. It scares them."

The running feet slowed but the dog continued chasing itself in circles, barking its ridiculous head off.

"Hello? I can hear you breathing. I'm blind, can you please answer?"

It was a mistake to let a stranger know she couldn't see, but she couldn't allow the dog to do as it pleased. It belonged on a leash, reminders were posted everywhere, and she could tell from the wide range of space it was covering, the sound of it racing back and forth, that it was unrestrained.

"Please control your dog."

There was no sound but the racing, barking dog.

"Being forced to run exhausts them. They need all their strength to hunt for food."

The dog's bark was faster, higher pitched. The animal sounded almost happy that it hadn't caught anything, gleeful at his success in disturbing the birds from their rest. "It's cruel. Torturing them like that. This is all they have — this beach — we're the pests."

She took a deep breath, wondering whether she'd be able to detect a scent above the smell of damp air and water. She took a few steps back. Where was he? If it was a he. The sudden fear was suggesting a he, someone who might hurt her. Women weren't usually violent, were they? It wasn't really true that they weren't violent at all, it was just more common in males, or maybe closer to the surface. They liked to intimidate.

"Hello?" Her voice was so soft she wondered if the other heard it.

She was never sure if it was an undetected odor, a shift in the air current, or a sound just beyond her conscious range of hearing, but she knew the man was still there. And it was a man. She could feel that too, feel the greater muscle mass, the aggression. He was moving closer to where she stood. The dog had stopped barking, stopped running as far as she could tell. Possibly it was stealthily moving closer alongside its master — if you could call someone a master who allowed the dog to indulge his primal nature without the guiding hand that made an animal a pleasant companion.

The wind had shifted and picked up slightly. She smelled sweat. She stepped back again, hoping for level sand, but even at its smoothest, sand always offered an opportunity to lose one's footing. If she stumbled, she'd appear even weaker than she already was. The dog and the man sensed her fear. Smelled it as vividly as she smelled perspiration and wet dog. She heard the soft flapping of the birds settling back down twenty or thirty feet to her left, foolishly confident the threat was gone. Waves continued their gentle lapping, like a baby's clapping hands, giving the false impression this was a safe and tranquil spot.

For a moment, the waves stopped, as they often did at low tide. She heard the breathing again. The man, filling his lungs deeply, huge sounds, indicating a large chest cavity. The dog panted, took several breaths for each of the man's. They sounded closer.

She took several more steps back. Her hood slipped off. She grabbed at the edges, but couldn't get it back in place. "Who's there?!" Her voice sounded unnaturally loud in her ears, and as shrill as the gulls' cries.

The breathing continued, then the dog turned and she heard his feet, thick toenails scratching and throwing clumps of wet sand. He barked furiously and once again the gulls began running before taking desperate flight.

She wanted to turn and flee herself, as best she could run at her age, stumbling quickly, escaping to the steps and the path where surely early morning joggers were passing by. Did any of them see there was a problem? Did they assume she was engaged in a friendly conversation? If she screamed, they would notice, if they weren't lost inside their own heads, ears plugged up and filled with their own music.

"Why won't you speak?" Her voice broke. She tried to slow her breathing.

The waves returned to their gentle lapping. "Hello?" She strained, turning her head slightly. The sound of the breathing had stopped. She couldn't hear the dog or the man. It was as if they'd vanished right before her eyes. Except her eyes were useless. They'd simply turned and walked away. He couldn't be bothered to dignify her with an answer, refused to alleviate the panic he'd surely sensed as she begged for an acknowledgment of her helplessness, her fear. Any person with a decent heart would go out of his way to give her a sense of what was happening around her. Of course, someone who allowed his dog to terrorize wildlife had a rather tarnished heart.

She knew the story — *It's nature*, a thoughtless dog owner would say. *Birds chase fish and crabs. Dogs chase birds. Wildcats chase dogs. The bird population is too large*, they'd argue. In her view, scavenging birds were a necessary part of the food chain, cleaning up the dead flesh of other animals. For that, they should be respected, even if humans found it repulsive. The gulls had a proud beauty and independence. And if anything was overpopulated, it was the dogs on the beach.

Species were either dying out at horrifying rates, or swelling their ranks to bloated proportions. But none of that mattered. It was terrible to see any creature suffer needlessly. She'd feel exactly the same if that man's dog were mauled by a mountain lion.

She turned and walked closer to the pier, moving diagonally toward the edge of the water.

"Mary!"

Following a lifetime of instinct, she turned her face up toward the pier, even though it made no difference.

"Come up and say hi."

The voice was Daniel's.

As if to confirm her recognition, he called, "I have bear claws."

How had she managed to give the impression she liked bear claws? Her stomach roiled, anticipating the sticky sweetness. She walked past the pillars supporting the pier. Pigeons clucked and warbled, as if the pier itself were making comforting sounds. She turned and went to the stairs. When she reached the middle of the pier, Daniel called out again, "Over here. To your right."

She followed his voice.

As she approached his side, he said, "I thought I heard you shouting."

"You did. A jogger was letting his dog terrorize the gulls."

"You sounded terrorized yourself."

"I don't like it."

"I know. But you can't stop it from happening."

"I can try."

"You shouldn't let it upset you so much. It's not good for your heart. Your blood pressure." He took her wrist and placed a napkin and half a bear claw in her hand.

"This isn't good for my heart either," she said.

"Just a little treat."

"Thank you."

"You can't stop the dogs chasing birds. Why can't you accept that?"

"I just can't."

She felt the movement of air as a pelican soared low above them. A moment later it plunged into the water with a loud splash.

"I hope that guy didn't get my fish," Daniel said.

Mary took a bite of the sweet dough and frosting. It felt good, comforting her from the inside out.

While Daniel talked about his grandchildren, she chewed and swallowed and let the breeze caress her face. She listened to the pelicans splashing around the pier, and the fishermen re-casting lines that sailed out past the railings like small, fishy birds themselves.

She'd hadn't always felt such an absurd love for the birds on the beach. Yes, she'd taught her sons to respect them, but she hadn't become hysterical like she was now. And hysterical was the only word for it. She felt a rage that could be described as murderous.

The change in her feelings about the gulls had come in the late nineteen-sixties. A seagull had saved her sanity, maybe her life. It was a ridiculous belief, but she'd never been able to shake it.

She'd been divorced then, abandoned by her first husband who had acquired a younger model of Mary. The world had changed since her childhood, when an abandoned woman was cast out of society, often left destitute, without any rights to her ex-husband's income or property. Women were coming into their own in the sixties. Henry had done well, and so, Mary did well. He was gone, but she had a house on the beach without a mortgage, and plenty to take care of herself. It wasn't as if she needed another man at all. Yet, she'd wanted one.

She should have seen that Gordon was trouble. Hanging out on the beach, using LSD like he was a teenager himself. He was several years younger than Mary, and she'd made an utter fool of herself over him. Proud that she looked thirty-five in her bikini when she was more than ten years past that birthday. Mary had behaved like a silly teenager herself — thrilled to compete with girls half her age, and win. Gordon was enthralled with her.

All of them were stoned, their senses distorted, laughing crazily at the simplest gesture, racing into the water and diving beneath the waves, immune to the icy temperature. They hadn't eaten all day and were probably dehydrated as well. They sat around on blankets, smoking cigarettes because the park rangers would chase them away if they found them smoking anything else. A fire crackled in the concrete ring designed to keep the embers contained.

Mary had drifted off to sleep or into some other sort of unconsciousness. She'd woken and found that all the others were gone — ten or fifteen of them. She heard faraway screams of laughter and the crash of waves. Everyone must have gone into the water again. She sat up and saw there were two others after all.

Gordon and a teenage girl sprawled on a blanket three or four feet away from her. They were naked, the sighs and sounds of their love making so distinct, it was as if she were lying on the blanket with them. The fire spun an orange glow over their bodies.

Mary looked away. She started to cry. Suddenly they were quiet. She turned back and Gordon was looking at her. He touched the girl's cheek and she turned to look. They giggled, then began shrieking with laughter, their cries drowning out every other sound. Mary stood up. They laughed harder, all the while continuing to stroke each other's bodies, Gordon on top of the girl, moving faster, laughing and moaning at the same time.

Mary turned, hurrying away from the light cast by the flames. Her foot caught in an abandoned towel and twisted, launching her onto the sand face first. Sand filled her nostrils. Her teeth crunched on granules as she tried to spit it out. Her tears made sand cling to her face. A few pieces slipped into her eyes. She rubbed them, crying more as sand scratched at the tender skin around her lower eyelid. She pushed herself up and began walking. Despite the soft sand, her knees ached from the force of her fall. She hurried into the darkness. The fog had come in and she was wearing nothing but a bikini top and cutoff shorts. She walked faster, almost running, unable to see where she was going, the moonlight failing to penetrate the thick film of tears across her eyes. She turned closer to the water, hoping the waves would drown out the sound of laughter and the cries of pleasure that followed her, filling her ears as if she were still right beside them.

When she reached the edge of the water, she ran along the shore for another quarter mile or so. Finally, she sat down, gasping for breath. She let the water come up around her ankles, creeping into her shorts, not caring if she was soaked and frozen. She put her arms across her bent knees and leaned forward, pressing her forehead against her arms. She cried for so long, she wondered how her body continued to generate moisture. Her house wasn't far away, but she'd left her bag with her keys and her sweatshirt by the fire. She couldn't go back. She had to wait until she was sure they were gone. It might be all night.

Slowly her crying subsided. She felt there was something, a presence, occupying the space around her. She tried to think whether it was the drugs distorting her brain cells, or something else. After a while, she'd lifted her head and glanced to her right. A huge white gull stood a few feet away. The moonlight made his white feathers glow as if he were lit from within. His orange beak was beautiful, and so distinct she could make out the small holes of his nostrils. He stared at her, unblinking. The look in his eyes was infinitely kind. He took a step toward her. She held her breath and watched him. They remained like that for a long time, possibly an hour, or maybe it just felt that way. Her senses were distorted by the LSD that swam through her nerves.

She was certain the gull had kept her from plunging into the water and ending her life. Shortly after that night, she'd woken from her drug-addled, sex-addled, delusional experiment and realized she was a middle-aged woman, walking along the edge of a razor that was going to tear her apart.

She never mentioned the gull. Anyone would have thought it was a hallucination, but she knew it was real. And she knew then, the gulls had intelligence. Feelings. They cared for other creatures, even human beings who were technically their predators.

Since then, she'd defended them as if they were her children.

The bear claw was gone.

"Thank you for the treat," she said.

"It makes me happy that you enjoy it," Daniel said.

"I hope you catch a lot."

"Thanks. You bring me good luck."

"I'll leave my luck with you." She got up and walked back along the pier, unsure how old she was or how long it had been since that night on the beach when the seagull saved her soul.

It was another life.

Eight

Corrine made red beans and rice with Italian sausage for dinner. They each ate two helpings and drank two glasses of Pinot Noir. When they were finished, Parker licked their plates, removing every grain of rice. Andy put the plates in the dishwasher while Corrine covered the pot where the beans and rice had cooked. She put it in the refrigerator and wiped the counter.

Andy picked up the wine bottle to pour the last of it in their glasses.

"Let's put it in plastic glasses and walk to the beach," she said.

"It's dark."

"Yes, I noticed."

He kissed her nose. "You're very clever that way."

She reached into the cabinet and took out two plastic glasses with short stems.

"No alcohol on the beach," he said.

"No one will notice. It's just wine. So you agree, it's a beautiful night for a walk?"

"Cold, but beautiful."

"Like you," she said.

He smiled.

She wished he would disagree. If he'd spoken those words to her, it would hurt. He seemed proud of being considered cold. She picked up the bottle and poured what was left into the glasses.

When they reached the beach, they left their shoes at the stairs, and walked almost to the surf line on soft, dry sand. It was cool, but not uncomfortable. They sat down. Parker sat beside Andy, looking out at the waves as if he wanted to make sure they stayed where they belonged. Andy and Corrine sipped their wine. She leaned her head against his shoulder. Parker lowered himself to a reclining position, but he didn't take his eyes off the water.

"What do you see out there?" Andy rubbed the dog's ears.

Parker made a smacking sound. They laughed.

Corrine glanced up at the pier. It was deserted, as it should be. She tipped her head back, trying to see past the railing. "I wonder if we'll see the ghost," she said.

"There's no ghost."

"You never know."

"Yes, I do."

She turned away from the pier. The more she'd thought about it, the more she'd become convinced it was entirely possible. There were thousands of unexplained things in the world, in life, why not the lingering essence of people who had died? When she passed the ship in the daylight, looking closely at its broken form, the bow pulled away from the rest, its two openings like vacant eye sockets, doorways to nowhere, especially prominent when the tide was low. It wasn't difficult to believe that at any moment, something indistinct, something unfamiliar, might emerge — a creature that had lived in the bowels of the ship for close to a hundred years. She shivered.

A wave broke softly, giving the impression it was a small one, but it rushed across the wet sand and up the embankment with breathtaking speed. A few fingers snaked close to their feet, quickly absorbed into the dry sand.

"It's coming closer. We should move back," Andy said.

"Sometimes I think you're afraid of the water."

"Not at all. But I take the ocean seriously. People don't realize how powerful the undertow is. How destructive the force of all that water can be."

"Most people do."

He patted her head. "You're so cute."

She sat up and pulled her upper body away from him. "What does that mean?"

"You assume the best about everything and everyone."

"Do I?"

"Sure. Gulls aren't scavengers, picking at rotting flesh, fighting with flies to devour a putrid piece of meat, they're god-like masters of the sky and sea. Old people are all sweet and good, simply in need of a little attention and then they won't realize they're decaying further every day, every hour. You don't see that most of them are nasty, sour people who have outlived their usefulness.

"That's a terrible thing to say."

"Sometimes the truth is terrible. I think a lot of old people know that. It's the reason they're bitter."

She dug her toes into the sand. "I don't think that's how it is at all."

Truth is not as terrible as a lie.

She turned toward the boat. "Did you hear something?"

"No." He slid his hand along the curve of her hip and thigh. "Don't you get tired of it?"

"Of being positive?"

"Of the constant death. You get so upset when you see a dead bird or seal, why do you want to put yourself face to face with human death every day?"

"Because I like old people. They know so much about the world."

"You have a lot of potential, and it's wasted at that place."

When they'd first talked about her job, he'd seemed supportive, interested in the details of some of the people she worked with. She couldn't understand why he was beginning to undermine her, trying to poison her heart. She folded her hands around each other and put them between her knees. She pressed her knees together, holding her hands in place.

Andy continued stroking her thigh. "Deb had the same problem."

"Deb?"

"My ex. I told you."

"Oh, right. Your ex-wife." She felt a surge of anger at being compared to his ex-wife. What did that mean? In the months they'd been together, she thought she'd learned everything about him, heard nearly all the important stories from his past. He'd given her all the details of his marriage, but now that she thought about it, they were facts — dates, employment history, family tree. He hadn't said much at all about why they'd split up. Nothing about his feelings or hers. And now, she couldn't remember the reason at all. "What problem did she have?"

"Didn't realize her potential."

"I'm using my potential. My career is challenging. It's different every day, and I love working with older people. And I don't like being compared to your ex-wife."

"I'm not comparing. You're in a totally different class. It was just an observation."

"A comparison."

He squeezed her leg. "You're nothing like her. I'm just saying you're beautiful and smart, and you're buried away in a warehouse full of people waiting to die."

She unclasped her hands and lifted his arm away from her. She stood up. Parker glanced at her, cocked an ear, and looked at Andy for direction. "Let's go," she said.

"Sure." Andy jumped to his feet and Parker followed suit, wagging his tail.

The wind whipped across her face, hair stinging her cheeks. Moonlight sparkled on the whitecaps. She raised her face, letting the wind blow the hair back off her skin. She squinted at the moon and tried to think what she wanted to say to Andy. She didn't want to be compared to his ex-wife, to any other woman, and she didn't like him talking about her potential as if she were a student or an improvement project. She had a satisfying career. She didn't need something different or better. And she didn't need exotic dresses or whatever else he had in mind. The wind was cold, but she didn't mind it. She liked how it made her feel alive. Yes, old people were decaying, as visibly as the boat sitting to her left, the whitish gray concrete brightened by moonlight. But every single breathing human being needed love and care, desired touch as much as a young person. They were all precious souls — the outside had nothing to do with what was inside their minds and hearts.

The waves were getting closer, every third one cresting the ledge of sand. It was eighteen inches high, formed by waves the previous week. Every eight to ten days, the ocean reshaped the beach, so that sometimes when she walked down to the shore she was disoriented, as if she'd come to the wrong place.

Andy stood waiting. It seemed as if he wanted her to

speak, but she still wasn't sure what she was trying to say. It wasn't like him to wait. He liked to fill silent spaces with words of authority. Even when he made idle chit chat, energy surged around her, giving his comments a cloak of importance they wouldn't have coming from someone else. He wanted to take control, keep moving, keep the action going. His face looked like a mask. He didn't turn in her direction, didn't move his mouth, and he hardly blinked. He seemed to be in a trance.

Above the center section of the ship, where the main cabin used to be, the sky seemed darker than everywhere else. It had the same thick blackness as if there were a mass of crows sitting there. But now, there were only a few gulls and pelicans, the rest of the boat was deserted. The black spot was devoid of moonlight, darker than the waves below. It moved slightly, flowing along the length of the ship. The moonlight had faded, or maybe the dark spot was spreading. She couldn't be sure. Still Andy remained silent and motionless. Her insides seemed to harden, as if the two of them were in some kind of tableau that she couldn't see for herself.

The chilling wind slipped beneath her jacket and its icy fingers stroked her ribs, reaching down to cling to the soft flesh of her belly. She felt as if she were alone, the dog as silent as his master. She turned toward Andy. His appearance was that of a man she'd never seen before, his hair the color of the boat and his face changing so it was both familiar but also the face of someone she didn't know. She shivered, but couldn't seem to force a sound out of her throat, couldn't form anything in her mind that might accompany the sound, if she could make one. The dark thing over the ship drifted like kelp on a swell of water, then arched up like a wave was lifting it into the sky, preparing to crash forward. It hung there and seemed to whisper, but too softly to be understood.

She touched Andy's arm. He continued staring at the water. Did he see the thing too? Or was she imagining it? How was it possible to see something dark and formed when the sky and water were equally dark? But they weren't. And the ship was white and chalky, giving the thing contrast.

A wave crashed and raced up the beach. It breached the embankment, heading toward their feet. She scrambled back. Andy remained where he was and the water washed across his feet and soaked the ankles of his jeans. Parker barked. Andy didn't respond.

"Andy?"

He looked at her.

"You're getting wet. We should go."

He nodded, tugged gently on Parker's leash, and turned in the direction of the steps up from the beach.

"Are you okay?" she said.

"Fine. We should head back."

"Yes."

"Did you see that…that thing?" she said.

"What thing?"

"Over the boat? The dark spot?"

"The sky?" he laughed.

"No. A shadow, or something. It was moving and changing shape."

"It's dark. How can you see anything moving?"

"The moon is bright. And somehow, I just could."

"I didn't see anything." He took her hand. His fingers were like iron rods.

She squeezed his hand. "Your hand is cold."

"Not really."

"Your fingers are like ice."

"I don't think so."

"You didn't see anything?"

"The moon. A few birds."

"I think she's right. It's haunted."

He stopped, let go of her hand, and faced her. Once again his face looked familiar, but she felt ill at ease, remembering clearly that a moment ago, he'd looked like someone she'd never met. As if she knew the exterior of him, but nothing about what was inside. She knew absolutely nothing except the well-connected stories and anecdotes he'd told her. She didn't know what he feared, didn't know what his dreams were — not really. She knew how many women he'd had relationships with — five. But she didn't know how many women he'd loved, if any, and didn't know the names of the people he hated, who his enemies might be.

Where had that thought come from? She didn't have

enemies and didn't recall thinking in those terms before, yet now, she was certain Andy was a person who did have enemies. Perhaps the spirit, that black presence, whatever it was, had peeled back Andy's skin and shown her there was a stranger inside. She wanted to cry, but there were no tears, just a sob deep in her bones, something that wanted to release in a piercing scream but couldn't find its way out of her chest.

"You go ahead and believe in ghosts," he said. "If that makes you happy. Although I think it's another indication that you're around too many people with dementia, including that crone you're stalking. But I think it's absurd, and I really don't want to talk about them. Indulging fantasies like those can take over your mind."

"Is that right?" she whispered.

He took her head in his hands, as if he were picking up a melon, checking it for bruises. Perhaps he was looking for soft spots that had allowed her to accept the possibility of supernatural beings and unearthly myths. He drew her toward him and kissed her gently. The things he'd said came from a man she didn't know, but his kiss was warm and familiar. The tears that hadn't been there a moment earlier, rose to the surface. They kissed for several minutes, moving closer, wrapping their arms around each other until she couldn't distinguish between his arms and her own, his mouth and her lips.

After a few minutes, she pulled back and he let her go.

They walked up the hill, Parker straggling behind,

investigating every clump of beach grass and fallen tree branch.

"You never told me much about Deb," Corrine said.

"Sure I did."

"Not what she was really like, or why you split up."

He put his hand on the back of her neck. His fingers were warm now, and he pressed them gently into the muscle. "Why would you want to talk about her? She has nothing to do with us."

"You compared me to her."

"I didn't."

"You said she didn't recognize her potential, like me."

"I think you mis-heard me."

The pressure of his fingers was no longer soothing. Now, her head ached. She was unsure of what he'd said, her memory clouded by the black object hovering above the ship. She moved out from under his arm.

"Doesn't that feel good?"

"It's hard to walk uphill, it feels like your hand is pulling me back."

"I'll give you a massage at home."

"That'll be nice."

They crossed the road that led from the State Park gate down to the beach and started up the stairs made of pebbled concrete. One side sloped up to houses above, the embankment covered with poison oak and wild vines. Trees covered the right side, forming a secluded grove where an occasional homeless person spread out a sleeping bag, until the Sheriff hurried them along. Once, she'd seen a man sitting on a mat playing a guitar and singing. It was one of those things that seemed like it should be perfectly natural, but it had scared her because it was so out of the ordinary.

She hurried up the stairs ahead of Andy, anxious to get out of the tangle of flowering shrubs and weeds and trees, out to the street where others were walking home from the Mexican restaurant.

When Andy caught up with her at the street, they turned and headed toward Corrine's neighborhood.

"I hate walking along here," Andy said. "It's so grubby. It needs spiffing up."

"It's a beach town. It's quaint."

"It's dirty. And there are some questionable looking characters hanging outside the bar."

"Whatever."

He put his arm around her again.

At home, she rinsed the plastic glasses and opened another bottle of Pinot Noir. She poured it into clean glasses and brought one to Andy in the living room. She sat beside him, touched her glass to his, and curled her legs to the side. "So why did you split up?"

"I don't get why you're fixated on that."

"I'm not fixated, just curious."

"Why?"

"Because it's important to know each other's history."

"I'm looking at where I'm headed, not where I've been."

"It's part of who you are now. And it affects where we're headed."

"Is this the relationship talk?" He took a sip of wine. "Because if it is, I'm not ready." He patted the edge of the couch. He lifted his hand and snapped his fingers at the dog. Parker looked at him, then put his head back down on his paws and continued staring at the darkness beyond the window.

"Not at all."

"Good. We're not quite there yet, agreed?"

"Absolutely," she said. "But I still think it's important to understand what came before."

"We weren't right for each other."

"That's not a reason."

"She wasn't right for me."

"That's not a reason either."

"I think it is."

"Why wasn't she right for you? And why didn't you figure that out before you were married?"

"Don't know."

"You met in college?"

"You already know the answer to that. Why are you asking me all this? I have no interest in talking about her."

"It's starting to feel like you're hiding something."

He laughed. "Do you seriously think that? I don't want to dig into an analysis of my first marriage, which has been over for three years, more than three years, and that translates to keeping a secret?"

"I said hiding something."

"Same thing."

"Is there something you don't want me to know?"

"There's something I do want you to know — I'm not going to dissect my deceased marriage. It was a mistake. It's over. I'm not hiding anything and my life is not influenced by any experiences with that woman." He put his wine glass on the table. The glass was nearly empty, but he didn't get up to retrieve the bottle. He put his hand on her leg and rubbed gently. He moved closer and kissed her eyebrow.

Corrine closed her eyes.

He kissed her other eyebrow and took the wine glass out of her hand. She heard it click on the table and the rattle of Parker's tags as he shifted position.

Andy kissed her, softly and then with a ferocity that tore at her lips and pushed her head back until her neck made a small cracking sound.

She pulled away from him. "What's that about?"

"Come on." He put his hands on either side of her face and kissed her gently. "Let's go to bed."

"It's only eight-fifteen."

"So?"

"I thought we'd finish the wine and watch a movie. I'm kind of hungry. Do you want some chips or something?"

"I'm only hungry for one thing."

She laughed, but it wasn't the playful feeling she was used to. "I asked you an honest question and I don't understand why you won't answer me."

"Because I don't want to talk about my ex-wife. It's starting to get irritating."

"Why?"

"I told you why. And I'm not hiding anything. We met in college, we were young. We thought we were in love, we let passion dictate everything and I didn't really find out we weren't right for each other until all of that wore off. Satisfied?"

She decided not to point out that he was working hard to cover up getting to know each other with passion right this minute. She was not at all satisfied. It was the same vague collection of facts he'd already provided. And not being right for each other could mean anything. She felt like an insecure teenager prying into the breakup of his marriage, but the more he resisted, the more certain she became there was something she needed to know, that he was indeed hiding something. Maybe nothing bad, or serious, but some detail he wanted to keep from her. An important detail.

Nine

It was five-thirty in the morning when Mary's phone rang. She was awake, she always was, and Thomas knew she would be. Her youngest son called every Thursday, already an hour into his work day in New York. He worked for a technology company, too many hours a day in her view — twelve in the office Monday through Friday and several hours most weekends. The price of success, he told her.

"Just checking in," he said.

"How is your day going so far?"

"Snow. High of thirty-seven."

She smiled. "I didn't ask for the weather report. I can get that on this phone that knows everything."

"My day is good. I'm off to London next week, and then Munich."

"It sounds wonderful. Still not slowing down, are you."

"Eat or be eaten."

"I hate that sentiment."

Thomas laughed. "I know, but it's true."

"You have enough money to last another lifetime. You're sixty-six years old."

"I like it."

"I know. Is Casey going this time?"

He explained Casey's schedule, which sometimes sounded worse than Thomas's, even though no corporation set the agenda — everything was strictly volunteer. Casey was involved with so many organizations Mary couldn't begin to remember them all.

"How are you feeling?" he said.

"Very well."

"No issues?"

"I said I'm doing well."

"You always say you're doing well. Still risking your life walking on the beach every day?" He laughed, but he sounded nervous.

She knew they worried. And it wasn't without cause. A blind woman battling crowds of people, walking across uneven sand, standing close to crashing waves was concerning. She didn't blame Thomas or her other sons for fretting about it. But still, what were they so worried about? One way or another, her life would end in the not-too-distant future. As much as possible, she planned to enjoy every remaining moment. It was the reason she still woke at five every morning. "I'd die without my walks to the beach."

"Don't say that. I saw there was a storm last week."

"Yes, but not enough rain. It only lasted a day and a half."

"How's your fisherman friend doing?"

"He's good. I did have an upsetting incident the other day." She bit her lip. She hadn't intended to mention it. Now, the rest of the conversation would go badly. It had popped out on its own momentum. That's what happened when she spent too much time brooding.

"What happened?"

She told him about the birds. She could have edited out the man silently facing her, trying to scare her, but if all she mentioned were the birds and her chastising, Thomas would know she'd left something out.

"That doesn't make me happy," he said.

"It didn't make me happy either."

"It's not nineteen-fifty-eight," he said.

"I know that."

"There are some scary people out there."

She laughed. "Why do all of you think there haven't always been scary people? Even in nineteen-thirty-eight. And in nineteen-sixty-eight. And nineteen-eighty. The world hasn't changed."

"It's changed a lot more than you want to acknowledge."

"People haven't changed," she said. She felt along the windowsill and picked up the small glass cow. Every windowsill in the house had part of her collection — miniature animals she'd collected over the years. This particular windowsill, facing the narrow street that ran past the front of her house, was filled with farm animals. The only disappointment with this collection was the baby chick. It was half as small as the cows and horses. She remembered how adorable the chick was — pale yellow with a tiny orange beak — but it didn't belong with the others. She rubbed her thumb over the cow's head.

"He didn't say anything at all? Nothing you're withholding?"

"Ha. I should have withheld the entire story. I blurted it out and the minute I began, I knew there'd be a lecture. The child becomes the parent."

"I'm not trying to be your parent. But I worry. We all worry."

"I don't need worrying over." She put down the cow and picked up the baby chick. Hens worried over their brood. Wasn't that the term? It shouldn't be considered a bad thing. When you thought of it for the hens, it was good, it was their care and attention to the well-being of their offspring. But this was all wrong — when offspring worried over the one who gave them life. She didn't like it. The reversal was nothing new, it had been going on for twenty years now, but it didn't annoy her any less than it had at the start, even though she knew there was more cause for it now. Or maybe the term was brood, not worry? Hens brooded over their brood? That made no sense. "I'm safe," she said.

"I don't think you are. Not when you go telling strange men what to do, acting as if you're everyone's mother, the mother of the birds, the patron saint of the beach."

"People need to respect wildlife."

"Well they don't. And you know that."

"It doesn't mean we just let them get away with it."

"You're ninety-one years old! You…"

"I know how old I am."

"You reprimanded a stranger. He's obviously not a nice character, frightening you like that. Who knows what else he might do. And now, you won't know if you see him again because you didn't see him. But he sure as hell knows who you are."

She curled her fist around the glass chick and touched her knuckles to the window. She guessed it was quarter to six, still dark outside. She walked into the kitchen. "You act like he's going to come murder a little old lady who gave a quiet reminder to restrain his dog."

"People are very territorial about their dogs. For some people, they're like children. And they don't take kindly to outsiders disciplining their children either."

"I didn't yell at the dog."

"Can you not do that any more? Can you mind your own business? In fact, can you find a companion to walk with you? What about…"

"I'm not discussing the companion subject again."

"Why are you so stubborn?"

"I'm not stubborn. I treasure my independence. Just wait until you're old."

"I'm already old, as you like to point out when you're trying to get me to hang up my hat."

"Precisely."

"Precisely, what?" he said.

"I don't need help. I'm not incapacitated yet. I can find my way around my house, and I know every inch of that beach. During every single season."

"You don't know every person on the beach. Look how crowded it is now compared to years ago."

"Thomas. I'm not getting a companion."

"Can you at least not talk to strangers any more?"

"Do you hear how that sounds?"

He laughed. "Okay, yes. But can you not do it? People aren't as civil as they were in your day. It doesn't take much to set them off."

"Beach rage?"

"Yes. That's a good way to put it."

She smiled and shook her head.

"And if that guy bothers you," Thomas said, "If he says something, call me. Right on the spot. You take your phone to the beach, right?"

She went back to the front window and felt for the black stallion that was rearing on its hind legs. She set the chick near the horse's hind legs.

"Are you still there?" Thomas said.

"I'm here."

"So I'm guessing you don't take the phone to the beach

and you don't want to lie to me."

"I didn't say that."

"Say what?"

"That I don't take it."

"You said nothing."

She returned to the kitchen and took an orange out of the bowl.

"Mother?"

"I'm here."

"Please take your phone everywhere you go."

She pictured the heavy black phone from her childhood house, and the slim princess phone on her nightstand in the seventies. She wanted to laugh at what it would have sounded like then — take your phone everywhere you go.

"Why have you gone silent on me?"

"Just remembering things."

"What things?"

"Nothing important," she said. "I'll take the phone."

"Thank you."

They talked about his trip, and before he hung up, he told her twice more to take her phone everywhere. When she ended the call, she put the phone on the table in the entryway where she always left it when she went out. If a man assaulted her on the beach, there wouldn't be time to fumble around and ask the helping voice to place a phone call. Thomas should know that. But telling him what he wanted to hear would help him concentrate on his work instead of worrying about his mother.

She went back into the kitchen and began peeling the orange.

At nine, Mary asked the robotic but soothing woman inside her phone for updates, marveled again that she had both feet solidly in the twenty-first century, robots and all, and went outside. She steeled herself against the wind, and patted her bag to be sure she'd actually packed her mug of coffee and another orange that she planned to take out to counter Daniel's bear claw. Once or twice a week was a pleasant burst of sugar, but every day and her pants would start to feel tight, her stomach would get angry and clamor for more awful things. You didn't live to be ninety-one eating donuts and hamburgers and drinking soda pop.

Her soft-soled shoes made only a whisper as she walked down the slight incline of the sidewalk, past the rows of beach houses. The soft tap continued across the bridge and along the path. Runners pounded by, slowing and leaving plenty of room, some tossing a *good morning* over their shoulders as they passed. When she reached the pier, her feet thudded on the worn boards. She walked down the center, knowing Daniel would already be here at this hour. He'd call out her name so she didn't have to stumble around, although many of the people who fished off the pier in winter greeted her, recognizing her, even if she couldn't recognize them.

It had only been four years since she'd lost her sight

completely. The dimming and narrowing of her vision had been gradual through her eighties. She smiled — sometimes she couldn't believe she was over forty, much less that she was so casually thinking back over her seventies or eighties.

She hadn't started talking to Daniel until about three years ago. But she knew his voice and knew the faint, somewhat lemony smell that seemed to float around him even though he spent half his day with fish. He had informed her he'd fished every day for most of his life. He came out to the concrete ship, and once that was closed off, to the pier. He threw his line in the water and sometimes he was lucky to catch something in the thirty minutes before he had to pack up and leave for his job as a high school teacher. He was retired now.

He called out to her and she walked to the railing and found the bench near him. "Why do you like to fish?" she said, wondering that she'd never asked him before.

"Fish is good for you," he said.

"I know you don't come out here every day just to be sure you have a healthy diet. Especially with all those bear claws."

Daniel laughed.

"There's more to it than that," she said.

"I've fished here since I was a kid. The thrill of being on the cement boat turned it into something magical, and that magic stayed with me. I'd pretend it was moving, that we were in the middle of the Pacific Ocean and I was hauling in huge tuna and swordfish."

"It sounds like a wonderful childhood."

"I've never been out in open water. Never fished off any boat but this one."

"That's too bad."

"I think I enjoyed it more in my imagination. The thought of being out there floating with no land in sight doesn't make me feel so good. I don't swim."

"Then I'm glad you got to enjoy this boat."

"When I got older, I just kept doing it. Habit. I'd be lost without the routine. It's nice. Standing here, not having to think much — looking at the water, watching the birds."

"The fish."

He laughed. "Yes, the fish. I do like to eat the fish too, when I'm lucky."

The wind was calming down. "Is the fog getting thicker?" she said.

"It is. You always know."

"The breeze died."

"I wonder about the things that pass right by me, since I have my sight."

"I suppose about the same number of things I miss, not being able to see. Did you happen to notice a man was talking to me the other day? Before you called out to me?"

"I don't remember."

"It was Monday. He was a jogger, and he had a dog with him. It was off the leash, chasing the birds. Barking a lot."

"That happens all the time."

"Then you didn't notice?"

"No, why?"

"He was…he frightened me."

"What did he do?"

Daniel's voice was louder. She heard his fishing pole tap the wood railing. The reel spun.

"I told him to restrain his dog, to stop tormenting the seagulls."

"And what did he say?"

"Nothing. But he came up close to me, and stood there for a few minutes. I kept asking him to speak, and I could feel him there, but he refused to say anything." The strong odor of fish wafted past her. "Did you catch something?"

"Three mackerel. But this latest is a clump of kelp."

"That's a good catch for the morning."

"I wish I'd seen that guy. What kind of jackass frightens an old lady?"

"I don't think of myself as an old lady."

Daniel was silent, and she imagined him smiling at the water.

"I guess the same kind of man who doesn't train his dog."

They fell silent for some time. Daniel didn't offer a bear claw. She took the mug out of her bag and sipped coffee while she listened to the gulls screeching and the fishing reels spinning as they let out line, then turning slowly as it was pulled back in. Occasionally she heard a grunt or exclamation of pleasure followed by the smack of a fish on the wood. She could feel the fog, the low, thick kind, heavy and wet on the backs of her hands. Her mug was almost empty.

Children were running in the surf, shouting. The sound made her happy, listening to their excitement over chasing waves that could never be caught, released from the fences and sidewalks of suburban towns on the other side of the hill. A child didn't need anything else if he had sand to dig in and waves to chase. She was glad her boys had the privilege of growing up in a coastal town. She believed it had made them into solid human beings with a connection to the earth and sense of their place in the world, no matter what they'd gone on to do — a big shot in technology, teaching, building custom yachts, and writing for a Northern California newspaper.

"I love hearing children scream when they're playing in the waves," she said.

"It can be grating," Daniel said. "It scares the fish."

"Can fish hear?"

"It's the vibration or something."

"If you say so. They sound so happy."

"It sounds more like terror," he said.

"It's play."

"They laugh like it's play, but they're playing with their nightmares. They know those waves are more powerful than anything they've ever encountered. They know what a six-foot wave can do to a child. They see the huge logs all over the sand. They know they could be tossed in the air and thrown a hundred feet."

"I don't remember thinking that when I was a girl," she said.

"It's not a thinking thing. It's the gut." She heard his fist pound against his belly.

"But they're having fun."

"Fun with terror. Listen, you'll hear it. That's one thing I know," he said. "Terror."

It was strange that after all this time together, all the chats about fish and birds, the ship and the weather, they were having another kind of conversation.

"What do you know about terror?" she said.

"Something that happened when I was a kid."

He sounded hesitant, as if he wondered why he'd mentioned it.

"You don't have to tell me."

"No, it's okay. But talking about it, I feel that panic like it was happening all over again, right now — that my life is over. I've never told anyone exactly what happened."

"I'm honored."

"We used to swim around the ship. It was…"

"I thought you couldn't swim?"

"I *don't* swim. I know how, but I never did again, after that."

"What happened?"

"I'm sure you know that back then, you could access the spaces below the deck. It was kid heaven. We dove and swam in there, looked at each other with our eyes bulging out. We gave hand signals to each other about how long we could stay down."

"It sounds frightening."

"That's not the terrifying part. The very last time I did it, I swam inside one of the compartments and my friends didn't follow. I waited a few seconds and when I knew I needed to go back to the surface, there was something spread across the opening." His voice grew quiet, as if he was so frightened, he couldn't find the strength to speak the words.

"Something?"

"An octopus." he said. "It was the size of a...its arms must have stretched ten or twelve feet, with hundreds of suction cups facing me." His voice shook.

"I don't want to dismiss your experience, but they don't come this close to shore."

"They can."

"I've never heard of it. They live in deep water, where it's colder."

"It was an octopus. Even now, those huge suction cups are there whenever I'm in a tight space and I close my eyes. The thing had grabbed either side of the entrance and...it was pulsing as if it wanted to eat."

"The ghost."

"What?"

"Nothing. I'm sorry for interrupting."

"I panicked."

He was crying softly now. She could feel he'd moved closer to the bench, turning away to hide himself from the other fishermen.

"It sounds terrible. What did you do?"

"I bit on my lips until they bled, trying not scream. I closed my eyes and said the rosary — letting the words run through my head."

"How awful."

"When I thought my lungs were going to explode, I opened my eyes and it was gone."

"It was the ghost."

"I…"

"It was the ghost."

"What are you talking about?"

"You've never felt it?"

The contents of his tackle box rattled as he dug around. A moment later, she heard him cast his line out. He was breathing normally now, the weakness and upset gone from his voice. "Felt what?"

"There's a spirit. It's around the ship sometimes, not always. I'm sure it's always here, but it only occasionally makes itself known."

"A ghost?"

"I think it took on the form of an octopus."

"I don't want to be cruel, but are you feeling okay? Is there some medication you're supposed to be taking?"

She laughed. "I'm not losing my mind. But a large octopus,

especially one large enough to cover a large opening as you described, wouldn't come into shallow water."

"It happened. And it wasn't a ghost. A ghost that takes on the shape of sea life? You're not serious."

"You should think about it," she said.

"It was a long time ago."

"It sounds awful."

"Ghosts are myths of the devil," he said.

"Possibly so. Everyone thinks the boat is a nice historical marker. A pleasant reminder of our past. But it knows terrible things."

"I can't see that at all," he said. "Yes, getting trapped down there was the worst experience of my life, and it turned me off swimming. But I've caught a lot of good fish from the boat over the years. Enough to feed a small village."

"The ghost…"

"Don't talk about ghosts to me. I don't want to hear it."

"I don't mean to offend you."

"If you go around talking like that to people, they're gonna' lock you up. You better be careful."

"I know what I've seen. And felt. I just wondered, since you were telling me your story, if you'd considered it, and…"

"Stop talking, Mary. I'm not listening to this."

"Are you afraid of it?" she said.

"I mean it."

Tears crept into her eyes. Most of her friends were dead. Her sons were far away and only visited occasionally. She'd come to think of Daniel as a friend, not a close one, but someone who cared for her, someone who was part of her days. And she cared for him. He sounded so angry. Did he think she'd ripped his story away from him, taken it on as her own? It might be he was ashamed of having told her how scared he was. He'd opened his heart and now he regretted it. He wasn't really angry with her, he was upset with himself. But being afraid was nothing to be ashamed of. When he'd first started telling her, he'd almost sounded proud — boasting that he knew all about terror, and noticing the terror in the children's voices. Now, she thought he might be right about that.

"Let me just say one thing," she said. "That boat is haunted. You might not take that literally, but it is. I hate it. I'm going to outlive it."

"If you hate it so much, if you think it's so awful, why do you come out here every single day?"

"So it knows I'm still here. That I'm still living. It can't kill me. Don't you see, it was trying to kill you."

"That's crazy. And I didn't die."

"It's a death trap. That's all it's been ever since someone got the crazy idea to make it a party place. They can make it sentimental and talk about dinner and dancing and band music, but it wasn't like that."

"You can't outlive a solid piece of concrete this big."

"I think I can. I'm healthy. Many people live past a hundred now. Except for my eyes, I'm in fine shape."

He didn't say anything. If her mention of the ghost made him think she was losing her mind, her plan to outlive a giant hunk of concrete and rebar must sound even more crazed. He wouldn't understand. But his story proved the ship was malevolent. It proved strange and inexplicable things happened on it, and beneath it. Everyone wanted to glorify it, as if life were so wonderful and perfect back then. How charming to dine on a ship. How lovely to dance at sea. They looked at the pictures and all they saw were the nice clothes and the pleasant looks on the faces of the dancers. They thought everyone back then was innocent. The human race never changed. All the ugliness and damage and horror might be more exposed now, but those things — the desire and lust and craving and crime were there since the first man and woman walked the earth. Those things were there — always.

People didn't know how it was during prohibition. They surely didn't think of it in terms of the boat. The lovely concrete ship moored in pleasant seaside Aptos. Thugs controlled everything. Liquor flowed as smoothly as it did now. People got drunk and ripped off their civilized masks. They said ugly things, they did ugly things. They turned into animals.

She hated it when the boat was viewed through sentimental eyes. She hated it when people spoke as if the world was decaying now and it had been wonderful back then. Times were simpler. Children were well behaved and marriages stayed together and everyone was kind and generous to each other. What a lie. She didn't understand why they wanted to believe such lies about the past, why they wanted to whitewash everything, go back in time. They pretended it was good because it had been good for them, maybe. But it wasn't good for everyone. Just because things were whispered about and then locked away so no one saw the truth didn't mean it was a beautiful time.

Ten

It was difficult to Google a guy named Andy Johnson. Was there any more common last name on the entire North American continent? Corrine entered his company name as well, but all she found was a photograph from a party in Spain in 2009 — part of the annual award trip for those in the salesforce who met their revenue quota. She could enter his college — UCLA — that might narrow it to twenty or thirty Andy Johnsons. He belonged to the SAE fraternity — ten or twelve Andy Johnsons.

After scrolling through the first of hundreds of thousands of hits, tapping back and forth to the images view, she put down her tablet. She went into the bedroom, calling for Cat. Googling the man you were in a relationship with was both normal and horrible. Everyone did it, so that made it normal. But feeling it was essential made her wonder if she should go further and hire a PI. Some women did. Her best friend's sister had done it and found out the guy she was seeing was associated with the Mafia. The *Mafia*! Clearly that woman had a gut warning. Was this thing with Andy the same? Or was she paranoid? Magnifying a minor annoyance, as he'd accused her of. No, she refused to dismiss her gut entirely. Since she'd seen the...whatever it was...hovering over the ship, coupled with Andy's oddly unresponsive posture, and the awareness that she only knew him on the outside, she couldn't quench the unsettled feeling in her stomach. How expertly he'd tried to twist it around and insist he hadn't compared her to Deb. He absolutely had.

Wasn't checking up on someone the first step toward the end of a relationship? If she didn't trust him, what was the point? If he wouldn't tell her about his past, what kind of future did they have? But searching for information was simply to ease her mind. To prove she was spinning up imaginative and fearful stories out of insignificant threads. She'd find nothing, and someday, soon, he'd casually mention why he and Deb split up. Pushing as hard as she had was a mistake. She'd forced him to dig in his heels.

She found Cat on the floor of the closet. Cat had pulled Corrine's flannel robe off the hanger and managed to shape it into a plump cushion. She was deep asleep, her head tucked upside down under her front paws. Corrine pushed the door back near the frame. She wished Cat would join her in the living room, but it wasn't fair to wake her from a solid nap and drag her into another room. She took off her long-sleeved shirt and pulled on a beige sweater. It was big, hanging in an uneven line around her thighs. The sleeves covered her hands up to the knuckle of her thumb. She made a cup of tea and went back to the couch.

After trying several combinations of Andy and Deb Johnson, and then Andy Johnson and Deb with no last name, she had nothing more than the photograph from Spain. It appeared to be everywhere. It seemed that half the people at the event had posted it on social media. It was a flattering picture of Andy. Finally she found a tweet that mentioned an @DebThurmon. Now she had something to work with. After some more surfing, she found Deb's Facebook page and was stunned to see that Deb had opened her profile to the entire state of California. Who did that? Was the woman stupid or one of those freakishly friendly, everyone-has-good-in-them people?

She put down her tablet and drank half the tea even though it was lukewarm. Cat wandered into the room and settled herself on the coffee table. Corrine would have preferred a nice lap snuggle, but just being in the same room together was nice, without the noise and smell of dog. Too bad Parker wasn't called Dog. She smiled and put down her cup.

She couldn't comprehend sharing photographs and parts of your life with a state inhabited by nearly forty million people. She clicked Deb's detail link. That explained it. She sold vitamin supplements. She had 3,782 friends. She was open to California so she could find new customers. Her feed was littered with information on vitamins, workout tips, and pictures of herself wearing skimpy, spandex outfits with matching shoes. It looked like she owned fifteen or twenty pairs of athletic shoes.

It was tedious work — tapping back through a timeline, but she discovered something that made her stop and defer the rest of the work until later. Deb and Andy's marriage had ended fourteen months ago, not three years. Deb announced it in an essay, much too long for Facebook, about first love and wishing the best for those who'd contributed to the shape of your life.

Corrine put her tablet next to Cat and went into the kitchen. She took out the metal shaker, a martini glass, and a jar of olives. She returned to the living room to the shelf where she kept a few bottles of alcohol. She picked up the Sapphire gin and vermouth. After mixing an icy cold drink, she poured it into the glass and stuck three large olives on a toothpick. She took a sip and stood for a moment enjoying the rush of alcohol into her blood.

It was dark and chilly outside but the drink would keep her warm enough. She opened the door that led from the kitchen to her enclosed garden. She sat on the metal chair and took another sip of the martini.

Drinking on top of discovering the mild, yet crucial lie, was not the best idea. It wouldn't be good if her dulled senses decided to send a friend request to Deb. She took another sip and vowed that she wouldn't go online, she wouldn't even pick up her tablet until morning.

Curiosity about the other information that might lie buried in Deb's timeline simmered inside of her. When the martini glass was empty, she had nothing, just an uncomfortable fizzing sensation in her throat, as if she'd drunk champagne that refused to dissipate.

None of this meant she should end it with Andy. She loved him. Or at least she was heading in that direction, but now she wondered what she loved? She certainly loved being with him, loved how he made her feel. Whatever she'd seen on the beach had been true — she knew part of the man, but had no idea how substantial a part that was. Snooping into his life wasn't the right way to know him better. She should be talking to him, but she'd tried and he'd slammed the door in her face. And slammed was not too strong a word. Now that she knew this about his marriage, it would be more difficult to ask questions because she'd have to keep information to herself. Continuing the search would make it worse.

She sucked on the last olive, letting it roll around in her mouth. When all the moisture had been sucked out, she chewed and swallowed it. She took her glass inside. She left it on the counter and went to bed. Morning would bring clarity.

For three days Corrine considered what she'd learned from Deb's lack of discretion. On two of those three evenings, Corrine and Andy ate dinner together and walked on the beach. She said nothing about Deb. During their walks, she hadn't seen any disturbances over the boat. She'd peered through the shimmer of moonlight, straining her eyes, doubting the shape of the night sky, one moment thinking something was there, and the next, mildly disappointed and also relieved it was only a piece of cloud or the movement of fog.

It was impossible to ask Andy about the timing of his marriage breakup. It was also impossible to feel good around him as she had before. She wondered if the apparition over the boat had distorted her perception of the world. Then she laughed at herself for indulging such primitive thoughts, and tried to figure out what she wanted. She loved him. She was sure of it.

She was sitting in her living room. Rain thundered on the roof and the trees in her small back yard whipped around like they were thrashing back at the wind. She'd made a fire in the wood burning stove, but the small room was so hot after an hour, she'd had to open the window. Cat was sitting beneath the window staring at the narrow opening as if she expected the storm to force its way into the house. Water dripped down the screen and was starting to pool in the window track, so Corrine was either going to have to hang out in her bedroom to escape the heat or put a towel along the windowsill. She took a sip of wine.

She looked at Cat. "What should I do?"

Cat turned and studied her. The expression on her face said — *How would I know?*

Corrine laughed. She unlocked her tablet and scrolled through email. There was nothing interesting. She checked her work email but there weren't any messages requiring action. She didn't recall ever having so much self doubt. Had it been dormant inside of her, slowly pulled out during the four months with Andy, as if someone were drawing a tapeworm out of her mouth, the entire, long ugly thing slowly emerging from her intestines?

If she returned to digging through Deb's timeline, she might find more. But once she did, she could never un-know it. Maybe she'd find nothing. Maybe the date discrepancy was the only thing. Or maybe Deb wasn't being truthful and there was no discrepancy. Maybe Deb had been so devastated it took her two years to recover her life to the point where she could post something so phony. And it *was* phony. Of course there were amicable divorces, but Deb's heartfelt essay, speckled with typos, sounded as if she was glad their marriage had fallen apart.

Corrine closed her email and opened a browser page. She Googled — *how to tell if your partner is lying*. Over three million results came up. Of course, every internet search brought up an insurmountable mountain of results, but it seemed telling in this case, as if the whole world distrusted the person sharing their bed. Topping the list were general Q&A forums with dubious answers that raised more questions than they resolved. She read them anyway. She read a few blog posts from psychologists fishing for clients, and from women and men who had lain traps for their partners. They were giddy with joy over their cleverness and the stealth with which they'd exposed the lies. It seemed they enjoyed the process of tearing apart their relationship and facing betrayal all because it had been so much fun getting the upper hand, winning — a treasure hunt.

She found a forum devoted to relationships in general. There was an entire thread about lying. One post was eerily similar to her own situation.

HurtingGirl: *I've been seeing a guy for five months and everything was perfect. I thought he was The One. He had a long relationship before me — five years. I thought it ended a few years before we met but just found out that they split two weeks before he and I hooked up. I feel like I can't trust him. I know it ended before me, but I feel betrayed. I'm thinking of hiring someone to check into him more, but if he finds out, we're over. Thoughts? Experiences?*

There were twenty-seven responses, evenly divided between *trust but verify* and *it's already over*.

One response stood out.

InLoveAfter50: *If you don't trust him, why do you want to be with him? No trust, no relationship. Everyone nowadays wants to expose everything. There's no privacy. Checking into every minor detail enflames distrust and paranoia. People misspeak, memory is faulty. In this case, maybe the relationship ended for him long before the actual breakup.*

With all this technology, we don't trust each other, we blow minor things into big problems and assume the worst about everyone. We live in constant paranoia. We don't need external forces terrorizing us, we terrorize ourselves.

In the replies to that post, a few commenters piled on top of each other to tell the person, presumably a woman, how naive she was, what a doormat she was. They flamed her for promoting a *boys will be boys* attitude, telling women they needed to forgive and forget. InLoveAfter50 didn't respond to any of the comments. Maybe that's why she was still in love. And apparently fifty years old. Unless it meant after fifty years of marriage.

Corrine closed the browser and put her tablet on the table. She took a sip of wine and raised the glass to eye level. She studied the light coming through the red liquid. The rain had backed off to a pattering sound and Cat had become bored. She was sitting on her haunches, eyes closed, still at the ready in case the storm reversed itself.

Corrine took another sip of wine and picked up the tablet. She opened the Facebook app and went to Deb's page. Deb had found something very exciting that was going to transform the energy her clients felt during their workouts. She was so excited, she'd posted four paragraphs about it, without the assistance of line breaks. Corrine's eyes ached looking at the thick rows of text. There were two-hundred-thirty-four "likes" and seventy-five comments. She scrolled past pictures of bottled supplements, luscious salads, and stir fry dishes. Every fourth picture was a shot of Deb with friends. Corrine tapped to expand the view of the page. She scrolled back up and studied Deb's profile picture. Why hadn't she seen this before? She'd been too caught up in the horror of exposing your life to millions of people, and with searching for information on Andy. She set her wine glass on the table and carried the tablet into the bathroom. She turned on the light and looked in the mirror, holding the tablet near the side of her face.

She shifted her glance back and forth from the tablet to the mirror. She looked an awful lot like Deb. Corrine's skin had slightly darker pigmentation, and she didn't wear make-up, but underneath the foundation, blush, powder, three shades of eye shadow, eye liner, mascara, lip color — Deb could pass for her sister.

She snapped the cover of the tablet closed and put it on the counter. She pressed her hands on the edge of the counter to stop their shaking and leaned forward. She took a deep breath. It was unnerving to see the resemblance but she didn't know why it scared her. Was Andy aware of it? Of course they said men had *types*. The same was said of women, although if she was asked, she couldn't say what her type was. Deb had the same pale brown hair and it looked to be thick and straight like Corrine's. Her smile was similar and the height of her forehead was the same. Beyond that, Corrine couldn't put her finger on specific similarities, but the resemblance would be obvious to a casual observer.

It wasn't as if Andy had met her at a party and been drawn to her because of her appearance. Their encounter was a complete accident and his suggestion they ride the roller coaster together had been immediate. It was dark, he'd hardly looked at her, as far as she could recall. Maybe he'd been watching them for several minutes, waiting for the disagreement with the surfer to escalate. It could be something he wasn't even aware of — attracted to her because she matched his first wife, in body shape and facial appearance. She opened the tablet again and stared at Deb's face.

She took the tablet back to the living room, swallowed the rest of the wine in the glass, and returned to the bathroom. She brushed her hair back and up and drew it into a ponytail. She secured it with an oversized barrette. Now she didn't even need the tablet next to her to see how much they looked alike. It was plastered all over her memory. The atypical hairstyle accentuated it — Deb's hair was in a pony tail in most of the pictures.

She took out the clip, shook her hair back into place, and went into the bedroom. She opened the closet door. As the door swung wide, a downpour started, hammering the roof and windows. The sky flashed with light. A moment later, thunder rumbled far out over the ocean. Cat raced into the bedroom and ran under the bed. Corrine slid the hangers along the pole, studying her clothes. Most of her tops were pastels, just like the clothes Deb wore in her Facebook photographs — sage and dusty blue and pale pink, a few yellows that could pass for white in a dark room. Corrine's work slacks were either gray or dark brown. When she wasn't working, she wore jeans or shorts.

Toward the back of the closet were two dresses — a navy blue bridesmaid dress from her sister's wedding, a black dress she wore to work parties, which were rare, and a suit she'd bought when she interviewed for her job at Fairhaven. She'd never worn it again. Deb spent her life in workout clothes, Corrine spent hers in jeans. She closed the door and went into the kitchen. She poured another glass of wine while the sky flashed and the thunder continued its low rumble. She returned to her tablet and visited the website for the clothing store where Andy bought the peach dress. She scrolled through until she found the dress, selected her size, entered her credit card, and ordered it shipped with two-day delivery.

Although she'd had moments of wondering whether Andy was trying to mold her into someone different, she certainly wasn't going to be Deb's look-a-like.

Eleven

Mary had always remembered it as the worst day of her life. Her father had locked her in her bedroom. He was determined she would not leave the house without permission, as she was prone to do. She rarely did as she was told. He was insistent on that point.

The weather had been stormy and part of the road down to the beach had washed out. Pedestrians could use it, but it was closed to automobiles. The beautiful ship had cracked, and Mary was worried she was never going to be allowed on the boat. It might fall apart before she was eighteen and allowed to participate in its *adult* activities. Although why a swimming pool was restricted to adults, she had no idea. She wanted to see that pool! She wanted to dive in and swim a beautiful breaststroke to the other end, hearing the gentle splashes of her body echo off the walls. She'd swum once before in an indoor pool and she knew how beautifully the water echoed — like a musical instrument.

She sat in the armchair in the corner for a while, thinking about how tiresome it was to be treated like a child. She was not a child. She had small breasts swelling under her dresses, but her father didn't know that. Even her mother didn't seem to be aware. The dolls sitting on the shelf across from her mocked her womanhood. They stared at her with their porcelain faces, the paint on their lips and cheeks making them resemble clowns, the glass eyes hollow and watery so they appeared infinitely stupid. And they were. She was too old for dolls. She wanted her mother to pack them away, but her mother said it was too soon. She'd regret it. Her mother had played with her dolls until she was thirteen. Mary laughed out loud. That was not going to happen. When she was thirteen, she would be sitting on the beach, watching boys strut past, trying to capture her attention. Before she was thirteen. Boys already glanced her way every single time she went out. Another thing her mother and father didn't seem to notice.

The dolls stared at her, laughing at her predicament. Locked in the bedroom like a lunatic was locked up. She'd read all about lunatics. Neither of her parents would have liked her reading about such sordid things, but they took her to the library where they expected her to stay among the children's books. It was their own fault for leaving her alone while they went outside for a stroll. Watching people look at them was more like it, admiring her mother's latest dress and her jewelry — a new necklace, freckled with gems, every year on her birthday. Mary had found a book about a woman who wrote for a newspaper in the late 1800s — Nellie Bly. She'd died two years after Mary was born, which was disappointing. Mary would have liked to meet her and ask her a few questions.

Miss Bly had pretended she was a lunatic and gotten herself locked up in an asylum for ten days. Reading about crazy people was interesting. Scary, but interesting. Mary liked the horror of how they did things no respectable person would do. They were so sad, so lost inside their own heads. How did the doctors decide someone was mad? Was there a test? It hadn't been very difficult for Miss Bly to pretend she was insane. She'd talked nonsense, expressed irrational fears, and that was it. Maybe they locked people up more easily back then. Proving she was worthy of release from the institution had been far more difficult for Nellie. People seemed eager to lock up anyone who didn't follow the rules. Sure, some of them rambled on with senseless stories, or abused their own bodies, or tried to kill themselves. They needed to be locked up, but not all of them.

Did her mother think Mary was a lunatic and tell her father to lock her up? Mary had also read that sometimes women who invited excessive interest from men were considered candidates for an asylum. Maybe her mother had noticed Mary looking at boys, or boys looking at Mary.

Mary's dresses were exactly the same as the clothing she'd worn when she was five — dresses like sacks that were only fitted to her figure when a huge sash was tied around her middle in a big fat bow. Her hair was long with little-girl ringlets, also topped with a bow. Mary was not to listen to grownup conversations or leave the house without Mother or Father. She wasn't to talk to boys at school. She ate early, before her parents, at a small table where her knees bumped the underside. Her mother sat beside her, watching her eat. It was difficult to chew her food with her mother studying her mouth. Mary didn't want to be a child anymore. She *wasn't* a child. She was tired of them pretending she was still a tiny girl, their precious, darling baby, as her mother liked to say.

And the dolls.

There were eleven dolls of varying sizes. Each one wore a unique outfit. Every year on her birthday — a new doll . Every year, less pleasure in their inevitable appearance when she lifted the lid off the gift box. She didn't remember how she'd felt about the dolls she'd received when she was two or three years old, but she did remember the doll on her fourth birthday. It was dressed in a red, white, and blue dress and held a little American flag in its stiff hand. Mary had been thrilled with that doll. She couldn't wait to take it with her to the Independence Day parade. The doll had long, dark brown hair and real eyelashes. When she was four, she didn't notice the horrific stare in those blue glass eyes. She didn't notice the lips were sealed closed with pink paint.

The dolls glared at her now, telling her she wasn't being very nice. They heard her thoughts, she was sure of it. Her mother said God watched everything Mary did, and noticed every single thought, but Mary knew better. The dolls were the ones who knew her thoughts. She couldn't see God, but she saw the dolls, and they saw her. It was difficult to sleep, knowing they sat on that shelf to the right of her bed, staring down at her, pursing their stiff lips at Mary's unladylike dreams. In her dreams, she saw the boy who sat in the back row in her class — a boy with black hair. He was several inches taller than Mary, with a tenor voice that made her insides feel like pudding. The boy stared at the back of her head until she could feel his eyes burning through her hair, lifting it up and exposing her neck. His name was Charles. In her dreams, Charles took her hand and held it in his. He kissed Mary's lips. He touched her hair and whispered that it felt like expensive silk.

When she woke from the dream every morning, she felt the dolls' eyes on her. They stared through her skin, their gazes penetrating her skull. When Mary had her back to them, they talked about her. Sometimes they spoke so softly, it was impossible to understand what they were saying. Their voices took on a hissing quality — *whisper, whisper, whisper.* It sounded like a shelf full of serpents.

The doll with blonde curly hair who wore a pink nightgown and pink slippers, each topped with a tiny white pompom, was the meanest. Mary had moved the matching nightcap so it covered most of the doll's eyes, but she still seemed to be able to peer out from under it. She got the others going. She murmured that if she were allowed to sleep beside Mary in her bed, like she used to, she would put a stop to those dreams. She would exert her purity and return Mary's thoughts to baby animals, and remind her to find pleasure in painting pictures of flowers and houses. The doll complained that she'd been stuck up on the shelf because Mary knew she was being a bad girl. It didn't prevent the doll from knowing what was going on. Oh, she knew. And Mary knew that she knew.

Mary stood up and slid her sash around so the bow was in the back where it belonged. She walked to the mirror over her bureau and looked at herself. The sash looked silly. She reached behind her and yanked on the tail of the bow. The ends slid away from each other and the sash fell to the floor. Her dress now looked like a tent, but it was better than that sash, tied around her like she was a birthday package. She leaned forward and studied her face in the mirror. Did anyone notice her baby fat was starting to slide off her cheeks like melting ice cream? Blue eyes stared back at her, full of life, eyes filled with the interesting things she'd read and all the interesting things she planned to do. They weren't vacant caverns like the dolls' eyes. Surely eyes like these, capable of bringing all the sights of the world into her mind, could figure out a way to escape from her bedroom with its ruffles and the parasol wallpaper and those dolls! She turned slightly so she couldn't see them reflected in the mirror. She closed her eyes and tried to think.

If she opened the window and climbed out, she risked hurting herself. Her room was on the second floor. There was a tree nearby, and she might be able to reach a branch, but it wasn't a very large one and what if it broke? She'd fall a long way and one of her bones might break. Her father would be angry. Furious that she'd disobeyed him, that she'd done something sneaky. He didn't like girls who did sneaky things. Her mother would cry. She would cry that Mary might have died, cry that her daughter wasn't happy to be like other girls, cry that Mary mustn't love her if she went to so much effort to escape. Without even turning to look, she felt the dolls nodding in agreement that those were exactly the things her mother and father would say.

But she didn't want to be here. Her father had been so eager to leave. The night before, Mary had to listen to all the crying from her parents' room and now her mother hadn't come out all day. Their house was a lunatic asylum. She wanted to escape and check on the boat. She needed to be sure the crack wasn't so big they couldn't mend it. If the boat split and fell apart before she was old enough to go dancing and dining and swimming there, she would die. It was the first day it hadn't rained in over a week. She needed to go outside and do *something*. She could not stay in this room with those dolls another minute.

She walked to the window, turned the lock, and pushed it open. She put the hook into the eye to keep it from sliding back down on her. She dragged the chair to the window and used it to pin the curtains to the wall so she wouldn't get tangled in them as she climbed out. No one could see this part of the house — it faced the side yard, so that was good. She put on a sweater. She took off her shoes and socks. She tucked her socks in the toes and dropped her shoes out the window. The brief silence followed by the soft thud as each one hit the ground made her feel as if her stomach had been hollowed out. She folded her dress up around her waist, grabbed the sash she'd abandoned earlier, and wrapped it tightly around her waist to make the dress shorter, and keep it out of the way.

She stretched her leg up and out through the open window, turned, and hoisted the rest of her body up onto the sill. She put both legs out and sat there for a moment. The tree was farther away than she'd realized. She was going to have to lean to grab the branch. She closed her eyes and pictured herself putting her feet on the branch just below, which was thicker and stronger than the one she had to grab onto.

There was no sense sitting around imagining it forever. Either the branch would hold her, either she'd be able to grab it without falling, or she wouldn't. If she did fall, it wasn't so good that no neighbors could see this part of the house. She might lie in the muddy garden for hours, until her father came home and nailed her window shut and made her go to bed without eating dinner.

She held the window frame with one hand, leaned out, and touched the branch. It swayed gently. She grabbed at it and pulled it down so she could get her other hand around it. Then she let her body fall away from the windowsill. The branch lunged down and the thicker one below scraped at her shins. She squeezed the branch, letting it move her up and down until it had adjusted to the extra weight. She kicked her legs, found the branch below, and curled her feet around it like the robins that perched higher in the tree and sang to her in the mornings. She stood there for a moment, still holding the branch above, steadying her breathing.

Once her heartbeat returned to normal, it was easy to climb to the ground as she'd done many times before, although not recently. They wanted her to be a child, but she was *too old to climb trees* — it wasn't *ladylike*.

She walked through the mud and picked up her shoes. As best she could, she wiped the mud from between her toes onto the grass and put on her socks and shoes. She untied the sash and draped it over the fence. She slipped out the gate and headed to the road leading down to the beach.

The boat looked whiter than ever under the gray clouds. A few fishermen were on the pier but the boat was deserted. Closed for the winter, and possibly longer.

She approached the pier and went up the ramp. She walked across the rain-soaked boards, hearing nothing but the thud of her feet and the roar of the waves. None of the fishermen turned to look at her. They stared over the railing, looking into the water as if they could find the fish by sight and move their lines to the right place. As she drew closer to the boat she saw there was a bar across the entrance area. It was secured with a chain and padlock, but it was only a single bar. How silly of them. She could slip under that without even putting her knees on the deck.

She glanced over her shoulder. The fishermen were still busy. She smiled at her good fortune. She couldn't imagine why no one was there, watching to see who might come on board. She ducked under the pole and hurried around the side, past the building that housed an arcade. She approached the larger structure. Above was the restaurant that had glowed with lights in the evenings. She stopped and looked through a window at the huge room — the dance hall, with a low stage at the front where chairs were set up for one of the bands. Waiting for summer. Waves crashed against the sides of the boat. Even though the storm had passed on, the ocean was still unusually rough. She turned and continued walking.

Now she saw why no one had been there to stop her from coming on board. Four men were on the left side near the bow, leaning over, looking into the water. How they could see anything but waves, she had no idea. They were talking loudly, but the surf covered over their words. It almost sounded as if they were shouting at each other. They must be discussing the repair. Maybe the crack was larger than they'd realized. Maybe the water crashing against the concrete was making it worse. She hoped not.

None of the men saw her approach. She walked right up to where they stood and still they seemed unaware of her presence. She wasn't sure why she was walking toward them, she should hide. The minute they turned they would hurry her off the boat, punish her for coming on without permission. She leaned over the side to see the crack. She hadn't noticed it from the beach, but surely it was visible here.

There was a short lull as the waves fell silent between swells.

"We need to call a diver," one said.

"We can't wait," another said.

"Do something. We can't just stand here talking about it."

It had cracked a week ago. Why were they so upset, as if something had to be done right that minute? She leaned over as far as she dared. She could hardly see the side of the boat. How were they able to see so clearly from where they stood? They were much taller, of course, but it was still an awkward angle.

Waves smacked the side of the ship. Salt water splashed up at her. She felt the spray on her cheeks and tasted it. If the sun was out, if it were summer, she would dive over the side and go for a swim, although if the waves were as fierce as this, they might dash her against the concrete.

One of the men cursed.

"Do something!" another one shouted.

A third man turned toward a storage bin. He dragged a large net and a pole with a hook on one end out of the bin. He handed the net to the others and they tossed it over the side of the ship. They pulled a rope that ran through the edges of the net. Two of them began dragging the net out of the water, rope scraping at the side of the ship, while the other two wrestled with the pole, helping to secure the weight of whatever they'd captured.

When most of the net was on the deck, the men with the pole dropped it and positioned themselves next to the railing. All four of them heaved something up out of the water and over the side. It smacked onto the deck.

Mary screamed. They turned. Their mouths moved, their arms waved, but she couldn't hear them. A roaring sound filled her head and her lungs, drowning out their voices and the ocean.

Wrapped inside the enormous net was a woman's body. Her hair was plastered over her face and twisted around her neck. Her arms were bound to her sides by a cream and turquoise shawl that Mary's father had given her mother for her birthday. The body was all wrong, like it was coming loose at the joints. The part of her face that was visible was purple and black with enormous bruises that ran into each other like splashes of wine.

Mary screamed and screamed. One of the men ran toward her. He grabbed her and turned her around so her back was to the others, and she could no longer see that awful thing in the fishing net. He hurried her toward the stern of the ship where it joined the pier. Behind her, despite the sound of the waves, she heard ugly thumps as they unwrapped the net from around her mother's body.

After that, she didn't remember much. The man hurried her off the ship and he must have asked her name. She remembered sitting on the pier, staring at the ship, thinking how stupid it was to have a boat made of concrete — something that sinks. She remembered crying and feeling sick to her stomach, throwing up on the pier. And then her father was there, carrying her down the ramp. He carried her all the way up the eroded street to where he'd had to leave his car.

They said her mother had killed herself. She didn't know how to swim. She'd gone out to the boat before dawn and pinned her shawl around her shoulders. They wouldn't say why. She'd heard them whisper there was no note. A few years passed before she understood what that meant. They whispered a lot of things — that it was for the best. That her father could make a fresh start. That Mary would have a chance at a decent life.

When she tried to ask her father about some of these things, he said it wasn't anything she needed to know. He said her mother was sick in the head and now she was at peace. He told her to pray for her mother. He told her to pray that she didn't follow the same path as her mother. He may have told her other things, but she'd forgotten them. Nothing made much sense, and things were impossible to remember when there was no logic to them. He might as well have been speaking a foreign language for all she could understand of what her father had to say.

Two weeks after her mother's body was pulled out of the water, Mary was walking on the beach by herself. Her father was no longer concerned whether she was locked in the house. All the dolls were gone. Mary said they made her cry and her father had them wrapped in paper and packed up in boxes, stored out of sight in the attic. He wasn't as concerned as her mother had been about ladylike behavior. He was as firm as ever about one thing — the ship wasn't for children. But Mary no longer wanted to be on the ship at all. She hated it. She wished it would crumble into a thousand pieces. She was glad it had cracked, and a year later, she was glad the dancing and dining were shut down and the whole thing was turned over to fishermen. There was nothing magical about it at all.

She walked along the shore with her back to the ship, but she always had to return in the direction she'd come, and then it was sitting right in front of her.

This time, she'd walked east, carrying her shoes so she could dip her feet in the lacy edges of the surf. It was early morning and the beach was shrouded in fog. When she turned to retrace her steps, the pier and the boat were hidden. She smiled. Maybe they'd be sucked out of there and disappear forever. As she came closer, the legs of the pier became visible first. After another fifty or sixty feet, she saw the dim, ghostly presence of the boat.

The air had changed. It was much colder, which was the opposite of how it usually was when the fog descended. The fog was wet and thick on her face, like soaked tissue paper gluing itself to her skin. She tried to wipe it away, but it just felt heavier, and her fingers came away numb. The boat began to take shape as she continued walking. She should turn and head toward the footpath, refuse to even glance at it, but something prevented her from looking away. It seemed as if the boat pulled her toward it, reeling her in as surely as the fishermen reeled in their lines. She often wondered if that was what had happened to her mother. Something evil in the dark, abandoned corners of the boat, pulled her toward it, filled her thoughts with death. She was compelled to throw herself over the side, taking extra care to make sure there was no possibility of fighting for her life once she was taken by the waves.

Mary didn't know why she was having these thoughts, but they seemed true. Truer than anything she'd ever thought or imagined before.

Floating in the fog above the center of the ship was a dark shape. It had no real form, but it had a mind and thoughts, a voice. This thing, whatever it was, could have saved her mother. Mary felt it was smug that it had managed to drag a human life beneath the waves, trap it near that split in the concrete, batter it until it wasn't breathing, tearing it to pieces as surely as a shark would tear limbs from a body.

Instead, this thing, harbored by the ship, lured her mother with its twinkling lights and promise of exciting parties, and then it swallowed her alive. As if it needed her mother. Her mother should have been locked up, not Mary. Then everything would have been different. They locked up suicidal people. Her father locked up the wrong person.

Mary fell on the sand and cried.

After quite a long time, she sat up and brushed wet sand off her shoulders and hair. She wouldn't tell her father about the apparition, he'd laugh at her. He'd tell her such things were impossible. But she knew. And she hated it. She wished they'd never dragged the ship into the bay and she vowed she would outlive the boat.

She remembered that ghostly presence and the day she saw her mother's smashed body like it had happened this morning. There were so many parts of her life that she didn't remember very well, parts that seemed like she'd dreamt them — heartbreak and loss and bafflement — things that had slipped beneath the layers of her mind. Events that were only shadows, some of them as dark as the thing that hovered over the S.S. Palo Alto. At this point in her life, she doubted they'd ever emerge from the darkness. They were better off forgotten. But that day, her mother's soaked and broken body, taken by the ship — she would never forget that, it would linger after she took her final breath.

Twelve

Andy was taking Corrine to dinner at Shadowbrook — a restaurant built on a wooded slope above Soquel Creek, featuring a charming cable car that took diners up and down the hillside to family gatherings and romantic meals. He'd closed a big deal, worth one and a half million dollars, with his top customer. He was *pumped*, he'd said. *Pumped!* They needed to celebrate *big time*.

Corrine stood in the living room, trying not to think how unlike herself she looked in the peach dress. She had to admit, the color was flattering. She would certainly stand out with all the exposed skin — legs, arms, half her back, shoulders, and a thin white strip below the tan line on her breasts. She supposed that was why Andy had been attracted to the dress in the first place.

She'd studied herself in the mirror three times since putting on the dress. She was determined to resist the urge to do it again. In the bathroom mirror, a stranger had looked back at her. A woman who wanted to grab attention, someone who needed to make sure she was the best looking woman in the room. Most women who dressed like this seemed to have a need to compete. It had always baffled her. Who were they competing with? If they were out to dinner with a husband or boyfriend, were they ensuring he didn't look around and find someone better? Did they really think that was all they had to offer? The only way to keep a man at their side — clothes and hair and make-up?

Competition was pointless and didn't lead to any kind of happiness or satisfaction with all the pieces of your life. And she wasn't competing now. But maybe Andy was. The thought made her want to change clothes, but he'd be at the door in two or three minutes, if the estimate in his text message was accurate. She dropped her phone into her purse and turned off the light. The doorbell rang and she went to answer, trying to suppress the blush blossoming behind her cheeks.

He kissed her on the lips. "You look good." He moved to the side to make room for her on the tiny front porch.

She locked the door and slid her left arm into her coat at the same time. Andy took the collar and held it while she wriggled her right arm into the sleeve. Maybe he hadn't noticed the dress in the dim light. She'd rushed to put on her coat, but it was cold. He'd get a better look in the restaurant, when they were seated across from each other, glowing in candlelight, drinking a glass of wine.

But he didn't. He ordered a bottle of Chardonnay. They ate an appetizer of baked brie with jalapeño jelly. They ordered salads and a main course. They sipped their wine. He smiled at her. He laughed. He told her all the details of his big win. Maybe he had noticed and decided not to mention it. Maybe all his charm and smiling was covering up anger that she'd bought the dress after dismissing his gift. He had to realize it was the same dress. It was such an unusual color. And the collar, with those beads around it. How could he not notice? How could he not remember? Maybe he wanted her to apologize, to admit he'd been right in suggesting it would look good on her. It did look good. She'd been to the restroom and finally seen the truth of that in the mirror.

You look great.

She'd glanced over her shoulder, but no one was there. Maybe she'd spoken out loud.

When she returned to their table, down two short flights of stairs, the last of which put her directly in Andy's line of sight, she knew he'd smile and tell her how pleased he was she'd decided to buy the dress after all. He'd tell her he was sorry she'd paid for it herself, and now he'd buy her another. But she'd refuse. She'd say, I feel like I'm someone else.

By the time they were eating cheesecake with a raspberry sauce and drinking brandy, she wondered if she'd gotten the wrong dress. Maybe this wasn't it at all. She'd hardly glanced at it when he gave it to her, pulled it out of the bag, seen the color and the beads — there were beads, weren't there? She'd shoved it back inside the tissue so fast, maybe she'd remembered everything wrong. It was night, the color might have looked different. Why wasn't he saying anything? Even if it wasn't the exact dress, it was close enough. And even if it wasn't close at all, if the one he'd given her was blue or green without a single bead, she was dressed in a way he'd never seen before. He'd said she looked good, but nothing more. She'd turned herself into this other, unrecognizable creature in her own eyes, but to him, she was the same.

The cheesecake was pasty in her parched mouth. It gripped the insides of her cheeks and her tongue as if it wanted to prevent her from swallowing. She didn't want to be having these thoughts. She wasn't trying to become someone else, she wasn't trying to get his attention with a dress, with an altered appearance, more make-up than she'd ever worn. She took a sip of coffee. It made the brandy taste too sweet, and the brandy turned the coffee sour. She pushed the cup and saucer to the side.

"No more coffee?"

"I just want to enjoy the brandy."

"Me too," he said. "And you, of course."

She smiled. She pushed her cheesecake plate until it clinked against the coffee saucer.

"I'll finish that, if you're all done," he said.

"I am." She nudged the plate in his direction.

"You're quiet," he said.

"Am I?"

"I guess I've been talking too much." He laughed and cut a piece of cheesecake. He held it on the fork. "The adrenaline rush from a big sale is a bitch. Next week I'm taking the rest of the team out for drinks. That'll help. I'm not sure I'm going to sleep more than a few hours tonight."

She smiled.

"I'll try not to keep you awake." He touched his brandy glass to hers.

"What about Parker?" she said.

"We'll stop by and pick him up on the way to your place."

"Or I could stay at your condo this time."

"We'd have to go get your things," he said.

"Wouldn't Parker be happier in his own home? I think he feels crowded at my house."

"Nope. He's fine. I like staying at your place."

"I thought my place needed remodeling? It's not really your style."

"I never said that."

"I think you did," she said.

"You *think* I did, or I actually said it?"

"I'm not trying to argue."

He finished the cheesecake and swallowed the rest of his brandy. He pushed the glasses and plate to the side, and held out his hands. "Give me your hand."

She placed her right hand in his, clinging to the brandy glass with her left as if it were a flotation device, the only thing keeping her head above water.

He squeezed her fingers. "I'm so lucky I found you."

"Was I lost?"

"To be honest, you looked a little lost when I first saw you that night. You always do. But that's why I'm here."

"I'm not lost."

"I love how determined you are. I love how you know what you want, even if it's unconventional. You know that I love you, don't you?"

She was trapped — one hand stuck between his hands and the other holding onto a glass, her entire arm immobilized because her elbow was pressed against the table. She couldn't move the glass without moving her entire body, tearing her hand away from his. With both elbows pinned to the table, she couldn't move her arm to bring the glass to her lips. Hearing those words warmed her for a moment, but there was something uncomfortable behind them. He hadn't said straight out — *I love you.* He'd couched it in extra padding, as if he didn't want to expose his heart. He wanted her to say it for him by responding with a *yes.*

"Do you?" he said.

"Do I what?"

"Know that I've fallen in love with you?" He smiled, lowering his eyes until he was looking at their hands, or some other spot on the table. Maybe the smear of raspberry that had dribbled off the cheesecake, as if she'd punctured her lip with the fork and the blood splashed on the white cloth.

"I didn't know it until just this minute," she said.

He continued to hold her hand tightly, locking her in place. "Now you do."

She didn't want him to ask whether she felt the same. It was too awkward, not being able to move, the jumble of words that didn't come to the point. The dress, the beaded collar pulling at her throat so she felt as if his grip wasn't just holding her fingers, it circled her neck as well. He had large, strong hands with smooth fingernails and pale downy hair scattered across the backs.

"How do you know you're falling in love?" she said.

"Does that mean you're not?"

"I'm not sure how to recognize it."

"Aren't you the analytical one. Don't turn it into something complicated."

"I'm just not certain how you know."

He pulled his hands away. "God, Corrine. I tell you I'm in love with you and you not only don't respond, you're going to interrogate me until I provide a detailed analysis of a topic the human race has never adequately defined?"

"I'm sorry." She wasn't sorry, but she knew she had to say it. She took a sip of brandy, glad of the chance to rearrange her arms so she wasn't pinned to the table like a butterfly on a display board. She put down the brandy glass.

He smiled and took her hand again. "It's not because I'm excited about closing the sale, if that's what you're thinking. I feel good when I'm with you. All the time."

"Me too," she said.

"Something about you makes me feel like your knight in shining armor, if that's not too ridiculous." He grinned and cocked his head, not unlike a bird eyeing another creature, not letting on whether it was looking for prey or afraid of becoming prey itself. "I rescued you, remember?"

That was funny. She'd always thought of herself as a rescuer. She'd rescued cats and lizards. She'd even rescued her sister once. Even funnier, she felt she'd rescued Andy, in a lot of ways. Rescued him from what had seemed like a mildly lonely, single note, overly sterile existence.

He lifted her hand and kissed her fingertips. She was glad he didn't push her to announce her love. She felt like a creep, withholding the words, but she wanted to be sure. And the past few days, she was less sure than she had been a month ago. She might love him, but how did you know? He'd said he felt comfortable at her house, yet every time he was there, he had a suggestion for how she might rearrange it, and plans for how it might be redone at some vague future point when she had that kind of money, which was probably never. She liked her funky, gently sagging house. It was a beach cottage. Then there was the dress. And her resemblance to Deb. And the growing sense that he considered her job beneath her, or maybe it was simply beneath a woman who was in a relationship with Andy Johnson. Did he love her, or the idea of her? Or someone else entirely?

They finished their brandies and rode the tram up to the top of the cliff. Andy dropped Corrine at her cottage and drove back to his place to get Parker.

Inside her house, Corrine picked up Cat and kissed her forehead. Cat twisted in her arms and Corrine let her escape. She went into the bathroom and looked in the mirror. There was Deb, grinning at her as if she'd won a battle Corrine hadn't known she was fighting. The same eager shine in her eyes, the same mildly uncertain smile. The thick long hair was the same, and the size of her breasts. Even the bones in her clavicle were identical in the soft light that reflected off the outdated burgundy and cream wallpaper.

In the bedroom, she kicked off her shoes and stepped out of the dress. She let it fall on the closet floor, covering her shoes. She put on a pair of jeans and a sweater and left her feet bare, even though it was cold.

On Saturday morning, Andy and Parker went for a run before Corrine woke up. When they returned, Corrine made breakfast. Andy took Parker home so he could do a few hours of work. "Mostly email," he said, "But I have to make a few calls to the team, which I should do at my place."

After Corrine cleaned the house, she made a turkey sandwich. She packed the sandwich, a bottle of water, and a handful of grapes into a canvas bag. She grabbed a hat, towel, and folding chair and headed up the street.

It was breezy with soft white clouds streaking the sky. At the top of the cliff, she looked down at the beach, dotted with runners and dog walkers and a few brightly colored umbrellas stuck in the sand. The boat was a chalky yellow color, crowded with gulls and a few crows — nothing haunted about it whatsoever. The tide was at an extremely low cycle and the waves were no larger than the wake of a motorboat. The sun was warm on the side of her face but she was still glad she'd worn a sweatshirt. She stood looking at the water for several minutes, captivated by the endless expanse of blue-gray that seeped into the sky at the horizon.

When she reached the bottom of the steps, she saw Mary, sitting alone on a blue canvas chair. She wore the cape she always had on, but the hood was down and her thick white hair was impossible to mistake for anyone else. Corrine kicked off her flip-flops, tucked them into her bag, and started across the sand.

"Mind if I join you?" Corrine said.

"Not at all." Mary smiled.

Corrine spread out her towel and put the bag on it. She opened the chair and settled herself beside Mary, close enough that she could rest her hand on Mary's forearm. "I brought a turkey sandwich. If you're hungry, we can share it."

"I'm fine," Mary said. "I don't need you bringing me food. I eat three meals a day."

"Do you remember my name? Corrine?"

"I'm not feeble-minded. Just blind."

"Okay, sorry. I wasn't sure."

"Are you trying to become a friend?"

"It's not like I set a goal." Corrine laughed. "It was fun

talking with you."

"Likewise."

"I love those birds with the long legs," Corrine said.

"Godwits," Mary said.

"Oh, I didn't know the name. They're so elegant. Their legs look so fragile, but they move so fast."

"I like them too."

"Do you miss being able to see them?"

"I can see them in my mind."

"That's a nice way to put it."

"That's how it is."

"Do you have family around here?" Corrine said.

"I have four sons. And nine grandchildren. Two greats."

"And they live nearby?"

"Why do you ask?"

"I was curious, that's all," Corrine said.

"Why are you curious?"

"Just making conversation."

"Are you in the habit of turning a conversation with an old woman into an interview?"

"Actually, yes, a little. I work at a senior care facility."

"An old folks' home," Mary said.

Corrine took the cap off her bottle and drank some. She screwed the cap in place and shoved the bottle into her bag. A gull swooped low, casting its shadow over them. It landed on the wet sand and began strutting toward the edge of the water. "We call it a care facility," she said.

"And what do you do there?"

"I'm a social worker. I help with assessments to make sure clients are well-integrated, work to identify signs of depression, interface with families, develop enriching social activities."

Two female gulls joined the male. They strolled back and forth along the edge of the water, stopping occasionally to burrow their beaks into the sand, chasing crabs. The smaller female caught one, bit at a it a few times to break up the shell, and swallowed it with an easy gulp.

"I don't want to end up in one of those places," Mary said.

"I hope you don't."

"That's not a very positive attitude for someone who works there."

"Ideally, people want to remain independent. Everyone feels that way. But sometimes there's no choice."

A four-year-old boy who had been digging in the sand, trying to form a large hole, not realizing he was too close to the water, slapped his shovel on the wet sand as a long, slender wave wiped out half of his hole. He stood up and threw the shovel. The male gull, about twelve feet away, hopped in the direction of the pier. The boy caught sight of the bird's startled reaction. He picked up his shovel and threw it at the female gulls. The male ran and flapped his wings, taking off. He screeched as he circled above. The boy screamed and picked up a rock and drew back his arm to throw it at the birds.

"Hey," Corrine said softly. She glanced to her left to see where the parents were. A man, presumably the father, was tossing a frisbee with another, older boy. The mother was on her back, a sweatshirt over her face. The small boy threw the rock. The birds squawked and hopped frantically away from him.

"What's going on," Mary said.

"A boy is throwing rocks at some gulls," Corrine said.

"Make him stop."

"How can I…"

"Make him stop!" Mary leaned forward in her chair. Her voice was shrill, a suggestion of tears in the back of her throat.

"I can't. His parents are right there."

The boy picked up another, larger rock. He was small and when he hurled it, the rock landed about five or six feet in front of him. The birds remained unmoved.

"Please make him stop."

"He can't throw very far. The birds are still there, I don't think they're intimidated."

"He needs to learn not to torment helpless creatures. It's not right."

"I know," Corrine said, "But his parents, I don't think they'll appreciate me interfering."

"I don't care. Please do something. Or I will." Mary pushed herself to the edge of her chair, ready to stand up.

Corrine put her hand on Mary's arm. "Okay."

She got up and walked to the spot where the sand dropped off. She hopped down and walked toward the boy. He looked at her, his eyes anxious and defiant at the same time. "Please don't throw rocks at the gulls," she said. "It's not nice."

"Stupid birds," the boy said.

She felt sad that a word like *stupid* was already part of his vocabulary. "They're not stupid. They're beautiful. Instead of trying to chase them, how about watching them. They can be interesting."

"They're stupid."

"You could dig for sand crabs and see if they come get them."

The boy picked up his shovel.

From the corner of her eye, she saw the boy's father slide down the ledge of sand. He walked toward her. "What's going on?"

"Just trying to explain it's not nice to throw rocks at the gulls." Corrine smiled in what she hoped was a non-confrontational way, but how could you tell the shape of your own smile?

"Leave him alone," the father said.

"Sorry, I just wanted to explain."

"He doesn't need any *explanations* from you."

"The gulls get stressed when…"

The father lifted his hand, palm facing her. "It's not up for discussion."

Corrine took a few steps back. She turned. Mary had

gotten out of her beach chair and was walking toward the ledge. Corrine hurried toward her. "Careful, it drops suddenly here."

"Why weren't you more firm with him? He needs to teach that boy some respect."

"Let's sit down," Corrine said. She climbed up the bank of sand and took Mary's elbow.

Mary pulled away. "I don't need an escort."

They returned to the chairs. "I feel a connection to the birds, too," Corrine said. "I wonder why that is? Not everyone does."

Mary didn't respond. Corrine looked at her. Tears dotted her bottom eyelashes. "Are you okay?"

Mary nodded.

They sat quietly for several minutes. The gulls had settled themselves closer to the pier. The boy had picked up his shovel and was continuing his futile efforts with the hole. The other boy was sitting beside his mother, and the father stood, half turned toward Corrine and Mary, as if he planned to keep an eye on them. She understood the impulse. But why did he allow his son to torment the gulls? Why did some people think it didn't matter how the birds were treated? Because they were scavengers they didn't deserve care or respect?

"If there's anything I can do…" Corrine said. "I don't know whether I've upset you. Are you sure you're okay?"

"I don't need your psychology or your help," Mary said.

"Yes. You told me that last time. I'm sorry if I seemed…"

"They're so helpless," Mary said.

"Their beaks give them some defense. And they can fly. The best escape of all."

"But when they're eating. Have you ever watched them? Really watched them?"

"I think so."

"They're frantic. They look so out of place on the earth. Trapped."

"Maybe. But they can break free at a moment's notice."

"They can't fly twenty-four hours a day."

"No."

"And when they're walking, grabbing at food with their beaks, no hands to help them get control of it, they seem nervous. They look foolish, running with their wings pressed to their bodies, as if half their appendages are missing. As if they're bound in a straight-jacket."

Corrine stretched her legs in front of her and shoved her feet beneath the warm top layer of sand. "I never thought of it, but they do look awkward when they run."

"My mother drowned," Mary said.

"Oh. I'm so sorry."

"It was a long time ago."

"Still. I'm sorry. That must have been awful for you."

"She couldn't move her arms. Her shawl was wrapped around her and it was as if she didn't have arms. It's what I think of every time I see birds trying to maneuver on land.

When I was losing my sight, I thought it would be a relief not to have to watch them and think of it anymore. But it's still there. I still see them. I see how they run, a little bit panicked, worried they can't get where they're going fast enough."

Corrine took Mary's hand.

"I hate seeing them run, seeing them so afraid. I think of her, trying to move her arms, trying to find her way to the surface."

"You must have missed her terribly."

"All my life. I was a child."

"Oh. I'm so sorry."

"Do you have children?" Mary said.

Corrine shook her head, forgetting for a moment Mary couldn't see her. "No."

"Are you married?"

"No. I have a boyfriend."

"Do you think you'll marry him?"

"I don't know. I've only known him a few months. It's too soon to think about."

"Waiting is good. When I was young, probably younger than you, we hurried things along. Meet, match, marry."

Corrine laughed.

"I'd known my first husband from a distance for a few years, but from the time we were formally introduced until we said *I do*, it was only four months."

"That's quick."

"Too quick. It didn't last, but it took a very long time to

crumble. Take your time."

"Don't worry," Corrine said. "I'm not in a hurry."

"Why do you like spending all your time around old people?" Mary said.

"They know a lot."

"Not really."

"Yes, they do. You do. Think of all the life you've lived that I haven't."

"That doesn't mean I lived it correctly."

"I don't think there's a single correct way to live. Besides, you know things."

Mary laughed. "I'm not sure they're very useful things."

Corrine reached into her bag and pulled out her sandwich and a napkin. "Do you want to split my sandwich?"

"Thank you, that would be nice. You won't be hungry?"

"I just need a few bites to take the edge off."

She handed half the sandwich and the napkin to Mary. "I have grapes too." She put the canvas bag between them and set the grapes on top. She guided Mary's hand too them.

They ate in silence, listening to the surf.

"Did your mother drown here?" Corrine said.

"Right beside that boat."

Corrine's throat tightened. "Is it..."

"It's not her ghost, if that's what you were going to ask."

"How do you know?"

"It's not."

"Then who is it? Why do you think it's here? The ghost?"

"I have no idea."

"Have you seen it often?"

"A number of times over the years. I've felt it more often than I've seen it."

"So the woman I saw on the boat wasn't real?"

"She's real. It's usually just a thick shape over the boat, but it's taken on other forms."

"I didn't know ghosts could do that. Of course, I know nothing about them. I never discussed ghosts until I met you."

"There's a reason you saw it. Most people don't."

"What does that mean?" Corrine put a grape in her mouth and held it there for a moment before she bit into it. Juice shot through her mouth. She wondered if it was time to leave. Andy might be trying to text and she'd left her phone at the house. Had Mary heard the question? Mary had finished the sandwich and eaten several grapes. Corrine regretted she didn't have another bottle of water to share, but she hadn't planned to share the sandwich either. She was still hungry. She ate another grape.

The waves continued to lap at the shore. The boy with the blue shovel was still digging. The tide had receded and was no longer washing out the side of his hole. It was surprising that such a small child had dug a good-sized hole. Especially with that plastic shovel. His brother sat on the towel, watching.

Corrine wanted to repeat the question. It hung in the air like something solid, but the empty space made her afraid of the answer. She wasn't sure if Mary wanted to upset her. A woman who had lost her mother as a small child might not have the kindest view of the world. The conversation had started out pleasantly enough, but now she wanted to escape back to her house. She wanted to curl up with Cat. She even found herself longing for Parker's protective presence. She laughed softly. Since when did she believe in ghosts? In anything supernatural? Ghosts were an archaic concept from the days when Mary was a child and superstition was entertained in every part of life. It had been proven that unexplained phenomena usually did have an explanation. Now, some people *wanted* ghosts to be real because they liked the excitement. Some people. Others were afraid of their own shadows, afraid of the world, afraid of life, and they projected all that fear into something outside of themselves. The woman on the boat couldn't possibly be the manifestation of a ghost. She laughed again.

"What's so funny?"

"Are you sure you aren't playing games with me? It was you I saw on the boat. Not a ghost."

"Believe what you want," Mary said.

"I'm not arguing with you."

"You certainly are. But it doesn't matter whether you believe me. You'll find out for yourself."

"How do you know?"

"The gate onto the pier is locked at night," Mary said.

"Yes."

"How would I have gotten through the bars? I'm not *that* small."

Corrine knew there had to be an explanation. The woman had worn a cape, she had white and silvery hair. There was no doubt in her mind at the time, and no doubt now, that it was Mary. Maybe Mary had lingered on the pier after sunset. Although there wasn't a place to hide. Still, huddled up in her cape, daylight fading, especially on a cloudy day, she might have gone unnoticed, looked like a coat left on a bench. A careless or distracted park ranger who wanted to get home. There were several explanations. A ghost was not one of them.

"I need to go home," Mary said.

"Are you okay?"

"Yes. It's just time to go." She stood and folded her chair.

"Can I help you carry that? It's awkward," Corrine said.

"I've already told you, I can manage."

They walked to the stairs and climbed to the top. Corrine put on her flip-flops. "It was nice seeing you again."

"Good-bye," Mary said.

Corrine watched as Mary turned and headed away from the boat. Corrine stood there for several minutes until Mary's caped body with its perfect posture disappeared behind the row of houses that lined the beach. Mary never moved the chair to her other hand, as if she didn't even notice the weight of it.

Thirteen

Late in the afternoon, Mary walked out to the pier. It felt deserted, but she could never be sure. Once they'd settled into place and between landing a catch, the fishermen were quiet. When families were about, they made their presence known with the layered sounds of their voices. Lovers, like the fishermen, often stood at the railing as silently as ghosts.

She felt badly that she'd lied to Corrine about the woman on the pier. Of course the woman was her mother's apparition, but there was more to it than that. If Mary was truthful, Corrine would never believe there was something more complex residing in that boat. Not if she could easily categorize it as a comforting specter formed in the mind of a bereft child. Corrine needed to know there was something disturbing out there. It had made itself known to Corrine for a reason. The thing would reveal itself and its purpose when it was necessary.

The other reason Mary had felt compelled to lie was less

altruistic. Not altruistic at all, as a matter of fact. Despite letting it come out that her mother had drowned, Mary was ashamed. All her life, Mary had been left to wonder why her mother couldn't manage to go on living. But trying to understand why a woman would kill herself, considering every possibility over and over, encountering the unanswered question in dreams and nightmares, for an entire lifetime, accomplished nothing. She would never know why, and she'd learned to live with that. Experiencing the pity of others was another story. Worse, it was impossible to live with knowing your mother didn't want anything to do with you. Your mother didn't love you enough to stay by your side. A child who wasn't important or special enough for her mother to bother keeping herself alive, didn't belong in the world.

She gripped the thick rail. Rough, splintered wood scraped her palms, but she didn't mind. It told her she still had flesh on her hands, nerves beneath the skin.

It had turned out that her mother wanted her after all. She couldn't be bothered to stay around and raise her daughter, but since her daughter had grown older, Lorene wanted her very much. She appeared frequently on the deserted ship, longing to take Mary with her to that other place, across that line over which you never stepped back. At least not in a way that you wanted.

Would her mother appear tonight? If there were others on the pier, her mother's ghost wouldn't make herself known. It had been easier when Mary still had her sight. Now she had to be alert to the shift in temperature, the sudden silence that meant her mother was walking near the rotting, sinking ship. Occasionally, her mother touched her hand. Mary both longed for it and fought the revulsion of something out of the grave touching her skin. She ached for it until the touch came, and then she recoiled.

If she told anyone about this — her sons, her daughters-in-law, Daniel — they wouldn't believe her. And if they did give her even a sliver of credibility, they would ask why she came out to the boat, knowing she might die. It was senseless, and yet, she couldn't stop. She wanted to encounter her mother's presence and she wanted to run for her life. She wanted to be near the ship and she wanted it to dissolve forever into the sea. There was no explanation for her desires. They fought with each other, controlling all her thoughts and everything she did.

When James was alive, it hadn't been difficult to avoid the ship. Unbelievably, at the age of fifty-one, she'd fallen in love. James had adored her beyond reason. They'd relished all the silly legends — two apple halves finding one another, soul mates, love at first sight. With James, there was a life to be lived — good food and conversation, gardening and walks on the beach. Card games and board games, books and television. Small parties and trips to other parts of the world.

Then, all of that had been stripped away. Half of it when James died, and the other half when she lost her sight. There wasn't much left now — just her desires — drawing blood as they fought inside of her. Nothing was left but the ghost of her mother. She would have preferred the ghost of James, but maybe that was too horrible. Her mother certainly was. You thought you wanted to have the dead come back to you, but it wasn't a satisfying experience after all.

There was a sudden drop in temperature. The wind hadn't picked up. She hoped and feared it was Lorene. The icy chill ran through her bones, starting from the center of her body rather than creeping in through her cape and sweater and pants and socks. She shivered and pulled the cape more tightly around her, keeping her other hand on the rail. The icy breath touched her cheek and she felt the tears start. She didn't want to die. Not yet. But the breath was there, whispering things she couldn't understand. Etching words and letters across her heart.

It wasn't that she was afraid of death. The endless sleep sounded comforting. But she didn't want it to be like this. She didn't want this specter threading its chill through her body, making her colder and more alone than she'd been during those weeks after her mother's body was dragged out of the salty water.

Her father had found a new wife, of course. And he had more children, of course. He tried to push them off as Mary's siblings, but she kept herself apart from them. Before the children came along, Verna had plenty of time to pretend she was a mother for Mary.

"Suicide is a sin," Verna said.

"I don't believe in sin."

Verna put her creamy face close to Mary's, her nose almost touching Mary's nose, her breath like overripe plums. "You'll be cast into eternal darkness if you entertain thoughts like that."

Mary said nothing. She dropped a sugar cube into her tea.

"I don't know why your mother taught you it was okay to use all that sugar."

Mary stirred her tea.

Verna rubbed her swollen belly. "I just want you to know that when the baby comes, there should be no more mention of the woman who brought you into the world. I'm your mother now. I'll take care of you — your father and I. We won't be talking about the lives of sinners."

Mary dropped another sugar cube into her teacup.

Verna reached across the table and grabbed the sugar bowl. "Enough. I'm trying to talk to you."

"I need five cubes."

"You do not need five cubes. You don't *need* sugar at all. Two is plenty. Now stop distracting me. I'm trying to explain something to you."

"I'm twelve," Mary said. "I don't need a new mother."

"Still a baby."

"I'm not a baby. Not even a child."

"Your mother committed the worst sin of all — murder. Taking your own life is just as terrible as taking another's.

That's why she was not buried in the church cemetery. That's why we shouldn't speak about her any more. She left you alone. But now you have me. And soon you'll have a new baby brother or sister to take care of."

"It's not my job to take care of your baby," Mary said.

"You'll enjoy it. You'll have practice for when you're a mother. And you'll be a good mother. I can see it in your eyes, that you care about life. As long as you learn some self control. With the sugar. And your vanity, always looking in the mirror. It's not nice."

"Maybe I don't want to be a mother."

"Every girl wants to be a mother."

"Not me."

"I know it's hard because your mother failed. But that doesn't have to be you. God will give you strength to fulfill the purpose He's given to women. You'll see. You're upset now, but once the anniversary of the…suicide…is past, things will change."

Mary picked up her tea cup. She reached for the sugar bowl and pulled it toward her.

"No more sugar," Verna said.

"I know." Mary tilted her teacup over the sugar bowl and let the tea run over the remaining cubes.

Verna shouted that Mary was a *very bad girl*. She sent Mary to her room to say the rosary three times. Mary put the rosary beads in one of her shoes that was too small. She sat in the chair and looked out her window, watching a crow try to balance on a branch that was too thin to hold its weight.

For many years, Mary had wished she could tell the ghost of her mother about the incident with the teacup. Being banished to her room for the night had been such a small price to pay for the pleasure she felt when Verna called her a bad girl. It was so satisfying, watching the tea soak up every single granule of sugar.

She often spoke to the spirit of her mother, but could never be sure whether she was listening. The spirit had her own agenda. Still, it was sometimes comforting to talk, knowing there was another presence nearby.

The cold was growing more intense. It always happened this way. She wanted to climb onto the railing and fall into the water, irrationally confident that even the numbingly cold water of Monterey Bay was warmer than this presence spreading its tendrils through her bones. But jumping into the water was exactly what Lorene wanted. She wanted her daughter to join her in a watery death, she wanted her daughter to give in to despair, to end her own life, to do the same as her mother, to be like her mother. Mary would not.

She stepped away from the railing. The icy breath continued to trace the letters across her heart. Whether it was trying to speak, whether Mary was supposed to string those letters together into words and sentences, she had no idea.

"I've met someone who saw you walking on the pier," Mary said. "She wondered whether it was you."

Her eyes ached from the cold. She closed them, but all that did was keep the chill pressed up against her eyeballs. She opened them again, seeing the same darkness. "I don't know if anyone else is out here. I don't hear anything. I hope not. They'd think I was mad, talking to myself. Unless you're making yourself visible, so I just look sad, talking to a woman who won't respond to me."

She let go of the railing and walked around the bench. She continued down the center of the pier, her footsteps echoed by those of her mother's ghost. The ghost that moved awkwardly, its arms bound to her side by the shawl. When she reached the iron fence that blocked access to the boat, she thought about the single horizontal bar she'd ducked beneath all those years ago. She could see the ship clearly in her mind. It wasn't the memory of the complete upper deck, outfitted with a restaurant and arcade, it was the eroded concrete, covered with bird droppings, that she'd looked at for so many years after. Once they closed it off forever in 2000, the pelicans and gulls took over. They seemed happy to rest there, safe from dogs and aggressive human beings. There they waited for the tide to go out so they could flock to the shore and dig for sand crabs, watch the surf for anchovies and squid. Out in the surf they competed with otters and seals and dolphins, but most of the time, there was enough to go around.

How long would it take that horrid boat to slip beneath the waves? It was ridiculous, surviving all these years. The thing was filled with disease. They'd removed the oil and opened the bunker tank that had been been trapping and killing birds, but still. It was never scrubbed of the occasional carcass glued to the concrete. She had to believe the birds picked up disease there. They might like having the convenient, protected resting place, but it wasn't good for them. It wasn't natural.

If she was honest, she wasn't going to outlast it, but she couldn't stop hoping. The thing might sit there in broken pieces for another hundred years. She shouldn't let it bother her. Where was the pride in outliving a concrete ship? It didn't matter. No one cared. They wouldn't even notice. The ship wasn't visible to her. She deliberately continued calling up memories instead of allowing them to die as they should.

The ice in her veins and bones had melted. It was still cold, but she could move more easily. She was alone again. She walked quickly back down the pier. As she passed through the open gate, she heard the ranger truck approaching. They would be locking the gate, thinking they kept the pier safe from intruders at night.

Back at her house, she took off her cape and hung it on the hook in the front hall. She moved the dial on the thermostat a quarter of an inch. The furnace clicked into action and even though she didn't yet notice the warm air, she felt better. She picked up her phone off the shelf and asked it to repeat any messages. It was silent. She carried it into the bedroom, attached it to the power cord, and left it on the nightstand. She changed into leggings and a long velour robe that zippered up the front.

She went into the kitchen, took a half bottle of champagne out of the refrigerator, opened it, and poured herself a glass. She allowed a small sip while she stood at the counter, then carried the glass and bottle into the living room. She returned to the kitchen and put a few handfuls of mixed nuts into a small bowl. She sat on the couch, sipping champagne and eating nuts, breathing in the warmth gushing through the living room. Her bones and muscles still ached with cold, but soon it would dissipate.

Nights were when she missed James the most. So many years and she still felt like it was only a few hours ago that they'd been seated on this couch, drinking champagne. Out of ninety-one years, she supposed thirty-odd good ones was more than a lot of people got. When she met him, she'd thought it was too late for her. She'd believed she was destined to live life unloved.

She'd been introduced to James at a party where she was one of three single women in a crowd of forty people. James was the only single man. In the nineteen-seventies, lots of couples were splitting up, forming new couples, like a square dance — a constantly shifting pattern. But the cultural upheaval was late coming to Aptos. People tended to settle by the beach when they were stable, set for life, whether by choice or inertia. James had come up behind her while she stood on a deck watching the sun go down. He handed her a glass of champagne as if they'd been together for years. He'd said she looked like a lady who drank champagne. She didn't have to ask what that meant. She'd finally met someone who saw into her soul.

Although Mary had advised Corrine that it was best to take one's time, James had moved into Mary's house within a few weeks of their first meeting and they were married three months after that. Of course, her guidance to Corrine was meant for someone never married before, who might not know that after a long, hopeless marriage, there was no doubt when you'd found the right person. It was advice for someone who might rely on an external knowledge, like Mary had the first time.

Despite her defiance with the sugar cubes and the rosary beads, despite her refusal to watch over the five children Verna eventually gave birth to, Mary found herself patted and molded into the woman Verna wanted her to be. Verna introduced her to the man who would become her first husband. Henry's marriage proposal was infinitely more appealing than living another day in Verna's house. And it had truly become Verna's house. Mary's father was rarely there — out on business most of the time. So sorry he'd missed dinner, the party, the walk on the beach, the game of cards. He had a lot of business endeavors. Mary had been happy to escape to Henry's home.

Henry was such a handsome man — taller than her father,

with dark hair and bright blue eyes. He smiled all the time. Everyone in town was his friend, but when he looked into Mary's eyes and smiled, she felt she was the center of his world. And she had been, until there were four little boys with dark hair and blue eyes and charming smiles, and she realized she wasn't the center of his world at all.

Just after Thomas turned eighteen, Henry had ushered her into the living room on a cold, wet Spring evening. He urged her to sit on the sofa while he mixed their drinks. Her white skirt fell across the dark green brocade like a blanket of snow on a shaded garden. He returned to the living room carrying two glasses with whisky and soda. He handed one to her and sat beside her. He touched the edge of his glass to hers, but didn't make a toast. It wasn't unusual. He hadn't toasted her for so many years, she couldn't remember the last time. She hadn't known it would be the last time, so it slipped by unnoticed, like so many last times did.

"There's no easy way to tell you this," he said.

She sipped her drink, worrying that something had happened to their finances. Maybe they were losing their gorgeous beachfront home. Or worse, maybe he had a life-destroying disease.

"I hope you'll handle it with your usual grace and dignity," he said.

She took another sip of whisky, slightly more frantic this time. It stung the back of her throat.

"I've fallen in love. With Alice."

The first thing that crossed Mary's mind was the day she poured the tea into Verna's bowl of sugar cubes. She should pour her whisky into Henry's lap. But that wasn't nearly enough. He deserved infinitely worse than a damp spot on his trousers. He deserved to have the sharpest knife she owned remove everything that was hidden beneath his trousers.

He put his hand on her wrist. "I knew I could count on your class. You're the finest woman a man could ask for to manage his home and raise his children."

The bile crashed in enormous waves through her stomach, tearing at the lining, fueling itself with whisky. Mary placed her glass on the table. She stood and walked out of the room. He called after her, but she didn't reply. She went into their bedroom and locked the door. She didn't come out for two days, subsisting on water and a stale package of saltine crackers she'd found in her bottom drawer. They'd been there for eighteen years, left over from when she'd eaten them to relieve morning sickness. She was amazed by their ability to survive, softened by the years, but tasting perfectly fine, filling her stomach for a while.

She had no idea where Henry slept, most likely with Alice.

During those two days, she'd tried to think of an adequate punishment for him. It was difficult. Murder came to mind more than once, but that wouldn't cause him any suffering. And she was going to find a way to make him suffer. He needed to know the shame of being tossed aside. He needed to know the shame of a sagging body that was compared with a body fifteen years younger, containing a yet unused womb.

Fourteen

Corrine couldn't think of anything but Deb. She looked at Deb's Facebook page with increasing frequency. At first it had been once or twice a day. Then it was six or seven times. Now, she found herself checking it every time she responded to a text message or scrolled through a news feed. Her behavior sickened her, but she couldn't stop. The more disgust she felt, the more driven she was to check for newly posted information as well as dig into past threads.

She was appalled by the lack of discretion in Deb's posts. Deb provided minute-by-minute details of a fight with her sister and her feelings about a guy *she'd hooked up with, but it didn't work out.* The shock lured Corrine to look even more. She was like the rubberneckers at a gruesome car accident — slowing down to catch a glimpse, driven to look, hungering for the shock of seeing mangled limbs, possibly brain matter spilled on the pavement. They wanted to see death. It wasn't as if she was looking for death, but she was definitely bordering on stalker behavior.

Never in her life had she imagined herself a stalker! What would it take for her to start pursuing personal information about Deb? To take a trip to Southern California and track her movements in real life, feeding her unquenchable desire for information? People who did those things were mentally ill. Was that happening to her? She was obsessed. She knew everything about Deb's life. She knew her birthday — that was easy. She knew what kind of car she drove — a Fiat. She knew Deb had three sisters, a chihuahua, and a group of close friends from high school who took a trip to Puerto Vallarta every year and called themselves the Skinny Bikini Clique.

To keep up her fitness and supplement sales image, Deb worked out with a personal trainer. That bit of information made Corrine smile. All she did was run on the beach and she looked just as good as Deb. Exactly like Deb. She'd seen Deb posing with the Skinny Bikini Clique, so she knew.

Deb visited her parents in Ohio once a year, she helped out in a soup kitchen during the Christmas season, and she had a tattoo of a pink rose on the underside of her left wrist. She was thinking of getting another — in a spot she didn't *feel comfortable broadcasting on Facebook*. That was a surprise, since she broadcast everything else. The forty million people in California could easily find out when Deb hit her sales goals — *Thanks to all my devoted and wonderful clients who give meaning to my life* — and when she missed — *no blame* (smiley face and a heart icon).

Corrine felt she could give Deb a call and have a thirty minute conversation without Deb ever suspecting they'd never met. Deb would have no idea she was being stalked by her ex-husband's new girlfriend.

It wasn't really stalking since she didn't intend any harm. What would be the point of that? It wasn't as if Deb were trying to get him back or wished him ill will. Deb wasn't a threat of any kind. And yet, she felt like a huge threat. She was a shadow hanging over Corrine's life, destroying her new-found romance, something she'd thought had a future. Was Deb the person Andy wanted Corrine to be? Or had he tried to make Deb into someone else and failed, leaving her half-finished? Maybe he'd found Corrine to be more malleable.

She slammed closed the cover of her tablet and went into the kitchen. Cat followed, eager for her daily treat of canned food. Corrine took out a can of food, peeled off the aluminum lid, and spooned pasty salmon flavored food into Cat's second bowl.

"Are you disappointed I never gave you a proper name?" she said.

Cat purred and took a portion of food in her teeth. She chewed. It was strange how she used such sharp teeth to chew the pulpy food. It could easily melt in her mouth and be swallowed without the use of teeth.

"I guess that means you're okay with it?" Corrine said.

Cat took another bite.

Corrine looked out at the garden. She was stalking a woman she didn't know and talking to a cat. Maybe she was mentally unbalanced. But if that were the case, she wouldn't see it so clearly, would she? Stalkers thought they were justified in their behavior. They had no idea they were creepy, overstepping boundaries, far outside of the norm. She also believed she was justified, but she was! She wasn't hurting anyone. She wasn't making threats, she wasn't even trying to frighten Deb. She hadn't *done* anything. She'd just read online posts that were visible to anyone.

The fuchsia in the brick planter across from the window nearly blinded her with its bright purple and pink blossoms, delicate pale green pistils with teardrop tips. Even in winter, the fuchsia flung out more branches, dangling new blossoms like tiny birds from its limbs. It made her feel sane. She wasn't deranged. She was unsettled. Anyone would be, seeing a twin of herself, fearing that the man she loved might not recognize why he was drawn to her. Even worse, maybe he did recognize it.

She filled the kettle with water and turned on the stove. She dropped a green teabag into a mug and waited for the water to boil. When the kettle whistled, she poured the hissing water over the teabag. She let it steep for twice as long as usual. When it was finished, she took the mug back to the living room. The fog was thick and low and damp. It was too cold to sit in the garden. Or was that just an excuse so she could return to her tablet? She was lying to herself now?

She blew on her tea, took a cautious sip, and picked up the tablet. She pushed the condemning thoughts to the side and opened Facebook. She took another sip of tea. It burned her tongue, but she didn't care.

Deb was at the gym.

Corrine closed the tablet cover and put her tea on the table. She picked up her phone and sent a text to Andy — *Do you feel like going for a run? I'm antsy.*

In less than two minutes, he replied. *Sure. Forty minutes?*

She tapped out her answer. *I'll be waiting.*

She changed into spandex pants, a white sports bra, and a navy blue top. She tied a sweatshirt around her waist and laced up her shoes. She dumped the tea down the drain and rinsed the fishy remains out of Cat's bowl.

When Andy pulled up in front of her house, she was on the porch, stretching her hamstrings. He gave her a quick kiss and tugged gently on the long braid hugging her spine. He clipped Parker's leash to the collar and they walked quickly to the stairs down to the beach. Once they were near the shore, they turned right and started a slow jog. The sand was soft, turning the easy jog into more of a slog, thick wet sand pulling at their shoes like mud. Parker trotted between them. He turned his head back and forth, looking up first at Andy, then Corrine. His tongue was draped over the bottom half of his jaw and his dark brown eyes shone. He panted with excitement rather than exertion, his pace little more than a fast walk. The waves sucked at the sand and rattled over a layer of pebbles that had been revealed as sand was pulled out with the tide. The beach was a constantly evolving landscape, with sporadic piles of rock and broken shells and pebbles, covered up for a few weeks by sand, then revealed again as the waves swept in ever changing formations.

Corrine dropped back a few paces to look out at the ocean without Andy's body blocking her view. Parker stayed beside Andy.

Waves swelled and curled and surged across the sand. A seal poked its head out, staring directly at her, then turned and dove beneath a wave. There were no pelicans cruising over the surface of the water today, and very few gulls. The ones who were in the area were huddled on every exposed part of the concrete ship. A few cormorants floated on the water, diving in beautiful curves every few minutes, resurfacing and shaking water off their feathers as they stuck their beaks into the air, hungry and searching.

She faced forward again. Ahead was a murre sitting on the moist sand. A shallow wave swept around it. The bird moved slightly but didn't get to its feet. As Corrine drew closer, she saw that it wasn't just squatting as they sometimes did. It had its breast and stomach feathers settled onto the sand as if it were nesting there. But they never nested in exposed areas like this.

Andy switched the leash to his left hand and Parker crossed in front of him, running through the water. They ran past the bird without looking at it, both of them staring directly ahead, as if they were eyeing a finish line they needed to cross at any minute.

Corrine slowed and stopped about three feet away from the murre. It turned its head toward her but didn't make any effort to change position.

"Oh! You poor thing." She moved back a few steps to keep from frightening the bird.

It studied her, tilting its head slightly. Still it didn't move except for the slight rise and fall of its breast. One leg was splayed out from beneath it, the webbed toes plastered on the sand. A wave came in and lapped around the bird's feathers, turning them a darker color as water soaked into them. The bird remained motionless.

"You can't swim? I wish I could move you. I want to move you." Her heart twisted. Her eyes filled up and when she lifted her head, she couldn't locate Andy and Parker. All she saw was water and sand and the liquid filling her eyes. She blinked hard, trying to make the tears stop.

The bird looked at her, pleading for help. Its eyes looked lost, confused, and frightened. It knew she was the last hope.

She knelt in the sand. "I'm so sorry." She put her hands over her face. Her heart ached with wanting to move the bird, but it wouldn't understand. And it wouldn't survive, even if she could get it into the water where it might start paddling. It certainly wasn't able to fly or it would have disappeared by now.

"What are you doing?" Andy's voice was firm. He and Parker had returned. They stood a few feet to her left.

"It's so sad."

"Stay away from it. You don't want to get bitten if it freaks out."

"It's not going to bite me. I wish I could help it. I think it's dying."

A wave came in, stronger and faster this time. It washed around the bird, leaving nothing but its head exposed. The bird didn't attempt to lift its head out of the water.

"There's nothing you can do."

She looked up at him. "I know that! But it breaks my heart. It's begging us to keep it safe."

"It's a wild animal. It's not expecting anything from you. In fact, you're probably scaring it, by staying so close."

She was almost sobbing now. "I care about animals, okay?"

"So do I. Domesticated animals. The animal I'm responsible for. You can't save every bird on the planet. Do you know how many birds die every year? Six or seven million are killed running into cell towers, and one to three *billion* are killed by cats."

"How do you know?"

"An article on climate change. Besides, it's nature. The weak die sooner. And eventually, they all die."

"You don't care if it's dying?"

"It's a wild bird."

"We can still care about it."

"I don't have the energy to care about every single bird and fish."

She stood up and tried to brush wet sand off her knees but it stuck like it had been glued to her skin. "It looks so helpless. It looks scared."

"Of course it's scared. Two huge human beings and a dog are crowding around it."

She took a few more steps back. She turned toward the ship. The incoming tide had filled the space where the bow was broken off from the rest of the ship. It looked like the tip was drifting out to sea on its own, leaving the rest of its body behind. She untied her sweatshirt from around her waist and pulled it over her head.

"Aren't you going to run any more?"

"No. I'm too upset."

"I don't understand why you fall apart over things you can't do anything about. Why you're more concerned about wild birds than you are with me."

"Because you're not sitting on a beach, helpless and dying."

"You only care about creatures that are dying? Is that why you like the old people?"

She glared at him, her eyes spilling tears. "I care about life."

He moved closer to her and put his arm around her waist. In a low, quiet voice he said, "You can't fall apart every time you see a dead bird."

"It's not dead!"

"Every time you see an injured or dead bird. You haven't

lived here long, but there are dead things on the beach all the time. Seals, too. It's the cycle of life."

"It's not the cycle of life. Half the dead animals are things we've killed."

He squeezed her and said nothing. She was glad he didn't try to tell her anything else about how she should think.

"Do you want to keep running?" he said.

"You can. I'm going home."

"Okay. I'll go with you." He tugged on Parker's leash and they started back the way they'd come. They climbed the stairs and walked back to her house without talking. Parker seemed to pick up on their mood — he didn't look as gleeful as he had when they'd started out.

They sat in the garden and drank a glass of white wine. Andy talked about work. Corrine tried to concentrate, but mostly she thought about the desperate bird. Her thoughts wandered to Deb. How did Deb feel about wild birds? Had Andy had been kind to her tiny dog? How had Parker and the chihuahua gotten along? Or maybe they'd never known each other. "How long have you had Parker?" she said.

"What makes you ask that?"

"Just curious. He's so devoted to you, I was thinking about it."

"Two years."

The answer told her nothing. It depended on which version of his and Deb's breakup she was going to believe.

Fifteen

All four of her sons called to check in on her. They didn't use that term, of course, but that's what it was. The cell towers must have been humming — Thomas calling or texting or emailing each of his brothers to give a report on their mother.

Mom doesn't take her phone to the beach.

I'm worried about her.

She won't listen to me either.

She thinks she's forty-five-years-old.

She acts like she's not blind!

Nothing's changed — she's getting into it with people who harass the gulls.

All this would fuel a discussion of her obsession with birds. Her inexplicable love for large, carcass-devouring birds. They would worry about her health and what she was eating. They'd worry about her falling, getting mugged. She had a feeling their biggest concern was that she'd become incapacitated, requiring one of them to take extended time off work. Decisions would have to be made. They'd be required to find a home and then they'd have to battle her stubborn refusal to accept reality. She'd never been one to put a lot of emphasis on so-called reality. Life reacted to you, not the other way around.

By the time she was done talking to Thomas, the last to call, as if they'd arranged to contact her in order of their descending ages, it was eleven-thirty, according to the woman inside her phone. The weather was cool and cloudy and windy. The forecast suggested a thirty-percent chance of rain. Wearing the cape in the wind was frustrating, but it kept her warmer than any coat. She put on rubber boots and tucked her pants inside the tops. She was sure she looked quite stylish for a ninety-one-year-old woman.

Just as she put her hand on the doorknob, her cell phone rang. She opened the door and stepped outside quickly, as if she needed to hurry or it might chase after her. She locked the door, dropped her keys in her pocket, and pulled her hood up. The wind wasn't noticeable as she walked down the sloping sidewalk between the tightly nestled houses, but once she passed out into the open space headed toward the creek, a gust caught her hood and blew it off her head. She tugged it back in place and held it with her left hand while she crossed the bridge.

Once she reached the sand, she walked quickly toward the water's edge. The knee-high boots with treaded soles made her less concerned about stepping into something too sharp or too soft. Something soft was the worst of the two possibilities — it could mean dog excrement or a decaying bird. She was still careful, aware of holes dug by children that had partially filled during high tide, but could still bring a sudden jolt downward, jarring her fragile bones. Her sons were right to worry about her.

She didn't like them worrying about her. They had every right, and they had good reason. Ninety-one *wasn't* forty-five. But what did she have to lose? She wanted to enjoy every moment she had left, and sitting inside her house, listening to the TV or an audio book, meeting a friend for a cup of tea, was not enough for a worthwhile life. She needed the beach, she needed the fresh air. She needed to hear the birds and the laughing, shouting children.

Once she felt wet sand beneath her boots, she stopped walking. The waves sounded rough, but she risked a few steps closer to the water's edge. Another benefit of her rubber boots — she could step into the oncoming waves and feel them push against her ankles. Her sons would be horrified by the danger of a rogue wave she'd never see coming. They were silent and unpredictable. A rogue wave would sweep up, faster and stronger than its predecessors, wrap its arms around her ankles, grabbing up to her calves and lashing at her knees, pulling her with it back into the ocean. She took two steps closer and felt the edge of a wave approach and lap over her left toe. It was okay. She was safe. She smiled and lifted her face to the wind. It was sharp and cold, but made her feel so alive. Feeling alive was what she needed more than anything, and her sons, and her few remaining friends, and possibly Daniel, and her new-found potential friend Corrine, did not seem to understand that.

What was the point of life if it was all lived in safety? Risk avoided, danger avoided, pain avoided, accidents avoided, and most of all, death avoided. She definitely wanted to avoid being confined to a place like Fairhaven, but not at the ironic risk of failing to relish the years she had left.

The wind whipped at her cape. It seemed to be getting stronger, but she couldn't go back home yet. It would be her only chance out here today if the rain arrived as promised. A gull cried overhead and she pictured it buffeted by the wind like a kite with a slack string. She heard a splash as another bird hit the waves in front of her. A dog began barking and everything inside of her turned to glass. Of course she couldn't distinguish the barks of different dogs, she'd never had one of her own, but she could tell by the excited undertone it was chasing the gulls.

A moment later the dog ran past within a few feet of where she stood, spraying her boots with flecks of sand, barking wildly, stopping and dashing back, then running in a circle around her, kicking more sand against her cape. The runner thudded past. He didn't command the dog to stop or heel. It was obviously off its leash.

"Put your dog on a leash!" Mary shouted the words, but it

seemed as if they were lost beneath the sound of rushing, churning water. "It frightens the birds, and wears them out when dogs chase them." Her voice faded. "They're so exhausted they can't hunt for food, and they starve."

The runner had stopped, but she wasn't sure where he, or she, was. She'd lost track of the dog's location as well. The dog barked. Mary whirled to her left. The dog was galloping through the waves, barking furiously. She heard the flapping of forty or fifty pairs of wings.

"Stop him!" she shouted. "Please stop."

The surf quieted for a moment between breakers. She felt the heat of another person standing a few feet to her left. It was the same man. She was sure of it. She felt the muscular tension of him, poised to run, or to grab her. She shrunk away, pulling her cape tightly around her. "Please leave me alone. Is it too much to ask that your dog chase a ball? That you not stand there trying to frighten me?" She wished she hadn't said that. She shouldn't let on that she was scared. She could imagine the chastising words coming from each of her sons and their wives, all eight of them harping at her that she was a fool. A blind old fool risking her life. She took a few steps away from the water. She shouldn't have admitted her fear, and yet, he knew she was afraid. It was the very reason he was standing in silence, hoping her fear would increase with each breath.

It was too windy for anyone to be fishing. And when she'd first come out, she'd been certain she was alone on this section of the beach. Could anyone see the man standing closer than he should — he'd taken a few steps toward her when she'd moved. She smelled his sweat, and possibly a whiff of unwashed hair.

"Please leave," she whispered. "Please."

He stepped closer. The toe of his running shoe bumped her rubber boot. She turned and walked several feet toward the pier. She felt him moving behind her, or was it the wind? She turned, breathing in salt air. The odor of sweat was gone, but she was sure he was still there, watching her, directing a tiny smile at her, aware that her eyes were vacant. She'd been right about the smile, because now he was laughing softly. Suddenly she realized — he understood what it was like to be missing one of your senses. He saw how weak she was without her sight, and by not speaking, he'd ripped away her hearing. All she had left was his scent and the intuitive awareness of his presence. Would he dare to touch her? Wanting her remaining senses to erupt in a maelstrom of irrational fear.

She should leave. There was nothing stopping her. But she had a feeling, maybe that intuition again, that if she demonstrated that much fear, he would follow her, possibly all the way to her front door. And then she'd never feel safe again.

If she'd brought her phone as Thomas had insisted, she could call the police. But even if they came, the man would be long gone. And what would she tell them?

She knew nothing. She could at least cross the beach and go up the stairs. There must be a jogger or two running on the path. She should scream. If anyone was up there, he would take off down the beach. Even if he wasn't caught, she'd be safe. She opened her mouth and tried to make a sound, but screaming at will seemed to be a difficult thing to do. A scream had to be visceral. She felt she was in a dream, terrified but unable to get her vocal cords to function.

He was touching her. Something tapped her tongue. She gagged. There was a tickle on her tongue and then the thing was gone. A sand crab? Had he truly put a sand crab into her open mouth? Tears filled her eyes. She turned. Her right heel skidded on loose sand. He grabbed the side of her cape and kept her from falling. Something touched her cheek, the same tickling sensation, thin, crusty legs squirming, trying to escape as surely as she was trying, and just as helpless, pinched between the man's fingers.

She began to sob. "Please leave me alone. All I did was ask you not to let your dog bother the gulls. Is that so terrible? Why are you doing this to me?"

He laughed softly, almost a falsetto — *hee, hee, hee.*

The best thing to do was to stop exposing her fear. Of course, it was too late for that, but she didn't have to continue until he knew she was paralyzed. She released the tight grip she'd had on the edges of her cape. She let her hood slide away from her forehead, pillowing around her hair as the wind tried to wind its way between the back of her head and the fabric. "It really is so unkind to let your dog torment the gulls. I hope you won't do it again." She began walking toward the pier. She planned to walk underneath it and take the steps that led up to the visitor's center rather than the set she usually used.

As she slid her feet forward, she realized the sand was littered with more dried seaweed than normal, but there didn't seem to be any large piles or long strands waiting to trip her. She moved carefully, making sure of each step. Aside from the obvious reasons for not wanting to fall, she didn't want to become even more helpless in front of him. She knew he was watching, deciding whether he would follow. The dog had been quiet for several minutes. Did that mean it had succeeded in driving all the gulls out to the protection offered by the concrete ship, or just pushed them further down the beach, and once the man started running again, the dog would go wild? She couldn't worry about it. She had to think of herself this time.

It seemed like it took her an hour to reach the steps, but she knew it was only a few minutes. As far as she could tell, the man had not followed her. She was safe, for now. And maybe she'd always been safe. But he was determined to destroy her sense of safety on the beach. She should stop shouting at him to leave the birds alone, but she couldn't help herself. It was so cruel and so unnecessary, and left her with a sick, weak feeling, as if she'd lost the use of her own arms and was condemned to stumble across the sand, exhausted.

It rained for three days after that. She was almost glad to be confined to the house, although a part of her wanted to chance going out despite the storm. She doubted the man would be running with his dog in the gusting rain.

On the fourth day, when the sky was reportedly clearing, she ate toast and a small piece of leftover swordfish with her second cup of coffee. She dressed and went out, reaching the pier as the sun was rising behind her. She could tell by the enthused voices there were more fishermen than usual, eager to get back to it after the rain. Eager to throw their lines into water that was likely to be replenished after the rough waves and the lack of predators.

She wanted to find a way to apologize to Daniel for offending him, without apologizing for the reality of the haunted ship. She would tell him she was sorry for trying to modify his story of the octopus, and she'd try to quickly change the subject to the man terrorizing her on the beach. She needed his help. That girl, Corrine, could help. She was certainly eager to do whatever she could to help Mary cope with old age, but Mary preferred asking Daniel. He wasn't trying so hard. And maybe she was more comfortable around men. Her relationships with women, except for a handful of friends, hadn't gone well — her mother, Verna, some of the women she'd known when she was single.

Besides, even though Daniel was old, he was tough. He'd solve the problem. She was sure of it. He was logical and easy going, but had a will like steel. He'd also insist she do her part, stop trying to police the beach. She'd have to consider that. Maybe her time was past. This was something for younger people — people like Corrine who had their eyesight, their strength, and more experience in the way the world operated in the twenty-first century.

She'd worn her rubber boots again, thinking of wading into the surf after talking to Daniel. The boots sounded like something inhuman on the wood planks. They echoed more darkly through the open spaces between boards as she clumped with an uneven gait. Many of the fishermen wore rubber boots, but she'd never noticed the difference in the sound until today.

Daniel had not brought a bear claw. He seemed more intense about his fishing than usual, and she was glad. The sweet rolls made her feel ill, but it wouldn't start the conversation on the right footing if she refused his gift. On the other hand, had he skipped the treat because he was more offended than she'd realized? But why?

"Hi, Daniel."

"Hi, Mary."

His voice sounded pleasant, no underlying tone that she needed to interpret.

"Has it been a productive day for fish?" she said.

"Yep. Five good-sized perch and the sun's just now coming up."

She smiled, hoping he was looking in her direction. "All

that rain, but still probably not as much as we need."

"That's what they say."

She settled herself on the bench. "I wanted to apologize for the last time we spoke."

"Why's that?"

There was a wet thud. From the sound of it, someone a few feet away had landed a rather good-sized fish.

"I think I offended you, talking about the ship being haunted."

"I told you I don't want to discuss it."

"But I don't want you to be upset with me."

"I'm not."

"Are you sure?"

"Yes."

"I didn't mean to twist the story from your memory into something of mine."

"Mary. I said I didn't want to talk about it."

"I took a frightening story from your life and put my own experiences into it. And you obviously don't feel a discussion of supernatural beings fits with your religion, and I know I kept pushing. I do that sometimes. I've been that way since I was a child. I can't let go of something and I can be bullheaded to the point of being rude."

"Mary!"

"I just want to make sure I haven't damaged our friendship."

"Please talk about something else."

"Is it upsetting to think about your experience inside the ship? Seeing that octopus, so big, and so ready to wrap its arms around you, attached itself to your body?"

"It's something I'd rather forget. I'm sorry I told you. I don't even know why I thought of it."

"Because it terrified you. We think frightening experiences have been put to rest, but they're not very far below the surface."

"Maybe."

"I can't imagine seeing something like that. I guess I never will now." She laughed.

Daniel was silent. She'd offended him again. It wasn't at all funny to him. She'd laughed at the idea of herself in any depth of water, and the fact she couldn't see. Was it possible Daniel hadn't realized that? He was locked inside his memory, thinking of the mouth of the octopus, all those arms and the enormous suction cups. She shivered. It did sound awful. He thought she was laughing at him.

"I don't remember what we were talking about," she said.

"Neither do I."

His plastic bucket scraped across the boards as he repositioned it. His tackle box clanked open and his fingers rattled around, looking for something.

"Do you know anyone else who's seen an octopus so close to shore?" she said.

"You are pigheaded."

"I said bullheaded. More persistent than stubborn. That's

nicer, don't you think?"

"Sounds pigheaded to me."

She thought she should laugh, to help him relax, to see that she could laugh at herself, that she hadn't been laughing at him a moment ago. "You don't want to talk about it."

"I think I made that clear. But I did hear about one once. About five years ago. It tried to grab a diver's camera. It was closer to Monterey. Pacific Grove, maybe."

"Oh, my."

"There was a video of it on the internet. You can …oh, sorry."

"It's okay." She said it softly, regretting all the things she'd never see.

She heard him cast his line and reel it back for a few seconds. There was another thud as a fish landed on the pier.

She pushed her hood off so the sun could get at her hair. "Do you recall that man I mentioned? The one who scared me? The one who stood right beside me and wouldn't say anything?"

"Yes."

"I was wondering if you could speak to him. As a favor to me."

"Speak to him?"

"Tell him to leave me alone."

"I can't do that."

"Why not?"

"First, I have no idea who you're talking about…"

"You could watch for me, and see if…"

"I don't think that's a good idea. I'm not responsible for looking after you."

"I wasn't asking that."

"If you ignore him, he'll leave you alone."

"I don't think I can, not now."

"Remember what we said about pigheaded?"

"Even if I don't speak to him again, I think he likes upsetting me. It's kind of sickening. That someone would take pleasure in that."

"You can't be telling people what to do. How to live their lives."

"I only asked one favor. To leave the birds alone. And everyone should do that. There shouldn't be any question about it."

As if they agreed with her, a flock of gulls flew low over the pier, squawking and calling out to each other. She smiled. Of course it was more likely they were excited by all the fish landing on the pier, secured in buckets by the fishermen before the gulls could make their approach.

"Well I can't be picking fights with strangers in your defense."

"It doesn't upset you that someone would torment a woman as old as me?"

"It bothers me that someone would torment a person of any age, but I can't help you. I'm not responsible for looking out for you. Where are your sons? Your grandchildren?

Maybe you need a companion."

"I don't need a companion. I have friends. Like you."

"I think he'll leave you alone if you stop shouting at him."

"I can't do that."

"You have to. And if you keep doing it, anything I would say, or even one of your sons, wouldn't make a difference."

"I thought you'd help."

"Sorry."

"So you are upset with me still?"

"No. It has nothing to do with that. I just can't be looking after you. I have a wife, a family of my own. It sounds harsh, I know. But you really need someone to help you. It's not safe, wandering around the way you do. In fact, I wonder about your sons, that they allow it."

"They don't live here."

"They should insist you have some help."

Mary pressed her feet together. It seemed as if they weren't there, all she could feel was thick rubber wobbling around her calves. "I don't need help."

"You asked me for help."

"That's a favor. For one problem. I don't need assistance to live my life."

"Look. It's great talking to you when I'm fishing. You're a sweet lady. A fixture at Seacliff, but I can't take on some guy who's decided to terrorize you. You either need to stay off the beach or get a companion. Even one of those dogs."

"A seeing eye dog?"

"Maybe. But at your age, I think you need someone to cook, make sure you don't leave the stove on, fix things around your house."

He wasn't going to help her. Maybe he was afraid of the man, or maybe she had imagined their friendship to be more than it was. She couldn't see his eyes or the set of his lips. She really didn't know how he felt about talking to her. His face might be covered with frustration when he saw her walking along the pier. She'd put more importance on the gift of the sweet rolls than she should have. He was just being nice to an old lady. He probably thought she didn't get enough to eat, that she was undernourished. In his eyes, she was a charity case. She stood up carefully, putting her shoulders back and lifting her chin slightly, even though he might not be looking in her direction. He might have all his attention on his fishing line. "I should be getting home."

She paused for a moment, thinking he would apologize, recognizing that this time, *he'd* offended *her*. More than that, he'd hurt her.

"Take care," he said. "And don't think you need to defend the birds. Let an animal rescue fanatic fight that battle. Then he'll leave you alone."

"You're probably right," she said.

She walked along the pier toward the footpath, feeling that she looked awkward and old and unstable in her rubber boots. She didn't go down to the edge of the water after all. Another day.

Sixteen

The internet was a funny thing. It was supposed to be bringing the world closer together, creating a global community where average people on every continent were able to connect with each other, do end runs around their governments, especially the oppressive and murderous ones. But mostly, it seemed to be dividing people — helping them build ever smaller, more homogeneous communities and construct ever more elaborate masks. They hid behind pithy sayings and entertaining video clips and *Likes* and *Favorites*. You never had to talk to anyone or even write a comment to maintain the illusion of a friendship: *Like. Like. Like. Like-Like-Like-Like.*

Deb had hundreds of likes on some of her posts. She had a lot of comments too — many of them superficial. And her responses to those empty thoughts made Corrine wonder whether Deb actually knew some of the people who were commenting, the people she got into lengthy pointless discussions with about her spiritual views and the importance of supplementing the inadequate American diet. Of course she didn't know them. They were customers. They lived all over California and she'd never met them. They were enthused by her enthusiasm. They loved her simple thoughts for the day and her two-sentence pep talks.

It was eleven o'clock on a Tuesday night. Cat was curled at the foot of the bed, purring until her whiskers vibrated, obviously pleased that Parker hadn't been around for two days. Corrine put her fingers on the bedside light switch. She needed to get to sleep. Six a.m. was coming fast, but she couldn't seem to stop scrolling through Deb's page.

She'd gone back on Deb's timeline to 2007, a long and tedious task, but she felt like she'd lived right next door during her marriage to Andy. She'd seen their vacation photos and heard about the gifts Andy gave Deb for her birthdays and Christmas. She saw their dinners out — Deb wearing heels every single time. Yet in all Deb's other photos, she wore workout clothes and athletic shoes. When she was with the Skinny Bikini gang, she wore flip-flops.

Andy had disappeared from Deb's photo gallery about two years ago. But it was hard to determine whether that was because things were getting rough between them, or they'd actually split. She was very cheery on Facebook, so there was no evidence of any emotional fallout. Aside from that one note about the wonder of first love and wishing him a good life, there was nothing about the end of their marriage.

Maybe Deb had a few ounces of discretion after all.

Corrine opened another tab and went to Google. She picked up her wine and took a long swallow. It was almost gone. She was going to do this. She wasn't going to analyze for one more day, one more minute, whether it was dishonest or shameful or creepy. She set up a new email account, calling herself Sara McGregor, and returned to Facebook. She logged out of her profile, and began the process of constructing a new profile. So easy. This was the problem with the internet. You could be anyone and you could be no one. She had to know whether he'd lied. If Andy was being truthful with her, calling him out on a minor lie would destroy their relationship. If he was hiding part of his life, her creepiness, her lack of trust, didn't matter.

She did an image search on fifty-year-old women and found a photograph of a woman who had her head partially turned away from the camera. It wasn't one of those cheesy photographs by people who deliberately hide their faces with their hair — too cute and too coy. The woman's hair was blonde with copper and brown streaks. A highlighting style that was a bit too old for her, but that made her a perfect candidate for a type that was searching for supplements to keep herself young and fit, to *push her workouts to the next level*. From what was visible of her face, the shape of the woman's smile made her look like someone you could share your secrets with, someone who would be understanding and keep a confidence, and almost always tell you what you wanted to hear. Even when it wasn't what you wanted to hear, she'd tone it down, soften it with caveats until her criticism was bland and unnoticeable. A perfect *friend*.

It was impossible to fake the timeline, so Corrine planned to post that she'd ...*finally caved and joined the online world after all these years, but I still really prefer people face to face.* Followed by an emoticon, or maybe an *LOL*. Did someone new to social media use LOL? She'd have to think about that. Finding friends was a bit more difficult. She spent another half hour searching for people who were loose with their profiles, people who boasted six or seven hundred friends, suggesting they befriended people they didn't know. If she could find twenty, that would give her a legitimate-looking profile. She found three to start with. She really needed to sleep, but setting up a false persona was strangely addictive and invigorating. She went into the kitchen, poured a small splash of wine in her glass and sat in the living room with the lights off, thinking about how to approach Deb.

Three of Corrine's clients had died during the night. She felt guilty. Of course all of her clients were dying. But she had the sense that her transformation from a kind, generous, and giving person into a woman who pretended to be someone else, who didn't communicate truthfully with her partner, who stalked a self-invented nemesis on the internet, was partially responsible for their deaths. In less than a month she'd become a total stranger to herself. A woman who looked like someone else. A shallow, insecure woman. Maybe all her flaws had invited more death into Fairhaven.

She tried burying the irrational thoughts under the tasks waiting on her desk and in her email in-box, but they wouldn't leave her alone. Crazy thoughts. Of course she wasn't some sort of angel of death! She laughed. She was tired. Not crazy, just too cooped up indoors. She hadn't been to the beach in several days, hadn't been outside at all except to walk to her car. She needed fresh air and common sense. The best thing to do would be to go home after work and before she ate dinner or poured a glass of wine, she would delete the phony email and Facebook accounts and go for a long walk on the beach.

The fake account isn't hurting anyone.

She didn't know where that thought had come from, but it made her realize she wasn't a bad person. She was curious and resourceful. Lots of people set up fake profiles online. Everyone had multiple email addresses, and it was only a small step to creating different lives. She wasn't doing anything illegal. She was simply reading what Deb put out there for all the world to see, and now she wanted to interact. She was being friendly to someone who looked very much like her. A look-alike would make anyone curious. Deb didn't know that, of course. Deb would know her as a fifty-something woman who could pass for forty-something. But what did it matter?

Telling the family of a death never got easier. Would it get easier over the years, by the time she was forty, or fifty? If she was still in this job. Andy's idea to look for something more uplifting, and more lucrative, was appealing in some ways. Especially today. The first family on her list wasn't a family at all. She placed the call to a woman named Betty Miller. Betty herself was in her seventies — her mother, Doris, had died in her sleep at the age of ninety-seven.

While Corrine waited for the call to connect, she wondered how long *she* would live, whether she wanted to go on for that long, if it meant lying in a bed or sitting in an armchair listening to mindless chatter or watching TV most of the time. Yet it didn't have to be that way. Look at Mary. She wasn't quite that old, but she lived alone, took care of herself, and charged out to the beach every day with the determination of a women thirty or forty years younger.

The end of Doris's life had been worthwhile, hadn't it? Corrine had had quite a few conversations with her, listening to her tales, even if they sometimes wandered, about working as a college instructor in a time when nearly all female teachers taught small children, and only men were allowed to lecture adults. Doris bent over in a full belly laugh when she described a man who walked out of her class after she gave him a B- on an essay. He'd said, *A girl isn't adroit with the English language.* He'd meant adept, of course. Doris giggled. *He was so pompous and I wondered if he'd go through his entire life using that word incorrectly, along with all his sloppy grammar. Everyone would laugh behind his back.* Corrine wondered how many people knew the subtle difference enough to laugh, but she loved watching Doris giggle. Doris talked often about how the world had changed and Corrine felt as if she'd made a friend. This was what made her job impossible. She had tears in her eyes and a swollen throat when Betty answered.

"This is Corrine Dunning from Fairhaven. How are…"

"Oh," Betty said. She let out a tiny whimper.

Then there was no sound but Betty's soft moist, breathing.

"She went peacefully," Corrine said.

"How do you know? Were you there?"

"No. But the staff…"

"Were they in the room?"

"No. But there were no signs of distress. She simply looked like she was in a deep sleep."

"We die alone," Betty said.

"Most of us, yes," Corrine said.

"Only the lucky few have others around. And really, it's still a journey we make on our own."

"Your mother was a wonderful woman. I'm so sorry for your loss."

"They think when someone is that old, it doesn't hurt as much. But they're wrong."

"They are," Corrine said.

Betty chatted about her mother's life, her career when most women didn't have one, and how lucky she was to have a happy sixty-seven year marriage, all of it making her last years at Fairhaven more tolerable. "Thank you for giving her some companionship when I couldn't be there."

"My pleasure."

After the call, Corrine went to the break room. She filled her white mug with water and put it in the microwave. She pulled a cinnamon teabag out of the box and waited for the water to heat. This was a wonderful job. How had she doubted it? Death came to everyone, and she was filling her clients' last days with a few moments of human connection. She held their hands and steadied their hearts as they prepared to release the tenacious grip on their lives. She wished she could see the wounded bird that way. Possibly her intense gaze into its eyes had made it feel loved and a little less scared. Possibly it understood completely why she couldn't offer it any help. It was exhausted and ready to fly into a different realm where its wings were whole and it never felt tired.

She dunked the teabag in the water and looked out the window. It was still cloudy, but the dark, almost black clouds made everything look quiet and mysterious. Not a single leaf moved on the Lemonwood tree that brushed against the window.

She took a sip of tea and carried the mug back to her office to make the other phone calls. These were more perfunctory, but the pleasant feeling she had from talking with Betty stayed with her.

Andy had made her doubt her choices. She'd decided on this career years ago. She loved old people. The world would be a better place if the elderly were given more prominence and respect. Sure, some of them were difficult. But a lot of children were difficult and so were teenagers and millions of adults. Most adults. How had it come about that a grouchy forty-year-old was given a pass because of job stress and a grouchy eighty-year-old was someone to be shoved aside? Thinking so didn't make Andy a bad person — his views were the same as most — but they were wrong. She'd had to fight her parents' opinions and suffer her friends' not so subtle belittling as she worked to get her graduate degree. All of them thought she was insane, making a terrible mistake. All of them thought it was depressing, thankless work. Andy wasn't any different from all the other people she cared about, but disagreed with.

She was overcome with a wave of guilt for secretly checking into his past. What had he done that was so terrible? Given her the wrong date for when his marriage ended, which was still up for debate anyway? He'd bought her a dress she didn't like. By some odd coincidence, she looked like his ex wife. It wasn't as if he'd chosen her because of that! Their encounter had been completely by chance. He wasn't even looking at her when he first inserted himself into the conflict. He'd been to her left, and slightly behind her. It was dark. There was no way he'd looked at her and thought — even on an unconscious level — *I'm going to ask her out because she looks exactly like my wife*. Ex wife. She laughed.

It seemed as if there was something wrong with her

recently. It felt as if some other creature, another personality with different thoughts, wild suggestions, was creeping about inside her head. Why had she hated the dress with so much ferocity? They hadn't known each other long, it was perfectly reasonable that he'd buy her a dress without fully understanding her tastes. She'd acted as if he were trying to make her into someone else. And then she went out and bought the same dress? Why? The dress was more than she could afford, a color and style she hadn't cared for. Why hadn't she told him she'd changed her mind? No wonder he'd said nothing about it at dinner. Men rarely noticed clothes to that level of detail. He'd never seen the dress on her and she wasn't even sure it was the same one.

She pushed her mug to the side and put her elbows on her desk. She rested her head in her hands and closed her eyes. Her head ached. It felt pickled in cinnamon now, so that every intake of breath was tinged with spice.

She sat up and pulled open the desk drawer. She found a packet of Advil and took two, washing them down with the last of the tea. The large gulp of cold tea made her stomach fold over itself. She sat up straight and tried to take a deep breath. She didn't know her own thoughts, couldn't make a decision. It might be a good idea to leave work early. Making so many calls in a single day had been difficult.

For the next half hour she deleted and filed emails. She checked that the pianist for next week's singalong was confirmed to start an hour earlier than originally planned.

Ordinarily, she would take an hour or so to go to the main sitting room and visit with anyone who was sitting alone, not engaged in a card game or at least listening to a book, but the headache was creeping down the back of her scalp. It had gripped the sides of her head and her eyes were blurry. Her stomach complained as if she hadn't eaten a cheese and tomato sandwich for lunch two hours earlier. It seemed as if her body wanted to dictate what she was going to do, force her to leave work early, force her to eat a large afternoon snack, and force her to close the blinds and crawl under the blankets until the pain stopped.

She sent her supervisor a text message that she was leaving. The idea of walking to the adjacent building to deliver that message in person was too painful to think about. The pain was spreading and growing like something had spilled on her head and was seeping through her brain. She picked up her purse, pulled out her keys, and walked out the door. She locked the office and started down the hallway to the back door, hoping to escape without seeing any of her colleagues. The Spanish tile floor and plain walls echoed her footsteps. Normally she loved looking at the beautiful tiles, listening to the clack of shoes across their surface, but today it felt as if the soles of her shoes were smacking the sides of her head.

Outside, the fog had turned damp and heavy. The leaves on the Lemonwoods brushed her shoulder as she passed beneath one that needed pruning. It left a smear of water across her jacket.

To the annoyance of every other driver on Highway One, she drove fifty-five the entire way home. She stayed in the right lane, but that didn't satisfy anyone but a few drivers of large trucks, and even they seemed to be trying to push her to sixty. She didn't care. Let them come up on her bumper and then heave themselves around her. A film of thick liquid across her eyes made everything look as if it were under water, and she didn't trust that she'd distinguish brake lights from tail lights as her eyes struggled to focus.

At home, Cat was waiting in the front hall. She yowled and preceded Corrine into the kitchen, seating herself firmly by her bowl. Corrine rinsed the water bowl and re-filled it. She sprinkled half a cup of chicken-flavored pebbles into the other dish, even though she knew she was being had. Cat was fully aware she only got a refresh once a day, but hearing the car arrive home in the middle of the afternoon must have told her the routine had changed and she could make a play for extra snacks.

Corrine got an apple and a handful of almonds and went into her bedroom. She kicked off her ballet slipper shoes, unbuckled her belt and removed her pants, and got into bed. She propped the pillows behind her and ate the apple in less than five minutes. Already her headache was easing. She felt as if she'd lied to herself, telling herself she couldn't work under the pressure of such intense pain, yet now, it was only a light throbbing near her left temple. She stood the apple core on its end and ate the almonds.

Now, she wasn't aware of any pain at all. What was going on? How could her head have ached so horribly she thought she couldn't drive, and moments later feel stimulated and eager to get to work? She wasn't going to drive back. Her supervisor had texted back that she should take care of herself. It would look ridiculous to return to work saying she was fine after thirty minutes. She got out of bed and returned to the kitchen. She got a glass of water and more almonds. She picked up her tablet from the coffee table and returned to bed. The sheets and blankets felt warm and cozy on her legs. Cat had already settled on the other side, stretched out so that she occupied as much of Andy's space as possible. Corrine opened the tablet and went immediately to Sara's Facebook profile. She hunted down twenty more friends and finished the almonds. She went back to the kitchen, mixed a martini, and returned to bed.

She felt as if she were outside of herself, watching a woman abandon her responsibilities without concern, drinking and sitting in bed in the middle of the afternoon. Who was this person? Was she turning into Sara? Would Sara drink in the middle of a weekday afternoon? She didn't think so. Sara was interested in health and nutrition. She wanted to *kick her workout up to the next level*. She couldn't sit in bed and drink for the rest of the evening.

Corrine decided she'd stay on Facebook a little longer, finish the martini, and after dinner she'd take a long walk on the beach.

She posted a comment on Deb's page. *It's been a long time, Deb! How are you? I'm finally getting back to weight training. Any inspiration you can give me?*

Deb was on Facebook constantly. Corrine was sure she'd answer in less than an hour. She put her tablet on the nightstand, finished the martini, and sucked on both olives at once. She lay down and slept. When she woke, it was six-thirty. She felt marvelous. Her headache was completely gone and her brain felt like it had been given a shot of adrenaline. She was starving. She got up, put on her robe, and heated a huge plate of leftover spaghetti. She poured half a glass of Cab and propped the tablet on the table in front of her while she ate.

Deb hadn't missed a beat. She didn't ask who Sara was, didn't put any kind of teaser question as if she wanted to solidify the woman in her memory. She posted two quotes about the strength and power of women who lift.

Corrine clicked *like* and commented about how inspired she felt. She scrolled through to see if she'd missed anything interesting among the bits of information about protein requirements and the glory of kale in tablet form. She *liked* a bunch of pictures of Deb at a party and *liked* a few comments Deb's other friends had made. She rinsed her plate and wine glass. She went into the bedroom and stroked Cat's belly for a few minutes. She hung up her slacks and dressed in capri length jeans and a black sweatshirt. She braided her hair and put on a Giant's baseball cap, weaving the braid through the opening in the back.

The fog had blown out to sea and the sky glittered with stars. The moon was a few days from being full. The fog-less air made the temperature drop. She went back inside took off her sweatshirt and put on a turtleneck before wriggling back into the sweatshirt.

When she reached the beach, she felt like going for a run. What was wrong with her? A raging headache, a martini, a three-hour nap, half a glass of wine, and non-stop eating since she'd left work. Maybe pretending to be someone else truly was messing with her head. She took off her flip-flops and left them at the bottom of the steps. The waves were crashing so loud they filled her head. She jogged to the edge of the water and began walking west. She hugged the top of the water line, letting icy cold water wash over her feet and touch her ankle bones, but making sure she stayed well out of the way so a large wave couldn't splash up and soak her pants.

On the opposite side of the pier, a man was fishing in the surf. It was kind of wild for surf fishing, but he seemed to be managing okay.

"Hi," she said.

He nodded at her and turned his head, fixing his stare on the spot where his line entered the water. The line shimmered in the moonlight, easier to make out than she would have expected. She hurried past him, feeling as if she shouldn't have spoken to him. She walked a few hundred yards down the beach and turned to look at the waves. The foam made white splashes across the dark water. Waves crashed and churned with no break between each swell, some of them doubling up on each other. She took a few steps back as they came in closer, washing across the sand and swirling behind her before moving in a large arc that curved back out, dragging huge amounts of sand with it.

She turned. The fisherman stood motionless, his line invisible from this distance. The concrete ship glowed white and pale gray. It was empty of birds. She turned slightly. A figure stood at the side of the pier, looking out at the boat. It wasn't possible. She closed her eyes, then opened them slowly. It absolutely was not a ghost, even though she couldn't see much more than the shape of a head, and the silhouette of a caped body. A wisp of white hair blew out from beneath the hood. It was Mary. There was no question. She turned and looked at the gate at the front of the pier. It was closed for the night. How had Mary gotten through? Did she have an agreement with the park rangers that allowed her access? Maybe she had a key. She'd lived in the area forever. There was no telling who she'd beguiled over the years.

Corrine began walking back toward the pier. The fisherman stared at the water, seemingly unaware of the woman above him. Corrine walked faster. The figure hadn't moved. Corrine moved further into the edge of the surf, thinking she might see the woman's face, but it wasn't possible. She'd have to wade in up to her hips. She veered back up the sand and hurried to where the fisherman stood. "Excuse me," she said.

He turned.

"Do you see that woman?" She pointed and looked up. The woman was gone. "I guess you can't see her from here. I don't suppose you'd mind walking over this way a bit?"

"I'm fishing."

"I know. I could hold your pole for you."

She couldn't see much of his face, but she imagined he was looking at her as if she were alcohol-addled. Why would he hand off his fishing pole to a strange woman who walked up to him on the beach and asked him to look at a woman standing on the pier?

"I'm sorry I bothered you," she said.

He didn't speak. She waited, hoping he'd give some kind of indication he was curious. He remained silent, staring out into the darkness, seeing nothing but the fringe of foam at the edges of the waves.

She made a wide path behind him and continued under the pier, quickening her pace as the support pillars seemed to crowd her, slick and dark with water, the bases bulging with clusters of mussels clinging to the wood. When she emerged on the opposite side, she walked another twenty or thirty feet and looked up at the pier. The woman was still there. She wanted to shout back at the fisherman — *Look! I told you to look. There's a woman up there. I thought it was Mary but she told me it was a ghost. She looks real, don't you think? Have you seen her before?*

She turned and walked farther. She stopped and looked up

again. The woman was still there, still staring at the sinking concrete ship. Corrine's brain ached. It was different from the ache she'd had earlier — a bona fide physical disturbance in the flesh of her brain, pressure on the fine web of nerves that made them scream out for food and rest. This was an ache of confusion. She couldn't trust her eyes, couldn't trust her knowledge of the world. She couldn't explain Mary's insistence it was a ghost, couldn't reconcile that with the very real form of a woman standing in the darkness. But neither could she explain how the woman had slipped past a locked gate.

The longer she watched, the more unreal the figure seemed. It wasn't moving now, and the strands of white hair that had been visible earlier were tucked beneath the hood. Unless those had been an illusion. Possibly it was a ghost and Corrine's confused mind had imagined the white hair to try to make sense of it, to try to mold the figure into something real that she was familiar with.

The last time she'd seen it, she'd known it was real. Wouldn't a ghost have something about it that would tell her she was seeing a being from another realm? But ever since she'd first seen the woman in the cape, her life had taken a strange turn. She'd become filled with thoughts she didn't recognize. Her view of Andy had twisted into something tinged with paranoia. At the same time, she felt she was pursuing truth that was being hidden from her. But wasn't that what all unbalanced, paranoid people thought? They believed the voices that echoed inside their own heads without any external source. They believed they were being lied to and they believed those thoughts were actually implanted by a foreign mechanism.

She wanted to turn and walk away. To forget about the woman and return to a normal life. To have fun with her good-looking, interesting, devoted boyfriend. She wanted to help the people she was responsible for, provide something of value to the world. But she couldn't stop looking, waiting for the figure to do something — reveal the truth of who, or what, she was.

Seventeen

A whimpering sound woke Mary. She turned on her side and tried to orient her thoughts. The whimpering was coming from her own throat. She'd had a terrible dream. She'd been repulsed, and frightened. She put her hand on her belly, it was cold and soft, the texture like a fillet of uncooked salmon, slightly tacky beneath her fingertips. She pulled her hand away. Some kind of clammy flesh had touched her in the dream. Was it simply her own hand on her skin? Too warm from sleeping in a cotton nightgown under a fleece blanket and a down-filled comforter? Beneath the clammy film that coated her entire body, her nerves shuddered.

She pushed herself up to a sitting position. She took her pillows and stuffed them between her back and the headboard. She felt on the nightstand for her phone and pressed the button to wake it as rudely as she'd been woken. "What time is it?"

"The time is three-sixteen a.m."

She put the phone back on the nightstand.

There had been something snake-like in her dream, something trying to hold her down. But that wasn't the entire reason for her whimpering. She now remembered trying to scream, unable to form any sounds but that terrified, helpless whimper. Her arms and legs had been bound tightly, the pressure so strong she wondered if her blood would stop flowing through her veins. Maybe she was dying. Was this the prelude? No one ever talked about these things. Perhaps her body knew it was reaching the end of its ability to keep its heart pumping, lungs pulling in oxygen, brain sending signals to maintain all of those activities, all of her organs following the commands in lock-step.

She put her hand on the night stand and inched it toward the center until her thumb touched the base of her water glass. She picked it up and took a sip. The water was still cold thanks to the partially opened window across from her bed. She liked the cool air when she slept, liked hearing the rhythm of the waves, liked smelling fresh air, the smell telling her the moment she woke whether it had rained during the night. The clammy feeling on her skin wouldn't go away. She took another sip of water. Her mind was still tired, collapsing back into sleep, serving up the disjointed thoughts that came before she fell over the edge into unconsciousness. Daniel was upset with her. Daniel had appeared in her dream. She'd never seen him in her waking hours, didn't know what he looked like, had never tried to form an image of him. All she knew was his voice. But in her dream, he was watching her, and she knew it was him. She felt his eyes on her face, unblinking.

The snake-like thing had covered her body, she was gasping for air as her ribcage was relentlessly pressed against her lungs.

An octopus.

Now she saw it in all its soupy, tangled, hideous presence. The large eyes that she could physically see looking at her. The eyes were enormous. They had crept behind the sightless barrier that covered her own eyes, had made their way inside of her head so they could stare with hunger and murderous desire. Daniel stood nearby, watching the thing watch her, immobilized by terror, allowing the thing to slap its clammy suction cups across her body, making her sticky and damp as it drew all the fluids out of her organs and onto her skin. She started to cry.

Why had Daniel's memory made its way into her dream? Was it regret because she had failed to comprehend how terrified he'd been? She'd tried to explain it away, turn it into that presence haunting the ship. It was rare to the point of disbelief that an octopus would come so close to a beach. Yet it wasn't unheard of. Still, it was difficult to believe it had trapped him so briefly and then disappeared without any other sightings. But why did she have to insist it was the apparition, making itself into an octopus or a decrepit old woman or a thick, malevolent cloud over the ship, anything it wanted, as if it knew your worst fears, your greatest sorrows, and adopted those forms.

She had to sleep. It was too early to get up. The gate to the pier would still be closed. Daniel wouldn't be casting his line into the water until after seven o'clock. She picked up her phone and requested the piano playlist that Thomas had set up for her. She put on Chopin and pulled the pillow from behind her back. She slithered down. Her skin was still clammy. How was it possible that a dream had created such a tangible physical response? Maybe the more her aging body relinquished its functions, the more powerful her mind became. An entire lifetime was folded into the crevices and twists of her brain, thousands of people echoing inside her skull, experiences that sometimes felt as if they'd happened just moments ago. Without her sight, the sights from her past had grown more vivid.

She tried to direct her thoughts to the music. Each strike of a piano key touched a spot in her brain like a physical sensation. It felt good, a massage of the flesh inside her skull — soothing her brain, untying the knots. Her thoughts became foggy again, senseless images floating past each other — Daniel, the octopus, birds landing a few feet in front of her, cocking their heads and looking at her. The faces of her children when they were babies. The stir fry she'd had for dinner the night before. A glass of champagne, bubbles exploding into the sky like the spray of ocean foam. She drifted to sleep.

She woke again. This time her phone announced in its melodic voice that it was six-forty-three a.m. She threw off the blankets and went into the bathroom. She filled the large sink with warm water. She stripped off her nightgown and stood on a rubber mat. She put the washcloth in the water, lathered it with a fresh bar of soap, and washed herself thoroughly. Rinsing herself left water in the grooves of the mat, but Jill, the daily home aide, would graciously rinse it and dry it when she stopped by later that morning to drop off a few groceries and do a bit of cleaning. Jill made everything possible. Truthfully, Mary absolutely wouldn't be able to live alone without Jill. She was so proud of being able to prepare simple meals and keep the house neat, but there were so many things she couldn't do. She refused to believe she needed a companion, but maybe Jill was already that person, without the actual companionship. If Mary was home when Jill came by, they exchanged pleasantries, but that was all. Mary knew she was arranging it in her own mind to feel that she was managing her life, but she was only telling herself a series of white lies. Maybe Daniel was right — she did need more than someone cleaning the place, dropping of groceries, driving her to an occasional medical appointment. But not yet. Not until it was absolutely necessary.

The smart phone had informed her it was currently fifty-five degrees Fahrenheit. The clouds would clear by eleven and the temperature by then would be sixty-one. She dressed in a long-sleeved soft cotton shirt and blue jeans. She still called them blue jeans, even though she knew no one under the age of sixty, possibly age seventy, used that term any more. But when she first became familiar with the idea that men's work clothes were available in all their comfort and durability for women, that's what they were called. She slid a belt through the loops and buckled it. For some reason, for whatever reason memories chose particular moments in time to resurface, she remembered the sash she'd yanked off her waist and used to hoist up her dress so she could climb out the window on that awful day. She'd started out so thrilled with her escape and ended utterly crushed by the sight of her mother's soaked and seaweed wrapped body.

She washed her face, brushed her hair, and went into the kitchen. Her house was an open floor plan which made it easy to find her way around. A counter with bar stools split the kitchen from the eating area, which flowed seamlessly into the living room. Beyond the large windows and sliding glass door was a wide deck that she rarely used now.

She took out a carton of eggs, an avocado, a tomato, and a bag of spinach. She put the small frying pan on the stove and dribbled in a bit of olive oil. Her sons did not like her using the stove, but what they didn't know wouldn't hurt them. It wasn't difficult to listen for the tick of the spark, then turn the flame to the desired level. If it didn't light, the faint odor of gas told her immediately she had to re-start it. And Jill was okay with it — every day she washed the frying pan and the wire whisk without a comment.

Slicing the vegetables was easy. She pressed the knife blade against her fingertips then moved it slightly to the left before making each cut. She cracked the first egg, inserting her thumb gently into the crack, and splitting it into unequal pieces. Egg white ran over her fingers. She thought again of the clamminess that had soaked her body during the night. The mucous texture of the egg white made it cling to her skin. For a moment, she couldn't continue. Her stomach shifted and she wondered if it wouldn't have been better to have a piece of toast and an orange for breakfast. She shivered several times in succession. She took a long slow breath, then gently nudged the yolk into the other half so the rest of the white could slide over the edge of the shell. When she had two whites in the bowl, she whipped them furiously and poured them into the pan. Like so many other things, when you'd gone through the same motions for seventy or eighty years, eyesight wasn't a critical component. Your body knew what to do. Although the result was more of an omelette than a scramble because she didn't trust herself to break the cooking egg into pieces without having a portion escape the pan and get caught in the flames.

After she ate, she left the utensils and dishes on the drainboard.

She poured another cup of coffee, brought her phone into the living room, and listened to an audio book — a novel about a British detective. She couldn't remember the title of this one, but the actor reading the book would remind her at the start of the next chapter.

At ten, she stopped the audio book and got dressed to go to the beach.

The sun was already trying to come out, she could feel a single ray making the light brighter than it was under a completely cloudy sky. There was no breeze, so she unbuttoned her cape except for the button right at her throat. She walked with her shoulders back, enjoying the pleasant air without the need to hunch over against the cold.

When she reached the top of the ramp onto the pier, she walked slowly, hoping to hear Daniel call her name. Until her foot touched the wood planks, she hadn't admitted it to herself, but she was terrified he wasn't going to call out to her. There would be no bear claw, much as it made her stomach bloated and her throat tight with too-sweet icing and thick pastry. There would be no leisurely conversation. He felt she was a burden, and maybe she was. She never should have asked him to confront that man. Why was that man's silent terror Daniel's problem? He was right, it was her fault for being a self-appointed champion for the birds against every single parent and dog owner who set foot on the beach. It wasn't her job. It did no good. It wasn't as if she could police the beach from sunrise until dusk. Children would throw rocks, untrained dogs would bark and chase wildlife. It was the way of the world, and she'd lost a tenuous friendship by taking it too seriously.

The gulls swooped so low, she felt the air shift as they soared overhead. They were envious of the fish being hauled out of the water by women and men lining the sides of the pier. She paused, certain that Daniel would acknowledge her. She imagined how she looked, small and thin, no bulk to her form beyond what her gently flapping cape suggested. She turned her head, the reflex of a lifetime spent turning to search for someone familiar in a crowd. She ached to be able to see the people fishing. Why did she have to be blind? She was shut off from the world. Men could stand on the beach and drape her with fear and she couldn't do a thing about it. She couldn't find her friend, couldn't know if he was looking directly at her, hiding himself by keeping silent. Tears flooded her eyes. She turned her head furiously from side to side, blinking as if the tears and her rapidly moving eyelids would allow her to see, even for a moment. He must be here. Was he so angry he wasn't going to speak to her, ever?

"Daniel?" her voice was soft. If he was more than a few yards away, he wouldn't hear her. She spoke louder, "Daniel? Are you here?" She froze. By calling out, she was announcing she couldn't see. They might all have turned to look at her. Some stares would be filled with pity, others with thoughts of crime, wondering how they might take advantage of her. She wanted to think of fishermen as inherently good, but it wasn't true. There might only be one, but there would be one who might follow her off the pier, along the path to her house. She felt exposed and utterly at their mercy. No one came to help her. The birds, to whom she'd given a lifetime of care and protection, flapped overhead, crying out for more food.

She wasn't sure how long she stood there, foolish and lost. If she were a little girl, standing alone, looking around her with a confused, sad expression, someone would hold her hand and lead her to one of the park rangers. She took a few tentative steps forward and turned slightly to the right, the side where Daniel had fished the last time she talked to him. She took a deep breath to quell the wavering that had echoed in her voice when she'd spoken his name a few moments earlier. "Has anyone seen Daniel?" She spoke firmly, in charge, hoping to ensure her slight build wasn't mistaken for weakness.

No one answered.

She took a few more steps. If she was in the spot near one of the benches, it was only another step to the railing. She put out her hand. Nothing. She continued moving and a moment later felt the railing against her hip. The smell of fish was strong, mingled with the aroma of chocolate laced coffee. Possibly topped with whipped cream.

"Have you seen Daniel? Daniel Sloane? He's out here every day. An older gentleman, not as old as me, of course." She smiled.

"Over there." The voice was casual, distracted.

"I'm blind," she said. "Can you tell me more specifically?"

"On the left side. A few feet ahead."

"Thank you."

She turned away. Surely Daniel had seen her. He must have heard her calling his name. Her heart was bruised, as if a concrete slab from the boat had broken away and was pressing down on her chest. It wasn't so terrible what she'd asked of him, was it? She should have backed down sooner when he'd begged her to stop going on about the ghost.

She thought about the dream. Daniel's octopus, wrapping itself around her and squeezing out her breath, gripping her skin with its tentacles, sucking at every part of her. The dream might have been letting her know that Daniel had abandoned her the way his friends had abandoned him in the bowels of the ship so many years, a lifetime ago. It was a fantastical idea, but she knew the creature had crept into her dreams from some part of her subconscious. A deeper part of her that knew, for whatever reason, she'd damaged their friendship far more than she'd realized.

"Mary!"

Someone touched her arm. She jerked away and nearly lost her balance.

"It's Corrine."

"Oh, hello."

"Are you okay?"

"I'm fine."

"Your eyes are red."

"It's the wind." The breeze was almost unnoticeable. She

felt Corrine take in the obvious lie.

"Do you want to join me for a drink?"

Mary laughed. "It's not even noon."

"By the time we get up the hill it will be close."

Mary tried to laugh, but she couldn't. "Sure. Why not?"

"Can you climb up the hill okay?"

"Not as fast as you, I'm sure. But it's not a problem."

As they walked along the path toward the visitor center, Corrine chattered about her cat and her boyfriend's dog. She told Mary about the construction project at Fairhaven which would provide several smaller social rooms to make it more home-like, rather than a single large room where everyone rattled around, feeling lost, and those watching TV were so far away, they turned up the volume and shouted down others who wanted to play cards.

At the top of the hill, they walked along the sidewalk until Corrine stopped in front of Manuel's Mexican restaurant. "Is Manuel's good? We can have some chips and salsa with our drinks."

"That sounds nice," Mary said. She felt unstable. She was being obsequious. Was she so hurt by Daniel she'd become desperate for someone to talk to? She had several friends left. She wasn't the only person who'd lived into her nineties, but it was getting more difficult. Some of her friends no longer went out. Two were now living at Fairhaven, but she wasn't going to give that information to Corrine. She needed some privacy. She still had the feeling Corrine was a little too helpful and a little too friendly. But today, after the shock of Daniel, she was suddenly forgiving.

They were escorted to a table in the front corner next to the window. Corrine ordered a Bloody Mary. She laughed. "How do you feel about the name of that drink?"

Mary smiled. "I usually drink champagne, but why not. Make that two." She lifted her face slightly to her left, knowing the server was somewhere in the vicinity.

As soon as the server moved away, another person placed a basket of chips and a small cup of salsa in the center of the table.

"We're just having drinks," Corrine said. "But you know what, salsa and a Bloody Mary sounds intense. Will you bring us some guacamole? My treat."

Once the drinks and guacamole were in front of them, Corrine ate five chips without pausing to talk. The hardened triangles of tortilla crunched and snapped between her teeth.

"Didn't you have breakfast?" Mary said.

"Just a bowl of muesli. After climbing that hill…" Corrine laughed. "Anyway, I love guacamole. I could eat the entire bowl myself."

"Help yourself," Mary said.

"I was kidding."

Mary picked up a chip. She put out her hand and located the stemmed bowl holding the creamy avocado. She scraped her chip across the surface and took a bite. She sighed softly. She couldn't remember the last time she'd eaten guacamole.

She finished the chip and picked up another.

"I saw that woman on the pier again," Corrine said.

"I wonder what she wants to tell you."

"You really think she has a message for me?"

"It's possible."

"I just don't know if I believe in ghosts. In anything supernatural."

"So you said. But you saw her." Mary pulled the celery stalk out of her drink and bit off the end.

"I've seen a woman. She looks like a real person."

"What do you expect an apparition to look like?"

"I don't know. I never thought about it. Transparent. Blurry without any substance, not three-dimensional."

"Why?"

"Because I do."

"You're influenced by films. Legends," Mary said.

"If they're real, doesn't that mean the legends are true?"

"Yes. But there are all kinds of stories. You saw her in the dark, from a distance."

"It makes me nervous. Thinking it could be true. I just don't think..."

"You don't want to think about it because it does make you nervous. But you know, in your heart, that there was no way for a living person to be on the pier when the gates are locked."

"Maybe someone let her in."

"And locked her out there?"

"I didn't go up and look at the gate," Corrine said. "Maybe it wasn't locked."

"Why do you want so badly not to believe? If you don't consider what she wants, you won't be paying attention. Things can happen." She took a few sips of her drink. She couldn't sense any movement on the other side of the table. The space around her felt vacant. There wasn't even a suggestion of Corrine moving her hands, breathing. She wanted to ask if Corrine was still there, but it always felt foolish when she had to ask that question. She'd rather not know the other person had left her alone, had silently pushed out her chair, stood up, taken her bag, and walked to the door. She'd had enough of that, wandering around the pier, calling for Daniel, feeling as if they were all watching her, pitying her. Most of the time, not seeing was okay. She'd accepted it. She could get by, with Jill's help. But she hated the pity. Hated feeling old and incapacitated. Hated everyone wanting to take her arm, to show her the way, telling her to watch out. She should be grateful for the kindness of the human race — most of them. But she wasn't. She hated that they felt she needed them more than they needed her. She hated their pity with every breath she took.

"What things?" Corrine's voice was a whisper.

There was still no movement on the other side of the table. As if Corrine were frozen in her chair, terrified by the memory of the ghost. Mary wished she knew what Corrine looked like. It was another disadvantage.

"It can get inside of you," Mary said.

"That's really hard to believe." Corrine's voice trembled. The Bloody Mary glass clicked against her teeth. There was a moment of silence and it clicked again.

"It insinuates itself into your brain, changes your thoughts."

"That's absurd."

"Yes, but it's true."

"How can a…I can't believe I'm having this conversation," Corrine said.

Mary felt Corrine's hand move out and pick up a tortilla chip. It made a tiny sound as it touched the side of the bowl on its way to scooping up guacamole.

"Would you rather talk about something else?" Mary smiled.

"Are you laughing at me?" Corrine said.

"Absolutely not."

"You smiled."

"I was offering you a chance to talk about something else. You seemed uncomfortable with the topic. With what the spirit can do."

"I thought they didn't do anything, just frightened people, maybe tried to fix their past or something like that."

"I thought you didn't believe in them," Mary said.

"I don't know."

Corrine sounded genuinely upset. It was more than simple annoyance or mocking dismissal that Mary had encountered when she'd tried to mention the ghost to others. Although Daniel had also been genuinely upset. Maybe people had been more open to ghosts years ago. Maybe technology and advances in science had slowly wiped out any belief in the inexplicable. With everyone cremating their loved ones instead of kissing them good-bye in coffins and placing them in a deep hole in the earth, covering them with thick, wet dirt, death had become an illusion. With physical remains reduced to nothing but ash, there was no possibility for a troubled spirit to remain in a particular place.

"You make it sound so real, so plausible," Corrine said. "It's scary."

"It is. But so is life."

"How can a ghost, if they exist, if she exists, get inside of you? I don't understand what you're talking about."

"It changes the shape of your thoughts." An image of the octopus formed in the center of her mind.

"My thoughts…"

"Have they seemed different? Foreign?"

"Maybe. But how could a ghost…"

"Like a hallucinogen."

"What?"

"A hallucinogenic drug. It alters the chemicals in your brain."

"But you put it into your body yourself."

"It can make you think people are out to get you," Mary said.

"Paranoid."

"More than that."

"So how does a ghost get inside your body and alter the chemicals in your brain?"

"The cloud over the boat…you breathe in the spray of the ocean and the fog…and that thing. Then it's inside of you."

"I'm not sure I want to talk about this any more," Corrine said.

"That's fine. It's frightening. I understand. But watch out."

"You're scaring me."

"I'm just telling you to be careful."

"If that happened, if something changed my thoughts, how would I even know?"

"They'd be unfamiliar. Very unfamiliar."

"Okay. And what would I do?"

"Just recognize it for what it is. Don't follow every impulse."

Mary felt Corrine press her elbows hard on the surface of the table. It shook slightly.

When Corrine spoke, her voice was muffled, as if she was bending over, hiding her face, her lips brushing across the heels of her hands. "I don't know what to think. I don't know whether you're just teasing me, playing games with my mind. I have a headache."

Mary picked up her bag. "Do you want a painkiller?"

"No. Not right now."

The ice in Corrine's glass rattled. A moment later, the glass thudded on the table. Mary felt a slight jolt as Corrine bumped the table, turning, likely looking for their server. Mary picked up her drink and swallowed the rest of it in three gulps. Half the drink. She'd regret that when she was walking home.

Eighteen

Corrine didn't care if some nefarious ghost, in truth, the figment of an old woman's tired imagination, was infiltrating her thoughts or not, suggesting she do things she'd always characterized as lacking in integrity or downright creepy. She had to know more about Andy. She had to know whether the stories he'd told about his life were true. She recognized that it was an obsession. The ability to recognize it proved there was nothing wrong with her thoughts. She wasn't being taken over by a force that had entered her mind to create paranoia. She was being cautious, as any woman in the twenty-first century should be.

She hated to think of Mary, or any older person, having a deteriorated, half-mad imagination. She liked to think the elderly kept their faculties, for the most part, and it was society's interpretations that made them seem delusional. It didn't mean she wasn't aware of the very real effects of Alzheimer's and dementia, and general loss of memory. She just didn't think of aging, even with those diseases, as something to be looked down upon. It was no different from any other disease or handicap. People endured memory loss and moments of confusion at every age. Society magnified those deficiencies in the elderly.

Still, Mary had some wild ideas. She might very well have some encroaching dementia. Even though Mary was articulate and focused in her speech, her ideas were preposterous. The woman Corrine had seen was *not* a ghost. There was a very real, flesh and blood woman walking on the pier in the early evening. And the dark substance Corrine had observed was nothing more than a small, low-hanging fog bank that had broken away from the rest.

Corrine imagined mentioning to Andy that she'd seen the woman a second time, imagined his laugh. They'd laugh about it together. See! She was not paranoid, not betraying him. She was simply showing caution, but it didn't mean she didn't love him. She was simply seeking a little bit of reassurance. Just because they were a couple didn't mean she had to tell him every single thing she did, how she spent each hour away from him. It wasn't as if she had a private investigator checking into him. All she'd done was befriend a woman he used to love in order to get a different viewpoint on him. She hadn't yet met any of his work or childhood friends. She hadn't met his family. That would come soon. In the meantime, she'd chat with Deb. There was no harm in that.

The false identity pricked at her heart, but she took a sip of her martini and the thorn dissolved, covered with layers of curiosity and a certain amount of pleasure at her cleverness.

She'd posted over fifteen comments on Deb's page, and Deb had either *liked* or commented back on every single one. Deb had given her advice on getting the most from her fabricated strength training regimen as well as her running. Posting comments about running made the strength training seem less of a lie, since she did actually run six days a week. She ran more miles than she'd told Deb. After all, Sara McGregor was fifty-two, she couldn't go too overboard. They'd also chatted about battling the snacking impulse, and how much alcohol was *healthy* — not a martini every day and a few bottles of wine on the weekends. Fessing up to the martinis made Sara real, vulnerable, someone who could be trusted.

Tonight she would send a personal message. She'd spent several days composing it in her mind. On her computer at work, she'd written a draft and revised it three times, mostly to make it shorter, more casual. Without a long, wordy introduction, it was difficult to explain to Deb why she was sending a private message and what she wanted to know.

She opened a message window.

Hi Deb. I hope you don't mind a personal message. Even though we haven't seen each other in forever, and only met so briefly, our chats on your page and all your help make me feel like we're good friends!

She added a smiley face after that line.

I thought it was very cool what you wrote about your ex. You're very centered. But it almost made me wonder why you split up, you seem so affectionate toward him. I don't mean to be nosey, just asking because I'm having some issues in my relationship and trying to figure out the next steps. Anyway, if you'd rather not discuss, no worries. She put another smiley face.

She re-read the message, looking for typos. She read it out loud. The sound of her voice made Cat's ears twitch, but she didn't turn her head curious over who Corrine might be talking to.

Corrine put the tablet on the coffee table, picked up her martini, and walked to the back window. She took a small sip, so small it was more like licking the gin and vermouth from the edge of the glass than actually swallowing alcohol. She took a deep breath and returned to the couch. She read the message a final time, typed in Deb's name, and tapped *send.* She settled back. She'd sip the martini and wait for Deb's reply. Her tablet and phone both gurgled with an incoming Facebook message. It was amazing how connected Deb was to her social media presence. It was as if the thing scrolled directly in front of her eyeballs at all times.

In her response, Deb assured Corrine it was not at all pushy or intrusive to ask about her failed marriage. She wrote that it had taken a long time to deal with what happened. She was anything but centered, but she felt she had to create a healthy story of her marriage to speak to the world, to use the power of that story to leach out the poison that Andy had poured into her. She said that she never considered herself a person with enemies, but that her former husband, the man she'd loved, had become her enemy. He'd tried to wipe her off the face of the earth. Not trying to kill her, nothing violent like that. He'd tried to erase her.

Corrine wrote a note expressing shock. Then asked what had happened.

Deb proceeded to send twelve consecutive messages providing *just the superficial details* of why her marriage had ended.

Corrine was stunned by all the information poured out to a person that Deb had no recollection of. She was also grateful that Deb was so free with the private details of her life.

Deb wrote that Andy was raised with an *attitude of entitlement.* He was an only child whose mother thought he was *god incarnate.* Deb said she *wasn't kidding at all.* The woman even washed Andy's car for him. *It was disgusting.* When Deb and Andy visited his parents' house, his mother gave him lengthy *shiatsu foot massages* while the four of them watched a movie in the family's entertainment center. She left *freakin'* chocolates on the pillows before Deb and Andy went to bed at night.

His parents gave him *private* golf lessons and *private* tennis lessons. He had a tutor for three years because he wasn't doing well in English classes and they wanted him to get into an AP class his senior year to assure his entrance to a *good university.*

Their house was average, so I think they went into debt to their earlobes to make sure Andy got everything he supposedly needed.

Being used to *mommy doing everything* made marriage *impossible.*

He had no idea he was expected to help out with even the smallest things — taking out the trash or hanging up his bath towel. We fought about it all the time. And even though it was petty, it wore on me and weakened the bond between us. Little things have a way of adding powerful energy to bigger things. It's what I teach in my personal training classes, like having cream in your coffee adds more than just the calories and fat in the cream, it's part of creating a whole picture of excess fat.

Then the scary stuff started. He decided he didn't like the things we'd picked out for our wedding. He decided all the color choices for the linens, the patterns for the flatware and dishes, everything, had been my choice. He said my mother had influenced me too much. I shouldn't have gone looking at things with her. He went along because he wanted to make his bride happy, but all the things in our house were wrong for our life. He took every single wedding gift to a thrift store and bought all new things. And he didn't consult me. Don't get me wrong, they were nice things. Nicer than some of the things we'd been given. But those were gifts from our families and friends. They were things we'd picked out together. It made me feel like he swapped out my whole house while my back was turned. Then he rearranged all the furniture and artwork. For a few weeks, I felt like I was living in another woman's house.

After we got past that, he started in on my hair — I should cut it, or highlight it. Every few days he got rid of some of my clothes while I was at work. I'd go looking for an outfit and it would have disappeared. He'd give me a box with something new, and yes, it was spectacular, but

I liked my clothes! I felt like a Barbie doll. He didn't think there was anything wrong with any of this. He didn't think it was weird, didn't care that no one I knew had done things like that.

He started telling me what to say. I needed to talk more about general interest things and lighten up on the fitness. He suggested I learn to play golf so I could discuss it intelligently. When I refused, he told me I needed to read a book about it and follow the tournaments.

He started brushing my hair and wanted to blow it dry and style it. It sounds sweet and romantic, but it wasn't. He wanted it to look a certain way. I think I finally realized we might be headed for a split after we had a family photograph taken at a studio for Christmas. When the proofs came, I realized I looked an awful lot like his mother. The color of my hair was now the same as hers. The shade of my lipstick that he'd suggested I try matched hers. Even my foundation — he said the one I used darkened my skin a little too much and I should try something lighter. It turned my skin tone into a reflection of his mother's. It made me scared and a little sick.

Corrine felt pressured to respond quickly. Deb had written back so fast, and she'd poured her heart out. It wasn't right to let the messages sit there unacknowledged. Especially with that damn Facebook feature that let Deb know Corrine had seen the messages. She pulled the olives off the stick and put both in her mouth at once. Sucking on them, she went to the kitchen and made a second martini. She'd regret it in the morning, but she needed her nerves to stop jittering beneath her skin as if a stream of ants had threaded their way into her blood vessels.

She took a sip in the kitchen and walked slowly back to the living room. She put the glass on the table and picked up the tablet.

She tapped the reply box. *Wow.* She hit send. She typed a second message. *That sounds unnerving. It's different from someone who's just controlling. It's not like he was abusive, but freaky.*

Deb wrote back. *Absolutely.*

Corrine wrote back that the story was very helpful. She really appreciated Deb's *candor.* She wrote that it wasn't exactly like her relationship, but it gave her something to think about regarding boundaries. She took a sip of her drink and typed — *How did you actually break up?*

Deb wrote back immediately. *I said "enough" when he told me I should get a little plastic surgery to adjust my smile, and maybe a little silicone to fill out my bra more than I do. I'm not going to cut up my body for anyone. I don't care how madly in love I am, or was. He didn't want a divorce. But even that was a bit odd. He said he'd invested too much in me. Not as much as if he'd invested in plastic surgery. LOL. He acted as if I was a project, or thing he was creating.*

Like Pygmalion, Corrine wrote.

Deb: *What's that?*

Corrine: *A myth about a guy who made a statue and fell in love with it. A Greek goddess brought the statue to life.*

Deb: *Maybe. He was trying to turn me into his mother!*

Corrine: *It's hard to find the right guy.*

Deb: *Isn't that the truth. I'm still single. But better single than the wrong guy. At least I recognize my dinner plates. LOL.*

Corrine: *Thanks for giving me so much to think about. I don't know what I'm going to do.*

Deb: *You're strong! You're smart! You'll find the right path!!*

Of course, Deb had no idea whether Corrine was smart. Deb obviously wasn't all that bright because she was telling her life story to a total stranger and she didn't even realize it. Corrine felt a pinch of guilt for misleading such an open, honest woman. But it wasn't lying, she *was* having trouble in her relationship.

She sent a few more words of thanks and signed off. She put her tablet beside her on the couch and settled back. She took a sip of her martini. Until this moment, she hadn't thought about what she'd do if she discovered something she didn't like. Deb had confirmed all her vague, slightly paranoid fears. She felt worse than she had when she was simply suspicious that Andy hadn't been straight with her about the timing of their divorce.

She'd seen a photograph of Andy's parents. Pygmalion had been the right illustration. Andy's appearance definitely reflected his mother's, and he wanted to create a woman who was a reflection of himself. Wasn't that what a statue was? He fell in love with his own creation. He'd already said he loved her. Maybe he'd lightened up after his split with Deb. Gotten the narcissism out of his system. A new dress and a few other oddities were nothing like what Deb had described.

And maybe Deb wasn't even telling the truth. She could be a pathological liar for all the information Andy had provided about her.

Corrine sat up straight and put her glass on the table. She pulled out the stick and sucked off the first olive. She wasn't any different from Deb — she was asking a woman she'd never met for information about her boyfriend. A guy who treated her like a goddess, a terrific lover, smart, interesting, and kind. He was good to his dog, he was affectionate with Cat. That told you a lot about a person, how they treated animals. Sure he was unconcerned with wildlife, but that was a common attitude. He'd made one slip in the date of his divorce — maybe — and she'd sprung into action with a false profile and a mini investigation into his background. What was wrong with her? And it wasn't a damn ghost sneaking around inside her head! She picked up the glass and took several sips. The alcohol raced through her, stirring up her thoughts, but soothing her fears.

She finished her martini, ate the last olive, and got out the cat brush. She picked up Cat and settled the warm, purring animal on her lap. She combed Cat's fur and thought of nothing, which was quite pleasant.

The weather had turned cold with gusting wind. The sky was a gorgeous blue on Sunday, but it was the kind of day to sit inside and look out the window. Andy suggested they take a walk to The Med for a drink or two and a game of pool. Corrine was happy to get out of the house, unbothered by the wind for the few short blocks, although she was relieved when they stepped inside the darkened bar and she could let her nose and lips thaw.

Three crusty-looking regulars, two men and a woman, sat at the bar, their backs to the pool table. Andy ordered a beer for himself and a vodka and tonic for Corrine. Two drinks could easily turn to three before they were finished playing pool, so a martini was out of the question.

Andy racked the balls and broke them with a resounding crack. No one looked their way or even flinched. He immediately sank the blue striped and red striped balls. Corrine felt defeated. When her turn came, she whiffed, but on her next turn, she sank the yellow and orange in corner pockets. Her confidence bloomed. When Andy said he was worried, she laughed. "Not that I have to win," she added.

"I won't let you win," he said. The words echoed with a double entendre in her ears, and she felt guilty for the way she'd stalked his background, lied to his ex-wife, and taken that woman's word over her own experiences. The words didn't even really fit what she was doing, but somehow, she'd felt they were in a battle, and she didn't want to be. She wanted to be in love. She wanted a stable, solid, and satisfying relationship. She wanted to be loved for who she was, and it seemed that he did love her. Buying a dress did not mean someone wanted to make you into a different woman, an image in his mind or a reflection of his mother. And maybe her job *wasn't* great for the long haul. Maybe she did have a lot of unacknowledged talent. It wasn't necessarily a good thing to stay in the same career your entire life. It was a good thing to have your guy praise you and want you to fulfill your potential.

She didn't exactly let him win the round of pool, but she pulled back her effort, unable to stop the words from knocking around her head like pool balls themselves — *I won't let you win.* It wasn't a contest.

After Corrine won three games of pool to Andy's four, they walked twenty-five feet to Pizza One and ordered a medium pepperoni, ham, mushroom, and Italian sausage. They sat at the counter looking out at the sidewalk, sweating from the heat of pizza ovens and too many people lined up in a small space, picking up pizza on a cold Sunday night.

When they got back to Corrine's house, Parker met them at the door. As Andy crossed the threshold, Parker jumped, slamming his paws against Andy's hips. Andy raised the pizza box over his head. "Hey. Settle down."

"He needs to go out," Corrine said.

"I know. But he shouldn't jump." Andy handed the pizza box to her. He swatted Parker's flank.

"Don't do that," Corrine said.

"He needs to learn."

"It's too far after the fact, he won't make the connection."

Andy picked up Parker's leash off the hall table. He hooked it to the collar and opened the door. "It'll just be a few minutes."

"He probably needs time to burn off some energy."

"I don't want cold pizza."

"I can microwave it."

"No thanks. He'll get a longer walk later, or tomorrow. He's fine." He closed the door.

Corrine took the pizza into the kitchen. She opened a bottle of Cabernet and got out two glasses. Cat appeared in the doorway. She meowed. Corrine dribbled fresh pebbles of food into her dish. Cat sniffed the food and meowed.

"Was Parker driving you crazy?" Corrine said.

Cat lapped at her water then walked to where Corrine was standing. Cat rubbed against Corrine's legs, spreading fur over her black leggings. "Thanks," Corrine said. She rubbed at the fur but all she succeeded in doing was moving it around.

She filled two wine glasses and carried them into the living room. She picked up the butane starter and lit the half-burned log sitting on the grate. She turned on one light and went back to the kitchen. Cat had disappeared.

The front door opened. A gust of wind blew into the entryway and made its way to the kitchen. The cold air was followed by Parker and Andy, the noise of them filling the small space. The hook for the leash clattered on the table.

"Down!" Andy said. He came into the kitchen and refilled

Parker's water bowl. The food bowl was nearly full of kibble.

They both pulled off two slices of pizza, carried their plates to the living room, and sat on the couch. Corrine inched closer until her shoulder was touching Andy's. He put his hand on her leg and squeezed gently. They toasted the end of an easy-going weekend and sipped their wine and gobbled down the first slices of pizza without talking. The fire spit and cracked.

Parker came into the room. He walked over and rested his head on Corrine's knee.

"Don't let him beg," Andy said.

"He's not. He just wants a rub." She scratched the back of his head and fondled his ears, stroking the silky fur. She was surprised how much affection she had for him. She still preferred cats, Cat in particular. She didn't want to own a dog. Exercise and trips outside to relieve himself had to be constantly at the top of their minds. And sometimes she liked to go to the beach without Andy hanging onto the end of a leash, talking to the dog as if there were a third person in their relationship. Although, if things continued on with Andy the way they seemed to be headed, she'd end up with a dog by default.

Parker kept his head on her leg while she ate the second slice of pizza. He seemed to blink with each bite, gazing at her with unrestrained longing as she chewed. She couldn't tell whether he wanted more head rubs, if he actually noticed her as a human being distinct from Andy, or if it was the pizza that interested him. She put the crust on her plate next to the crust from her first slice and picked up her wine.

Andy talked about Saturday's round of golf while they finished their wine.

She stood and added a smaller log to the fire and went into the kitchen for the wine bottle. When she returned, Parker was in the same spot, taking note of every step and gesture. Andy stood up and took the bottle from her. He refilled their glasses and put the bottle on the table. Corrine picked up the plates, stacking hers with the leftover crusts on top of Andy's. Parker stood and walked toward her. He pressed the side of his head against her leg and whimpered. She took a piece of crust off her plate.

"Don't give him that. Cheese isn't good for him."

"There's only a tiny bit of cheese."

"I don't want him to have it."

"It's one small treat. He was very good while we ate."

"He's supposed to be good. I don't want him thinking he can eat off our plates. Ever."

"Oh come on." She held out the crust.

Andy grabbed her wrist. "I said, no."

Parker barked.

Corrine twisted her arm but Andy held it firmly.

"Let go!" She yanked harder.

Parker lifted his head up, glaring at Andy. He barked several more times.

"Parker!" Andy said.

The dog turned and jumped up, slamming his front paws against Andy's thighs. Andy stumbled back, dragging Corrine with him. The plates slipped out of her hand and fell on the floor. The top plate cracked in half.

"Now look! Let go of my arm. It's just a piece of pizza." Her voice was loud, hysterical-sounding. She could feel herself over-reacting, maybe. Or maybe not. She wasn't sure, her thoughts blurred with vodka and wine, her body numbed with cheese and warm, chewy pizza dough.

Andy slapped Parker's nose. "Don't jump." He let go of Corrine's wrist and she knelt to pick up the plates.

Parker jumped again, barking repeatedly.

"Stop it!"

Andy sounded nearly as hysterical as she had. She felt like crying. It was such a nice evening. *An easy-going weekend*, they'd said as they smiled and took their first sips of wine.

Parker jumped on Andy again, barking. Andy slapped his flank this time and the dog dropped back. He lunged for the plate and ate the pizza crust.

"Dammit," Andy said.

"Sorry."

"I'm sorry I grabbed you," Andy said. "Sorry this happened."

"Me too," she said.

"Sorry about your plate."

"I don't like it when you hit him," she said. "And I definitely don't want you to grab me. Ever."

Andy sat on the couch. He picked up his wine glass. "I know. Okay. I don't know what happened. I don't want a dog that jumps. Or barks in the house. He's not allowed to bark at me. Lunging at me like that." He took a swallow of wine. "It seemed like he wanted to take me down."

"I guess he's grown fond of me," she said. "He didn't like you grabbing me."

"I'm his master."

"He spends a lot of time here. He wants to protect me as much as you."

"Maybe."

"It's a good thing, don't you think?" She took a sip of wine. She sat beside him, although she didn't press her shoulder against his as she had earlier. She wasn't sure how to feel about what had just happened. And she was angry at herself for not being sure. He'd grabbed her like she was a disobedient child. It was aggressive and controlling and all those other bad things you were supposed to run away from as fast as you possibly could. But he wasn't those things. She didn't want to make excuses, but the situation had just gotten out of control. He was upset about the dog. Andy took good care of Parker — didn't let him eat table food, made sure he got his exercise. A dog that was too big for her tiny living room. Ninety pounds of muscle and bone. She shouldn't have held out the pizza crust for Parker. She knew it wasn't that healthy for him, and he wasn't her dog. Andy had asked her not to. It hadn't been her decision to make.

"I guess we should have you give him commands sometimes," Andy said. "Since we're here so much. So he knows to listen to you. He should not be allowed to jump on me like that. On anyone, unless we tell him to. I don't understand why he's started doing that."

"He's cooped up."

"We're all cooped up." Andy laughed. He moved closer. "I know I need to take him out for a good run every day. It's been a rough week. And he didn't get his run yesterday because of golf."

She felt he was hinting around for her to offer to take Parker running after work, or during golf. The next thing, when he traveled for work, he'd ask her to take Parker. The dog was too big for her house. What would happen if they eventually moved in together? Got married. His house or hers? She knew what Andy would choose, but she adored her cottage. It was silly to think in terms of love, as if she loved the cottage and her quiet life with Cat more than she loved Andy. Did she love Andy? How did you even know?

Nineteen

Mary sat on a blanket listening to the waves. She turned her face up toward the sky, letting the sun warm her skin and the breeze tickle her neck. Beside her was a small insulated bag holding a half bottle of champagne and a delicate flute. Next to the cooler was a cloth bag with a container full of red grapes, some sliced cheddar cheese, and wheat crackers. She was looking forward to her small picnic. Sometimes companionship wasn't as wonderful as people made it out to be. The cries of the birds were often more pleasing than listening to one of her friends complaining about ungrateful grandchildren.

She regretted the things she'd said over drinks with Corrine. She hadn't been able to stop thinking about it all week. The woman worked for a senior care facility. There was no telling what kind of contact she had with other social workers and government agencies. What if she informed them there was an elderly woman who needed assistance? A blind woman, wandering alone on the beach, living by herself — a threat to her own safety, and others'. A woman who was clearly out of her mind, talking about a ghost haunting a half-sunken ship, suggesting some sort of hostile entity was creeping inside of people and altering their thoughts. Corrine could easily make Mary sound like one of those tinfoil hat types. Corrine might raise an alarm — what if this blind woman left the stove on and escaped gas caused an explosion, killing herself and her neighbors?

Her wounded feelings over Daniel had caused her to talk too much. Another mistake — letting a relative stranger become overly important in her mind. She'd magnified their casual greetings and those damn sweet rolls into something significant. It was nothing. She'd acted like a silly young girl chasing a boy. Her face burned, thinking about it. Although she enjoyed her own company, had accepted the gradual shrinking of her social life as the world died out around her, she was lonely. Daniel had been a fixture in her life, but blindness distorted her perspective, making her think she meant more to him than she did. That, and the spirit inhabiting the ship. One time her mother, another time something else, creeping inside to twist her thoughts in every direction.

Daniel's inclination to shut her out of his life was devastating. Yes, she'd allowed him to take up far too much room and importance in her mind, but that didn't mean she didn't miss him. There had to be a way to get his attention, to smooth over whatever had caused his violent rejection to the topic of ghosts. Most people simply dismissed her talk as fancy or stupidity. She'd never had someone tell her to stop talking, demand that she change the subject, and then end a friendship over it.

Maybe she could discuss it with Corrine. But telling Corrine would allow her to acquire even more ammunition for interfering in Mary's life — worry over her extreme reaction to a fisherman ignoring her.

She pulled out the container of grapes, plucked two off the stem, and ate one. She chewed slowly, letting the waves and a few shouting children, who sounded very far away, wash over her thoughts. A dog ran past, spraying sand across her bare feet and ankles. A couple followed, talking and laughing, calling the dog — Bruce — to come back. They passed so close she felt their shadows fall across her face, but they didn't apologize for the spray of sand, for a dog racing toward a woman trying to enjoy a small picnic. She brushed the sand off her feet, which was a rather futile exercise when she was sitting with her feet on the sand, but she felt she had to do something to assert her presence.

Was Daniel on this side of the pier? Had he seen the dog run too close to where she was seated? Was he concerned, or simply shaking his head at her stupidity? It wasn't right that everyone assumed you had to stay inside your house, or that you had to be watched over like a child because you'd lost your sight. It wasn't as if she was incapacitated. She only needed to move slowly, deliberately. There was no reason to shrink her life into a tiny space inside her house, shrink her self-reliance into nothing more interesting than brewing a cup of tea — everything else turned over to a cook and cleaner and errand runner. They might as well put her on a leash and lead her out to the beach.

She opened the insulated bag and removed the bottle and champagne glass. She peeled off the foil, untwisted the wire, and eased the cork out. It popped and fizzed lightly, but didn't explode in her lap. She poured a third of a cup into the flute and nestled the bottle inside the container. She raised her glass in the general direction of the ship. "I'm well on my way to outliving you! Cheers." She took a sip. She propped the glass beside the half bottle and placed her sliced cheese and crackers on a small wood cutting board. She layered a piece of cheese on a cracker and took a bite. She sipped her champagne and ate the rest of the cheese and cracker.

The edge of her blanket pulled slightly and she felt the movement of someone sitting beside her. A current of fear raced through her shoulders. "Corrine?"

It was him. She swallowed. The dog stood a few feet away. His breath was loud and panting. She couldn't hear the man's breath, but she could feel him shifting slightly, pulling the blanket this way and that.

"Who are you?"

The man let out a deep sigh.

"What do you want?" she said. She was hungry. Another

piece of cheese would satisfy her, but she couldn't eat with him watching. Her champagne would grow flat and warm while he sat there. Now, she didn't just want to enjoy the drink, she needed it to settle her nerves. What was wrong with him? "Please leave me alone."

The man took another extraordinarily loud breath. She turned her head frantically. She could call out for help, but she couldn't hear any nearby voices. Anyone casually observing them would assume he was an acquaintance. They'd see nothing but a small woman huddled in a cape and a man sitting beside her.

"Go away. You're bothering me."

She felt him move. The insulated bag crinkled slightly. He bumped the glass in her hand. She felt champagne dribbling into it. She pulled the glass close to her side and some of champagne splashed onto her lap. She didn't care. How dare he do these things? Even if she did cry out, would he explain to anyone who might come to help that she was simply his feeble, confused grandmother? He'd explain that she no longer knew who he was, no longer remembered his voice, ranted senselessly, but he wanted to bring her to the beach. She needed fresh air and a chance to get out of her claustrophobic environment. She imagined him speaking. At least then she'd know his voice, but what good would that do?

She did not want to drink the champagne he'd poured. It would be an acceptance of his help. And yet she wanted a sip of nerve-calming alcohol more than she remembered wanting anything else in a very long time.

The bag crinkled again as he replaced the bottle.

She stretched out her arm and poured the champagne out of her glass onto the sand.

He clicked his tongue on the backs of his teeth.

She grabbed the bottle by the neck. She refilled her glass and drank the entire contents. The carbonation bit at her throat like tiny pins stabbing tender flesh. She swallowed. It made her thirsty. She poured more into the glass and drank it in one swallow.

When the bottle was empty, she put it in the bag, packed up her food, and shoved it into the cloth bag. She felt a little tipsy from drinking the entire half bottle with a minuscule amount of food to absorb the alcohol. She loved her champagne, loved the celebratory feeling it gave her on an ordinary day, and this monster had spoiled it. She was not asking him again to leave her alone. She would not speak to him. She had all the time in the world. Outlasting him was easy. He'd get bored of his silly game. Thinking of it like that made her feel more relaxed. There was nothing to be afraid of. There were other people on the beach and fishermen lining the pier. It wasn't as if he could hurt her in broad daylight. Just because it was always nighttime in her world, didn't mean he was protected by darkness. She laughed. Why hadn't she seen that when he'd bothered her before? She was perfectly safe and now that she knew that, she had an advantage over him. It was impossible for him to frighten someone who had no fear.

After a while, she felt the blanket tug beneath her legs. He was leaving. She wondered what the dog had been doing while his master sat there, trying to make her uncomfortable. She realized she hadn't heard it panting after she started drinking the champagne.

She started to stand up but her head spun. Was it possible he'd put something in the champagne? But no, she'd poured that out in the sand. Had he slipped it into the bottle? She rose unsteadily. Something wasn't right. She sat down again. Less than half a bottle shouldn't make her this light-headed. Was something else wrong? This couldn't be it. The end coming at last. She would not die on this beach, right in front of that damn boat. She took the food out of the cloth bag and put it in with the empty champagne bottle and glass. She folded the cloth bag into a small pillow and lay down on her side. The sun was warm. Inside of her head, everything tilted and spun like a carnival ride. She took a long slow breath and tried to relax her muscles. A little nap would take care of everything.

Mary!"

A hand gripped her shoulder, shaking her gently. She was so relaxed, the shaking seemed to rattle her bones like a fistful of chopsticks inside a container. She tugged the makeshift pillow closer to her jaw.

Corrine's voice sounded far away. "Mary! Wake up. Are you okay?"

Mary nodded. The canvas bag rubbed against her cheek, brushing grains of sand across her skin. It made her itch, so she nodded more vigorously, wanting to burrow her whole face into the fabric.

"Can you sit up?"

Mary nodded. A hand slid beneath her left shoulder and pressed up, like someone was trying to lever a dresser into the back of a truck.

"What happened? Talk to me," Corrine said.

"I fell asleep."

"You seem like you're drugged. Did you pass out?"

"Sleep. I fell asleep."

Corrine's voice wobbled as she spoke. "I thought you were dead."

"I'm fine," Mary said. "Stop worrying."

"Then why won't you sit up?"

"I'm tired. I needed sleep."

"On the beach? You could have been hurt."

"How would I be hurt?"

"Please sit up." Corrine pressed her fingers against the underside of Mary's wrist.

"I don't need my pulse checked. I'm fine." She yanked her arm away from Corrine's grasping fingers. She pushed herself into a half sitting position, leaning on her left arm. The dizziness was gone. There was no need to mention it.

"You look pale."

"That's good. I could have gotten burned napping in the sun."

"Why were you sleeping? It's not safe."

"Don't fret so much," Mary said. "I needed a nap. That's all. I drank a little champagne and it made me sleepy."

"Champagne?"

"It's how I celebrate the day. Every day should be celebrated. Especially when you're my age." She laughed.

"I can see that."

"Can you?"

"I'm sorry. That wasn't a good way to put it."

"No need to apologize. Our language is filled with phrases like that. We all take our sight for granted. We take everything for granted until we don't have it. Even life."

"I guess so," Corrine said. "Can I help you up?"

"No."

"You should be getting home."

"Why?"

"It's close to sunset. What time did you come out here?"

Mary waved her hand. "What does it matter?"

"I'm worried about you. I wonder if I should call the paramedics."

"Don't be ridiculous."

"Then will you stand up for me?"

"What's the rush?" Mary said. "I took a nap, I'm still waking up. So it's getting dark. It makes no difference to me."

"Okay. But it's dinner time. When did you last eat? Have you had any water? You might be dehydrated."

She hadn't thought of that. Perhaps that was what caused the dizziness and the long nap. If it was getting dark, that meant she'd been out there for five or six hours. Would she be dizzy if she tried to stand up? She felt fine. Very thirsty. Dehydration made perfect sense — the sun, the champagne. She didn't want to stand up and possibly lose her equilibrium, collapsing into Corrine's arms. Corrine would spin into a frenzy of assistance. Why was the woman so determined to help her? She was letting her job bleed all over the rest of her life.

"I'd just like to sit here for a few minutes," Mary said.

"I can't let you do that. It's getting cold. Raccoons could come onto the beach. So many things could go wrong."

"Stop worrying! You're annoying me."

"I'm sorry."

"I'll be fine. You can get going now."

"I'm not leaving you alone."

"Who made you my caretaker?"

"Why are you fighting with me? I'm trying to help you."

"Because I don't need help. I've told you that before. Several times."

"We all need help at one time or another."

"Is that right."

"I could use your help," Corrine said.

Mary felt the blanket slide around the sand as Corrine

settled next to her. Why did people feel they had the right to sit on her blanket? Was her little piece of sand some kind of public gathering spot? She wanted to scream. In her own way, Corrine was as frightening as the man who wouldn't speak to her, who wanted to intimidate her, or whatever it was he wanted. The man who might have drugged her, but she had no way of knowing that for certain. She couldn't imagine why he would want to. She shoved her hand in her pocket. Her house keys were safe. It wasn't as if she carried cash on her, although he didn't know that. Maybe he'd looked. Maybe he had slipped something into the champagne bottle, walked away, and returned later when she was dead to the world.

"Your hands are shaking," Corrine said.

"I'm fine."

"I don't believe that. Something isn't right and I wish you'd trust me."

Mary settled her hands in her lap. "Why do you need my help?"

"Do you know anything about social media?"

"I know what it is. I was already starting to lose my sight by the time it started taking over the world. And it has taken over the world, hasn't it? I hear them talking about hashtag this and that on half the TV shows, even the news."

"I did something wrong," Corrine said. "And I feel terrible."

"What's that? You twittered something you shouldn't have?"

"I pretended to be someone else."

Mary laughed. "From what I've heard, that's what the internet is for."

"Not for most, not for normal people."

"Who's normal? What does that even mean?" She felt the blanket tug slightly.

"I have a bottle of water," Corrine said. "Do you want some? You still look really pale."

"I thought you said it was dark."

"I said it was getting dark. And cold. Aren't you cold?"

"What did you want to ask me? And yes, I'll have a sip of water. Thank you." She took the bottle. The water was so smooth and cool. She felt she hadn't had a drink of water in days. It had definitely been dehydration. She'd had a mild hallucination — the idea of the man slipping a drug into her champagne. It was ridiculous. And the feelings of dizziness. It all made sense. Perhaps, she'd even imagined the man. And the dog. It could be the ghost playing games with her sanity. She should have considered that before. She took another drink of water and handed the bottle back to Corrine. "Well? Why did you pretend you were someone else? And what happened?"

"My boyfriend was married before I met him. I found his ex-wife on Facebook and pretended to be an old acquaintance so I could find out about him."

"You don't trust him?"

"I do."

"It doesn't sound like you do."

"I was curious. And it's so easy to find things online."

"And do you still trust him? Now that you have new information?"

"Yes."

Corrine's voice was so faint, Mary thought she'd moved off the blanket and was standing several feet away. She put out her hand and felt the other woman's foot, tucked under her thigh as she sat cross-legged at Mary's side.

"I told you to watch out," Mary said.

"For the ghost?"

"I told you she plays tricks with your mind. You saw her, and now she's toying with your thoughts."

"I just can't accept that." Corrine coughed several times. "I'm so confused."

Mary waited.

"You probably think she's caused that, too," Corrine said.

"Why are you confused?"

"I feel guilty for checking up on him. Now I feel guilty for not telling him I did it, but I know I can't. And I feel like... I'm not sure if he loves me or the idea of me. Or some idea he's created in his head, or..."

"You do sound confused."

"You've been in love, haven't you?"

"Three times. But I was only loved back once."

"Oh, that makes my heart hurt."

"I survived."

"How did you know you were in love?"

"If you have to ask, then you probably aren't," Mary said.

"Why do people say that? It's like a secret club. No one will say what it's really like."

"Because if you love someone, you don't try to explain it. You don't question yourself. You hardly think. You just feel."

"Well how did you know you were loved back? That the person you are inside, the real you, was loved?"

"That's a more difficult question."

"So what's the answer?"

"Maybe because when I met that man — James — I was exactly who I am on the outside as well as the inside. I didn't hide my opinions. I didn't do anything I didn't enjoy, eat or drink anything to be polite, accept invitations to events that bored me. So when he loved me, it was for all of those things. I think with my first husband, he never really loved me because I was making myself into the person society told me to be. A young woman meets a man and gets married and starts a family. She hides parts of herself. I was drawn to him, I enjoyed his company, and he asked me to marry him. I didn't think much about love."

"I feel like I'm betraying him, trying to get information from his ex."

"Then stop."

"And the person who loved you back, how was that?"

"It's hard to describe without sounding trite," Mary said.

"Give it a go."

"You're lost in the other person. You feel like you're one being with two brains. More than anything, you want the other person to be happy."

"Okay..."

"I said it badly."

"I don't think so," Corrine said.

"So what's the favor?"

"I think I just needed someone to listen. I needed to confess what I'd done."

"You can't confess to one of your friends?"

"Strangers are better," Corrine said. "Should we get you home? It's cold. And it's completely dark now."

"If you need to get home, go ahead."

"I'm not leaving you here by yourself."

"I don't need an escort home. I don't need a babysitter. Or an elder sitter. Whatever they call it. I'm not arranging my life to make you feel better."

"Aren't you hungry?"

"Yes. Now that you say it, I am." Mary stood up. She shoved her sandals in the canvas bag and moved both bags off the blanket.

"I'll shake it out and fold it for you," Corrine said.

"Thank you."

Once all of her things were loaded into Corrine's arms, they began walking across the sand. Carrying the blanket, Mary's two bags, and her own bag thankfully prevented Corrine from taking Mary's arm. She walked slowly, feeling

Corrine match her step for step.

When they reached the footpath, Mary said, "If you'll tuck the blanket into the canvas bag, I can carry everything home." She slipped her sandals onto her feet without bothering to brush off the sand.

"I think I should walk with you."

"Why can't you understand that I walk everywhere in the dark? I'll be fine. I know every split in the sidewalk."

"Because I worry about you."

"Because I'm old? Because I'm blind? It's very thoughtful of you, but I'd rather take care of myself."

"I know."

"If you don't trust your boyfriend, you don't love him. If you can't talk to him about your questions, you don't feel loved. Love feels safe."

She stopped speaking for several minutes. She wondered if Corrine would say more, wondered if she was wasting her breath to mention what she was really thinking. What did it matter? "Or, the ghost is making you fearful and distrustful," she said. "Something to think about. Have a nice evening." She turned and walked quickly along the path toward the bridge. She hoped Corrine didn't follow, but there was no way to know, and no way to prevent it. If she stopped to listen for footsteps, Corrine would think she was afraid.

Twenty

Corrine stood on the path and watched Mary walk toward the bridge. It crossed over the trickle of Aptos Creek, which cut through the sand and seeped into the ocean. It didn't take long, with the black cape covering most of her, for Mary's body to be enveloped in shadows.

Corrine shivered. It seemed as if the elderly woman had been swallowed whole. She seemed to have no care for her life, and yet she didn't show any of the signs of giving up, or releasing her hold on whatever years she still had coming to her. She fought to keep herself firmly entrenched in the world. She walked with determined steps, whether she was on the pavement or struggling across soft, unstable sand. Her mind was crisp and her voice was clear and steady. She spoke with authority, even when she veered onto the topic of ghosts. She didn't *sound* delusional. Maybe in some way the idea of a ghost comforted her? Made her feel safe, as if someone were watching over her. That way, she didn't have to admit a need for assistance. But she seemed at odds with the ghost. As if the ghost had interfered in her life, was the cause of a tragic experience. Did she blame the ghost for her mother's drowning? Corrine could understand how that might be a child's response. And over the years, she'd never let go of that belief.

The path was deserted on both sides of the pier for as far as Corrine could see. The beach was dark and silent. She turned slowly, as if something were pulling her hips and shoulders, lacing cold fingers around the back of her neck and turning her head, forcing her to look at the ship. The water shimmered around the sea-washed concrete. Above the spot where the main cabin had been was the darker vaporous substance she'd observed before. It settled in the night air like a cloud, yet thicker. It looked as if it had weight, pressing down on the ship. The rest of the sky was clear, with a thin layer of fog hugging the Monterey peninsula.

She crossed the path and leaned on the wood railing. She stared at the thing above the boat. The pier was empty. She felt she should go home. She didn't have to stay and experience this dark, brooding presence, its weight reaching out, bearing down on her shoulders and the top of her head in the same way it pressed down on the remains of the ship. But the sleeves of her coat felt as if they were growing around the wood, grabbing at her arms, preventing her from leaving. If she pulled back suddenly, she was sure it would cause huge tears in the fabric. She closed her eyes. The thing over the ship wanted her to watch, to study every fracture in the boat. It wanted her to look at the smear of algae covering the lower half, the dark stains of oil and water and age, the crusted covering of bird droppings, hardened into a shell that covered every flat surface.

It was impossible to believe the things Mary said. How could another being enter your brain? And yet, even as Corrine turned the thought over in her mind, inspecting it from all sides, she felt as if something was causing her brain to change shape, digging out small holes where she could no longer locate her thoughts, and other spots blistering, previously unnoticed fears and doubts creeping out from breaks in the membrane, settling down in new places.

She wasn't sure if the peach-colored dress was a generous gift or a threat to her psyche. She wasn't sure if buying the identical dress had been her own choice or if she'd been compelled by something unrecognizable to make the purchase. Had that been after she'd first seen the so-called ghost? She wasn't sure. She couldn't remember the sequence of any of the events of the past few weeks. She had to force herself to believe she'd met Andy before she ever spoke to Mary. How did the human mind organize experiences on a timeline? It couldn't be trusted. Were the hours pretending to be an old friend of Deb's distorting her perception of reality?

And maybe it hadn't been the ghost at all that was twisting her thoughts in upon themselves. It might be Andy. How had he even found her that night they first met? It was strange that when the disagreement between Josh and the surfer started, Andy was suddenly standing there. How quickly he'd moved to replace Josh at her side, as if he'd known Josh was leaving. As he'd been absolutely certain she wouldn't care that her boyfriend had vanished. And she hadn't seemed to care. She'd gone off and enjoyed the rides with Andy, thrilled by his glowing good looks, his overwhelming physical presence.

Had he stolen her right out from under Josh's nose, as if she were a carnival prize? She hadn't thought so at the time, but now her head ached with trying to remember how the evening had played out. Had Andy been there watching them the entire time? Of course he had. He stepped in the moment the exchange started to get tense. But why? Maybe he'd done something to launch it, motioned the surfer to cut in, then moved out of their line of sight? She pressed her hands against her face. Why was she even thinking about that night at The Boardwalk? She was transforming it into something false, molding it into various shapes until she recreated the event. She could turn it into a hundred different things.

Even though her hands covered her eyes, she could feel the dense, dark cloud sitting there. It seemed to be waiting for her to figure something out, trying to lead her thoughts in a direction it had chosen.

"Leave me alone," she whispered.

Echoing inside of her head, the sound of her voice was very much like Mary's. No, her imagination was tricking her again. It was a common phrase — *leave me alone.* That didn't make her anything like Mary, a confused woman overtaken by whatever clung to the boat. That's what the thing was trying to tell her. She was too attached to Mary, too invested in her, worrying about someone who wasn't Corrine's responsibility. For whatever reason, Mary was trying to suck Corrine into her fantasy world. Loneliness, maybe, but it wasn't Corrine's job to alleviate all the loneliness in the over-seventy population up and down the Central California coast. It wasn't! Mary had tried to make her feel as if Andy didn't love her. Mary was lonely and bitter and grieving for her own lost loves. She wanted Corrine to suffer. She'd insisted Andy didn't love her. She'd tried to persuade Corrine to believe she didn't even love Andy. What kind of game was that?

Love wasn't some magical blanket that swept you up into a perfect world. Why had she even asked Mary's opinion of love? Being old didn't make her an expert. She was a complete stranger. A lonely old lady wandering the beach, and sneaking about on the pier at night, trying to draw people into her ghost stories, creating an imaginary world so she could cling to some purpose in her life. Corrine had seen it before, older people who allowed their imaginations unfettered control, creating a mythical place for themselves in a world they could no longer tolerate.

She moved her hands away from her face. The thing was still there, but it was simply a low cloud. Not a being trying to get inside her brain. How ridiculous. And it hadn't turned itself occasionally into a human form that walked on the pier. That had been a flesh and blood woman. She wore the same cape and had the same long, silvery hair as Mary.

She no longer felt as if the railing wanted to tear her sleeves. That, too, had been absurd. She backed away from the fence and turned to walk toward the road that led to the top of the cliff.

She could feel the thing hanging behind her. Despite her jumbled thoughts, she was certain it was not some ghost prowling about inside her skull. It was not some other entity at all. It was her own confused thinking. She'd given away her power to that woman, questioned her own judgment and acted like a child, seeking advice. Confessing! She couldn't believe she'd said that. Her research on Deb's profile page demonstrated good sense. And what she'd discovered was that Deb was crazy, telling wild, meaningless stories about her ex. What man cared so much about household things he purchased all new plates and linens? She laughed. Her voice echoed along the empty path and out over the beach. The sound was beautiful. She laughed harder and felt that her voice and her confidence and her entire being floated out over the ocean, gaining strength, reassuring her that she was a strong, confident woman, in control of her mind. She'd found a great guy and their future looked promising.

Andy picked her up at five. They were joining his co-worker and fiancé — Dillon and Sonya — in Capitola for dinner and then heading over to a club that featured live music. The fact that Corrine was finally meeting someone from his office was further confirmation they had a strong, healthy relationship. All that frantic speculation, paranoia, reading something sinister into common occurrences had started after she first spoke to Mary. Ghost indeed. She laughed, a quick short, sound, a bit like a parrot, or some other large bird.

She wore the peach dress and brown calf-high boots, which might have been a poor fashion choice, but it was cold. At least her toes didn't hurt, even if goosebumps ran like tiny waves from her bare shoulders to her wrists.

Sonya was dressed head to toe in gold, including gold flecks on her eyelashes and a gold headband that was unnecessary for her short-cropped, platinum blonde hair. Next to Sonya's brilliant gold, Dillon looked drab in dark jeans and a forest green shirt. However, his face was anything but drab. He produced a smile that made him look as if every moment was the most exciting fragment of his life. He grinned when he was introduced to Corrine, smiled continuously as Andy explained what she did, and flashed another smile while he held open the restaurant door and gestured for Sonya to enter first, followed by Corrine. Then, for a brief moment, he wrestled Andy for the edge of the door as if the loser would also lose the eventual battle over who was picking up the check. In this case, losing meaning not having the opportunity to be the magnanimous man in charge.

Over cocktails, Sonya fired questions at Andy regarding effective sales strategies, gaining and retaining loyal customers, and his thoughts on global warming, immigration, and legislating the right to die. She kept her right shoulder turned inward, giving Corrine a view of her milky pale skin and the sharp knobs of her spine. Dillon smiled steadily. Andy began to develop a slight sheen of sweat, as if he were under industrial spotlights, being interrogated in front of a live TV audience.

By the time the main course arrived, Corrine was exhausted from listening to Sonya and watching the effort Dillon was undergoing to keep his lips curved and his teeth exposed. Hopefully a plate of oysters and clams would bring some relief. It was said that frowning required the use of more muscles than smiling, but Corrine wasn't sure. She yawned. Andy gave her a sympathetic smirk that said he'd be yawning also, if he wasn't so busy articulating his viewpoints. It wouldn't look very impressive to yawn at your own thoughts.

They drank two bottles of wine, leaving a glass each to accompany the cheese and fruit plate Sonya ordered for dessert. "We don't need more sugar with all this alcohol," she said. "Especially since we're going for more drinks right after this. Our bodies will just turn it all into sugar."

When it was time to leave, Andy hurried to Corrine's side of the table. He held her coat while she slipped her arms into the sleeves. He bent down and kissed the side of her neck. She shivered and he kissed the same spot again, sending a spiral of pleasure through her body. He put his lips close to her ear so they were brushing against the ridges of flesh. "You look fantastic. I hope you had a good dinner. Sorry for the weird dynamic." He put his hand on the back of her neck. He followed closely behind her as they wound their way between the tables to the door.

They walked four blocks to the club. Corrine was pleased she'd opted for flat boots, as Sonya teetered on the thin, extraordinarily long heels required to accompany the thick platforms under the balls of her feet. The sloping and occasionally uneven sidewalks were no help, and Corrine felt helpless and awkward watching Sonya wobble ahead of her, forcing Andy and Corrine to take small, hesitant steps. Sonya talked to Dillon, some of her words impossible to hear with traffic, other people walking, and the crash of waves two blocks away. From what Corrine could hear, she had some sort of complaint about Dillon's lack of engagement in the *fascinating and stimulating* dinner conversation.

Surely Sonya had been stimulated by her own rapid-fire questions and possibly fascinated with Andy's responses, but calling it a conversation was a stretch. Corrine smiled. After the past few hours, she wasn't sure whether Dillon and Sonya were both friends of Andy's, or if there was a working relationship bogged down a few times a year by Sonya, who seemed to be preparing her audition for a spot on a daytime news show. Nothing about either one of them provided any insight into the kind of people Andy liked to spend time with. She knew she shouldn't be viewing the evening as a fact-finding mission, but these were the first friends she'd met. But now, she wondered whether Andy and Dillon were close friends after all. She realized Sonya was a new entrant into Andy's life who didn't know him any better than Corrine did.

Still, Andy had been more solicitous than usual, keeping a proprietary hand on her waist while they walked, on her shoulder when they entered the club, and on several other parts of her body as they were seated and ordered drinks and sat back to listen to the bluesy music. He seemed to relax his posture as he realized the volume of the music would make conversation nearly impossible.

That didn't stop Sonya. She shouted into Andy's ear. This time, Corrine couldn't hear a word and she wasn't sure whether she was relieved or anxious. As the evening went on, Sonya leaned closer and closer to Andy, resting her fingers on his wrist, touching the edge of his glass. Still, Corrine felt a strange lack of jealousy. Somehow, despite the gold-clad woman wrapping herself around his arm like a shimmering, metallic python, Andy managed to keep his eyes on Corrine. He gave her looks of such longing, she knew she'd come dangerously close to undermining the best thing that had ever happened to her. She was flooded with warmth toward him. She wanted to touch his pale hair that now seemed to belong solely to her.

Andy lifted Sonya's fingers off his wrist. He adjusted his

chair so it touched Corrine's. He put his arm across her shoulders. As Sonya continued speaking, he turned toward Corrine and kissed her ear. He whispered that he was tired. "It feels like she's sucking my brain out of my head." He laughed and bit her ear lobe gently.

Sonya tapped his shoulder. When he didn't turn, she edged her chair closer. She rose slightly and put her hand on his shoulder as if she meant to position him like a department store mannequin.

Corrine glanced at Dillon. His grin was molded into the same shape it had been all evening. She wasn't sure if he was drunk, or high, or just very, very strange. Andy had talked about him as if he were a crack sales guy, one of the best on the team. *Very sharp*, Andy had said. Dillon had given no evidence of that. He made Corrine think of a sociopath, grinning constantly and inappropriately from a stark photograph as a news anchor read a list of heinous crimes.

It was all too much. Without thinking about what she was doing, Corrine stood and walked around Andy's chair, positioning herself between Andy and Sonya. She put her finger on Sonya's jaw and turned her head so she was facing Corrine. "Stop talking. We're here to listen to the music."

Sonya stood up. She reached out and ran her fingers along Corrine's exposed collarbone. Then, smiling and looking directly into Corrine's eyes, she slid her hand down the open slit of the dress, over to the side, and pinched Corrine's nipple.

"Ow! What the hell?" Corrine pushed Sonya. She stumbled sideways and red liquid from her freshly served cosmo splashed onto the table.

Dillon grinned. "Ooops!"

Andy stood up. He pulled out his wallet and drew out a few bills. He dropped them on the table. "Corrine and I are going to call it a night. Enjoy." He grabbed her coat and purse from the back of her chair and waited for her to step in front of him.

Corrine thought about speaking the niceties of *thanks for the evening* and *good to meet you*, but then decided the situation was too bizarre to bother with that. She hurried toward the door, Andy so close behind her that she felt she could smell his skin. A smell that reminded her of wheat growing in hot sun, a smell she would know anywhere. She was definitely in love. She was consumed by him, by the entire physical presence of him. She ached with a swollen, overwhelming love for the sound of his voice, his views of the world, his job, even his dog. There was nothing she didn't adore about this man! She was all in, as they said.

It was after eleven, and they were both a little tipsy. The temperature had dropped to the mid-forties, but still they changed into jeans and sweatshirts. Corrine wrapped a scarf around her neck, Andy hooked up Parker's leash, and they headed out for a walk. Parker had made it clear they'd have a restless night if he didn't get a little room to move around and consume some of the energy firing through his muscles. Corrine felt it wouldn't hurt her and Andy either. Her muscles were as tight and twisted as Parker's, as if they wanted to grab hold of her bones and shove them out through her skin. Walking on the cold, dark beach, followed by the effort of climbing the hill would sooth her frenzied nerves, allowing her to fall into a deep sleep where her dreams played out the madness inside her head, leaving her mind washed clean by morning.

They didn't speak as they walked past dark houses. The streets were empty of traffic. It gave Corrine the feeling that everyone else was still out at a club or had left town for the weekend. She and Andy and Parker were the sole remaining inhabitants of her neighborhood. Scattered leaves crunched under her feet, but otherwise their footsteps were eerily silent and the only sounds came from their lungs — all three of them breathing hard as the cold forced its way inside their bodies.

Andy took her hand and held it until they reached the stairs. They descended single file, Parker leading the way, straining at the leash as if he wanted them to run down the steep staircase.

On the beach, they walked under the pier, keeping well back from the edge of the surf. The waves were large, the high tide close to six feet, thundering onto the sand.

"How long have you known Sonya?" She'd managed to avoid the question on the drive home and while they were changing their clothes. Andy had vaguely apologized for the evening. She'd brushed it off as not his fault and he hadn't said anything more.

"I only met her one other time."

"I guess she wanted to get to know you." Corrine laughed. The sound was shrill and she tried, but failed, to soften it. She took his arm and leaned against him.

For once, Parker walked sedately beside Andy.

"She's a weird chick," Andy said.

"I don't like that word."

"In her case, it fits."

"How long have they been engaged?"

"I'm not sure."

That seemed odd, that he wouldn't know. "Is Dillon always so…smiley?"

"What do you mean?"

"He didn't talk at all. He just…smiled. Grinned, actually." She giggled.

"Did he?"

"It was a little creepy."

"He's a smart guy."

She wasn't sure what to say. Dillon certainly hadn't done anything to introduce her to his supposed intelligence. The lingering impression was still that of a sociopath. She didn't think she'd want to be alone with him. "How many years have you worked together?"

"Not sure. Five, at least."

"So he met your ex-wife?"

"I can't recall. Why do you ask?"

Corrine shrugged. She didn't like the direction her thoughts were taking. Less than an hour ago, she'd felt everything was settled. Why was she having these feelings of distrust, again? She turned and looked at the ship behind them. The thick cloudy substance was near the bow, a smaller piece of cloud, as heavy and solid-looking as it had been before. She strained further to see whether the woman was on the pier.

Andy stopped. "You're twisting my arm. What are you looking at?"

"The ship."

"Why?"

"I don't know." She turned back and tightened her hold on his arm. "You're sure you've never seen that woman on the pier at night?"

"No. But I don't come out here at night, except when I'm with you."

"I like it at night. Less crowded."

"To me, the point of the beach is sun and surf, but if you like it, I'll tolerate it."

"Tolerate?"

"Yup."

It wasn't as if he had to love everything she did, or look at life the same way she did, but it sounded condescending. It sounded temporary, as if he'd put up with it for now. "Is Dillon always so quiet?"

"Why do you keep harping on him?"

"I'm not harping." She let go of his arm. "He didn't say a word."

"Sonya talks a lot."

"So when she's not there, he talks?"

"Absolutely."

"But she wasn't talking the whole time. You had a lot to say."

"She kind of controlled things," he said. "Why are we discussing this?"

"Isn't that what couples do? Debrief on the evening after they go to a social event?"

He laughed. "It sounds like you're critiquing my friends."

"Not at all. And you said you'd only met Sonya once. She's not really a friend."

"She's Dillon's fiancé. That makes her a friend."

"Okay." She turned her head slightly. The cloudy thing was still there, lower than before. She turned back but not quickly enough.

"Why do you keep turning around? Should we head home?"

"I feel like the ship is watching me."

Andy laughed, but the sound was tinged with worry.

She wanted to cry. Why had she said something so absolutely crazy? Where had the thought even come from? Mary was messing with her head. It was that ominous tone in her voice, the warnings. The insistence that something had found its way inside of Corrine, and now she was doubting every thought. She was thinking too much, over-analyzing. There was no ghost.

"Are you listening to that crazy old woman again?"

"Don't call her that."

"She is. They all are. When you get old, your blood vessels get stiff and you can't think clearly. It causes hallucinations."

"It does not."

"I think it does."

"You can think whatever you want, but it's not true. Not the way you're thinking of it."

"Well stop listening to her. The ship isn't haunted. If you pay attention to that kind of thing, you can start to believe it just because it keeps repeating itself in your head. I don't want a crazy girlfriend."

"Like Sonya?"

"She's not crazy." He tugged on Parker's leash and turned. "Let's go back."

"Did you see what she did to me?"

"Yeah, I saw. Why do you think we left?"

"It's the most disgusting thing I've ever experienced."

"She was trying to get attention."

"I didn't like it."

"And that's why we left," he said.

Corrine looked at the pier, squinting slightly, as if that would help her make out the figure of the old woman, the ghost...or Mary. She shivered.

Andy quickened his pace.

"I don't like her," Corrine said.

"Ignore it. I'm sure it won't happen again. Dillon adores her."

That proved there was no explaining love. They walked quietly for a while. As they drew close to the pier, Corrine looked up. If she saw the woman, she could get Andy to tell her whether it was a ghost or a human being. She shivered.

Andy put his arm around her. "Why so cold, even with your scarf?"

"I keep thinking about that woman walking around."

"You shouldn't come out here at night, then you wouldn't get caught up in all this nonsense about ghosts." He laughed. "I thought you were more intelligent than that."

Corrine huddled close to him. He was right. She was much more intelligent than that. She'd thought she could be friendly with Mary, but it was looking like that wasn't a good idea. Still, she liked talking to Mary. And it was difficult not to worry and want to take care of her. All her life she'd been compelled to take care of people, to rescue them. There was something inside of her that couldn't stop. Maybe that's why she was drawn to Andy. There was something about him that needed rescuing.

Andy leaned close to her. "Thank you for wearing that dress. It looked amazing on you. I'm glad you like it."

A high pitched tone started up inside of her ear. It sounded as if Andy thought she'd kept the dress he'd given her. Did he not remember taking it out of her closet? Had he noticed she wore it when they went to dinner at Shadowbrook? She pushed the thoughts away. It didn't matter.

"The boots were a little funky," said Andy. He poked her gently in the ribs. "We need to get you some better shoes."

"It was cold. And they're easier for walking."

He didn't say anything.

As they passed beneath the pier, she felt once again that the ship was watching her.

Twenty-one

Baking chocolate chip cookies was not easy when you were blind. It had taken Mary the entire morning and half the afternoon, but she'd managed. She hadn't told Jill about her plans. She'd needed to do it herself. She needed to know she was capable of doing it herself. She'd made a mess, she was sure, but she'd managed to identify each measuring cup by re-nesting them each time so they could be chosen by their relative size. She'd done the same with the smaller measurements, using a stainless steel set that had only four spoons.

Setting the oven temperature had been challenging, but she had a lifetime of instinct regarding how far the knob needed to be turned, and she kept it lower than necessary, just to be sure, checking the cookies with the tip of her finger and a toothpick every five minutes. Now, the cookies had cooled enough for her to taste one. It was perfect. It wasn't just pride in what she'd accomplished — the cookie was truly one of the best she'd ever tasted. Maybe she'd let go of this too easily. Although now she felt she needed a nap, so maybe yielding her love of baking had been for the best. It was tiring, straining with every cell to be accurate and cautious. Her neck and shoulders ached. Her knees hurt from standing on the tile floor for so many hours.

When the cookies were cooled, she began packing them in a tin she'd found in the bottom cupboard. She hoped it wasn't a Christmas theme painted on the tin, but she supposed it wouldn't matter terribly if it was. The cookies were a gift for Daniel. It was the only thing she could think of to gouge an opening in the concrete wall that had formed between them. She still had to figure out how she was going to get his attention. If he didn't respond to her calling his name, would she have to approach others, asking whether they knew Daniel and could lead her to him? And if he rejected the cookies...she wasn't sure what she'd do.

There were two cookies that she hadn't been able to squeeze into the tin without breaking. She took a bite of one and placed it on the table. She carried the measuring cups and spoons and spatula to the sink. She put the mixing bowl and beater beside the sink. She finished the cookie, then went into the bedroom and stretched out on her back on top of the quilt. Tears pooled in the corners of her eyes. All those years she'd made cookies — as a child, as a new wife, later teaching her boys to make cookies, even though most boys weren't taught such domestic skills. Baking for her teenaged sons, for her grandchildren, she'd never known what a privilege it was. She closed her eyes and slept.

After her nap, she felt less sorry for herself. She spent the rest of the afternoon listening to her audio book. Just before dinner, she opened the window a half inch so she could hear the ocean more clearly. She poured a glass of champagne and sat on the couch, sipping it slowly. For dinner she heated leftover steamed broccoli and the other half of a chicken breast that Jill had prepared the day before. She poured a second glass of champagne to accompany her dinner while she listened to the news. Tomorrow she'd look for Daniel.

Mary was in front of the gate at the north end of the pier at six a.m. The park ranger wouldn't be around for at least half an hour, possibly longer. After a while, two fishermen joined her outside the gate. They greeted her by name, then began a conversation in Spanish. She wondered how they'd learned her name. Were all the regulars familiar with her face, her shape, her unseeing eyes? When she'd stood alone in the center of the pier a few days earlier, immobilized by shame over her vulnerability, perhaps all of them truly had been looking at her. But they'd also known not to speak, not to make her feel as if she needed an arm or a hand to help her. The two men chatted with each other. Mary stood quietly, letting their words wash over her like a soothing mantra.

Three teenaged boys walked up the ramp to the gate, arguing about something she couldn't understand. Finally it emerged they were talking about several musical groups — debating which was more deserving of an award of some kind. By the time the ranger showed up to unlock the gate, she still wasn't sure whether the boys were referring to a national award ceremony or a reality TV show where people demonstrated whatever talents they did or didn't have. She wasn't familiar with the shows. Reality TV was one of those things that she'd enjoyed mildly when she still had her sight, but had lost interest because there was too much nuance to be missed when all you had was the auditory piece. Reality TV was one of those incomprehensible modern developments, and she often wondered what her mother would have had to say about it.

The gate swung open. A few others had joined the pre-sunrise group, but she couldn't be sure how many there were. She spoke in a loud voice — "Has anyone seen Daniel?"

Several of them responded verbally rather than shaking their heads as people often did. The Hispanic guys picked up the gist of the question — they repeated Daniel's name and said no.

She walked onto the pier and remained just inside the gate. There were no benches close to the gate, but she didn't mind standing for twenty or thirty minutes. He wasn't going to get past her. She was sure he would speak to her if she was standing directly in his path. If he continued to hide himself in silence, he was no better than the man who came up to her on the beach, taking advantage of her weakness.

After a while, her legs began to ache. She took few steps back, reaching behind her to find the rail. If she leaned against it for support, she'd last longer.

Seven or eight people had gone past, wire handles rattling on plastic buckets. She pictured their poles pointing into the sky, bending gracefully like stalks of sea grass, some with lures already attached, swinging in time with their steps.

Her fingers were numb. She wished she'd worn gloves. It was colder than she'd realized. She was so eager to arrive early, she hadn't checked the weather. She held the tin in one hand and shoved the other hand in her pocket. After a few minutes, the wrist and hand holding the tin ached from the weight of the cookies. She moved it to the other hand, warmed the cold hand for a few minutes and then went back to using both hands. Moisture began to collect at the edges of her nostrils and she was sure her nose was red. She must look pathetic, holding her unwanted gift, possibly marked with Christmas designs which would give the impression she was too poor or too cheap to buy something new. There was a sour taste in her mouth, and she began thinking about the bear claws. How unappreciative she'd been, always believing she was doing Daniel a favor by eating his treat. Maybe he'd seen the lack of pleasure on her face. He could see everything and she could see nothing.

Part of her wanted to walk to the end of the pier and drop her baking efforts over the rail, pleased when she heard the heavy splash as the loaded tin hit the water. Suddenly, she was angry. She'd been polite and charming to Daniel. How dare he treat her like this, refusing to let her know what she'd said to offend him, becoming so outraged because she asked for a simple favor. All he had to say was *no*. He didn't have to cut her out of his life. He wasn't worth having as a friend. What had she been thinking? He was a guy who liked to fish, who bought too many sweet rolls and couldn't finish them all so he gave them away.

He's not your friend.

She bent down and set the tin on the ground and pressed her hands over her ears, as if that would silence the voice. She turned and gripped the railing. She could walk to the bench and wait there. But she'd chosen this spot so no one could pass by without her noticing. There hadn't been any footsteps for quite some time. Maybe she'd gotten so buried inside her thoughts, she'd missed hearing them. She leaned on the railing, aching for Daniel's friendship, however frail and obligatory it had been.

Below her on the sand, a dog barked. She released her grip, picked up the tin, and walked back through the open gate. She went slowly down the ramp, listening for footsteps or buckets or tackle boxes. The dog barked again, furious. Probably terrorizing the birds. Tears rolled down her face. She tugged her hood forward and clutched the tin to her chest. She walked quickly along the path, across the bridge, and up the narrow sidewalk to her home.

Inside, she put the cookie tin on the end table and tossed

her cape on the sofa. She sat on the sofa, her face turned toward the windows. Her phone rang. She picked it up and stroked the side, wondering who it was. Thomas had said he'd set different sounds for each of the people in her list of phone numbers, but he hadn't gotten around to it the last time he visited. A moment later, the phone blurped with a voicemail message. She didn't care who it was. She put the phone on the coffee table and leaned her head back.

Her world was collapsing to a small dot inside her head. Her thoughts swam in circles, full of bitter words she wanted to speak to Daniel, angry at Corrine for constantly pointing out that Mary was frail and elderly, disappointed in her sons for...she wasn't sure why she was disappointed. They treated her well. It wasn't their fault their jobs had taken them away.

She sat up. Maybe it wasn't Daniel at all. She'd been so busy warning Corrine about the spirit, how it might stir up dreadful thoughts, she hadn't been paying attention to her own mind. Or Daniel's. Perhaps he hadn't abandoned her at all. She knew better than anyone what that thing could do, how it twisted your mind, how it made you afraid and tried to drive splinters into your heart. It wanted the death of everything. It was dead and it wanted to drag every good thing and every scrap of love into the grave alongside it.

Several days passed, during which Mary ate all but ten of the cookies. She guessed there'd been close to three dozen. She'd eaten five a day — two with her lunch, two with dinner, and one before bed. With the bedtime cookie, she had a small glass of milk. She felt like a little girl and the feeling was wonderful. At what point in her life had she stopped eating cookies and drinking milk? It was a heavenly snack that made everything sweet and satisfying and good. It brought her the sleep of a child, her dreams unremembered.

There was plenty of time to think. Missing the beach was a deepening ache, but she felt she needed to decide how she was going to reassert herself. Each experience had torn at her confidence. She couldn't sit peacefully on the sand and listen to the water, or chat with a friend on the pier. It was kind of ironic. Corrine wanted to babysit her and Daniel wanted to get as far away as he possibly could. Maybe she should ask Corrine to confront the cruel stranger after all. Corrine certainly had an authoritative way about her. Still, a man would be better. The guy felt large and powerful and he was obviously a bully. It had to be done by a man.

Finally, she decided the best thing to do, the only thing, was to continue her habits. A daily walk to the pier, a daily trip to the beach, standing close to the waves, listening to the gulls. Habit and routine served you will in surviving the world. In surviving your life. Sometimes habit and routine were all you had, and they would carry you to the next dry rock, passing over the waters raging around.

On Saturday, she dug around in the cupboard and found a smaller tin. She was positive this one was a Christmas theme. She remembered getting Almond Rocca in it. The images were snowflakes and angels. What an odd combination. It didn't matter, all that mattered were the cookies, not quite as fresh as they had been a few days ago, but still chewy and good. She'd tasted another one to be sure.

She walked to the pier and made her way boldly down the center. When she was about halfway to the end, she paused to see whether Daniel would call out to her. It was windy but she could feel the sun bright on her face. After a moment, she turned to the left and sat down on one of the benches. She took out her travel mug and sipped her tea and forced her mind not to think of Daniel. Routine. Habit. Maybe she'd meet someone else, someone who wasn't as touchy as Daniel. Maybe even someone interested in ghosts. Not many were. She'd thought Corrine would be, since she'd seen the ghost herself, but she was beginning to wonder whether Corrine knew her own mind, with or without the influence of the spirit.

The tea was too hot and her tongue was stinging, but she continued taking small sips. She pulled Daniel's tin out of her bag, pried off the lid, and took a cookie. She replaced the lid and tucked the tin into her bag. She ate the cookie slowly. The waves broke steadily. Her breath moved with the same tempo, as it often did, oxygen rushing into her lungs when they crashed to the shore, slowly seeping out as the wave receded.

When the mug was empty, she put it into her bag with the tin of cookies. As she was about to stand up, she felt the jolt of someone sitting down hard on the opposite end of the bench. A dog grunted and sniffed vigorously at her knees. It settled a few feet away, shifting between heavy panting and barely perceptible whining.

"Mary, isn't that right?"

"Yes. Who are you?" she said.

"You really can't see at all?"

"Who are you?"

"Andy Johnson. You know my girlfriend, Corrine."

"Oh. Yes." Mary nodded. She pulled the bag close to her side and held onto it as if she needed to protect the cookies.

"I'll get right to the point," Andy said.

"Certainly."

"You need to stop filling Corrine's head with your notion of ghosts."

"Is she incapable of expressing her wishes to me?"

"She's too nice."

"Too nice for what?" Mary hugged her bag more tightly. The waves continued breaking with the same rhythm but her breathing wasn't anywhere close to their pattern.

"She's fixated on the elderly. She has some sort of compulsion to help them, and she's become quite attached to you."

Mary wasn't surprised by the compulsion to help, but the fact that Corrine considered herself attached gave her a strangely warm feeling. She smiled.

"What's so funny?"

"Nothing. Go on."

"I'd appreciate it if you'd stop telling her your fairy tales."

"I see." She was not going to debate the reality of ghosts with this man. Perhaps he'd find out for himself. Perhaps not, but he wasn't someone worth arguing with. It was all over him, in the tone of his voice and the hostility radiating from him, as if he fancied himself in charge of the entire world. As if he thought he could dictate Mary's behavior. How on earth did someone become so arrogant yet retain such stupidity that they truly believed they possessed so much power? "Why do you think she fixates on the elderly, as you so nicely phrased it?"

"I'm not trying to be rude. It's not only the elderly, it's anyone, or any *thing* that's helpless, or weak."

"And you think I'm weak?"

"As people get old, they grow weaker, yes. And Corrine has an over-developed sense of responsibility."

"Do you think she's weak?"

"Not at all."

"Then shouldn't you allow her the dignity of speaking for herself?"

"The ghost thing is upsetting her. And it's not necessary. I'm only asking you to cool it on the scary supernatural stories, not saying you shouldn't be friendly."

"I hope not."

"Good," he said. The dog stood up and moved closer to the bench. It pushed its nose against Mary's leg. It lifted a paw to her knee. She knew it wanted her to pet it, but its body was tense, as if it wouldn't take much for it to assault her, the smallest gesture from Andy, a sound.

"Corrine is an adult, we can talk about whatever we please."

"I'm asking a favor," he said.

"I think it shows character that she wants to help people you consider weak."

"It's a pathology."

"How would you know? Aren't you inclined to help people who are weaker than you? It's a normal, civilized instinct."

"Not everyone can be helped. It's not possible to rescue every wounded bird. Not possible to alleviate the loneliness of every old person, hold every single hand in the face of death."

"What are you so afraid of?"

"I'm not afraid of anything."

"I think you are."

"I'm not."

"You're afraid Corrine will talk about things that make you uncomfortable. Growing old. Death."

"Don't tell me what I think, Mary."

"Then why do you care what she talks about with me?"

The dog started pacing in front of the bench.

"I think your dog is done talking," Mary said.

The bench shifted as he stood up. He snapped his fingers and she heard the dog trot behind the bench.

"It's a simple favor," he said.

"Wouldn't it be rather weak of me to change my behavior based on the interfering request of someone I've never met?"

"It's for your own good. She's extremely bothered by it. If you keep at it, she might start avoiding you."

"Thank you for letting me know."

"Enjoy the weather. Gorgeous day," Andy said.

"You'll be old some day."

He laughed. She felt them move away. The dog's feet tapped on the worn boards as he hurried to get to the beach. The man sounded high strung, determined to convince himself he was reasonable. Aside from treating his girlfriend like a child, he'd made it clear he was afraid of becoming old and weak. Terrified, almost.

Twenty-two

Corrine's grandmother had died when Corrine was nineteen. Corrine had been home from college for the three week winter break. She'd seen her grandmother on Christmas Eve when Corrine, her sister Maggie, and her parents gathered at Grandma Ruth's house. Her grandmother seemed fine. More frail, maybe. Her wrists were thinner than ever. Her delicate platinum watch dangled like a bracelet, the weight of the timepiece pulling it upside down so the face wasn't visible, as if it were looking down at the table, or searching the floor for something it had lost.

Grandma Ruth's house was a rambling ranch style, stretched out on a corner lot. It had five bedrooms and four bathrooms, a family room and a formal dining room, in addition to a breakfast nook in the good-sized kitchen. They'd eaten clam chowder at the kitchen table while choral renditions of Christmas carols played on the stereo in the living room. Ruth's old records glided gracefully around the turntable without a single imperfection to snag the needle.

Corrine and Maggie slept overnight as they'd done since they started junior high school. The next morning they made pancakes for Grandma Ruth and cleaned up the kitchen. As they were leaving, their uncle came to pick up Ruth. He would drive her two hours east to his home in Sacramento, where Corrine's father politely declined to join the other side of the family as he had no interest in watching his sister drink herself to death.

When Corrine and Maggie left that morning, Grandma Ruth patted Maggie's shoulder then turned and wrapped her thin arms around Corrine.

"I adore you girls."

"We know, Grandma," Corrine said.

"Don't wait so long next time. Will you come visit before you go back to school?"

Maggie kissed her grandmother's cheek. "I can't. I have to work like twelve or fifteen hours a day over the holiday. For the internship I told you about?"

Her grandmother let go of Corrine and nodded. She looked up at the ceiling, as if she'd find her memory hanging from the overhead light. "You did. I forgot." She turned to Corrine, a fragile smile on her lips. "Corrine?"

"You know I will, Grandma. I'm home for two more weeks."

Her grandmother squeezed her hand.

Ever since she'd acquired a driver's license, Corrine had

visited her grandmother every week. They talked and drank tea and played pinochle. Each time she left, her grandmother squeezed her hand and told her she was special. Corrine was certain that her grandmother's words, and the hand squeeze, which was almost a secret handshake of sorts, meant something. She was her grandmother's favorite. Without a doubt. She knew she shouldn't have such thoughts, knew it was an outgrowth of sibling rivalry, one of the basest forms of sociological malfunction, but she couldn't help it.

In the hallway on Christmas morning, the squeeze of her grandmother's thin, still strong fingers said it again. Corrine was the one she really wanted to see. "I'll come over next week. Is Tuesday good?"

"Any day that's good for you."

But then Corrine met David. She'd gone to a party the day after Christmas and fallen for him the moment she saw him. They'd packed an entire year into those two weeks — a trip to San Francisco with a walk across the Golden Gate bridge. A drive to Monterey to visit the aquarium, hiking in an open space preserve. They went to movies and ate pizza and Chinese food and drank beer. She'd remembered her Grandmother the day after New Year's. She called, pouring out her apologies. Her grandmother understood perfectly. Corrine was young. She should enjoy life. It was too short, and youth was even shorter.

On January third, Corrine was packing her suitcase when her mother came into the room and said Grandma had suffered a stroke. It happened right in her front garden. The neighbor called the paramedics, but Ruth had died instantly, lying among her roses. She'd been cutting them back for winter. Possibly the heavy clippers were too much for her. Or it was just time. It was a blessing she'd gone quickly and without pain.

Corrine disagreed. Her grandmother's pain must have been enormous. Missing her granddaughter, her hopes raised all during that long week — the dullest week of the year between Christmas and New Year's. Waiting for Corrine, then telling Corrine not to worry — it was okay. But it wasn't okay at all. Life was far too short, shorter than Corrine had ever realized.

After the funeral, while they ate lasagna, made by Corrine and her mother from Grandma Ruth's recipe, they drank wine and told stories. Maggie and Corrine washed the dishes.

Corrine tore off a sheet of foil and folded it over the leftover lasagna. "I feel so bad. I promised I'd visit, and I didn't."

"I'm sure she understood. We're busy."

"I said I would."

Maggie turned a glass upside down into the dishwasher. It was still half full and water splashed across the front of her slacks. "Aw shit."

"I promised I'd go over. At least once. To play cards."

"She understood."

"You don't know that. I didn't have to spend every second

with David. I should have gone over. She was looking forward to it."

"So what. She's dead, she doesn't care," Maggie said, rubbing a towel across the front of her slacks, as if that would make the dark spot go away.

"Don't say that. She cared when she was alive."

"Stop beating yourself up."

"She died without anyone," Corrine said. "No one should have to do that."

"Usually, that's exactly what they have to do."

"It's not right. Someone you love should be there, someone to say good-bye, to hold onto us while we leave our bodies."

"You're too idealistic. And way too sentimental," Maggie said.

"I don't think I am."

"I know you are."

Tears flooded her eyes. She couldn't see the handle of the drawer where the foil was stored. She blinked and tried to swallow the moisture that rushed through her head like a river swollen with melting snow. She felt Maggie's hand on her shoulder. "You can't do this to yourself. We loved her. We spent a lot of time with her."

"I hate it that she died all alone."

"It was fast. She didn't even know."

"I still hate it. I didn't say good-bye."

Maggie spoke softly, not her usual harsh, firm opinion. "That's you. Feeling bad for yourself. Grandma didn't know.

And wherever she is, she's okay now."

"She shouldn't have been alone."

Her sister pulled her hand away. "God, Corrine. We're all alone. Death is lonely. It's not the buddy system. Stop making it so dramatic."

They'd finished cleaning the kitchen without speaking to each other. When Corrine was back at school, she talked to a counselor about focusing her studies on geriatric care.

"It's a booming field," the counselor said. She smiled. "Very altruistic of you. It's not well-paying."

Corrine had managed to withstand Maggie rolling her eyes and fixing looks of pity on her face at Corrine's career choice. She hadn't been as strong during her last year of graduate school. Maggie, whose preferred method of communication was an occasional public post on Corrine's Facebook page, called on a Saturday morning.

"Hey, Sis. I have a huge problem."

"It's good to hear your voice," Corrine said.

"You too. So I have this situation…it's really awful. I put all the money Grandma left me into this, I guess you could call it a start-up. Like I was an angel investor."

"What happened?"

"The details don't matter. The point is, I owe…I put up money for my friend, too."

"It doesn't sound like a legitimate investment — putting in money for a friend."

"Maybe not, but the point is, the money is gone, and I owe

a hundred and thirty-seven thousand dollars. I thought you could spot me."

"That's a huge loan."

"I wasn't thinking a loan at all."

"That's what *spot me* means."

"Oh. Well I know Grandma left you more than she left me, and I never thought that was fair."

"It was her decision."

"I'm dying, Corrine. I'm really...I'm in a lot of trouble. Please? I don't know what else to do." Then, her sister started crying.

Corrine didn't recall Maggie ever crying.

After she'd written the check, she knew she'd done the right thing. She'd felt good that she was in a position to help. She was certain her grandmother understood.

It didn't matter if her views were unrealistic in the extreme, she'd never been able to let go of the belief that no one should die alone. Yet, in her experience, people seemed determined to die alone. As much time as she spent with the residents of Fairhaven, they always died after she left the room. They died before they were transported to acute care facilities and someone would at least be present during the drive. They died watching TV when no one from the staff was in the room and the other residents were occupied. They died within hours of their families walking out the door after a visit. And they died at night.

It was as if they wanted to slip out of the world quietly. They didn't want a farewell or the experience of helplessly watching someone's grief. They crept down an empty corridor and opened the back door, looked around to be sure no one was watching, and stepped out. Maybe she'd been wrong about her grandmother. Maybe dying alone in her garden, without lingering pain, without prolonged awareness of saying good-bye, was exactly what she'd wanted. Still, Corrine deeply regretted not keeping her promise to visit. She would regret it forever.

She wondered what Grandma Ruth would say about her behavior now. Creating a fake persona and stalking a woman on social media. It was embarrassing to even think about it, and she worried her grandmother might hear her thoughts. Who knew where the dead resided. They might follow you around like so many molecules clinging to your skin. They might appear in a room, summoned by your thoughts of them. Perhaps when you recalled their words, they were actually there speaking those words to you. Of course, that made no sense when you thought about the process of recalling what the living had said to you. But maybe your ghost came into being while you were still alive, some other part of you, and those thoughts about the words of others were their ghosts, not the neurological performance of memory. No one really knew, did they? Even her thoughts right this minute might be her grandmother, whispering in her ear.

It was possible Mary was not losing touch with reality at all. She might know more about how things really were than anyone. She'd spent her whole life living with the ghostly remains of her mother.

"I'm sorry," Corrine said. She closed her eyes for a moment. "You see why I'm doing this, don't you? It's not that I don't trust him. I just don't know him that well, yet. And I don't want to believe everything he says without question. Which I guess means I don't trust him. What do you think, Grandma?"

The room was silent. And no words that her grandmother might have said, no paraphrase of something she'd said at one time, came into Corrine's head. She opened her eyes and picked up her martini. She was the one who was losing it. Talking to a woman who had been dead for over ten years. A woman who couldn't possibly haunt Corrine's home, if you believed in that sort of thing, because she'd never crossed the threshold of the cottage where Corrine sat tapping at a device her grandmother would have found mystifying.

She took a sip of her drink. The crisp, cold, silky liquid quenched her thirst, although later, the effects of the alcohol would make her twice as thirsty. She took another sip and put the glass on the table. She tapped her way to Deb's page. Her finger began to ache as she scrolled through updates about supplements and exercise. Working out wasn't that complicated. Did it really need to be discussed at this level of detail? She supposed strength training was more complex, but if people just went for a run, or a bike ride, they'd feel great and stay in shape. Look at Mary. She was thin and sharp-witted and appeared quite healthy at ninety-one years old. It was incredible. And she drank champagne every day. Corrine laughed.

The desire to know more about Andy's past consumed her. Meeting grinning Dillon and golden, freakish Sonya had done nothing to alleviate the sense that she didn't know this man at all. That she had invited a man into her house, her bed, her heart who had some sort of plan for her. A desire to replace her with a reimagined version.

The evening with those two had been a dream of some kind with no tangible human connection. Sonya, dressed for display, hadn't interacted with Dillon at all. Her outlandish insertion of her hand in Corrine's dress was frightening in its boldness and its desire to cause pain — and its freakishness. Andy said that was why they'd ended the evening, but why had it even begun? His insistence that Dillon was so very intelligent was contradicted by the idiotic expression he'd worn all night. Corrine wondered if Andy was mocking her, playing some other game with rules she couldn't decipher. Testing her to see whether she believed a man with no evident personality, no thoughts, and a frightening expression was what Andy said he was. Simply taking Andy's word in the face of all evidence to the contrary. What did Dillon's crazed, frozen grin, hiding something she didn't want to imagine, say about Andy? She took a healthy swallow of her martini.

Maybe she should just break it off. It was torture, living in this constant state of questioning and uncertainty. But who did that? Who dumped a good-looking, warm, gracious, interesting man because he had bizarre friends, or because his ex-wife passed along questionable stories? She felt she was losing her mind, unable to know what her true thoughts were, watching them slide around like spilled bits of mercury from an old-fashioned thermometer that had shattered, spilling its poisonous guts. Talking to Mary hadn't helped at all. She'd thought an older, experienced woman who had known the world and its twists and turns for nearly a century would have some useful wisdom. Instead, Mary couldn't stop talking about ghosts, feeding more doubts into Corrine's thoughts.

If all these doubts about him were simply paranoia, she'd be a fool to break up with him. How did you know if something was wrong with your thought process, if you had a mental illness creeping into a corner of your life, waiting to take it over?

For some reason, right that minute, it seemed as if chatting online with Deb would be a comfort. It would clear her thoughts. Or was she fooling herself? Maybe she was simply addicted to snooping. She was enjoying the anonymity and the knowledge that she was getting the upper hand with Andy by acquiring information he didn't know she possessed.

She wasn't sure if it would look suspicious launching into more questions about Deb's ex without a small talk preamble of some kind. She sipped her drink. She didn't feel like composing a lame question about fitness or diet. She wanted to know more about Andy. She had to know. She opened a message window.

Hi Deb. Sorry to bother you again, but I think the guy I'm with is very similar to your ex-husband. What was his name again?

Deb answered immediately: *Andy. BTW, I looked up that Pygmalion thing you were talking about. I think I can see why you mentioned it.*

Corrine: *I feel like I'm obsessing. Looking for problems. He bought me this dress that isn't like anything I wear. And he makes little comments about how I could be different and I'm not sure if it's the same thing as what you went through with Andy.*

Deb: *For me, it was obvious, like I told you.*

Corrine: *How long did you know him before you were married?*

Deb: *Two years.*

Corrine: *That's a long time.*

Deb: *Apparently not long enough.*

Corrine: *Did you have any clues before you were married?*

Deb: *Looking back, it was pretty clear, but I didn't notice at the time.*

Corrine: *Do you know where he is now? Is he remarried?*

Deb: *He was engaged, I'm not sure if they got married. We lost touch. Or rather, I broke off communication. LOL.*

Corrine: *Why?*

Deb: *I didn't see the point.*

Corrine: *Did he have a lot of other friends?*

Deb: *Not really. He wanted to be with me all the time.*

Corrine: *That seems romantic.*

Deb: *Not really.*

Corrine: *Did you meet his friends?*

Deb: *I said he didn't have any.*

Corrine: *You said "not really", I thought that meant not very many.*

Deb: *Nope.*

Corrine: *So the plastic surgery was what made you end it for good? Were you thinking about it before that?*

Deb: *Wouldn't you?*

Corrine: *I think so, yes. I don't even like the dress. I told him I didn't want it, and then I went and bought the same dress. I'm not even sure why.*

Deb: *That's weird.*

Corrine: *I know. So I met some friends of his…and they were… strange. To say the least.*

Deb: *Well at least the guy you're with has friends. Look, I really can't tell you what to do. I know I give a lot of advice on my page, but that's about things I know. I've never met the guy you're with. So he might be completely different from Andy. In fact, to be honest, I can't remember you that well, so I feel a little uncomfortable.*

Corrine: *I'm bummed you don't remember me. ;)*

Deb: *Sorry. I meet a lot of people. LOL. Don't mean to be cold.*

Corrine: *You're not cold. Not at all. You are so sweet.*

Deb: *Aw. Thanks.*

Corrine: *Did you ever meet the new fiancé? Did she also look like his mother?*

Deb: *Never met her.*

Corrine: *So my boyfriend's friends...they seemed like they were insane. Not fun "insane" but really disturbed.*

Deb: *Creepy.*

Corrine: *The woman's clothes were wild — all gold. And the guy didn't talk. He grinned like a maniac all night. And I mean ALL night.*

Deb: *Maybe they were just people he found and asked them to pretend to be friends. Ha ha.*

Corrine: *Are you kidding? Why would you say that?*

Deb: *I don't know. It just popped into my head. It's possible, right? It sounds to me like you should get out of the relationship.*

Corrine: *Why do you say that?*

Deb: *It feels like you're asking me questions but you already know the answer. You feel uncomfortable.*

Corrine: *But I love him! It's so hard to know!!*

Deb: *It sounds like you're almost afraid of him. You don't trust him at all.*

Corrine: *I just don't know.*

Deb: *You need to listen to your instincts.*

Corrine: *I do.*

Deb: *Do you?*

Deb: *Look, I gotta run. Talk to you later.*

Corrine: *Did Andy ever do that? Introduce you to fake friends? Is that what made you think of it?*

The icon popped up showing that Deb had seen the message. Corrine ate an olive and waited. After several minutes she typed a question mark. The icon didn't appear.

She ate another olive. After a few more minutes, she typed: *Okay. Thanks for listening. Bye.*

Soon, the screen dimmed and then went dark.

Corrine finished her drink and ate the last olive.

She was mildly frightened. Part of her mind insisted she was creating drama. She was manufacturing all kinds of things in her mind. She was talking to Mary, to Andy's ex, to her dead grandmother, even. She was entertaining the possibility of a ghost manipulating her thoughts. She laughed, embarrassed with herself. She was doing everything but talking to Andy. The guy she was supposed to be in love with.

Twenty-three

The ghost that drifted above the concrete ship, and walked along the pier, sometimes taking the form of a woman, had haunted Mary for most of her life. She'd never talked about it much because mentioning you'd seen a ghost made everyone think you were an imaginative child, or tripping on LSD, or suffering dementia. Once a ghost was mentioned, no one believed a word you said, and many people didn't even want to spend time with you. She wondered if that was at the root of why Daniel had turned his back on her. He'd written her off as an old woman who had stumbled outside the boundaries of sanity.

Occasionally, thoughts had entered her mind that seemed to materialize out of nowhere. She'd assumed it was the inexplicable firing of neurons inside the brain, a massive network the size of the universe, generating images, picking up bits and pieces of information every nano-second of the day. Of course, the concept of a nanosecond wasn't understood when she was a child. The brain put all those bits and bytes together in a million, a billion, possibly a trillion, or more, different ways.

But one night, Mary was walking on the beach and the woman had materialized out of nothing. The ship was barren, then suddenly, the woman was standing there. She wore a cape like the one Mary's mother had worn, her head and face obscured by the hood. The woman had walked up and down the length of the ship as Mary stood mesmerized, her feet sinking into the soft wet sand.

The woman hadn't spoken. There was no voice, no sound at all, even from the waves. But somehow, in a way that was unquestionably another's, the woman's voice echoed inside Mary's head.

I'm here, watching. I'm here, listening. I'm here, speaking, if anyone wants to pay attention.

Mary could never determine whether the woman wanted to weave fear and despair into her mind, or if she wanted to reveal the truth, turning Mary's thoughts in a new direction. Sometimes, fear and despair were merely stepping stones toward the truth. So maybe there was no malevolence in the ways the apparition twisted people's thoughts, maybe the end result was always the truth.

Corrine had seen the woman but stubbornly refused to accept that it was an entity from beyond the grave. She'd rather invent impossible ways for Mary to get to the pier through locked gates. Now, Mary wondered if Corrine wasn't as disbelieving as she pretended. Andy had suggested that Corrine couldn't stop thinking about the ghost. She'd obviously talked to him about it. She'd mentioned it enough times that he was worried. And Corrine had told him she felt a connection to Mary. Or at least he'd said that. Maybe it was his opinion, not a thought Corrine had expressed at all. Until Corrine approached her again, she wouldn't know. It was painful, losing control of life like this. Sitting in her home or on the beach, the victim of others' whims. She had no idea where Corrine lived, no way of contacting her. A person who could see would ask for a phone number, but unless Mary took her only partially useful mobile phone to the beach and asked Corrine to enter the number, there was nothing she could do. Her sons gave her that phone to give her a sense of security, but all it did was make them feel safe. Her sole connection was to those four boys. Most of her older friends, the ones she could also no longer be with because they were trapped in their own frail bodies, didn't have mobile phones.

Despite her walks on the beach and her illusion of independent living, she was a prisoner. Her eyes were closed to the world and that world was shrinking around her until she was squeezed as surely as that octopus had squeezed her in the dream, hardly able to breathe. Perhaps that was the meaning of the dream. It wasn't a dream she could tell her sons about. They would laugh. They would tell her something logical and scientific about the function of dreams, working out your anxieties, not a vehicle for messages from an outside force. They would brush it off as meaningless.

Talking to Corrine would be wonderful. If Mary could talk about her experiences of the ghost for more than five minutes at a time, if Corrine would open her mind and listen. If she'd entertain the possibility...

She went into the kitchen and put the kettle on the stove. She took out a teabag and her travel mug. While she waited for the water to boil, she ate a chocolate chip cookie. She might as well finish them off. And there would be no more baking. She opened the refrigerator. An orange would taste bitter after the cookie. She took out a bag of baby carrots and ate three. The water boiled and she poured it over the teabag. She screwed the lid on the container, put on her cape, and went out.

Several days passed before Mary ran into Corrine again. Mary was sitting on the sand in the early afternoon on a Saturday. The beach was quiet, sparsely populated with a few families and couples who were willing to tolerate the heavy fog and the rough surf. She remembered when she used to see people swimming in dangerous surf on beautiful days, unaware of how threatening the waves were, how wild the rip-tide. They were deluded by the cloudless sky. When it was foggy and the same surf conditions existed, people stayed out of the water. It seemed as if they needed a dark sky to warn them of danger.

The blanket was folded in half, protection against the

possible appearance of her tormenter — there was no room
for him to sit down this time. Beside her was the insulated
pack with a bottle of water, two crystal flutes, and a half
bottle of champagne nestled between flexible ice packs. Her
canvas bag had a container of pretzels and a small covered
bowl with red seedless grapes. Jill had done a superb job
finding grapes. They were the size of the giant marbles the
boys played with throughout their childhoods — the
shooters. They were firm and sweet, triumphing over the
cloying taste of chocolate chip cookies.

She took a few sips from the water bottle. The champagne
would remain sealed until — if — Corrine stopped by. She
should have invited Corrine to her home. If she hadn't been
so standoffish, so worried about making sure no one insulted
her pride with unwanted offers to help, maybe they would be
closer friends by now. Still, it wasn't too late to start over.
Hopefully she hadn't already chased away Corrine as firmly as
she'd alienated Daniel. She plucked off three grapes and ate
them. She was hoping to save those as well, but she was a
little hungry, her appetite inflamed by too much sugar.

After thirty minutes or so, the fog remained heavy and
damp. The waves began to crest the ledge of sand. She stood
up and dragged the blanket and bags ten or twelve feet back
toward the sea wall. Maybe Corrine had other plans for her
Saturday. Maybe the fog and damp were keeping her away this
time. She unzipped the bag and put her hand around the neck
of the champagne bottle, reminding herself she was

following her routine, keeping with her habits. If that was the case, perhaps opening it and pouring a glass would bring Corrine to her side.

She let go of the bottle and zipped the bag. What if Corrine had seen her and turned away? The blanket was folded into a tiny rectangle. By trying to prevent the man from intruding, she'd given the unspoken message to Corrine that she didn't want company. Maybe Corrine was watching even now. She stood up quickly. She paused for a moment, lightheaded from the sudden movement. She placed her bags on the sand and pulled the blanket open into a large square. She put the bags back and settled down again, shifting her legs to the opposite side.

It seemed like another half hour passed. She might as well open the champagne. One day, Corrine would show up on the beach again when Mary was there it just might not be…

"Hi, Mary."

She smiled. "Hi, Corrine. I'm so glad you're here."

"Can I sit down?"

"Yes, please do." Mary scooted to the right, even though it wasn't necessary. There was plenty of room. "I brought two glasses for champagne. Would you like some?"

"Sure."

She felt the tug of the blanket as Corrine settled next to her. Mary unwrapped the foil and removed the wire clasp. She eased out the cork. The pop always made her feel satisfied, as if life were simple and filled with hope. She had no idea why.

She believed it was a long-forgotten association from her childhood, but was never sure whether that meant there had been some happy moments after her mother drowned or if the pleasant association came from much further back. She poured a bit into the first glass and handed it to Corrine. She filled her own glass and wedged the bottle back in place. She held out her glass. Corrine touched the edge of her glass to Mary's.

"To friends," Mary said.

Corrine answered softly. "To friends."

Mary sipped her drink. "I was worried I'd scared you away. I can be prickly sometimes."

"I understand," Corrine said.

"How is your job?"

"It's going well. The construction is on schedule. I've been distracted, and feeling I don't enjoy it as much. I've been questioning it. My boyfriend says I should consider other careers that might be more satisfying longer term, but I don't know. I'm not sure I agree. I think I need to spend more time there and remind myself why I love it, why I chose it."

"I met your boyfriend a few days ago," Mary said. "He suggested your interest in old people might be...unhealthy." She laughed, somewhat nervously, she thought. "But I think it's nice."

"You met Andy?"

"Yes." Mary sipped her champagne. It had a lovely cold bite to it. She was glad she'd brought two ice packs. In fact, waiting all that time for Corrine, it had grown more chilled than it had been when she'd taken it out of the refrigerator.

"How?"

"I was sitting on the pier. He came up to me and introduced himself. His dog was with him."

"Parker."

"He didn't introduce the dog, but the dog tried to. He kept nudging at me."

Corrine laughed. "He's friendly. I don't think all Rottweilers are. What did he say?"

She'd debated whether it was right to tell Corrine. But if she didn't tell, she would have felt she was keeping a secret, hiding information because the not telling would be as deliberate as the telling. If he was going to be crass enough to talk to a stranger behind Corrine's back, trying to control her friendships, then Mary could be equally crass. She also had an ulterior motive. If Corrine was anything like her, in fact, like most people, knowing someone didn't want her to do something would make her quite eager to do that very thing. A common feature of human nature — rebelling against rules. Especially unreasonable ones. And if Andy was trying to make rules about what Corrine could and could not talk about, Corrine was going to develop an overwhelming desire to talk about the very subject he forbade — ghosts would consume her conversation and her thoughts. Andy had shot himself in the foot, as they said. "I hesitated about telling you."

"Why?"

"I don't want to upset you. But then I decided you have a right to know."

"Know what? What did he say?"

Mary ate two pretzels and held out the container for Corrine. The plastic box wobbled in her hand while Corrine burrowed around for pretzels.

"He asked me to stop talking to you about ghosts."

"That's insulting," Corrine said.

Mary sipped her champagne.

"Why would he do that?" Corrine said.

"I don't know. There's no harm in discussing ghosts."

"Absolutely not. It's embarrassing that he would talk to you about me. Who else is he contacting behind my back, trying to manage my life? I feel like he wants to turn me into his own idea of the woman he wants to be in love with."

"I don't know about that," Mary said. "But he doesn't seem to think very highly of your independence."

"No. He doesn't. I can talk about whatever I want."

"I agree."

"In fact, I saw her again."

"The ghost?" Mary said.

"Yes."

"And what happened?" This was more than she'd hoped for. Andy's interference had shoved Corrine through a curtain into another world. Now, Corrine absolutely believed that the figure on the pier was not a living human being. Mary took several small sips of champagne to hide her smile.

"I thought a lot about what you said. That she manipulates thoughts." Corrine began pouring out a confusing jumble of paranoid thoughts, swings from loving Andy to mistrusting everything he said. She told Mary about his strange friends, and her sense that Andy's colleague was a sociopath, the fiancé too, for that matter.

When she was finished, Mary picked up the champagne bottle. It was empty. She'd been pouring dribbles throughout the telling of Corrine's story. She was disappointed. It hadn't occurred to her that she usually drank the entire half bottle by herself. She replaced the bottle and put her empty glass in the bag. "What are you going to do?"

"I don't know. I love him. I see all these facets to him. All the things that bother me are coming from outside — my impression of his friends, his talking to you. Maybe I'm making more of it than it is. Maybe he was just worried about me. Maybe that woman, that ghost, is trying to drive a wedge between us."

"Maybe."

"If the ghost plants thoughts in your mind, how would I know which ones are true? Which ones belong to me? I...it's too strange. I feel like I don't know my own mind."

"Maybe we never do," Mary said. "Maybe the human mind is impossible to know. Even at my age, my thoughts surprise me and frighten me. They turn every which way at a moment's notice."

"I thought that, someday, I'd reach a settled point in my life."

"Never."

"I love him."

Mary didn't say anything. She was happy to have a friend, and happy to know that there would be future conversations about ghosts. There would be more champagne and more secrets shared. She was content for now.

Twenty-four

Andy had to travel to New York for five days. He left on Sunday and would be home late Thursday. He asked Corrine to take care of Parker. She felt she couldn't say no, although the exchange had a surreal nature because one part of her was planning to tell him everything. She would ask him all the questions she'd asked Deb, possibly tell him about Deb's complaints. She'd demand an explanation for why he'd gone behind her back to tell Mary what she could and could not talk about. It felt strange to be caring for his beloved pet when their relationship might crumble within the week.

As much as Parker could be enjoyable, as much as she loved his unabashed adoration, he was big. Even when he was lying on the cushion Andy had provided for the corner of the living room, so deep in sleep he was completely motionless, his presence dominated the room. His breathing was audible from the couch, his smell, even after a bath, was distinct. At the same time, he'd spent so much time in her house, the rooms had a slightly hollow quality when he wasn't there. The feeling confused her and she wondered whether Cat experienced it the same way. The day before Parker came to stay for the week, Cat had sniffed at the dog's sleeping cushion. She sat down next to it and cocked her head. Then she'd curled up at the edge, her back pressed firmly against the cushion.

In the evenings, Corrine took Parker to the beach and they ran for three miles. Parker easily kept pace with her and then ran faster, urging her to increase her speed. She felt better than ever after her runs with him.

For three nights, Parker sat on his cushion and stared at her. Every time she glanced up from reading her tablet, or watching TV, he was looking at her. When she made a martini, he followed her to the kitchen and watched, ears perked, while ice clattered into the metal shaker. He sat down and relaxed his ears when she measured gin and impaled the olives on a stir stick.

While she sipped her martini, she stared back at him, trying to fathom what he might be thinking. How self-aware were animals? Was he wondering where Andy had gone or did Parker's life have an out-of-sight, out-of-mind quality to it? Was he thinking that he now lived at her house rather than at Andy's slick, spacious condo? Maybe he thought nothing, only observing the sights and sounds around him.

He must know secrets about Andy. He would have seen and heard things that Deb had no clue about. He knew everything that happened in that condo, everything but Andy's thoughts. And possibly, he'd heard those as well. Unfiltered comments uttered out loud, if Andy was as crazy as she was and chatted to his pet. She was pretty sure most pet owners did.

On the fourth night, she began speaking to the dog. "What do you think, Parker? You know Andy better than anyone. Does he love me?"

Parker stared at her.

"You're right, I think the better question is do I love *him*?"

Parker put his head on his paws.

"I mean, that matters more. But it also matters whether he loves me. Because even if I do love him, I shouldn't stay with him if he doesn't love me. I don't know what you thought of that dress, but it really put a bad taste in my mouth. It seemed as if he'd never noticed anything I'd worn. And then when I dared to wear it with boots…and what about looking like Deb? Do you think I look like her? Does Andy know how much we look alike or is he completely unaware? It gives me the willies. Should I tell Deb? Maybe I should out myself. But then she'd tell him. Or not."

She sipped the martini. "Mmm. This is so good." She took another sip. "I'm really confused. Mary tells me the ghost is causing my confusion. But it's also Andy himself. I feel like the man I know, except for the dress, is not the person other people tell me he is. I mean, Dillon was a freak. You didn't meet him, but I wonder how you would have reacted. You would have made the truth clear right away. And now Andy's telling people whether they can talk to me? What's that about? I bet you'd also know right away whether the ghost was real. I should take you out there at night."

She stood up and swallowed the rest of her drink. Not now. She couldn't go for a walk after slamming down a martini. But tomorrow. After dinner, they would go for a walk and possibly the woman would appear. If it was something that wasn't human, Parker would know immediately.

On Thursday night she sliced up a leftover chicken breast and made a salad of butter lettuce, chicken, tomatoes, and avocado. She spent an hour reading the news, and then watched an hour of comedy news. She'd already changed into spandex capri pants and a sports bra after work. She put on a tank top and sweatshirt and sat on the floor to put on her shoes. Parker scrambled to the entryway when he heard her running shoes on the tile. She clipped on his leash and they went out.

They trudged across loose dry sand and turned right, passing beneath the pier. The tide was low and the wet sand was packed hard, perfect for an easier than usual run, but watching to see whether the woman would appear was more important. There was no way to know what her reasons were for walking on the pier at night, how she chose when to come out. Corrine paused a few yards past the pier. She should go up and check the gate to see whether it was truly locked. Why hadn't she thought of that before? She glanced out at the boat. The thick cloudy thing was near the center, but there was so much fog she couldn't decide whether it had a different substance than the clouds, or was simply more of the same.

She turned and cut diagonally across the sand to the steps. Parker followed eagerly, unconcerned that their walk might be cut short, only interested in what was currently happening. He seemed content to be walking instead of running, as if he'd picked up her desire and wanted to support her plans. She laughed. Was her constant need to attribute human motives to animals something she'd had all her life, or had it become more prominent since she first encountered the...the whatever it, or she, was?

They climbed the steps and walked to the ramp leading up to the pier. She went to the gate and touched the lock. She pulled gently on the bars. It was definitely secure. The pier was deserted, as it should be. She stood for a few moments. Waiting here, rather than walking on the beach with her back to it, would allow her to observe the woman's arrival. If she suddenly appeared, Parker's help wasn't even necessary.

She stood there for several minutes. Soon, Parker began to whine. He circled her legs, looping the leash around her knees. She passed the leash to her other hand and unwound it. "We'll go in a minute."

The dog went to the gate and shoved his nose between the

bars. He remained like that, staring down toward the boat which was hardly visible, since it had sunk over the years to several feet below the level of the pier. Gulls and a few pelicans sat on the bridge, their backs to Corrine and Parker, looking out toward the horizon, which was invisible in the darkness.

Parker pulled his nose out from between the bars. He sat down. He looked up at her and whimpered.

"Okay. We'll go for a run. I guess she's on to my trap."

They walked back down to the hard-packed sand, and began running toward New Brighton beach, but didn't go all the way. Even without a ghost, it was nerve-wracking being out this late. The beach was deserted. She had Parker to protect her, and he was probably the best protection there was, but she still felt uneasy.

She turned and walked for a while, heading back toward the boat, then began running again, faster this time. Parker loved it, trotting to keep pace with her. As they drew close to the boat, she slowed to a walk, keeping her head slightly tipped back and her eyes fixed on the pier. It was still empty. She stopped. Nothing. Maybe she'd ask Andy to let her keep Parker another night. Suddenly she was overcome with grief. If she told Andy all her fears, told him about Deb, told him about her distrust, he was likely to break up with *her*. And if he ended their relationship, she'd never see Parker again. She started to cry.

Parker stayed over Friday night because Andy's flight got in late. Corrine took the dog to the beach. She walked for a mile or so, then turned back. The woman didn't materialize on the pier. Or on the ship, for that matter. If she truly was a phantom, she surely wasn't limited to the pier.

On Saturday night, Corrine made a curry stew with potatoes and peas and chicken, served over jasmine rice. When Andy's car pulled into the driveway, Parker sat up. He trotted to the front door. Andy unlocked the door and before he crossed the threshold, Parker jumped, planting his thick, meaty paws on Andy's thighs and pushing him back outside.

"Hey!" Andy swatted Parker's flank. "Not the greeting I expect. Haven't you been keeping him under control?" He put his arm around Corrine's waist and kissed her lips.

"He hasn't jumped all week."

"Is that right?" He pulled her closer, kissing her more deeply. "I missed you something bad." He let go, took her wrist, and pulled gently, tugging her toward the bedroom.

"Later. I have dinner ready. There's plenty of time."

He turned his lips down into a childish pout and they went into the kitchen. Parker returned to the living room and settled on his cushion. Cat had disappeared into the bedroom.

When they were seated at the table, a coastal Pinot Noir glistening like an enormous jewel in each wine glass, two candles with bright, barely moving flames, and the golden curried chicken with brilliant green peas on white plates, she took a slow breath and a sip of wine. Delaying her questions until later would make her more anxious. Andy would brush off any attempt at a serious conversation once they finished eating. "How was your trip?" she said.

"Good, from a business perspective, but a bit rough in parts. I thought I'd hear from you more. A guy doesn't like having doubts about the woman he loves. It seemed that I wanted you, and you were off doing…I don't know, chasing ghosts?" He laughed. "I thought about you all the time. Even when I was out at an unbelievable steak place with a customer Wednesday night. I thought I was going to have a panic attack. The need for you was that intense." He grinned.

"That's nice," she said. "I suppose I didn't text much because I was thinking a lot. I was going to…"

He leaned over and kissed her lips. He licked a grain of rice off the corner of her mouth. "Mmm." He took a sip of wine and pushed his chair a few inches away from the table.

"I wanted to…"

He held up his hand. "In fact I missed you so bad, I did something crazy." He reached into his pocket and slid his hand out. Pinched between his thumb and forefinger was a platinum ring with an enormous diamond solitaire. It sparkled like a star, drawing the light away from the glasses of wine, as if the candle flames were leaning toward it. "Will you?" He smiled. He looked slightly worried, more vulnerable than she'd ever seen him.

She stared at the ring, hating herself with a ferocity that

made her feel nauseous. She felt like a silly, giggling girl on a reality TV show, unable to take her eyes off the diamond or suppress the irrational joy that bubbled inside her chest. The thought of challenging his integrity while he sat there holding out the ring was beyond cruel. And completely impractical. Already the moment was decaying. His fingers trembled slightly and his face had taken on a rigid quality. His words hung in the air, crept across her brain, hitting it with tiny hammers. A sharp pain sprang up below her left ear. The seconds were sliding by, turning to minutes.

Andy lowered his hand. "Okay. Not what I expected."

All she could think of was that he'd said the same thing to Parker. "It's just that I..." She wasn't sure what to say. Maybe not mention Deb, as she'd planned. Not confess to what she'd done. But was she thinking in that direction because she wanted the ring and the idea of being engaged and married and having her life settled, and if she told him she distrusted him so deeply she'd effectively spied on him, the ring might disappear back inside his pocket? And his atrocious seeking out of Mary, trying to control her friendships, wanting to put boundaries around her experiences.

"I did have the impression you were in love with me," he said. "Despite your relative silence this week."

"I think..."

"You think? There's no way that sentence can end well." He put the ring on the table and picked up his wine glass.

"I was going to talk to you about some things."

"More important things than this?" He pointed the base of his glass at the ring.

"No, but things that are bothering me." She ate some curry and rice. It was cooling fast, too fast. How long had she sat there, not answering him? "It seems like you want me to be someone different than who I am."

"Where did you get that idea?" As he put his glass down the base clanked against his plate.

"You seem to want me to wear clothes that aren't me. You seem to want me to look different than I do. And my job…"

"Because I bought you a dress? What's the matter with you? What woman would turn a gift into something like that?"

She couldn't tell him it was because she looked like Deb. She couldn't. It might all be her imagination anyway. A lot of people resembled each other. The mind searched for similarities, glancing at a photograph. How hard had she really studied it? No one looked like themselves in a photograph. There was some essential thing missing. Maybe she and Deb looked nothing alike if someone saw them together in real life. Andy hadn't seen Deb for a year or more. And what else had bothered her? Oh, the date of his breakup. And talking to Mary. He'd said she was *fixated* on old people. Well maybe she was. There was something unusual about it. Her over-developed need to help, to ease pain. The pain she wanted to alleviate couldn't be touched, so what was she thinking? Andy was right — she couldn't hold the hand of every single dying person. And what about all the other suffering? It wasn't just elderly people who faced death. There were cancer victims and people with early, debilitating strokes. But the dress. He thought she was rejecting his gift and he didn't see that he wanted to alter her appearance. "You didn't like it that I wore boots with the dress."

He laughed. "Are you kidding me? If you don't want to marry me, just say so."

She took a sip of wine. She picked up the bottle and refilled both their glasses, even though hers didn't need it. She took a few bites of curry and rice. It was definitely cold. She'd spoiled dinner, his charming, eager proposal, and maybe their relationship. She stared at the ring. Lying on the table, it looked dull, like a piece of glass. Part of her wanted to pick it up, but that would be tacky. Or confusing. Or something. She felt like crying. "Do you love me the way I am?"

"I wouldn't have asked you to marry me if I didn't."

It sounded so true. He'd answered so quickly, not as if he had to pause and consider what the question meant, look beneath it for hidden meaning. She swallowed. "You love me working with old people? You love me living in a rundown cottage?"

"Is this some kind of bargain?" he said. "I have to accept that we aren't going to change and evolve when we're together? Either I like every single pair of shoes and every corner of this house, or you don't want to be married to me?"

"That's not what I meant." She looked at the ring. How had she managed to botch things so completely? She had no idea where to go from here.

He slid the ring under the lip of his plate.

"I'm sorry." Her voice was tight, as if she'd stopped breathing.

"For what, exactly?"

"For messing this up."

"So that's a no?" He stood. He tossed his napkin onto his plate where the cloth clung to the curry sauce. He picked up his glass and gulped down the rest of the wine. He shoved back his chair. It teetered and crashed to the floor.

Parker barked and charged into the room. He jumped at Andy, shoving him against the table. The candles wobbled and crashed over. One of the flames licked at the edge of the napkin and caught. Parker began barking, pawing at Andy's legs, concerned about the disarray and the slowly spreading flame.

"Stop that!" Andy grabbed Parker's collar and yanked him back.

Corrine ran to the sink and filled a glass with water. She tossed it on the flame. It sizzled and went out.

Parker continued barking, straining against Andy's grip. He lunged at the table. The plates and flatware clattered. One of the candles rolled off the side and the ring bounced to the floor. Andy let go of the dog's collar and knelt to pick up the ring. Corrine bent down to pick up the candle. Hot wax spread across her hand. She cried out. Parker jumped onto Andy's back and growled. Andy flipped around, shoving Parker, but the dog didn't budge. Andy dropped the ring and Parker growled from deep in his throat. Corrine whimpered and Parker began barking again, so loud her ears ached.

"Stop making that sound!" Andy said. "You're upsetting him."

She stood up and put the candle on the table. She went to the refrigerator, took out some ice, wrapped it in a towel, and pressed it on the back of her hand.

Andy stood up. The ring was on the floor.

Corrine dropped the ice on the counter and knelt down. She picked up the ring and slid it onto her finger. She felt numb, as if everything that had bothered her was nothing but a confusing, meaningless dream. All she could do was try to fix what had happened, to turn the night of their engagement back into something good and beautiful.

Parker was lying with his head resting on his forelegs. His eyelids were partially lowered, giving him a contrite expression.

Andy was watching her. "So? What the hell?"

"I'm sorry." She walked over to him and slid her arms around his waist. She pressed the side of her head against his chest. "I think I'm scared."

"And I'm not?"

"We haven't known each other very long."

"That's what an engagement is for," he said.

"Yes."

Hadn't Mary insisted the ghost tried to insert foreign thoughts into your mind? The creature had filled her mind with paranoia and distrust and worst of all, self doubt. She'd known the minute she met him that Andy was a terrific guy — her white knight. He'd soothed that entire situation at The Boardwalk. He'd treated her like a queen, and continued to do so ever since. She loved him. There was no doubt in her mind.

Twenty-five

The smart phone informed Mary it was a gorgeous day. The woman's voice had a smooth, cultured tone. So human, yet so perfectly digital. Of course the voice didn't specify *gorgeous*, it said sunny and clear with temperatures in the high fifties. The memory of the blue sky and sparkling water on such days filled her with optimism. She poured coffee into her mug, added a generous helping of cream, and screwed on the lid.

She walked slowly to the pier, relishing the sun on her shoulders. She strolled along the pier, keeping her thoughts on the rhythm of her footsteps, and the breeze touching her cheeks like her lover's fingers. She would not think about Daniel. If he called out to her or didn't, there was nothing she could do. She'd simply take her daily walk to the end of the pier and pause to remember the sight of the decaying, rotting, guano-covered ship. First, she recalled the chalky concrete and the dark algae, then she pushed her mind back to the days when children ran around the stripped boat, thrilled at its size and mystery, and then farther back, to when it was new. Others must have had pleasant memories of dancing and dining, parties and flirtations and laughter. She didn't have any of that. Countless times she'd wondered whether the ghost had haunted that ballroom from the start.

After the images in her mind had run their course, she turned and walked back, faster and more determined now. She would not look as if she was searching for him, would not give him the impression, if he was watching, that she longed for the simple friendship they used to have.

When she reached the sand, she finished the rest of her coffee. She slipped off her shoes and placed the mug and shoes in her bag. She walked across the sand. When she reached the line of dried seaweed marking where the last high tide had reached, she rolled up her pants to mid calf and walked slowly toward the water. It was quiet, an extremely low tide where the waves flattened until they assumed the form of a mountain lake. She moved carefully until the water lapped at her toes. It was cold, but not unbearable. She let her mind drift, listening to the distant voices of the fishermen leaning on the railing, discussing sports and fish. She strained to hear Daniel's voice, but either he wasn't on the east side of the pier, or he wasn't talking. Maybe he wasn't there at all. For all she knew, he hadn't come out to fish since the last time they'd spoken.

There was a change in the texture of the breeze on the back of her head. Someone was standing close behind her.

She took a few steps to her right. The person behind her moved also. She turned her head, wanting to speak, but not sure if she was mistaken. She walked toward the posts supporting the pier. The sound of the water changed, echoing against the wood above her. A moment later, she felt him beside her. *Him!* His presence shoved against the space around her. She felt her breath tightening as surely as if he'd put his hands around her neck, squeezing hard until she coughed and then lost even the thread of oxygen, choking until her lungs screamed in pain.

Beneath the pier, no one could see her, unless one of the few people walking along the shore happened to pass at the right moment. "Why are you doing this?" she whispered.

His arm brushed against her. She started to cry. Now his entire arm was touching her side. She edged away and he came closer. He put his hand on the back of her head.

So brittle.

The voice was inside her head, a searing whisper. Not male or female. Possibly inhuman.

She was sobbing now. "Please leave me alone."

You don't belong here. You're an eyesore. People want to enjoy the beach, not a decaying woman, muttering about ghosts.

She should scream, someone would come. Or…there was no one there at all. They'd label her mad — hearing voices.

She clutched the edges of her cape and hurried across the wet sand. Her feet sank deep, slowing her progress. She tripped through a pile of wet seaweed and lurched forward.

She was almost running, as much as it was possible for her to run any more. She felt a body right beside her, walking with long, easy strides, almost gliding across the sand. She heard breathing. There wasn't anyone beside her at all. Perhaps there had never been a man. She'd shouted at him to control his dog and the ghost had appeared that very first time, while the man ignored her and continued running down the beach. If she screamed, someone would come and tell her she was all alone. There was no man, there had never been a man. It was all inside her head, a spirit that wanted to frighten her to death.

She rushed into the house and fell on the couch. She tore the cape off her shoulders. She was breathing hard. He was not going to keep her from going to the beach. He wasn't allowed to make her feel so helpless, so weak, so terrified for her life. And what did her life matter? She was ninety-one years old! Yet, it did. She didn't want to yield it to violence. Unless it wasn't him.

Her phone trembled and played an electronic sound that made her feel like robotic beetles were crawling inside her head. She grabbed it and sat up. She swallowed and took a slow breath and answered.

"Mom?"

"Yes."

"It's Thomas. I called and you weren't there. I've been calling for over an hour."

"Oh, yes, Thursday. Sorry."

"That's all? Sorry?"

"Yes, sorry I missed your call."

"Where were you?"

He sounded like a ten-year-old. Mary grimaced. A prisoner. She truly was a prisoner. "I went for a walk. Like I always do."

"You know I call on Thursdays."

"I didn't go out until eight. You usually call before that."

"I had an early meeting," he said.

"How was I supposed to know that? You expect me to sit here all morning and wait for your call?"

"What's wrong? Are you feeling okay?"

"I'm fine. I just don't think I need you checking up on me."

"I'm not checking up on you. I care about you. I want to talk to you. I didn't intend to come across like I was keeping tabs on you."

"Thank you."

"You sound…anxious."

"I'm not."

"You're feeling okay?"

"I had coffee — too much caffeine."

He laughed. "Okay. Now I get it. So what's new with you?"

She told him about Corrine, taking a deep breath before using the word *friend*. Thomas was pleased and sounded much less wound up than he had at the start of the call. Perhaps he'd had too much caffeine too, or would use that as a cover to avoid saying he worried himself sick over his mother's well being. She should be touched by that. It was sweet. And she was lucky to have doting sons. She didn't tell him about the thing that had just happened. She wondered whether she would ever be able to go out to the beach again. How could she be so old, so close to the end, yet so frightened?

When Henry had left her to live with Alice in 1963, Mary wouldn't have felt more ashamed if all her clothes had been stripped off and she'd been left on the beach during a holiday weekend, her stretch marks and sagging breasts and lumpy stark white thighs exposed to the world. She wasn't sure why that image came to mind or why she found her overripe body shameful. She should be proud of having given birth to four healthy sons. Bringing them into the world and raising them into educated, charming, successful men required strength and stamina. Henry didn't seem impressed by that feat. Henry wanted a woman who didn't place family demands on him, a woman with whom he was the nucleus of the universe. Even more, he wanted a woman who would strut along the beach in one of the scandalously small bikinis that young women were wearing now, looking firm and fresh as she exposed nearly everything she had to public view.

After spending those two days in her room, as close to fasting as she'd ever come, her eyes devoid of tears and her heart devoid of sensation, she'd decided there was only one satisfying path to revenge. She couldn't make Henry love her. She couldn't make him desire her well-used flesh. She couldn't make him turn away from Alice. Time might take care of that, but it was out of Mary's hands.

Despite his lack of appreciation for all she'd done to create four outstanding men, Henry adored his boys. He craved their attention and admiration. He wanted that almost as much as he wanted to grow his business and build a respectable fortune. But her sons' minds were in her hands. They were adults, but she was still the primary female in their lives. It was her voice that had been stamped into their tender brains before they were born, and her words that shaped every corner of their psyches. With patience, and a gentle tone, and a forgiving and long-suffering demeanor, she would mold their hearts until they loathed their father.

It was absurdly easy. The boys were already unhappy their parents were divorcing. They weren't inclined to spend a lot of time with their father and his new sweetheart, and their father was not inclined to let go of Alice's hand for even a moment, unless he was attending a business meeting or sitting behind his massive oak desk.

Her sons asked whether she was okay. *I'm used to it.* She smiled, her expression mirroring the Virgin Mary's beatific smile. They demanded to know what she meant.

I don't want to speak badly of your father.

It wasn't a shock.

Alice is certainly his type.

He needs to feel young.

He's needed to feel young for years now.

I really don't want to say more.

You owe him your respect. Her smiles were filled with light and charm and tenderness.

By the time Henry and Alice were married, the boys refused to visit their home. In their minds, Alice was only the latest in a long string of females who were not their mother. Despite their father's tearful pleas, they quickly and silently removed him from their lives. The beauty of it was, Henry never knew. He also believed Mary was gracious and forgiving.

She never forgave. If she'd been given an opportunity, she would have murdered Henry. Of course, an opportunity would mean she would have to be provided with a gun, the knowledge to handle a weapon, the skill to aim, and an army of supporters to clean up the evidence. Instead, she spent many evenings sipping champagne, listening to Vivaldi, and going over the scenarios in her mind. Rehearsing them was almost as satisfying.

Henry had died a slow, torturous death from brain cancer when he was sixty. His boys weren't there to say good-bye. The boys didn't attend his funeral. Even when he was buried, Mary continued to entertain her occasional fantasy of firing a gun and watching his chest ripped apart, his heart riddled with holes.

She wondered if she should have experienced guilt for the pleasure of those fantasies, but she didn't. The lack of guilt occasionally provoked secondary guilt, but it was easily washed away by a glass of champagne and a walk along the beach.

She worried the walks on her beloved beach were going to be torn out of her hands. If that man, if that man and the ghost, were going to brush against her, whisper their hateful words into her ears, weave them through her mind, the beach would become a place of horror rather than solace and peace. Maybe someone, or something, finally wanted to kill her. After all these years, the things she'd said to her sons, and her murderous thoughts would be punished with a protracted, agonizing death.

Twenty-six

Corrine poured a small glass of white wine. She set it on the coffee table, picked up her tablet, and unlocked it. She opened the Facebook app, logged out of her account, and logged into Sara McGregor's. She didn't pause to look at updates, keeping her gaze in the middle distance so she couldn't see the details of Deb's face. She tapped the menu bar and clicked the link to delete the account. It disappeared before she blinked. She doubted whether Deb would notice. Deb had so many people sending her messages and posting on her page, Sara McGregor would slip unnoticed out of her life, just as she'd materialized out of nowhere, a ghost herself.

Next, she opened her email and deleted Sara's account. For half a second, it felt as if she'd committed murder. Needy Sara with her fitness plan and ulterior motives, uncertain about the man she thought she was in love with, but able to gather information about Andy. With Sara's death came the loss of access to any further knowledge. She didn't need it.

The stories Deb told might not even be true. Of course he hadn't replaced all of his and Deb's wedding gifts. It was laughable. Deb had invited forty million people to be friends on Facebook — she was clearly unbalanced. There was something very disturbing about a woman who allowed millions of people access to significant pieces of her life.

She snapped the cover into place and put the tablet on the coffee table. The moment she set it down, Cat jumped onto the couch and began kneading her paws into Corrine's thigh. Her sharp claws stung, but the pressure was a tiny massage and the purring was a warm rumble echoing inside her own chest, so she didn't mind.

A little pain is good.

She wasn't sure why she thought that, but it was true. The mild pain kept her alert. Her mind was focused on the sharp punctures through her pants, into her skin. The pain prevented her thoughts from going too far off course.

She leaned forward carefully so she wouldn't disrupt Cat's preparation for settling on her lap. She picked up her wine glass. She stretched out her legs and Cat stepped firmly onto her thighs. Corrine took a sip of wine and rubbed her finger along the bridge of Cat's nose. She took another sip of wine. She held out her hand, spread her fingers, and studied the diamond. After all the chaos she'd created when Andy had presented it to her, she'd expected him to slip it back into his pocket and walk away forever. But he hadn't. He seemed to forgive her outburst and lack of trust. He seemed...she wasn't sure. The best way to describe it was that he seemed satisfied.

Andy was working late and the evening stretched ahead, vague and relaxing, but maybe too vague. Most women in her situation would be paging through websites, planning wedding details, texting friends with questions about colors and appetizers. But she wasn't quite ready. Andy hadn't said anything about setting a date. She was content to get to know him better. He'd said that was the purpose of an engagement, although she wasn't sure he was right about that.

The moment the water touched Corrine's feet, she knew she was being watched. It was a terrible feeling, and yet part of her wanted to laugh. She'd come out here with Parker for protection, for the company of another living creature nearby — breathing, blood pumping through his body, a solid physical presence, with all his glorious muscle and strength — and the ghost had been absent. Now, when she was alone and vulnerable, the oppressive sense of something other-worldly was so thick she felt she was breathing in thick smoke.

She stopped beneath the pier, as if it wouldn't be able to see her beneath the worn planks. It was dark, how did it see her anyway? Yet, it was watching. The posts holding the pier were black, indistinct in the darkness, and before she'd stepped under the platform, the boat had been a ghostly white. It was funny how that term sprang to mind, yet this ghost, if it was a ghost, came as a dark, cloudy substance, or a woman wearing dark clothing. The only thing close to white was her silvery hair.

Corrine was afraid to walk out from beneath the pier. Could the spirit touch her? Drag her into the ocean and hold her there until she drowned? She shivered. She wrapped her arms around her waist and bent over slightly, but the shivering increased. She couldn't control her muscles. Her teeth began to chatter. It wasn't from the cold, exactly. It was something else. Something inside of her.

Waves splashed up the posts as if they wanted to climb up onto the pier, reaching higher each time. The water echoed in the narrow space and very faintly she could see the back end of the ship. The pigeons that normally roosted beneath the pier, warbling constantly, were silent. They were either asleep for the night, or their sounds were drowned by the surf. She unfolded her arms, turned and began running. The sand felt good on her bare feet — solid and real. She felt she had a better grip than she did with running shoes. She was more connected to the earth.

She ran as fast as she could. She kept her head down, watching the sand for rocks and broken shells and the worst, the partially rotted bodies of dead birds. Running felt good. It made the shivering subside, but it did nothing for the sensation of being watched. Any sane person would have returned home. She never really knew if the beach was safe. It seemed like there was always someone around — the tourists sleeping in their RVs or someone out walking. She didn't ever recall being the sole human being on the entire stretch of sand. But sometimes that other person out walking was speaking with loud, angry words, gesturing and shouting at unseen faces, glaring at her, contemplating whether to release internal demons on her, then, turning away, unable to see her at all.

The awareness of being watched was getting more intense. She felt the entire sky was filled with eyes, looking down at her, studying her, trying to peer inside her mind. Her heart thudded and her breath heaved in and out of her lungs. She slowed to a walk, unable to keep up the pace in the wet, soft sand. Her breath still came in gusts. She turned and looked at the boat. The birds that usually sat on the bridge, perched on the iron rods that protruded from the concrete, and clustered together near the back were gone. There were two rectangular openings in the broken piece of the bow. During the day, they gave a menacing promise of passages to some place dark and dank. In the moonlight, they were less distinct but still suggested the presence of a chamber that hadn't seen human life for decades. As the openings held her gaze, a figure emerged from one of them. It seemed to walk on nothing but the mist of the crashing waves as it climbed to the tip of the bow. It was the same woman Corrine had seen on the pier. Her hood was down and her long hair flowed behind her, drifting on the breeze, shimmering like foam.

Corrine could no longer reassure herself that the woman she'd seen was Mary, possessing private access to the pier. It wasn't possible for Mary to be out that far on the broken piece of the ship. Even if Corrine entertained the idea of Mary taking a boat and rowing out to the bow, it defied probability she could enter the bowels of the ship.

The woman turned toward Corrine, but no face was visible. Still, Corrine felt the eyes watching her. She wanted to race across the sand, scramble up the steps, and run as fast as she could up the paved road to the park entrance. Yet something held her in place. She wasn't sure if it was the specter itself or her own terrified fascination.

Water washed over her feet and splashed up her legs. She took a few steps to her left to make sure she was out of reach of a larger, faster moving wave. She walked forward slowly. It seemed as if the woman on the ship and Corrine were approaching one another, both uncertain about whether she was recognized by the other, waiting to form a definite impression, their breathing wary.

Everything grew silent. The woman's shape became indistinct and a moment later, something rushed at Corrine like a gust of wind. Wrenching pain spread across her head, accompanied by a terrible ripping sound. Her hair was being torn out by the roots in huge fistfuls. She put her hands on her head and felt another pair of hands, large and strong, stripping the hair from her head, pulling pieces of her scalp along with it. Her lips and nose felt as if they were being clawed off her face. She screamed, hardly able to take in air between her cries. She felt her skin being peeled away like bandages removed without pity off the seared flesh of someone who'd been badly burned. She fell on her knees, screaming. It seemed as if blades were being dragged across her body, leaving deep, bloody crevices. She tried to crawl toward the water but couldn't make any progress. She stopped, realizing the salt would make it so much worse, if that were possible. She screamed louder, begging in wordless cries for the hands to leave her alone.

As quickly as it had begun, the pain stopped. The hands held her face, patting it as if to reshape it into something unrecognizable. Slowly, the pressure of the fingertips grew less distinct, and then the hands were gone.

She put her own hand on the top of her head. Her hair was still there. It was slightly damp from the mist but there were no clots of mangled flesh. She put her hands on her face, everything was intact. Her nose and lips and eyebrows all felt as they should. There were no wounds, no wet smears of blood. The pain was completely gone.

She looked up at the ship. The figure was still there, still facing Corrine, the hair still floating on a soft breeze. The sound of the waves had returned and the ocean continued its steady beat, pouring water across the sloped bank of sand. Her thoughts twisted and tightened around each other. She sat back and crossed her legs at the ankles.

The hands that tore at her hair, peeled off her skin in bloody sheets felt unmistakably like Andy's. The same delicate hair on the backs, as fine as a baby's. They were the same size and shape, the short nails, a slight ridge in the center of the right ring finger. How could the hands belong to Andy? Perhaps she'd fallen asleep and had a nightmare, dreaming of him trying to mold her into someone else? But she felt fully awake, her senses sharp and still burning with remembered pain.

Words formed in her mind, as if the woman on the boat was speaking inside her head. Outside, all Corrine heard was the sound of the waves, but inside, deep in the center of her brain, she knew, and felt, a soft voice.

I'll make you mine. I'll form you into the woman I need.

She put her hands over her face and cried. This wasn't her own mind, these weren't her own thoughts. They didn't even seem to belong to the woman on the ship. They appeared to be from Andy himself. She lowered her hands. The figure on the boat was watching her.

Corrine stood up and started to scream. The figure on the ship wasn't just molding Corrine's thoughts as it pleased, it seemed to know what was already in her mind. She ran wildly along the shore, beneath the pier, and turned toward the stairs away from the beach. From the footpath, she raced up the wooden steps to the parking lot and ran all the way home, not caring that gravel and pavement tore at the bottoms of her feet.

At home, she mixed a martini, wrapped a blanket around her shoulders, and sat in the dark garden. When the drink was gone, she made a second one. She slept for eleven hours.

In the morning, she knew it had all been a dream. After eating bacon and toast and drinking two cups of coffee, she was able to look out at the pale sky and laugh.

Corrine stood on the path and studied Mary's back. The elderly woman sat with perfect posture, not an easy thing to do on the sand at any age. Her hair was held with a barrette and clipped at several spots along the ponytail, keeping it all in place. She could have been sitting in a bistro eating a light lunch. Beside her was a green bag, presumably holding her champagne and glasses. There was something appropriate about drinking champagne at the beach. Corrine stepped out of her flip-flops and shoved them into her bag.

The sand was warm even though it was cloudy. She walked quickly to where Mary was sitting. She said hello and sat down on Mary's blanket. Mary opened the champagne and they each drank a glassful. The pelicans dove for fish, smaller birds dogging their every move, screeching, hoping to catch the fall-out. They talked for a while about Mary's sons and Corrine's job.

All of her co-workers had commented on the beautiful diamond. Of course, Mary wouldn't know it was there until Corrine told her. She hesitated, knowing Mary was likely to have a less than enthusiastic reaction to the news that Corrine planned to marry Andy. The words echoed strangely in her head and she wasn't sure why. Was it the traumatic circumstances of their engagement? It might be the vivid and awful dream from the night before. But she was absolutely certain there was no such thing as a spirit capable of inflicting physical pain. And ghost or not, she didn't believe an external force could penetrate her thoughts. Her fears were fed by Deb's tales suggesting that Corrine would be slowly, imperceptibly re-shaped by Andy. Corrine had worked very hard at putting those stories out of her mind. Every moment she was with him, she listed his good qualities to herself. Then, she had to battle the feeling that a woman in love, engaged to be married, shouldn't have to put so much effort into creating mental lists.

Not telling Mary about the ring was as deceitful as what she'd done with Deb. It seemed she was a very deceitful person overall — masquerading as someone else, withholding from Andy the stories she'd heard about him.

Mary refilled her glass.

"Why did you bring a whole bottle this time?" Corrine said.

"I always drank the half bottle myself. With two people…"

Mary's face was turned toward the water, but Corrine saw the edges of her mouth turn gently upward.

"It's nice to have a friend," Mary said.

"You don't have many?"

"A lot of them are dead." Mary gave a sharp laugh. "Or they're in care homes. Or they just can't go out. I'm lucky to live where I can walk to the beach without climbing the hill or that impossible flight of stairs."

"You are."

"I was friendly with one of the fishermen for several years, but I did something to upset him."

"What was that?"

"I don't know. Talking about the ghost, possibly. Although it sounds silly to say that. He won't acknowledge me. Unless he's given up fishing. Anything is possible. I have no way of knowing."

"Oh."

"Yes, *oh*."

Corrine took a sip of champagne. "I had a strange… dream…" Corrine described the ripping and tearing at her hair and flesh, the unbearable pain, the realization after that nothing had happened, yet the gripping fear. "I'm not sure it was a dream," she said softly. She explained her desire to forget. She didn't mention the suggestion that had formed in her mind as if another person were speaking. That was the most important part, but she couldn't bring herself to utter something so ridiculous, and something so damaging.

More deceit.

These words came to her as if from somewhere outside, over the water, perhaps. "It wasn't a dream." She took a long swallow of champagne. "It was like you said. I felt something was inside my brain. I've felt that way quite a few times recently."

"Yes," Mary said.

"I don't understand. This isn't how I see the world — inhabited by phantoms or ghouls or whatever it is. I feel like my life is being turned inside out." She gulped more champagne. "Andy asked me to marry him. We're engaged."

"Congratulations," Mary said.

Her voice didn't sound cold or condemning, but it did sound very far away. Disappointed, maybe. "It was a surprise, but a good one."

"Was it?"

"Why do you say that?"

"Was it a good surprise? I thought you weren't happy that he appears to want to manage your life," Mary said.

"I think I took it the wrong way."

"Did you?"

"I really do love him," Corrine said.

"You don't have to persuade me."

"I'm not trying to. I just thought it needed to be said."

They sat quietly for a few minutes.

"Has she…it…the ghost ever put thoughts into your head? Made you confused or paranoid?"

"Yes, I told you that."

"It was hard to believe, I guess. But it seemed like I was becoming suspicious of Andy, spying on him, and not trusting him. Making small things into something big."

"In my experience, she stirred up some fears."

"So it wasn't true? Just feeding paranoid inclinations?"

"The truth can be frightening," Mary said.

"What do you mean?"

"She creates fear, mistrust. Terrible feelings, confusion. But those things can be stepping stones to the truth."

"You're giving me a headache," Corrine said.

"I wasn't trying to." Mary poured more champagne in both glasses.

"I shouldn't be drinking this," Corrine said. "I'll feel terrible walking up the hill."

"There's water in the bag."

Corrine wedged her glass in the sand and took out a bottle of water. "Thanks." She twisted the cap and took several long drinks. It was so cool, so smooth and clean-feeling. She felt she was washing out her throat, sending waves of curative liquid through her brain. She took another drink. She laid the bottle near her knee and picked up her champagne flute.

"When is the wedding?" Mary said.

"We haven't gotten that far."

"I see."

"See what?"

"You seem unsure."

"It's a big step," Corrine said. "It just happened a few days ago."

They sat quietly for several minutes. "Do you really believe the ship is haunted?" Corrine said.

"I know it is."

"Whatever I saw, it was quite terrifying. I hate to say this, because I know Andy won't like it, but I think I do believe there's something out there. I saw the woman, and she was on the very end of the boat. She came out from one of those openings that looks like a door. And the pain — I've never felt anything like it." She shivered and champagne splashed out of her glass. She set the glass in the bag and hugged her arms close to her sides. "It was more than just unfamiliar thoughts, fear and all of that. There was a voice inside of me, but not audible. I can't explain it."

"What did she say?"

Corrine was cold, so cold she could hardly move her lips.

"You don't have to tell me, I was just curious," Mary said.

"No. No, it's…it wasn't her voice. It seemed like it might have been…it might have been Andy's voice. But I don't see how that can be."

"She knows what he thinks," Mary said.

"I don't know. How can that be?"

"You'll see," Mary said. "She knows."

Mary emptied the rest of the champagne into her own glass without offering more to Corrine. It was okay. Corrine didn't want another drop of champagne. Her head felt like it was ready to split open, as if someone had wedged an axe into her skull.

Twenty-seven

After Corrine left, Mary ate a handful of grapes. Corrine had complained of a headache, attributing it to the champagne, but there was a reason that girl's head ached and it had nothing to do with carbonated alcohol. She packed up the empty bottle and glasses and lay down on her side. She was ready to enjoy a nap on the warm sand. Nothing soothed her to sleep like the sound of the waves, close enough to feel as if they were stroking her shoulders, whispering lullabies.

As she lay there waiting for sleep, she thought about Corrine, wondering what Corrine looked like. She imagined an open, welcoming expression in her eyes, a kind smile. Corrine was a bit of a fool. She worried about Mary walking on the beach without assistance, but thought nothing of tying up her entire life and her well-being with a man who had proven he was controlling. What would happen when the couple began to experience the bumps and bruises caused by the constant, daily, intimate contact of sharing a home and a life? The man wanted to take hold of Corrine's soul and possess it as if she were his latest acquisition. Mary had known from the tone of his voice that he wasn't someone you disagreed with.

There must be a way to help Corrine see that she should give serious thought to attaching her life to that man's universe. Corrine was sensitive and kind and in touch with the pulse of the world around her. Andy was determined to force everything and everyone into a shape that suited him. He would destroy Corrine's spirit. Before long, she'd consider giving up her career, defeated by his subtle, but constant suggestions. She'd be manipulated into giving up her friendship with an old woman who murmured about ghosts.

Maybe her concern for Corrine was pure selfishness. She'd lost one friend, she didn't want another slipping through her fingers. That was part of it, but it wasn't everything. She truly was concerned. That man would suck the life out of Corrine and leave an empty shell with no thoughts or feelings or desires of her own. It was impossible to see that, until it had happened to you.

She turned onto her other side so that her back faced the water. Why couldn't she sleep? Usually she had no trouble drifting into a soft, dreamless nap. Now, her brain darted and lunged like a pelican splashing into the sea, coming up with a maw full of writhing fish, water streaming off its beak. Pelicans had to be the most efficient sea bird in existence. In one scoop they brought up an entire meal. She used to love watching them. They glided like B52s, racing over the waves, never touching the water, their speed incredible — up to forty miles an hour — silent, wings motionless. Then they rose higher, searching from a vantage of fifty or sixty feet, before locking on a school of fish, and diving as if they'd been dropped like a dead weight from the top of a cliff. They hit the water with a splash and settled in with full mouths and smug expressions.

They seemed to look up toward the pier, mocking the fishermen who stood with their inadequate lines dangling over the railing, weighted with lures or sardines, hoping to interest a single fish, hoping they didn't get the line caught up in a snarled mass of kelp.

Some people fished because they enjoyed the tranquil nature of it. They even joked that they went *fishing* in order to spend a day alone outdoors. She didn't think that was the case for many of the fishermen on the pier. There was an intensity about them, more focused on the capture of a decent sized meal than on the kind of atmosphere a man or woman in waders looked for at the center of a mountain stream. She didn't know why Daniel fished every day, whether he needed the food for his family, or just enjoyed a healthy meal like she did. It seemed unlikely that he would give it up altogether, no matter how badly she'd upset him.

She sat up and rearranged herself, then lowered herself back to a fetal position.

At this point, she was beginning to reconcile herself to

never talking to Daniel again. She wasn't going to walk up and down the pier every day, like a beggar, hoping he'd toss a friendly word into her tin cup. It was shocking how much she missed talking to him even though all she remembered over the years were mornings of casual chitchat. The first real exchange of life stories had been his memory of the octopus and his fear at being trapped inside the ship. Maybe he was ashamed of his fear. A lot of men were. Women too, but men seemed to go to greater lengths to over-compensate.

She sat up and drank half a bottle of water. She laid down again, and finally, after thinking of Daniel's warm voice, and the bear claws that now seemed like the most wonderful dessert in the world, she fell asleep.

Out of some dark corner she hadn't looked into for years, came a memory of a fisherman she'd met. Was she awake or dreaming? Something grazed her cheek. She put her finger on the bone to brush it away, but nothing was there. She'd had a thought about touching her skin and now she'd done it — a conscious effort prompted by conscious thought, she must be awake. The thin skin and bone felt familiar. Her skin was slightly damp from the fog, although it didn't feel like the low fog which tended to make her skin wet. Had she cried in her dream? She ran her fingers across the lower part of her cheek. It was moist. She wasn't ready to sit up. There was something soft and barely formed in the back of her brain, trying to make its way to the surface. A fisherman.

You've forgotten.

What had she forgotten? She put her hands over her face and tried to press her thoughts into something soft and yielding.

She'd been walking on the pier the week after James died. Her eyesight was weak, but she could still find her way easily, could still see the water splashing against the ship. She carried a small handful of his ashes. Scattering human remains into the water off the side of the concrete ship was forbidden, but that's exactly what she planned to do. It was only a few tablespoons. Of course, if everyone broke the rules, there would be a problem, but everyone didn't. She held the ashes tightly. She didn't want them drifting between her fingers. Neither did she want her mind to drift, causing her hand to spontaneously unclench, scattering ashes before she was ready. They were meant to go on the water, not across the weathered boards of the pier.

As she drew near to the point where the pier joined the ship, she saw a fisherman who'd caught a large salmon. The glistening, thrashing fish was two feet long, maybe more. The man who caught it was having a terrible time wrestling it over the railing. He was balancing on aluminum crutches to walk, with bands designed to support his forearms. The lower part of one leg was missing just below his knee, and his other leg was weak and wobbly. Trying to maintain his balance, keep the crutches in place, and hang onto the fishing rod seemed almost impossible. If she wasn't holding a fistful of her husband's ashes, she would offer to help.

She considered quickly tossing the ashes into the water. What did it matter? James was gone. It was symbolic for her, it comforted her that part of him would be in the ocean, but it was only for her. He didn't care anymore. Still, it was impossible to let go of that promise. She'd assured him she would do this for him. And she wanted to do it. There were others who could help the man land his huge fish.

She stepped onto the ship. She walked as far as she could up the port side. It was a terrifying walk, remembering her walk along this section of the boat in the moments before her mother's body was pulled out of the water. She wasn't sure why she hadn't chosen the opposite side.

When she reached the farthest point, past where she'd gone that day as a child, excited at her clever escape from the house, not knowing what was waiting, she stopped. She leaned over the side. She brought her fist up to her face and kissed her knuckles. She closed her eyes and thought about James. She whispered, *Are you here?*

Her skin was warm despite the fog. An equally warm feeling ran through her bones and convulsed across her belly. She opened her eyes and slowly uncurled her fingers. Some of the ash was stuck to her skin. She held her hand out and let the loose ash fall over the side. It caught on the breeze and hung for a moment. A breaker swelled up beside her and caught the remains. She smiled and brushed the rest off her fingers. She stood for a few minutes, thinking of nothing.

When she stepped off the ship, back onto the pier, the fisherman was still wrestling with the salmon. Two others were helping — a teenaged boy and a thin man with a San Francisco Giants hat. One of the man's crutches lay on the ground and he leaned precariously on the remaining support. The boy was acting as the second crutch, while the other man had both hands on the pole. They arched their backs and stepped as if they were in some kind of strange ballet dance, moving slowly, with an oddly pleasing grace. She watched for several minutes, excited by the possibility of that large fish and the delicious meal it would make.

The man in the Giants hat re-positioned his hands so the man on the crutches had better access to the reel. The fisherman turned the crank, straining at the resistance created by the weight and violent movement of the fish. Slowly the fish came closer to the edge of the railing. Another boy ran to the side and grabbed the fish. He pulled it over and it flopped on the pier.

The man with the crutches cried out with childlike joy.

The man in the ball cap shouted, "Great catch, Daniel!"

The teenaged boy picked up the abandoned crutch and repositioned it. "Daniel! You the man."

Mary sat up. Her eyes flashed open, as if she were younger, still able to see when she opened her eyes after a nap and the floating, indistinct scenes of a dream clung to the backs of her eyelids. Was that her Daniel? Had she met him when she could still see? Forgotten him?

She opened the water bottle and took a sip. It was only one week after James had died. She was living in a strange, vacant world. But why had the memory resurfaced now? Because Daniel had been constantly on her mind, his name echoing through her head when she was awake and whispering in her sleep? She'd talked about him, grieved for him. She didn't know if it was the same Daniel. The name was common. It was ages ago. Still, Daniel had told her he'd been fishing off the pier for years.

Her eyes filled with tears. Of course he couldn't help her with that monster who wanted to frighten her. He probably couldn't even walk on the sand, much less take on an enormous bully.

What difference did it all make? Unless Daniel called out to her as she walked on the pier, she'd never talk with him again. He might as well be fishing off a pier in New Zealand.

Twenty-eight

Corrine hadn't been able to turn away after talking to Mary. Instead, she'd gone up the steps and positioned herself at the railing near the path. She studied Mary's narrow back and shoulders, her small head. Even the blanket surrounding her looked enormous compared to her tiny form. There was something brave yet incredibly thoughtless about her own life that allowed Mary to sit unseeing on the vast expanse of sand. She seemed like one of the gulls, so proud, yet fighting every moment to keep herself fed and mobile. Was that what life was distilled to over the years? Or maybe life was that way from the start, and there were so many glittery distractions when you were younger you didn't see what was at the core.

Mary was eating a handful of grapes and sipping water. When she was finished, she packed up her things, lay down on her side, and curled up.

Corrine shivered as the old woman made herself even smaller, more vulnerable. She couldn't imagine sleeping on the beach without a companion nearby, unaware of a sudden change in the weather. Not knowing if the tide breached the ledge of sand and a rogue wave rushed toward her, if someone approached and took her belongings. Even the birds might be provoked to attack her motionless body. Corrine wasn't sure why yielding conscious awareness in a public place struck her as frightening. It wasn't as if someone would murder a sleeping woman during daylight hours when there were people looking down from the pier, jogging past, or walking their dogs. What was she afraid might happen if she slept on the beach? She supposed it was the shear terror of knowing her animal instinct was deadened.

It was pleasant standing still, mesmerized by the waves, but after a while, her legs began to ache. Hopefully Andy wasn't worried, wondering why she wasn't home or answering text messages. She hadn't brought her phone and wasn't sure of the time. He didn't know she'd gone to the beach, but she was not going to leave her post until Mary stood up and folded her blanket.

Three gulls arrived, landing about thirty feet from where Mary slept. A few minutes later, six more joined them, followed by another seven or eight. Soon there was a huge group — proud males with gleaming white feathers and their companions, streaked brown and gray. They positioned themselves in rows, keeping an unwavering watch on the ocean.

A few minutes later, Mary sat up slowly. Corrine was

relieved. She was tired of standing at the rail, but the longer she'd remained, the harder it had become to consider leaving. Mary took out a bottle of water and drank some. She put the bottle away. She continued sitting with her face to the water, mirroring the stance of the gulls, hardly moving.

The breeze was growing stronger. Charcoal clouds were replacing the whitish fog. Corrine took out an elastic tie and secured her hair. She needed to pee, but watching Mary, waiting to be sure she left the beach safely, had started to feel like a mandate, as if she'd been tasked with a guardianship. She really needed to use the restroom. She should have left ages ago, not hovered like the ghostly presence that brooded over the concrete ship. She turned slightly, pressing her hip bone against the railing. Mary still hadn't moved. She faced the water as if she wasn't blind at all and was watching for something.

It had started to rain, just a light mist, but the beach was emptying fast. There were only two people left on the pier, their fishing poles extended out over the water. Why was Mary still sitting there? Didn't she notice the rain? Maybe her hood blocked the moisture from her face. Corrine glanced over her shoulder. She couldn't contain half a bottle of champagne and nearly a full bottle of water. She darted to the restroom.

When she returned a few minutes later, her hands were wet because the restroom hadn't been re-stocked with paper towels. A man was standing in front of Mary's blanket. Andy.

His height and broad shoulders and white-blonde hair were unmistakable.

Twenty feet to his right, Parker was running in circles, barking, making periodic dashes toward the birds. The birds ran, flapping their wings madly as if they hoped to be able to find a new, safer spot on the sand. Eventually, a number of them took flight. Parker's leash was nowhere in sight.

Corrine shouted at Andy. "What are you doing? Make him stop chasing the birds!"

Parker ran faster, barking, reversing direction, then repeating his concentric circles. Most of the birds were gone now, scattered across the sky. Some remained overhead, scolding him with raucous cries, others had flown out over the waves and hovered on the wind current.

Andy was looking down at Mary who sat huddled inside her cape like a child. Even from where Corrine stood, the shaking of Mary's back and shoulders was pronounced.

"Andy!"

He didn't look up. Was it possible he couldn't hear her? Maybe not, over the gulls' cries and Parker's barking, which hadn't abated despite the fact he'd cleared the area of every single bird.

Corrine took off her flip-flops, ran down the steps, and stumbled across the beach. It was almost impossible to run in dry, loose sand. The light rain had done nothing to make the surface easier to navigate. Her bag flapped against her hip. The arch of her foot slammed on a thorny weed that had torn loose. She cried out but kept running, and then, as she tried to favor the foot with the thorn digging into her flesh, she turned her ankle slightly and stumbled sideways.

Andy hadn't mentioned he was coming to the beach. Had he gone to her house earlier than planned? He wasn't lecturing Mary on her interest in ghosts, telling her to stay away from his brand new fiancé, was he? Tears pricked at the corners of her eyes. His disparaging comments about Mary and her belief in the supernatural resurfaced in Corrine's mind. If he'd ever experienced a painful, frightening encounter like she had, he might view it differently. She should have told him about her experience with that thing on the beach. It might have helped him understand Mary, made him more tolerant. Getting married meant no more secrets. The things she'd kept from him before were now in the past, but she was creating a weak foundation for their future together if she continued hiding parts of her life from him.

She reached the edge of the blanket, panting as if she'd run three miles, not thirty feet. "Andy."

"Andy?" Mary's voice shook with a mixture of anger and a stomach-twisting sob. "You're Andy?" She leaned forward and tried to push herself to her feet.

Corrine stepped closer. "What's going on? Why isn't Parker on his leash?"

"Just going for a walk," Andy said.

"It's him," Mary said. "The one who refuses to speak."

Corrine put her arm around Mary.

"She's not your grandmother, Corrine."

She squeezed Mary's shoulders, feeling she was eighteen, holding onto her grandmother. "What are you doing?" She looked up at him. His eyes were glassy, the pupils so small she couldn't see them. It gave the impression there was a thin layer of frost across the shimmering pale blue iris.

Parker bounded over and thudded his ribs against Corrine's legs. "Where's his leash?"

"Calm down," Andy said.

"You stood here, knowing she couldn't see you? Saying nothing until she was absolutely terrified? What the hell is wrong with you?"

"Don't get excited," he said. "It was just a game."

Corrine took her arm away from Mary. She moved to the side. "That's despicable…I don't even know…why would you…" She shoved the heels of her hands against his ribs.

Andy stumbled back. "Don't."

She shoved him again.

"Get a grip. It was a game. I didn't do anything. She was shouting at me about those damn birds, screaming like a little piss ant. It would have been funny, if it wasn't so irritating. She was hysterical, as if my dog doesn't get to run on the beach and be a dog. Dogs chase birds. It's the law of nature."

"So you tormented her?"

"She needs to stop acting like she owns the beach. Like a bunch of scavengers are more important than human beings and their pets."

"I'm so ashamed of you!" Corrine heard her voice, outside of her head, screaming as fiercely as the gulls. From the corner of her eye she saw Mary flinch.

"Don't scream at me. You sound like her. Men hate hysterical women. You should know that."

Corrine wasn't sure why she should know that, but she was filled with such self-loathing she couldn't think. He disgusted her. He looked like an other-worldly monster, unmoved, with his icy eyes and his unnaturally light hair. His lips were thin and blanched from the wind. She stepped off the blanket, trying to think what she should do. What kind of man wanted to terrify an old woman? What kind of man treated any human being like that? Any creature at all?

She kicked his shin.

Andy laughed as her bare foot brushed ineffectively against his jeans. "Come on, Corrine. Don't do this. Let's go home."

She swung her leg harder, aiming for his crotch. He jumped to the side and grabbed her ankle. The force of him half-falling and his grip on her ankle put more pressure on the weakened ligaments, sending a bullet of pain up her leg. She cried out.

Parker barked repeatedly.

"Let go of me!"

Parker's barking grew louder, more anxious. He ran around Mary, turned and raced back, moving with erratic bursts between Andy and Corrine.

Andy let go of her ankle. She dropped to her knees for a

moment. Then, she stood slowly and moved toward him. "I don't know what to say to you. I don't know who you are."

"Oh, come on," he said.

She stood silently, breathing hard.

Andy seemed to feel her tension. He took a few steps back. Parker barked louder, also recognizing what was going on inside of her, racing through her body, roiling in her stomach. She stepped back and charged at Andy, ignoring her aching ankle. She shoved him harder than she thought possible. He took another step back and she kicked his shins. She slammed her fist into his stomach.

"Stop it, right now," he said.

"You're an animal."

"You're the one acting like an animal. A crazy, shrieking bird." He laughed.

She kicked him again.

He lunged at her and grabbed her upper arms. He spun her around so her back was pressed up against him. "If you stop that shrieking, you're actually kind of hot when you're like this." He laughed. "All that fire in your eyes, thinking you can hurt me."

She screamed and twisted in his arms. "Get off me. I hate you."

He grabbed her hair and yanked her head back. His breath was warm on her cheek. "You don't hate me, you love me, you can't tear yourself away from me."

Corrine screamed.

Parker stopped barking and jumped at Andy, a guttural sound surging out of his throat.

Andy kept hold of her hair. She twisted and thrashed, screaming.

He shouted at her — "Stop making that noise! You're upsetting the dog."

She let out a prolonged scream that seemed to come from a place so deep inside she hadn't known it existed.

Andy tightened his grip.

She squirmed and angled her legs back at him, landing her heels on his shins, but it had no effect. She was crying. Mary was saying something, but Corrine couldn't make out the words. She twisted her body to the right, trying to get away from the blanket so Mary wasn't caught in their scuffle, which possibly sounded worse than it was. She glanced up at the pier. It was empty now. Of course that's why nobody had intervened — the three of them, locked in a raging struggle, were completely alone under the vast expanse of descending clouds.

Andy's grip had relaxed slightly. Breathing softly, she twisted herself violently and managed to hurl both their bodies onto the sand. Now she could hear Mary crying softly, pleading with them to stop. Parker lunged at them, planted his forepaws on Andy's arm, and growled.

Andy shook him off and tightened his grip around Corrine.

She kicked him. It was much easier to have an impact on

his legs now. From somewhere far away, Andy was yelling at her but she had no idea what he was saying. All she could feel was blood pounding in her head, flooding the backs of her eyes, thudding against her ear drums. He had hold of her hair again and it hurt as badly as it had on the beach when the ghost, or her own mind, assaulted her.

He yanked her arm and she heard something crack. She felt her mind floating. Everything was silent except a horrid cry coming out of her. There was a loud growl right near her ear and Parker was on top of them. The dog opened his mouth, saliva pooling around his gums, his teeth glistening only a few inches from her. He clamped his jaws around Andy's lower arm. Blood shot out of the tender flesh underneath his wrist. Andy howled and let go of her. She rolled away from him, gasping for air. She pulled herself up to a crouching position.

"Parker! Corrine…tell him to stop!" Andy roared. "Tell him."

His words disappeared in a great cry of pain — the most awful sound Corrine had ever heard.

Parker growled and tore into Andy's jaw. There was so much blood. The more Andy bellowed, the more vicious Parker became. The sounds coming out of him hardly sounded like a dog. Andy's upper body was coated with blood. The side of his face was torn away. Corrine cradled her damaged elbow and pressed her forehead against her bent knees. She couldn't look. The noises from Andy and Parker were awful enough.

She should do something. But if she had her phone, she wasn't sure whether she would call anyone. She was as sick to her soul over what Andy had done to Mary as she was over Parker's brutal attack. Andy deserved it, maybe. The thought made her so ill she wondered whether she was going to lose consciousness. Did anyone deserve a brutal death? Or death at all? She was probably wrong about that, but she'd think about it another time, because right this minute, it seemed like the truth. Of course truth didn't adjust itself moment by moment, but it still felt true. Andy brought it on, maybe that's why. She was sickened that a pet, considered his best friend, could so easily become an enemy. The warning signs had been there. Andy had underestimated the strength of his dog and he'd underestimated how fond the dog had grown of Corrine. He underestimated everything — Mary, Corrine, the possibility that the dead might linger behind a thin curtain, longing to touch the world they'd left behind. She hoped that wasn't the case for Andy.

After a while Parker backed away from Andy. On her good arm, Corrine dragged herself toward him and pressed her fingers to the wrist that hadn't been bitten. There was nothing. She sat back in the sand and tried to think. Mary was standing a few feet from Andy's head, clutching her cape around her throat. Parker sat beside her, watching Corrine, waiting to see what she would do.

It was raining harder now.

"I love him," Corrine said.

"How can you, after what he did, after...?" Mary shuddered. She moved away from Andy's body.

"He's an animal, he did what his nature dictated."

"That's a poor excuse."

"Parker."

"The dog?"

"Yes. If someone sees this, they'll take him away. And I love him."

Both of them were silent for quite a long time.

"Can I ask a huge favor?" Corrine said. "It's dark."

Mary nodded.

"Would you stay by his...with his body? I'm going to take Parker to my house and clean him up. I'll be back in less than an hour."

"That's fine," Mary said.

"Did he say anything to you?"

"It was hard to understand everything. He spoke in a whisper. He said I don't belong here."

Corrine let go of her throbbing elbow for a moment. She snapped her fingers and Parker trotted to her side. He looked up at her, his eyes guileless. He wagged his tail. "What else did he say?"

"That old people should check out when it's time, or at least stay out of public view."

Corrine opened her mouth, but she saw Mary had more to say.

"He said we shouldn't inflict our decaying lives on the world. That he planned to leave with dignity."

"That didn't happen, did it?" She didn't wait for Mary to say any more. She began limping across the beach. Parker followed her easily as she made her way to the stairs and along the path. He seemed oblivious to what he'd done, trotting by her side, looking up at her with warm, soft eyes. He stayed close, as if his leash were attached and she held the end.

When Corrine returned to the beach, Mary was still standing several feet from Andy's body. Her blanket was folded in a small square, sitting on top of the insulated bag.

Corrine pulled out her phone. "I'm going to call 9-1-1."

Mary nodded.

"They'll know he's been dead for more than a few minutes. Eventually."

"Yes," Mary said.

"I want you to go home. I'll say I didn't have my phone. It's true. And it took me a long time to get home because of my ankle. I'll say that I don't know where his dog ran off to. Later, can I bring Parker to your house? I'll stay, if you don't feel safe with him."

"I'm not worried," Mary said. "It wasn't only him."

Corrine looked at her. "Wasn't...?"

"The spirit."

Corrine swallowed. The slight movement of her mouth and throat made her feel queasy again. "Maybe. I don't know.

If they talk to anyone who might have seen us earlier, do you have a problem telling this story?"

"No. I didn't see anything."

Corrine smiled. Mary smiled also, as if she'd seen the expression on Corrine's face.

Twenty-nine

Parker, Corrine, and Cat stayed with Mary for five days. Over the course of those five days, Corrine began to feel as if she'd atoned for neglecting her grandmother. It was senseless, and it wasn't that atonement was required, or that her grandmother had even expected it, but she felt it nevertheless. Living in close proximity to someone so old brought so many memories of her grandmother to the surface she could hardly hold them all in her hands. For so many years, she'd held onto that single broken promise like it was a family heirloom. Because the invitation was the last thing her grandmother had said — those words had swollen into terrible disproportion. Now she saw that they were simply the last, and no more significant than the thousands or hundreds of thousands, possibly millions of other words exchanged with her grandmother.

People told the police they had seen Corrine and Andy on the beach, but they hadn't taken much notice. Another person might have been with the couple, they weren't sure. It was raining and they'd hurried home. Corrine explained how she and her fiancé had argued. It got a little physical — *he grabbed me* — she said. The dog wanted to defend her. It attacked his master. He was so big — ninety pounds of pure muscle and bone. There was nothing she could have done with a sore ankle, a dislocated elbow…the dog ran down the beach and didn't return. Animal control would be looking for him, they said. If she saw the dog or if by chance it found its way back to her house, she shouldn't approach it. She should call for help. They were very kind to her, sensitive to the trauma of watching a pet maul your fiancé. A female police officer advised Corrine to see a therapist. To take a few days off work. Corrine adopted the second suggestion, and when her supervisor heard what had happened, Corrine was told to take care of herself for the entire week, to not return until she was ready.

The executor of Andy's estate contacted her — Deb Thurmon. When the email appeared in her in-box, Corrine lost her breath for a moment. She stared at the familiar name. Slowly the oxygen made its way back into her lungs and she laughed at her initial panic. Deb had no idea who Corrine Dunning was. It turned out Andy hadn't kept his life as orderly as he'd kept his condo, which was now in Deb's hands. Corrine didn't care, all she wanted was Parker. And as far as Deb knew, Parker had disappeared, most likely devastated over what he'd done.

Deb was unsympathetic enough to tell Corrine that her life would be better without Andy. "Not that I wished him dead." Deb laughed. Her voice over the phone was shrill. It sounded nothing like what Corrine had imagined when they were chatting online and Deb came off so centered, almost wise.

"Of course not," Corrine said.

"But he was a messed up dude."

"How's that?"

"He practically thought he was god. He wanted to re-make the entire world to fit what he wanted. Starting with me. And I'm sure he would have moved on to you next."

Corrine laughed.

"It's not funny. The guy wanted me to have plastic surgery."

"What for?"

"To adjust myself into his vision of the woman who should be his mate. I think he wanted us to look like brother and sister."

"That's weird. Why…"

"Yes it is."

"Did he say that?"

"No. But I have a resemblance to his mother. The clothes he bought me, the way he wanted me to fix my hair — all made me resemble her. He wanted my hair color lightened to be closer to hers."

"He said that?"

"He didn't *say* anything. I have eyes. I saw how she looked,

I saw photographs of her when she was my age. He was like Pygmalion."

"Oh," Corrine said. She didn't want to talk to Deb any more. She wanted to forget about Andy and Deb and everything that had happened in the past six months. Except for becoming friends with Mary. And finding out she cared about dogs. "Do you need anything more from me?"

"No. I just wanted to let you know how things are. As a courtesy. That you're not in his will."

"Fine by me," Corrine said.

"I haven't heard anything about his dog. Which is just as well."

"I guess someone picked him up," Corrine said.

"It sounds that way. Andy appointed some guy named Dillon as the caretaker for the dog. But no one wants a dangerous animal. I mean, I feel sorry for the thing. I wouldn't want to be the one to put him down. I'm sure this Dillon will be relieved when I tell him."

"Thank you for getting in touch with me," Corrine said. "And for letting me know how he was."

"I thought it might make it easier."

"Good-bye," Corrine said.

After she ended the call, she changed into running clothes and flip-flops. She went to the beach and ran barefoot for more than four miles — up to New Brighton, then turning and running back, beneath the pier and up another mile around the curve of the bay toward Monterey. Every time the image of Andy and the woman he was trying to sculpt pushed their way into her thoughts, she ran faster. Finally, she slowed to an easy jog and looked out across the water, letting the endless blue wash over everything.

The last night at Mary's, Corrine made clam chowder. They ate it with sourdough bread and unsalted butter. Corrine had white wine and Mary drank a glass of champagne. Corrine told Mary about the things Deb had said and Mary listened without comment.

While she was inserting the bowls in the dishwasher, Mary said, "Should we go down to the beach?"

"Why?"

"It's pleasant when there's no one about."

"Things happen at night."

"Not always," Mary said.

"Almost always." Corrine ladled the leftover chowder into a container and put in the refrigerator. "Maybe. But if I go, I'll bring Parker."

Mary laughed. "She's not intimidated by a dog."

"I don't know if I want to go at all."

Mary called Parker and he trotted into the kitchen. "He wants to go out," she said.

"You tempted him."

"Don't be afraid. She's never hurt me. She only wanted you to know what you were up against."

They dressed for the cold night air. They went out and

walked quickly past the houses, down the incline, and across the bridge. Small puffs of vapor came out of Parker's nose as he ambled beside Corrine. When they reached the beach, they walked for a while on the wet sand. It was packed hard, like concrete beneath their feet. The impact jarred Corrine's bones and made her knees stiff. It didn't seem to bother Mary, or if it did, she didn't complain.

When they turned back, the woman was on the ship, facing toward them. There was no wind, yet a few strands of hair drifted around the edge of her hood like seaweed floating on a calm, low tide. Her face was hidden by the hood, if she even had a face. Corrine shivered. The woman wasn't moving, she simply faced them as if she wanted an acknowledgement of her presence, a chance to make some kind of contact. It seemed as if Mary knew she was there, and was unsurprised and unruffled by the ghostly presence. The chill wafting through the air was much deeper than the winter air they'd faced when they were walking. Had Mary summoned the woman to join them?

Parker whimpered, but he didn't seem to be looking at the ship — as if he felt her presence but couldn't see her, whether she was too far away, or something about her form was invisible to him and some other aspect of her presence had aroused his animal sense.

"Did you *know* she'd be out there tonight?" Corrine said.

Mary didn't answer.

After a few minutes, Corrine spoke in a tiny voice that had

lost its authority. "What does she want?"

"I've never understood. Not with any certainty."

"How long has she been there?"

"Since I was a child."

"And it's not your mother?"

"Sometimes. But not always."

"What do you mean?"

"She takes on different forms."

"What do you *think* she wants?"

Mary was quiet. They continued walking, more slowly now. As the woman drifted along the corroded deck of the ship, Corrine felt that Mary, like Parker, saw the ghost with some faculty beyond physical sight.

"It's difficult to believe that something…someone who's dead can influence the thoughts of people that are alive. My thoughts only belong to me. Only I can touch them," Corrine said.

"A lot of things are hard to believe."

Corrine thought of Andy.

"Until it happens to you," Mary said.

"And after all these years, there's *no* explanation of what she is or why she's there?"

"As far as I know, not that many people have encountered her."

"Should I feel honored?"

"I don't know," Mary said. "If you want to."

It was a strange response. Corrine wasn't sure how to

interpret it. Despite the eerie goings on in her mind the past weeks, despite the physical sensation of being attacked by something she couldn't see, she couldn't accept Mary's explanation. "I don't like not knowing. I want to know who it is, why she's there."

"Some things you can't ever know," Mary said.

"Have you given her a name?"

"What an odd question. Why would I do that?"

"If you've seen her so many times, it makes sense. You have a connection, doesn't a name make the connection stronger?"

"I haven't given her a name," Mary said.

Corrine wasn't sure why she'd asked the question about the ghost, because when she spoke, she hadn't been thinking of the ghost at all. She'd begun to realize she needed to give Cat a proper name. It would put Cat and Parker on a more equal footing. Solitude might be a good fit. It wasn't really a name, but the word came to her, thinking of her life without a man to love.

They walked under the pier and stood watching the waves in the darkness.

"Being alone is better than being with the wrong man," Mary said. "There are so many damaged people in the world."

"Everyone's a little damaged," Corrine said.

"But some need to inflict their wounds on others. You don't want to be with a man like that."

"No."

"And some become more lovable because of their wounds. That's the sort of person you'll find."

"Maybe."

"I did." Mary took Corrine's arm and pulled her close. Her hand crept up Corrine's sleeve and touched her hair. "You have such beautiful hair. Long and thick."

"Like yours," Corrine said. "And hers."

The wet sand was softer now. They walked away from the boat past the steps leading to Mary's house, continuing along the beach until they were pleasantly tired and turned back.

Thirty

The day after Corrine took her animals and returned to her own place, Mary went out to the beach at six-thirty in the morning. She was prepared to make a fool of herself. There was no other way to find Daniel. She supposed she could have asked for Corrine's assistance. Now that she knew Daniel used crutches, she had something to go on. Still, something prevented her from asking Corrine. She wanted to talk to Daniel herself, without Corrine's ever-available help. Besides, it felt mildly demeaning to point Daniel out as the man with crutches.

When she arrived at the gate, two fishermen were talking quietly about a football game.

"Do you know Daniel Sloane?" she said. "He comes out here all the time. He…"

"Sure. Daniel," one of the men said.

"Have you seen him recently?"

"Every day."

Her pulse slowed its movement through her veins. Thick, wet cement seemed to fill every chamber of her heart. She had hoped he was housebound with the flu or a winter cough. "I'm blind," she said. "I need help finding him."

"Yes. I've seen you around."

"When he comes, will you let me know?"

"Why?" The second man's voice was deeper. He sounded as if he thought she wanted to create some kind of trouble.

"We had a disagreement. He's been ignoring me."

"Doesn't sound like Daniel," said the man with the deep voice.

"It doesn't. But I want to apologize. Will you let me know when he comes?"

"No problem," the first man said. "We can do that."

After the gate was unlocked and people began making their way onto the pier, Mary said, "Will you come find me? If it's not too much trouble? I'll be sitting at the first bench."

"No problem," the man said.

Mary took her seat. She heard footsteps and the rattle of tackle boxes, people talking. She began to get hungry. She'd forgotten to bring a mug of tea or coffee. There was half a bottle of water in her bag. She drank that, but her stomach continued to complain. Finally, when the sun was warming the back of her hood, soaking into the wool fabric, spreading across her scalp, climbing toward the top of the sky, the man with the deep voice spoke. It surprised her — he'd seemed the less helpful of the two. "Daniel's here, setting up. Should

I walk you over?"

She stood up. "Yes. Thank you."

They walked thirty or forty steps and turned toward the right side of the pier. "Daniel," the man said.

There was a brief pause.

"Hi, Mary."

"Thank you," she said, unsure whether the man was still there. She spoke to Daniel. "I'm so sorry. I remember you now. I met you a long time ago. Before I was blind. Well, I didn't meet you, but I saw you."

"The cripple," Daniel said.

"Don't. I didn't…" She wasn't going to lie to him. "I mostly noticed that huge fish. A salmon."

"And that my legs are useless."

"Yes, I remember."

"It hasn't changed."

"Don't be angry with me."

"So, now you understand, I can't help you with anything."

"Can we sit down for a minute? I baked you cookies." She laughed and felt tears spill out of her eyes. "I don't have them. I ate them all, looking for you every day."

"It's okay. I have a bear claw. Do you want some?"

She nodded. She made her way around the bench. It shifted slightly when Daniel sat beside her. She reached over and found his shoulder. She patted it, feeling as if she were patting a dog, but he didn't seem to mind. A moment later, he handed her half a bear claw and a paper napkin. She took a bite. It was so soft and so sweet. She chewed slowly and swallowed. "I've missed you."

"Me too," Daniel said. "Now you know…I'm weak. I've always been weak. I cried like a baby when I was trapped under that ship. I couldn't see where I was going — my lungs were exploding and I was lightheaded. I ripped up my legs on the rebar when I was trying to get to the surface. The leg got infected. They had to remove part of my left leg and the right one has never been much use. I'm a sitting duck for any thug or bully."

"I'm so sorry."

"No one believed me. They all said exactly what you did — an octopus would never come so close to shore."

"I said it was probably the ghost, but I know what it's like to have no one believe you."

"I told you what happened to me, the worst experience of my life. And you tried to tell me it was my imagination."

"It's not your imagination. The ship is haunted."

"Maybe. Haunted or imagined, both are the same — not real."

"It's very real."

"That's a lot to swallow. I remember every detail, even after all these years. I can close my eyes and see that thing sucking at the water, trying to get to me."

Mary licked the frosting off her index finger. She didn't want to argue with him. It wasn't as if a ghost was something easily explained and understood. Did it really matter whether

Daniel knew what had tried to take his life? The point was, his legs were permanently damaged, his life altered, but here he was. Fishing, enjoying the ocean, talking to her.

"When you asked me to help defend you from that guy," he said, "It was too much."

"You're not weak."

"Yes, I am." He added in a low voice, "Not really a man, at least not a man who can take care of himself, and the people he loves."

"A man who admits his weakness is more of a man."

"What do you know about it?"

"I know a lot about men — two husbands, a lover, four sons."

"All my life, after I lost the use of my legs, I remembered that octopus. I told myself I was lucky to be alive. Even if I can't walk. But when you told me what that guy was doing to you, I felt it all over again. Helpless. Completely useless."

"It doesn't matter now, he's dead."

"Dead?"

"A dog attacked him," she said.

"That's something."

"Can we start again, where we left off?"

"I think so," he said.

They sat quietly, eating their halves of the bear claw.

"I saw your new friend running on the beach," Daniel said. "She has a dog."

"Corrine?"

"I don't know her name. She's out there now, running near the water."

Mary stood up. "Where?"

"She went past the pier about fifteen minutes ago."

Mary walked to the railing. "When she comes back, will you tell me?"

He got up. They stood beside each other. After a while, Daniel said, "Here she comes."

"Describe her to me."

"She's thin. She has long legs. I can't see much of her face from up here. Her head is shaved."

"Oh. I see."

"It wasn't before," Daniel said. "She's smiling, laughing at the dog when he splashes in the water."

Mary thought about the shaved head. She guessed no one was going to tell Corrine how to live her life from here on out. Or maybe Corrine simply didn't want the ghost to find its way inside of her skull without her noticing.

She smiled.

"You look happy, too," Daniel said.

Mary lifted her arm and waved her hand.

"She's waving back at you," Daniel said.

Mary lowered her arm and looped it through his. Daniel patted her hand. They stood listening to the waves for a long time.

About The Author

Cathryn Grant is the author of Suburban Noir novels, ghost stories, and short fiction. Her writing has been described as "making the mundane menacing".

Cathryn's fiction has appeared in *Alfred Hitchcock* and *Ellery Queen Mystery Magazines*, *The Shroud Quarterly Journal*, and *The Best of Every Day Fiction*. Her short story "I Was Young Once" received an honorable mention in the 2007 *Zoetrope All-story* Short Fiction contest.

When she's not writing, Cathryn reads fiction, eavesdrops, and plays very high handicap golf. She lives on the Central California coast with her husband and two cats. Visit her website at SuburbanNoir.com or email her at Cathryn@SuburbanNoir.com

Book two: Slipping Away From the Beach

The second book of the Haunted Ship Trilogy takes place in 1967 — the Summer of Love. Mary's four sons are grown. Her husband has left her for a woman who is young, beautiful, and unencumbered by children. He also left her with enough money to live comfortably in an ocean-front house on the edge of Rio Del Mar beach.

Mary is eager to inhale the music and freedom, the sex and altered states of consciousness that have permeated Santa Cruz and most of California. This might be her last chance to feel young, find love, and regain her spirit.

After witnessing a gruesome death, the summer of love grows cold and dark as Mary questions the circumstances of the death and wrestles silently with the ghost haunting the concrete ship.

Coming in February 2016.

Book Three: Haunting the Beach

The third book of the Haunted Ship Trilogy is set in 1930. The S.S. Palo Alto has been towed to its final resting place at Seacliff Beach. Ten-year-old Mary is captivated by the party boat.

In books one and two, Mary recalls horrifying events from her childhood. Now, the circumstances leading up to that terrible day unfold before her uncomprehending eyes.

In the final chapter, ninety-two-year-old Mary finally confronts the ghost that's haunted her since the ship first appeared in her life. Her adult perception of her childhood allows her to make sense of her life.

Coming in May 2016.